SPRING THAW

Donna Minnix Proctor

DC PUBLISHING, LLC

PUBLISHING, LLC

SDC Publishing, LLC was established to promote and encourage aspiring writers and artists. It is a family oriented vehicle through which they can publish their work.

Contact SDC Publishing, LLC at
allenfmahon@gmail.com

Or on the web at SDCPublishingLLC.com

This is a work of fiction. The events and characters described herein are imaginary and are not intended to refer to specific places or living persons. The opinions expressed in this manuscript are solely the opinions of the author and do not represent the opinions or thoughts of the publisher. The author has represented and warranted full ownership and/ or legal right to publish all the materials in this book. No part of this book may be copied or reproduced without express written permission.

"Only an act of true love can thaw a frozen heart."
Olaf (Frozen)

The Frozen Heart by Robert Herrick

I freeze, I freeze, and nothing dwells

In me but snow and icicles.

For pity's sake, give your advice,

To melt this snow and thaw this ice.

I'll drink down flames; but if so be

Nothing but love can supple me,

I'll rather keep this frost and snow

Than to be thaw'd or heated so.

Donna Minnix Proctor

ONE

Sean Cody watched his latest client stride across the tarmac toward the hanger and groaned. Her type always meant trouble for him, with their regal manner, expensive shine, and unending demands. This one exuded the innate confidence that seemed to go hand-in-hand with old money – obscene piles of it. He disliked her on sight.

His short tenure with Baldwin Aviation had taught him that, whether they were the pampered wives of well-to-do businessmen, or successful entrepreneurs in their own right, the women who chartered his services as a helicopter pilot, were spoiled, entitled, and exceedingly unappreciative. Since the same adjectives applied to James W. North, President and CEO of Baldwin's parent organization, North Star Enterprises, Sean expected nothing less from the tycoon's overly-indulged wife. The pilot dreaded this hop.

Shouldering his backpack, he groaned again, took a deep breath, and stepped out to meet her. Instead of dropping the overnight bag she was carrying into his outstretched hand, as he'd expected her to do, she slipped her palm into his, her grip firm. She surprised him again with a genuine greeting. "You must be Mr. Cody. I'm Diana North. It's good to meet you."

"He grunted in acknowledgement, not trusting her casual, almost friendly, demeanor. "Call me Sean, Mrs. North. It's easier."

"Okay, Sean. Then I'm Diana. Her bow-shaped mouth drew into a sad smile that made the man wish he could see her eyes, which were hidden behind designer sunglasses.

"Uh, I'll take that," he offered belatedly, uncharacteristically shaken.

"Thanks," she accepted, handing him the leather carryall. "Let me get my coat and briefcase out of the car, and I'll be ready to go." He watched her backtrack to a sleek, wine-colored Jaguar, parked at the end of the long, metal building which housed Baldwin Aviation's office and maintenance garage.

He'd learned from experience that it was best to ignore the women Vic Baldwin paid him to fly up and down the east coast, women like this one, indecently wealthy and unbelievably arrogant. But for reasons he couldn't fathom, Sean couldn't ignore Diana North. From the tip of her highly polished, black leather boots, to the top of her elegantly coifed, platinum head, she seemed to be exactly what rumor claimed she was – cool as the proverbial cucumber, completely unapproachable, and all business. And yet, there was something about her…something he couldn't quite put a finger on…something that, against his best judgement, drew him in.

Sheila Stewart, Vic Baldwin's outspoken,

diminutive office manager, had dubbed Diana the "Ice Queen." Noting the expertly tailored, charcoal wool suit, which she wore with class and style, Sean understood the nickname the petite secretary had chosen for the woman. Mrs. North's tall, broad-shouldered frame dwarfed that of the tiny, voluptuous younger woman. Diana's long legs, aristocratic neck, prominent cheekbones, and halo of white blond hair, pulled back into a tight chignon, made for an unusually handsome package, and one that accentuated her decidedly superior demeanor.

Despite the warmth she'd shown him thus far, Sean silently agreed with the precocious Miss Stewart's derogatory assessment of his latest client, feeling certain that she'd be an icy bitch when the mood struck her. Still, his curiosity was piqued. Shaking off the apprehension clawing at his belly, Sean turned his back on Diana's rapidly approaching form, and circled the hanger to the waiting helicopter.

He loaded their bags into the storage compartment, helped her pull on a long cashmere coat, wrestle with a tan leather briefcase, stretched to its limit, and climb into her seat. Then, he sprinted around the helicopter and took his place, fastening his safety harness and clipping on the headset.

Radioing a few terse words to Vic, who barked a response, he fired up the engine, bringing the huge, sweeping blades to life. Moments later they lifted off. Sean busily clicked off the steps in his flight routine, thankful for his passenger's undemanding silence. As soon as they were airborne, he veered west.

"Things could get bumpy over the mountains," he warned a while later, feeling strangely compelled to initiate conversation. Though his instincts told him to stick to his customarily silent, efficient operating style, something about Mrs. North made him want to draw her out. "Let me know if you get queasy."

Pulling off the reading glasses she'd donned in place of the dark lenses, she glanced up from the computer she'd opened on her lap and smiled, that same sad, forced smile, and leveled her eyes, a frosty, cobalt blue, directly at him. The look hit him like a punch in the gut.

"Don't worry about me. I don't get air sick," she assured him briskly, before replacing the frames on her upturned nose and returning to her work. Sensing a dismissal, Sean took the hint, hunched his wide shoulders in resentment, and made no more attempts at small talk. *So, that's how it is, huh?* he thought angrily. *Shut up and drive. Well, that suits me just fine, lady.*

Almost three-quarters of hour passed before Diana folded up her laptop, slipped it back into her portfolio, and turned her gaze on him. He could feel her chilling, laser-blue stare boring holes into the side of his face, and his jaw clenched tightly, telegraphing his annoyance and sullen determination to keep his silence.

Her deeply sensuous, Kathleen Turner voice, broadcast from her headset to his, sent an electric jolt down his spine. "Sorry I haven't been good company. I'm preoccupied. Business on the brain, I'm afraid." In an obvious effort to make amends for cutting him short earlier, she added, "I'm glad for the chance to fly with you. James speaks highly of your expertise."

Still miffed by her earlier reproof, Sean grunted. "I'm surprised he mentioned me."

"Even the great and powerful James W. North, III, honors skill and competence when he sees it. You've impressed him, Sean. He's even a little jealous of you."

"Of me?" Sean's full, melodic baritone rose in disbelief. "A poor hop-jockey, bumming around the world from job to job? Can't imagine why he'd be jealous of me."

"Lots of reasons," she replied with a dismissive wave. "You're strong, healthy, and attractive. You have the freedom to come and go as you please, working a while here or there, then moving on to someplace new as the mood strikes you. You're very good at what you do. Plus, you don't have to answer to anyone. My husband resents and envies you for all of those things."

Sean tried to concentrate on her words, but he kept getting hung up on one. *Attractive, attractive,* kept bobbing around in his brain, like a silly teenager with his first crush. *She thinks I'm attractive.* He wasn't sure what surprised him more, that she'd noticed him in the first place, that she'd openly voiced her assessment of him, or that it mattered so much. *Stop it, Cody!* He ordered himself. *The woman is nothing but trouble.*

Clearing his throat self-consciously, he forced a

response. "Yeah, it's nice to take off whenever you want with no one to tie you down, but a man with a bank roll the size of your husband's should be able do whatever he wants whenever he wants. He's the boss, isn't he?"

"Oh, yes, he is definitely that," she agreed, her tone dripping with antipathy. "James North loves being the boss, telling other people what to do; unfortunately, it's that very need of his – for power and control – which limits his freedom. All the people he keeps waiting around for his next edict depend on him, and he's responsible for them."

"You don't paint a very complimentary picture," Sean noted.

She shrugged her graceful shoulders. "I think the facts speak for themselves. Here's an example," she ticked off the point by tapping her index fingers together. "If James weren't such a driven man, NSE wouldn't own Baldwin Aviation."

"That so?" Sean was curious but skeptical.

"A couple of years ago, the company's management was kicking around the idea of purchasing a helicopter for short trips around D.C., and to Philadelphia, Boston, and New York. As luck would have it, and James is nothing if not lucky, one of his banker buddies tipped him that Vic's new shuttle service was struggling. So, James took advantage of your boss's temporary insolvency to poach his business.

"It was quite a cutthroat move, actually. Vic Baldwin was demoted from owner-operator to North Star flunky, in one fell swoop. One might despise James's methods, but his successes must be applauded. The investment has been a good one." Then she seemed to reconsider and paused, chewing her lip. "Of course, I could be giving James the short shrift, since I'm exceedingly angry with him."

"Why's that?" the pilot asked, beginning to warm to the conversation, despite the warning bells clanging in his head.

"For forcing me to take this ridiculous trip to West Virginia, of all places, when there are much more important things needing my attention."

"You aren't up for a relaxing weekend in the mountains?" Sean teased, trying to bring back that small, sad smile.

"A relaxing weekend?" She sniffed in annoyance. "Hardly. This trip is all business. James insisted that I go to 'wild, wonderful West Virginia' to check out the Mountaintop Meadow Resort. He thinks it's ripe for a takeover. Apparently, the parent company is on the brink of bankruptcy, so he believes it's a prime opportunity for North Star to expand again." She took a deep breath and studied her short, pale pink nails.

"And you're the only person for the job." he declared.

"It is my area of expertise, though we have others who could do an adequate job. But James claims that he wants to keep it all hush-hush, so speculators won't get wind of it and push up the purchase price. As far as the resort is concerned, I'm the spoiled wife of a wealthy businessman, taking a relaxing weekend away from my busy schedule of shopping, visits to the salon, and other assorted frivolity."

Surprised by her self-deprecating humor, that so closely reflected his initial assessment of her, he cut his eyes at her sharply. She rewarded him with another of those small, sad smiles.

"I have a new project I want to explore, but James keeps me busy following his agenda instead. And so here I am, flying with you over the beautiful Appalachian Mountains.

"He hates my idea. But I've convinced several of the more open-minded members of the board to consider my designs. A couple of them view my plan favorably. That's why I'm so angry. I'm missing an important director's meeting today, one that could change the way this company operates."

"You think your husband devised this trip to get you out of the way," Sean concluded insightfully, suspecting that self-serving manipulation of his wife would be standard operating procedure for a man like North, and hating him for it.

"Obviously. But he won't get his way this time. James thinks he's already won, by keeping me away from that meeting, but he's in for a huge surprise." Diana's voice held a determined edge.

"That's why I was so engrossed earlier. I was putting the final touches on my proposal and rationale, so I can email it to the board's Vice-Chair, as soon as we get to the resort. He's agreed to present my prospectus, and to actively champion it for me." Her tone was calm and confident, but the telltale way she chewed her lower lip, and clenched and unclenched her fists, gave evidence to the worry and uncertainty gnawing at her.

As she spoke, Sean wondered what would make a woman with her wealth, her connections, and her privilege, look so completely forlorn, so utterly defeated. Noticing the silver hairs streaking through her pale blond ones, the beginning of tiny lines around her eyes, and the softening of the skin under her jaw, he guessed her age to be about ten years more than his thirty-three. It impressed him that she took pride in her maturity, and hadn't sought out a plastic surgeon to keep her looking fresh, flawless, and foolishly young. He ignored the escalating screams of the little voice in his head and asked, "How'd you get hooked up with Mr. North?"

"That's a long and boring story, and I've already said too much." She smiled her practiced smile once more, and it touched him deeply.

He could hardly believe his own ears when the words tumbled out of his mouth, "Hey, I got nothin' but time. Tell on."

"Well…if you insist." Her lips widened into a sincere grin that showed her very white, very straight teeth. "James and I met in college, in a class on small business development. The professor paired us up to work on a project and we've been a team ever since."

Ivy League college I bet, Sean thought with disdain. Pushing down his in-born resentment of her blue-blood privilege, he guessed, "You were business majors?"

"James was, of course, but my major was psychology." Regret was thick in the deep, almost whispered tone of her voice. "I wanted to be a professional counselor, and took the business class as an elective, to find out if I had what it takes to run my own practice."

"But you never did the counselor thing."

Shaking her head, she elaborated, "That assignment changed the plans I had for my life. James didn't want to be partnered with me, because I wasn't a serious business student, but the professor refused to budge on the assignment. It was one of the few times when my husband's skillful negotiation strategies weren't successful, and he ended up stuck – with me.

Finding himself being drawn into her story despite his continued misgivings, Sean quizzed her, "What was the project?"

"Each team had come up with a new product or service, develop a workable strategy to deliver it, and a comprehensive marketing plan. Surprisingly, James and I made a great team. His strengths complimented mine and vice versa. I'm the one with the big ideas. James has the skill, and the backing, to make my dreams a reality."

She paused thoughtfully. "I looked around at the other students like me, moving in and out of dorms or cramped apartments every year, their cars overflowing with leftover junk from their parent's attics, and it seemed like a terrible waste of time and effort. So, I suggested that we develop a leasing business, providing all of the essentials students need to make their lives comfortable – everything from lofts and refrigerators to sound systems and mood lighting. We'd rent a big warehouse to store our products in the off season, and hire a few beefy, financially-strapped fraternity boys to deliver them.

Students would order from catalogues sent home to their parents. A pre-payment and damage deposit requirement would protect our assets."

"Sounds like a great idea. Bet you got a good grade."

"We got an A. James fleshed out the plan and took care of the details, including conducting a market survey, to determine the inventory we'd need to carry. He found the least expensive sources for the items we wanted to stock, and drafted the catalogue and distribution schedule. The professor was very impressed. But not being one to do anything in a small way, the ambitious young heir of the North family fortune talked Daddy into putting up the capital to start up our little venture for real."

"And North Star Enterprises was born," Sean completed for her.

"That's right." She nodded pensively. "The company name was also my idea. The star connotation tickled James' fancy. He says it symbolizes his 'meteoric rise to success, his sparkling business acumen'."

"Not a modest man, is he?" His clever understatement brought a sincere chuckle out of the older woman. The light, airy quality of her laughter charged the air and raised the hairs on the back of Sean's neck.

"The man's ego is vast, and possibly limitless. Though, he does have a few things to be proud of. He parlayed that little college endeavor into a company producing profits in excess of ten million a year. From there we went into land speculation and development, creating planned communities in some of the fastest growing cities in the country. His business sense and investment savvy have made a lot of money for a lot of people, not the least of whom is his own family."

"But he couldn't have done it without you. You showed him the way." The pilot glanced away from his instruments to give her a long, hard look, his respect for her growing grudgingly.

"Maybe. James goes after anything he wants, and he's very persistent. He saw something in me that he needed, and grabbed onto it with both hands. After our success with that project, he became my constant companion. Despite my repeated attempts to free myself, he eventually offered me a deal I couldn't refuse. We were married soon after graduation." Tears unexpectedly welled in her eyes.

Sean didn't want to feel sympathy for the woman. To be brutally honest, he didn't want to feel anything for her, but he couldn't seem to help himself. Those unshed tears moved him. "It wasn't a love match?"

"More like a hostile takeover." She sighed and lowered her face. "To his credit, James never claimed that our marriage was anything more than a good business deal. He never pretended to love me."

Beginning to think that he may have misjudged Diana, Sean felt a resistant empathy growing. "Why'd he insist on marriage? Wouldn't a partnership have served him just as well?"

"James wanted the exclusive and universal rights to my vision. A simple corporate partnership would have given me too much freedom, power, and control. I could have walked away from NSE at any time, as long as I had the resources to pay a competent lawyer. No, James wanted to own me, and the only way to do that was to offer me a bribe so large that I couldn't pass it up, and to make me Mrs. James W. North, III."

The matter-of-fact way she laid bare the circumstances of her unusual relationship with her husband dismayed him. He'd had the guy in his helicopter often enough to know that James North was not to be trusted. He was a barracuda, the kind of man who made you stay on your toes, always watching your six, ready for a surprise attack. North was ever on the lookout for any opportunity that could be turned to an advantage, and Sean refused to provide him with one. How Diana had lived in a loveless marriage with such a selfish and unprincipled husband was completely beyond him.

"You went along with it," he concluded, his tone conveying more concern than he intended.

"Yes, I sacrificed my one true love, and happily ever after, fantasies for a life of wealth and privilege." She stared at him, her startlingly blue eyes still wet with tears. "Does that sound cold and calculating?"

Unwilling to admit exactly what he was thinking about her or her decision, Sean scrunched deeper into his battered leather jacket. "I'm not one to judge."

"That's exactly what it was," she told him frankly, "but I had my reasons, which seemed like good ones at the time. And for years, I had no regrets."

"I hear a 'but' in there somewhere," Sean concluded.

"But…my personal circumstances changed about a year ago, and I started thinking more and more about how I'd never accomplished anything with my life, except to help already well-to-do people make more money than they could ever hope to spend. So, I decided to use my gifts and resources to make a few changes in the way NSE does business."

The expression of expectant defeat, bordering on hopelessness, disappeared from her face as she spoke of her plans. Her eyes sparkled. "North Star communities have, up until now, exclusively catered to the upper crust – large homes, luxury condominiums, health clubs, and golf courses. You get the idea. It troubles me deeply that we've perpetuated such artificial socio-economic stratification, when we should have been building a society that is more diverse, using our vast profits to create a comfortable, safe environment for hardworking people."

"Hey, what are you, a bleeding-heart liberal in conservative wolf's clothing?" he teased, surprised by her revelation.

Her laughter echoed in his headset. "I guess I am at that. For years I've put up a good front, but after serving a long sentence in my make-more-money-at-all-costs prison, I'm breaking out. My new community designs include affordable, handicapped-accessible homes, public transportation, day care and community centers, and plenty of open green-space where children can play safely."

"Seems like a socially responsible plan to me; but let me guess, your husband isn't impressed with the plan."

"Oh, he hates it. He says it's a ridiculous notion, a totally stupid, professionally suicidal idea. We've been arguing over it for months now. James has been furiously adamant in his position. But for once I'm standing firm, too, despite the considerable pressure he applies to bring me to heel. James can't abide disobedience and dissention, especially from the family. Everything has to be his way – or else."

On the occasions when Sean had shuttled James North to New York or Boston, he'd not only learned to watch his back, he'd developed more than a vague distaste for the man. The former Marine could respect the entrepreneur's ruthless drive and determination, but North's overbearing rudeness and smug self-importance, were impossible to tolerate. Preferring the posh NSE private jet, James made no effort to hide his annoyance when circumstances forced him to use the services of Baldwin Aviation's premier copter-jockey. Diana's description of the man's hostile takeover of Vic Baldwin's company, and his unfeeling manipulation of her, congealed that nebulous dislike into a strong aversion.

Unusual readings flashed on several of the helicopter's gauges, drawing Sean's attention away from his passenger. Diana's words faded to background noise as he attended to the urgent demands of his job.

While the pilot was busy flipping switches and adjusting knobs, Diana Grayson North studied the sharp planes and angles of his face. *He's gorgeous,* she thought, carefully absorbing every detail. His close-cropped hair was a deep sable brown. The beard stubble sprouting along his strong jaw was a shade lighter, as were the thick, expressive brows arching over his deeply alluring eyes – eyes like twin pools of warm maple syrup. A slightly crooked nose ended more than a finger's width above his full mouth, the corners of which turned up slightly, in a perpetually mocking grin. A small scar bisected his right eyebrow and another slashed across the point of his prominent chin, giving him a rakish, almost dangerous look.

As she watched his long, tanned fingers deftly and efficiently manipulating the controls, she couldn't help wondering how it would feel to have those skilled hands on her, exploring her curves with the same intense concentration. She shivered involuntarily, surprised by her visceral reaction to him, and thinking that she couldn't remember when any man had, by the simple act of being, aroused her senses any more.

Taking a deep, calming breath, she inquired, "What's wrong?"

"A couple of gauges malfunctioned briefly," he explained. "I was afraid we might have a glitch in the electrical system or something wonky with the onboard computer, but everything's working fine now." The steadiness of his voice reassured her.

"Go on," he urged. "You were saying that you're planning a surprise for your old man."

"No, it's your turn. Tell me about yourself, Sean Cody."

Clearly unaccustomed to his wealthier passengers, particularly those of the feminine persuasion, displaying any interest in him beyond his ability to fly the chopper, the confident, but guarded pilot hedged. "What do you want to know?"

"Well, let's see." She drummed the tip of her index finger against her lower lip. "How did you get to be such a good listener?"

"Sisters," was his simple, cryptic answer.

"Sisters?"

"Four of 'em, all older. They spoiled me rotten and I adored them for it. Still do." He scanned the instrument panel once more before adding, "My folks had given up on having a son after my youngest sister was born, but I surprised them eight years later."

"I'll bet you were pampered unmercifully."

"Spoiled is the word for it." He shot her a devilish smirk. "And I was a quick study, too. It didn't take me long to learn the many benefits of listening to the women in my life."

"I've always wanted a sister." Her frosty eyes misted again. "Tell me about yours."

Falling into a comfortable pace, Sean spoke of his siblings, his face glowing with pride. "Melissa's the oldest. Next comes Kathleen, who's three years younger than Missy, and then Ellen, who was ten when I was born. She just turned forty-three.

They're all married now, except Bridgett, the youngest, with kids of their own. Only Missy and her brood still live at home, but Kathleen and Ellen have places in the same county, near Mom and Dad. Missy's husband, Nelson, will eventually take over the farm when Dad retires, but everyone helps out in busy seasons."

Diana quickly did the math, calculating the pilot's age at thirty-three. For the first time in her life, she wished she could turn back her biological clock a decade or so. Not wanting to think about that, she re-routed the subject a bit. "Your family means a great deal to you. So why did you leave the nest?"

"I was a stupid kid, bored with the tedious routine of farm life. I wanted to see the world, have an adventure. Right after high school graduation, I enlisted in the Marine Corps. My parents were furious. They'd planned for me to go to Virginia Tech to study agriculture, so I could take over the dairy business someday. But to be good at farming you have to love it, and I don't.

"Military life was a better fit. I needed more action than I could get driving tractors and milking cows. The discipline was good for me, too, and I learned to fly. I was planning to go career, but changed my mind and hung up my boots after fifteen years."

"Wasn't as glamorous or as exciting as you'd imagined it would be?" she hypothesized.

"Definitely not glamorous, but I did get more than my share of excitement and adventure. I've seen parts of the world I never even dreamed existed."

She watched him shudder as if he was haunted by unpleasant memories, but she persisted anyway. "Why did you quit?"

He shrugged noncommittally. "My last tour did nothing to uphold the goals I'd vowed to achieve when I enlisted – serving my country and protecting our freedom. The modern military leadership worries more about serving questionable political allies and protecting oil fields and other economic interests. I got fed up."

"Something we have in common," she noted. "We're both trying to get our lives back on the right course. It just took me a few years longer to wise up."

Sean's only comment was a muttered curse. "Shit!" followed by a flurry of desperate action.

"What is it?!" Diana shouted.

His hands flying over the controls, he shouted, "The computer's gone haywire. Electrical system's shorting out!"

Flipping a toggle, he screamed a distress call. "Damn! Radio's dead." Electronic crackling filled the air and a shower of sparks flew out of an instrument array. Sean reached beneath the console and felt around frantically. Cursing again, he jerked his fist back and grabbed the stick in both hands, dipping the helicopter downward and losing altitude rapidly.

"I'm guessing this isn't good," his companion said grimly.

"Nope," he confirmed. "There's a clearing over

there." He waved toward an opening in the trees, just ahead. "I've got to set this baby down." Expertly handling the lurching vehicle, the pilot maneuvered into position and descended sharply. "Hold on! Landing'll be rough. Power could go any second."

As if fulfilling his prophecy, the console went black and the motor died. The silence was deafening. The disabled helicopter fell the last few feet, landing with a tooth-rattling jolt. Sean grabbed off Diana's headset as she clawed at the buckle of her safety harness. "Get out, now!" he yelled. "Run! This thing's gonna blow."

She obeyed without question, throwing open her door and sliding down from the high seat. The pilot followed, pausing only to grab their luggage out of the rear compartment. He rounded the cockpit, ducking under the still vibrating rotors, and sprinted after his passenger. When he'd caught up with her, dropping the bags at her feet, Diana turned, and looked back.

The force of the ear-splitting explosion propelled the man forward, striking the woman's smaller body full-on, and throwing them both to the ground. Using his large frame as a shield, Sean ducked his head, pressing his lips into her hair, and raised his arms to protect her face from the burning debris raining down on them. The air was filled with a choking black smoke. The heat of the flames lapped at his back and his ears rang from the concussion.

But what disturbed him more than the smoke,

or the heat, or the narrowness of their escape, was the intimate contact with the woman lying beneath him. Diana's body was generous and soft, welcoming and comfortable. Her silver locks, streaming loose from the twisted knot on the nape of her neck, smelled of lavender. His lips brushed her temple when she turned her face toward him, and a familiar surge of desire tugged at his groin. He groaned.

"Are you okay?" she whispered hoarsely.

Prompted by her breathless whisper, he hauled himself up and helped her to her feet. "I'm fine. How about you? Any damage done?"

"I don't think so," Diana reassured him, brushing ash off her coat.

"I didn't hurt you when I fell on you?" He appreciated the blush of high color that slid up her long neck and across the fair skin of her prominent cheekbones.

Shaking her head, she told him, "You sure are a handy man to have around in an emergency. Thanks."

"That's what you pay me for," he snapped. "Come on, let's get out of here." Shouldering his knapsack and her suitcase, and taking her arm, he guided her from the clearing and into the edge of a thick pine forest. In the distance, the twisted remains of the helicopter, a grotesque metal skeleton, glowed ominously. Plumes of acrid smoke rose skyward.

TWO

"Shouldn't we stay near the wreckage?" Diana asked the big man as he charged ahead through the underbrush. "What if someone heard the explosion or saw the fire and called 911? The searchers won't know where to look for us if we stray too far."

Sean trudged on, never slowing. Unreasonably, he seemed to be trying to put as much distance as possible between them and the crash site. "I doubt anyone saw anything. We'd been flying over remote forest for some time."

"Give me your cell phone," she ordered. "Mine was in my brief case."

"Don't carry one," he barked.

"Are you kidding me? Who doesn't carry a cell phone?" she asked shrilly.

"Don't need one. Helicopters have radios," he declared.

"You're unbelievable!" she told him with a shrug of frustration.

Pausing to pull a stocking cap and a pair of gloves out of his jacket pocket, he asked her, "What time were you expected to check in at the lodge?"

"Around one. The board meeting starts at three-thirty, so I planned to get there in time to email my prospectus prior to that. I don't like cutting things too close," she answered breathlessly, struggling to keep up with the younger man's ground-eating strides.

"You reserved your room with a credit card?"

When she nodded in the affirmative, he continued, "Then the resort won't care whether you check in or not. They already have their money. Your co-conspirator on that board won't get concerned until just before the meeting, when he hasn't gotten the info you promised to send. He might assume that you've gotten cold feet, but even he is worried, he won't be able to follow up until the meeting's over, because he won't want to tip his hand to your husband."

Diana lowered her head in defeat, but stubbornly refused to confirm that his deductions were accurate.

"How long do those board things usually go?"

"Depends," she hedged.

"Take a guess," he prompted sharply.

"Two hours, sometimes more," Diana admitted.

"So, it could be late afternoon before anyone checks on you, right?"

"I guess it could," she admitted reluctantly. "But won't Vic expect you to report in upon arrival?"

"I only notify him when there's a problem. Since I was staying over to fly you home tomorrow afternoon, he won't suspect that something's gone wrong for twenty-four hour or mores."

That revelation did nothing to calm her fears. Assuming the practiced, superior attitude she always used when she felt threatened, Diana tried to force him to backtrack to the chopper. "I still think the wisest course of action would be to stay near the clearing, where we could be seen from the air. You're an employee of an NSE subsidiary, so technically that makes me your boss. As such, I insist that we turn around immediately."

Rounding on her, his face twisted in anger, he snarled. "It's a good thing one of us knows something about wilderness survival then, isn't it, Miss High and Mighty?" His irritating tone dripped sarcasm.

"In case you haven't noticed, we've landed on a deserted stretch of mountain-top, and the temperature's dropping. It may be mid-March, but it's still winter at this altitude. The sky looks like it's going to drop some snow or freezing rain at any second. There was no shelter anywhere around the crash site, and I don't have tools in my pack to build one. So, unless you make it a habit to carry a hatchet in your Louis Vuitton, Mrs. North, I suggest we keep heading downhill, with our eyes open for a place to hole up, if the weather breaks bad."

Hurt and humiliated, Diana sniffed back stinging tears, as she picked her way through a patch of prickly vines, following Sean's broad back as he moved away from her rapidly. Small openings in the tree branches overhead, through which low clouds of a leaden gray peaked, gave evidence that the man was right about the probability of precipitation, and her apprehension grew. Diana quickened her pace to catch up and apologize for pressuring him, but when she approached, she heard the pilot muttering under his breath.

"Damned rich bitch, I knew she'd be nothing but trouble. Should have listened to my gut and turned down this hop."

Diana tucked her face into the collar of her coat and muffled the apology. For what seemed like hours, while they trudged on, the silence was broken only by the chatter of squirrels and chirp of birds moving in the canopy and underbrush. It began to snow. Large wet flakes plopped and crackled when they struck the leafy forest floor and started to dissolve.

It grew steadily colder. The flakes stopped melting and began piling up. Soon there was a thin blanket of white covering everything. Sean glanced at Diana, clearly still angry about her high-handed attempt to intimidate him, and shot her an I-told-you-so stare.

When his warm brown eyes met her cool blue ones, the accusing look evaporated. The wind had whipped her hair until it hung in loose, wet strands. Her nose was as red as her lips were blue. Even with the vigorous exercise and expensive coat, wrapped tightly around her, she was shivering.

He swore again. "Aw hell, Diana, you're freezing. Why didn't you say something?" Kneeling down, he unzipped her overnight case and fumbled through its contents.

It was the first time she'd heard him speak her given name, and despite his use of it in conjunction with the expletive, it sounded wonderful. Rolling off his lips, it echoed in her head and rushed through her veins, lessening the chill a bit.

"Didn't you bring any practical clothing with you?" he snapped in frustration, finding only a plastic bag of toiletries, a pair of silk pajamas, and a change of lingerie. "You were headed for a resort, for crissake. Don't you society broads believe in jeans and sweat shirts?"

Stuttering through chattering teeth, she defended herself. "It was a business trip. The relaxing weekend bit was a front. I didn't know I was going to need sports clothes, but there's a cable-knit sweater in the bottom of the bag."

Pulling the desired garment out with an annoyed sigh, Sean threw everything else back into the case and ripped the zipper closed. "I can't believe I risked my life to save your underwear and toothpaste. Here, I'll hold your overcoat while you put this on."

She tried to unbutton the heavy topcoat, but her numb fingers refused to cooperate. Tucking her sweater under one arm, he pulled off his gloves and pinched them against his side with the other elbow, so he could help her. By the time he slipped the last button through its hole, his hands were shaking almost as badly as hers, making Diana wonder if the cold temperatures were having more of an impact on him than he was letting on.

"I'm sorry, Sean," she breathed as he pulled the long coat off of her shoulders. "I really appreciate your thoughtfulness, and I'm sorry for putting you in danger."

"Forget it," he snapped, apparently still irritated. "It's not your fault." Once she'd tugged the sweater over her suit, he folded her back into the cashmere coat and fastened it up tightly. Then he handed her his gloves, and transferred the knit cap from his dark head to her fair one.

Doing up the top hook on his leather bomber and jamming his hands deeper into his pockets, he asked her, his tone a bit softer, "Better?"

"Much, thanks," she murmured, offering him that familiar, sad smile.

"Let's move," he ordered. "We've got to find shelter and make a fire. It'll be dark soon." She nodded and started after him, grateful when he slowed the pace.

As they trudged on, she studied him, thinking that all he needed was a white scarf, flung around his neck, to make him look like a WWI flying ace. "Why helicopters?" she asked.

"What?"

"Why not airplanes? Big, bad jet airplanes? You seem like the kind of guy who'd be dashing off at mach three, into the wild blue, not puttering along a couple of hundred feet above the ground."

"I'm too big for jets," he explained. "I don't fit into those tiny, cramped seats. Helicopters are more my style. Us Marines prefer to leave jets to the show-off Navy and Air Force hot shots. Give me a good, reliable chopper anytime."

Stopping to take a long look around, he changed the subject abruptly. "See that rocky ridge?" He indicated a rugged hilltop sticking up above the treetops. "It looks promising. Let's angle over that way."

When they rounded a small, raised knoll, they broke through the foliage and into a small, cleared depression about ten feet wide. The narrow ribbon of white snaked through the surrounding forest in both directions. "It's a logging road," Sean said, stating the obvious.

"Which way should we go?" Diana asked, a spark of hope flashing in her clear blue eyes.

He pointed to the right, where the road veered around a sharp bend. The going was much easier on the cleared ground; but even so, dusk was falling heavily before they reached the ridge, where the small roadway tapered into a dead-end.

"What do we do now?" The tired woman sighed, her shoulders drooping in defeat.

"Hang on. There's something over there, tucked under that outcropping. I'm gonna check it out." Jogging ahead, to get a better look in the rapidly diminishing light, he called back to her, an excited lilt in his tone, "Hurry! It's a hunting cabin."

By the time she got close enough to make out the outline of the tiny wooden structure, that had been built under a rocky overhang, Sean had the door open. "It wasn't locked," he said, grinning widely. "I guess the owner's not worried about burglars, this far out in the boonies, or else there's nothing here worth steeling."

Placing a wide palm in the middle of Diana's back, he guided her into the dim interior. "Let's get some more light in here." Dropping the bags onto the dusty floor, he crossed to a large window, leaned over a beat-up sofa, and pushed back the tattered canvas curtain. The dying rays of the setting sun shone through the streaked glass, giving the room an eerie glow.

Diana looked around her. The cabin consisted of one room, with a slanting roof that dipped down in the back, where the structure had been constructed to follow the hillside behind it. Near the front was the kitchen area, complete with a sink, hand pump, and rough Formica countertop. A heavy woodstove stood out from the wall, halfway back. Behind it, under the low part of the ceiling, was an old, iron-framed bed. The battered sofa, sagging under the one large window, and a scarred cupboard, small table, and four chairs were the only furnishings.

A bare bulb hung from a porcelain fixture in the middle of the ceiling. Sean jerked the string with no effect. "There's no electrical service, so there must be a generator outside somewhere. I'll go see if I can locate it. While I'm gone, look around for some candles."

Pulling off his hat and gloves, and tucking them into the pockets of her coat, Diana searched the white enameled cupboard. In it, she found a lighter and an antique oil lamp.

When Sean shouldered the door open once more, his arms full of firewood, she had already placed the lamp on the chipped table and lit it. The kerosene-yellow glow cast ominous shadows around the room, but made the cabin decidedly more inviting.

"There's a generator in a shed around on the side, but no fuel." Dropping his load beside the cast iron stove, he opened it and began pushing logs inside. "If we can get a fire going, this place should warm up pretty fast. I see you found some matches."

"Better than that," she smirked, handing him the long-nosed lighter she'd removed from the cabinet drawer.

"Now all we need is some dry kindling. These pine needles are wet from the snow." His hands on his hips, he pivoted, his sharp brown eyes scanning the room.

"How about paper? Would paper work?" she offered.

"Sure, if we had any," he grumbled, dismissing her, and returning to his vain attempt to ignite the wet tinder. Reaching into a cardboard box she'd noticed, pushed up under the cupboard, she pulled out several old newspapers, rolled them into a tube, and tapped him lightly on the shoulder.

"Stop playing around!" With a backhanded swipe, he whirled around, glaring at her. She just smiled and waved the papers in his face.

"Thanks," he growled, snatching them out of her hand.

While Sean started the fire, Diana went back to the cabinet, where she located a variety of canned goods and cooking utensils. Using an ancient, crank-type can opener, she peeled back the lid of a large container of beef stew, dumping the contents into a clean saucepan. She placed the pot's blackened bottom on the top of the stove to heat, and turned back to the sink, cranking the hand pump until it flowed with clear, cold water.

Sticking a battered coffeepot under the flow, she filled it. Then she opened a can of fresh coffee and shook the aromatic blend into the aluminum basket. Soon, the pot was perched atop the rapidly warming stove, bubbling merrily. Diana warned her companion, "It's been a long time since I brewed coffee like this, so I can't guarantee it. At least it'll be hot enough to warm you from the inside out." Securing small jars of sugar and powdered creamer from the cupboard, she added, "We may need these to make the stuff palatable."

"Won't hear me complaining," Sean said, pulling off his jacket and dropping it over a hook on the wall behind the door. "I'm just glad I didn't have to carry the wood, build the fire, and cook the food. I figured you to be too spoiled to pitch in."

The sad smile sliding across her lips, she sniffed, "Not that it's any of your business, but I haven't always been wealthy. I learned how to take care of myself when I was very young, and that's something one never forgets. No amount of privilege can wipe out the lessons learned as a result of deprivation." Her voice had a sharp, wounded edge.

His apology took her by surprise. "I'm sorry, Diana, that quip was uncalled for."

"Forget it," she snapped back, her tone mimicking the one he'd used on her. "I know how you feel about me, Sean. You've made it quite clear. Unfortunately, it looks like you're stuck with me, maybe for quite a while. You'll get to see that I don't always live up to my 'Ice Queen' nickname. Not entirely anyway."

Staring at her in stunned silence, his warm brown eyes wide, his jaw slack, Sean didn't seem to know how to respond.

Laughing at his discomfort, Diana asked, "Surprised you, didn't I? Bet you had no idea that the derogatory label had reached my overly-indulged ears."

"No... that is..." he stuttered.

"It's okay. Name-calling is one thing I've endured, in one form or another, all my life, so I'm quite immune to it. Actually, James picked up the latest tempting slur on his most recent trip with Baldwin Aviation. You did the flying, I believe, and your Miss Stewart went along for the ride. He overheard her using the clever insult and immediately claimed it as his own. He thinks it's very appropriate and uses it on me quite frequently. When he's around, I do my best to prove that I deserve the handle."

If Sean had any thoughts about her revelation, he didn't voice them. Considering the matter closed, Diana turned back toward the stove to check on the progress of their dinner.

The small room was warming nicely, so she shrugged out of her long coat, and placed it on a hook beside the pilot's leather bomber. Then she pulled off the cable knit sweater, removed her jacket, and slipped the sweater back over her head. Picking up her overnight case from the spot on the floor where Sean had dropped it, she carried it to the back of the cabin and laid it on the bed, draping her suit jacket over it.

"That stew's probably ready." Noting the time on her white-gold Rolex, she added, "And the coffee should be done, too."

Moments later, she ladled two chipped bowls full of the savory stew, and poured the steaming brown liquid into heavy mugs. Moving from the place he'd staked out on one end of the worn sofa, Sean joined her at the table, inhaling deeply.

"Smells wonderful," he offered, dipping out a large spoonful and blowing on the contents to cool them.

"Only because you're famished," she admitted. "Saving damsels in distress from exploding helicopters has a way of whetting the appetite."

His only response was a grim, one-sided grin.

Both the stew and the coffee proved to be passable, and they consumed them in silence, filling their empty stomachs and driving away the last of the chill. Breaking the atmosphere of quiet acceptance that was beginning to grow between them, Sean shocked her by asking, "So how long were you married before your husband started fooling around?"

Diana's frosty blue eyes measured him warily, taking stock, and weighing the sincerity of his words. When she didn't answer immediately, he conjectured, "I guess you're wondering how I know about Mr. North's indiscretions."

"No," she declared quietly, pausing to pull the last of the pins from her disheveled coiffure. "You're a bright guy. I'm sure you figured out that there was no reason for my husband to take your little office manager along on a business trip, other than hanky-panky. But I am surprised you've deduced that I'm not blissfully ignorant of James' many affairs.

"He usually shrouds his liaisons in the utmost secrecy, pretending that he wants to keep me in the dark. He likes to portray me as the big, dumb blonde – the stupid cow of a wife, who doesn't have a clue what's really going on. So how did you arrive at the astute conclusion that I'm on to James and his numerous indiscretions?"

Diana noted that Sean was regarding her intently, and she wondered what he was hoping to find. A chink in her protective armor perhaps? Well, that was unlikely. She hadn't been bothered by James' cheating for years. The same couldn't be said for the pilot's steady regard, however. That bothered her – big time. Nervously, she shook her head until her platinum curls fell over her face. She couldn't bring herself to meet his gaze.

"From Sheila. She bragged about the affair and told me that you know about it," he admitted. "Her relationship with your husband is all she talks about anymore. But not at first. Early on, it was like you said – top secret. I suspected something was going on between them and confronted her, only to have her deny it. But following the New York jaunt, things changed. I've had to hear every detail of that trip, repeated, over and over. Sheila's convinced herself that your husband's going to throw you over for her. It pleases her to think that she's beaten you in a contest for him and she's gloating over the victory."

Diana sighed, picturing James' classically handsome face, surrounded by wavy auburn hair styled to perfection, a small widow's peak framing the top of his elegant forehead, and intense gray eyes, peering out over an aristocratic nose. His smile was a testament to orthodontic perfection, and his fine-boned chin was cleft by a deep, irresistible dimple. It was no wonder women swooned over him. "She wouldn't be so proud of her accomplishment, if she knew that she's merely the last in a long line of conquests."

"Probably not. This is nothing new?"

"Hardly. James has always made it clear that he isn't attracted to me, physically. I'm not his type. He much prefers petite women, like your Miss Stewart. Tiny in all dimensions except the chest, of course. Maybe it's because they make him feel big, and strong, and decidedly superior; but whatever the reason, he's almost always has one of his little tarts on the string."

Diana was surprised to note that Sean seemed honestly disturbed by her husband's blatant disregard for her feelings, and for the sanctity of their wedding vows. "I can't believe your marriage has been completely, uh..." he stuttered, searching for the right words.

"Celibate?" She provided, grinning knowingly. "Of course not. James didn't want to give me the option of annulment, so he quickly made sure our union was properly consummated. After that he ignored me, until he decided that he wanted an heir to the North fortune. Then, for over a year, he turned my life into a continuous conception project.

"It's almost funny really," Diana said, without humor or even the hint of a smile, her heart lurching. "I had to take my temperature every morning, to determine when I was ovulating. Then he'd come by to service me at the appropriate time, like it was just another task on his endless to-do list. Board meeting – check. Contract negotiation – check. Sex with wife – check. Workout at gym – check. You get the idea."

"How many children do you have?" Sean queried, somewhat hesitantly.

"None, thank goodness. When I didn't conceive after several months of trying, James insisted that I see a fertility specialist. He was sure that I was the problem, because of my 'unfortunate upbringing,' as he calls it. Being an old-money, New England blueblood, his genetic makeup is beyond reproach. They put me through every test imaginable, but could find nothing wrong. Finally, James agreed to testing himself and found out that he's infertile. There's no hope that he will ever father a child. So, that was the end of that. He stopped visiting my bed."

"Sounds pretty cold-blooded," the pilot noted, his brows pulled together in a frown of obvious resentment.

"Yes, well, I guess it was, but then I knew what I was getting myself into," she admitted without apology.

"Don't you think you deserve more?" The calm, accepting way she spoke of her unfulfilling marriage seemed to distress him.

"More? Like what? True love? Come on, Sean, I'm a middle-aged woman, and a realist. I traded those childish fantasies for a fat bank account. I have regrets, of course, countless regrets. I've never stopped wishing for a caring husband, a true life-partner, not one who just tolerates me because of the business success I bring him. But I don't fool myself. Pure, self-less love only exists in fairy tales."

"That's not true. I know people who are deeply in love – my parents, my sisters and their husbands, for example," Sean insisted, trying to get her to see the possibility.

"A few, very lucky people might be fortunate enough to experience a pale imitation of love, for some small portion of their lives, but I'm not one of them. I gave up my chance at love, bartered it away, when I married James." Not wanting him to see how much this discussion hurt her, she lowered her face to hide the painful tears stinging her eyes.

Sean sat by speechlessly, watching the teardrops slide down her cheeks. He reached across the table and took her hand in his. She knew her fingers felt cold and practically bloodless. After a few seconds, she pulled away, rubbing the hand he'd held with the other, and raised her eyes to look at him squarely, issuing an unspoken challenge.

"My father ran off a week after I was born, and my mom struggled to raise me alone. She had no education, and few skills, so she worked part-time, wherever she could, whenever she could, at menial, low-paying jobs. We moved from one dilapidated, roach-infested apartment to another, one step ahead of the bill collectors. The food stamps usually ran out before the month did.

"College was a dream I never expected to attain, but thanks to a very special high school guidance counselor, who encouraged me and made me believe in myself, I got up the courage to apply. When I was accepted on a partial academic scholarship, Mom was thrilled. I had to work hard to make it through, but it was worth it. James' marriage proposal included an offer to take care of my mother, for the rest of her life. Accepting it meant that she would never have to work again, or want for anything. I couldn't bring myself to refuse."

Why are you telling him this? she demanded of her willful heart. *Why is it so important for Sean to understand the truth about you, about your past?* Those were questions she couldn't answer, didn't want to answer. Wiping away a tear with the back of her hand, she sighed. "There you have it. My story. Whether you wanted to hear it or not, there it is. Maybe now you can see why I don't believe in happily ever after."

Sean squirmed in his seat and nervously cleared his throat. "Guess you've got reasons for being such a cynic." After a pause he added. "I have one more question."

"Shoot," she breathed.

"Why didn't adopt a kid? You have the money."

"I was willing, but James wanted no part of it. His blue-blood heritage means too much to him. It was a stretch for him to accept me as a suitable mother for his child, since I come from such inferior stock; but ultimately, his huge ego took over, assuring him that his superior genes would make up for any deficiencies I might bring to the mix." Choking back tears again, she turned her face away.

"James said adoption was too much of a genetic crap shoot. The truth is, he can't bear the thought of any child without so much as one drop of precious North blood, inheriting his fortune and the company he's worked so hard to build. So instead, he's taken a nephew under his wing, his brother's youngest son, Justin, and he's grooming him to take over NSE."

Once she had her emotions under control, and the sad smile pasted back in its customary place, she looked at him again. Sean asked her, "That's okay with you?"

She nodded as she spoke. "Justin's a good kid...or man, I should say. He has one more year at the University of Virginia, and then he'll go to work for the company, full-time, next summer. I'm not sure James realizes the kid's full potential, though. He has that rare combination of vision and business sense. Before long, he'll be putting his old uncle to shame."

"I'd like to see that," Sean admitted.

"I take it you're not particularly fond of my husband. He hasn't won you over with his overwhelming charm and personal warmth?" Sean's disapproval of James pleased Diana. A twinkle flickered in her bright blue eyes.

"'Not particularly fond' is a considerable understatement. He's egotistical, phony, and untrustworthy. Of course, he's never gone out of his way to impress me. Why would he? I'm just a glorified chauffeur." Sean leaned back in his chair, stretched out his long legs, and crossed them at the ankles.

"I think you have the man pegged, and I'm glad you can see through him. Most folks can't." Running her fingers through her hair, she leaned across the table and grinned at him, glad she'd opened up.

"I have no idea why I'm telling you my life history. I'm not usually so forthcoming, not with all the gory details of my personal life. The years I've lived under the watchful eye of the great and powerful North family have taught me to guard every word I say, and to keep most things to myself. But, you asked, and I trust you. I guess that's what you get for saving my life – my eternal trust and devotion." She offered him another of her sad smiles.

"Okay, that's enough about me and my crazy, mixed-up sham of a marriage." Her smile transformed into a genuine, teasing smirk, and her eyes twinkled with azure highlights, an unusual mischievousness bubbling up inside her. "What about you, Sean Cody? Why haven't you fallen prey to some determined female with her cap set for you? You're a big, strong, good-looking guy. I know you've had more than your share of offers."

Clearly embarrassed by the question, Sean tilted his head sideways, and looked at her out of the corner of his eye, his arms folded across his chest.

Undaunted by his silence, she prodded, "Come on, Sean. I have no romance in my long and unfulfilling marriage. You must let me experience it vicariously, through you. I want juicy details!" Lowering her voice to a husky whisper, she taunted,

"Tell me about your love affairs."

"Not a chance," he protested, an attractive blush rising up his neck.

Refusing to be outmaneuvered, she teased, "What else do you have to do? It'll pass the time. Besides, you owe me. I bared my soul to you."

Giving in with a resigned sigh, Sean laced his fingers on the top of his head. "I was engaged once, to a girl from my home town – my high school sweetheart, Patti Martin. We were planning to get married after I'd completed my first two-year tour. She was anxious to travel, to get away from rural life and see exciting new places, but she agreed to wait for me till I'd earned my stripes, and was making enough money to support a family."

"But she didn't."

"About six months after I graduated boot camp, I got the 'Dear John' letter. She was all apologetic, begged for my forgiveness, said she hoped we could still be friends, wished me luck in my career…blah, blah, blah. You know the rest of that story."

"Who was he?" Diana asked, intuitively sensing where his tale was headed.

"A new dentist who'd moved into the area after I left." Sean licked his full lips, which were drawn into a grim line. His rugged jaw twitched with suppressed pain. "I guess she figured he'd be able to give her the things I wouldn't. They were already married when I got her note."

"That must have been terrible. I'm sorry," Diana offered sincerely.

He gestured widely, waving off her sympathy. "It's water under the bridge. What's past is past.

You can't change it, so you just have to learn to live with it."

"Maybe, but rejection still hurts. I know." The fair woman's eyes touched him softly and her heart ached. "Has her life been better with him than it would have been with you?"

"Probably," the handsome pilot admitted. "She's got a huge house on the lake, three spoiled kids, a garage full of fancy cars, and a membership at the country club. Plus, she's the reigning queen of the local junior league. I would have dragged her all over the world, to some of the most remote and uninviting places, and left her alone for weeks at a time while I was out on assignment. She would have had a very lonely life."

"Maybe," Diana conjectured, "but she would have gotten to travel, to see the world. Instead, she gave up her dream of an exciting life in foreign lands for a comfortable life in the old hometown she was so desperate to leave.

"I know what it's like to make compromises, and to live with regret," she whispered, her eyes misting again. Sniffing back the tears, she added, "I wonder if your former sweetheart's been content with the sacrifice she made."

"Who knows and who cares?" he snapped, his irritation obvious.

Diana ignored his reticence and persisted. "You were a young Marine, foot-loose and fancy free, as they say. Who was your next conquest?",

Sighing again, Sean reluctantly admitted, "After Patti dumped me, I was pretty bitter. Refused to let any woman get close to me. I had a few flings.

Guess I was the typical guy with something to prove. But my lifestyle didn't lend itself to long-term relationships. None of my many girlfriends stuck around more than a date or two – three at the most."

"Your life is certainly more predictable now, since you've been flying for Baldwin Aviation," his lovely companion offered. "Haven't you been looking for a nice girl who wants to settle down? There must be thousands of eligible women in Northern Virginia who'd jump at the chance to go out with a guy like you."

"I wouldn't know. My flight schedule's pretty full. Most of the women I've met have been clients. And so far, few of them have done anything to make me want to spend any more time with them than is absolutely necessary. I had my fill of being ordered around when I was in the military." Stretching his arms over his head, the pilot yawned widely. Clearly, he was exhausted from the grueling day, and in desperate need of a few hours of shut eye.

"You're holding something back, I can tell," Diana quipped, probing. "There's been at least one lady-love in your life recently, hasn't there? You're looking much too smug and self-satisfied. Out with it. Tell me everything."

Groaning, he shifted forward and propped his elbows on the table. "Damn, woman. You're persistent. As much as I hate to admit it, I dated Sheila a few times. She's a terrible flirt, and I desperately needed an ego boost, so it was inevitable that we'd hook up. Vic warned me off her but I didn't listen. Any woman who's been married and divorced three times, before thirty, is trouble waiting for a place to happen.

"It didn't last long. I got fed up and cut her loose. She was really ticked at me – stayed mad for weeks. Keyed my truck, not that you could tell – thing's a piece of crap – called me out on social media, texted continuously, followed me home and sat outside my apartment, etc., etc. I was beginning to think it was fatal-attraction time, then she landed your old man and let me off the hook."

"Why didn't it work out between you?" Diana asked.

"Sheila might be your husband's type, but she's not mine. She's whiny and manipulative, which I hate. And, she's too short. I don't like doubling over to kiss a short woman. Breaks my back. Then there's the sex." He flushed hotly again. "Let's just say I don't like having to search around to find the woman in my bed."

"I get the picture," Diana whispered, feeling a blush spreading across her face as well, and thankful for the inadequate illumination the lamp produced. Surprising herself with an uncharacteristic boldness, she challenged him. "What sort of woman is your type, Mr. Cody?"

If he responded to her question, the words were clipped off before they could escape his lips. The long hard look he shot at her before pushing himself up out of his chair sent a chill down her spine and told her she'd gone too far.

"It's getting late and I'm beat. Let's see what we can do about sleeping arrangements."

Accepting the brush-off with relief, she agreed. "I'm tired, too, and nature's calling. Since I don't see any sanitary facilities in here, I assume they're out there somewhere, in the dark."

"There's a pit privy down the hill to the right, about thirty yards," he said, confirming her fears. "It's still snowing, so be careful. Take the lamp. You'll need it."

"That's not necessary." She slid her chair back and crossed to the cupboard. "I saw a flashlight in here somewhere." Rifling through the drawer, she pulled out the desired item and slid the ON button forward. A thin beacon of white light shot out of the unit, slicing across the shadows. "Looks like it works." Tugging on her coat, she added, "I'll be right back."

THREE

When Diana returned, shivering, Sean had already turned the lamp down and curled up on the sagging sofa under a light blanket, his leather jacket rolled up under his head. "I found another blanket, a pillow, and a sleeping bag. The zipper on the bag is broken but it should work as a comforter."

"Thanks," she acknowledged, through chattering teeth, noting that he had spread a blanket over the bare mattress, covered it with the unzipped sleeping bag, and topped it with a flannel-covered pillow. "The wind's picking up."

"I can tell." He wiggled deeper into the bend of the couch, pulling the thin cover up tightly under his chin. "I stoked the fire, but this place is drafty as hell. The window leaks like a sieve."

The cuffs of her wool pants were wet from the snowdrifts she'd trudged through on her short trip down the hill, so Diana decided to change into her nightclothes. Her silk pajamas might be thin, but thin and dry was preferable to heavy and wet. Glancing in Sean's direction, she was relieved to see that he'd turned away from her, and was facing the back of the sofa.

She quickly donned the bright blue pajamas,

thankful that she'd elected to wear thick socks under her boots. She hung her pants over the footboard, where the hems could dry, tucked her jewelry into her overnight bag, and climbed into the tall, iron-framed bed.

Though the rest of the room was growing steadily colder, the low roof at the back of the cabin trapped the warmer air, transforming Diana's bed into a cozy nest. Exhaustion soon overtook her and she drifted into a deep sleep.

The big pilot was not nearly so comfortable. The sofa was lumpy and too short for his long legs. The frigid air, seeping in around the large window above him, chilled him through the threadbare blanket, heavy jeans, and thick knit shirt he wore. He had a sweat suit in his knapsack, which he debated putting on, too, but the cold made him unwilling to move.

Grumbling to himself, he wondered what Diana had done with his hat and gloves. Reluctantly, he unfolded his jacket and slipped his arms inside it, sacrificing his pillow for the added warmth. Just as he'd made up his mind to go in search of his stocking cap, an explosive crash split the air, followed by several smaller, but no less alarming, thuds.

Startled out of her dreams by the sound, Diana gasped, "What was that?"

A grating screech sounded against the tin roof overhead, setting Sean's teeth on edge. "Sounds like something fell on the roof," he conjectured. "I'd better check it out." Grabbing the flashlight off the table where she'd laid it, he barked at her, obviously irritated, "Where're my hat and gloves?"

"Oh, sorry," she whispered, contrite, "I'll get them." She threw back the covers and started to slide out of the bed.

"Stay where you are," he ordered. "There's no use in both of us freezing our asses off. Just tell me where you put them."

"They're in the pocket of my coat, on the hook by the door," she said meekly.

Locating the desired items, he jerked the cap down far enough to cover his ears and tugged on the gloves. When he threw open the door, a blast of arctic-like air whooshed in, making the lamp flicker. "Be careful!" she called after his disappearing back.

Moments later he reappeared, snow swirling in behind him. "The wind splintered a tree on the top of the cliff. A huge limb has dropped onto the roof. It brought a shower of rocks down with it. I can't see much from the ground, so I don't know if there's been any damage." He crossed to the cabinet, searched the drawer, and pulled out a large, serrated knife.

"What are you going to do with that?" she asked, her sapphire eyes shining.

"A hacksaw would be more efficient, but this will have to do. Debris may be blocking the chimney. I've got to get up on the roof to find out for sure. I might have to cut away some branches."

"Is there anything I can do to help?" she asked.

"Yeah, sure. You could give me a boost up onto the roof!" he snapped sarcastically, as he reached for the doorknob. Then he paused, his well-entrenched training forcing him to troubleshoot this potentially hazardous situation prior to jumping into it. His dark eyes quickly scanned the small room, looking for any useful tool which might have escaped his notice.

When his gaze fell on Diana he froze. She looked so worried, and so vulnerable, that he scolded himself for his insensitivity. Deliberately softening his tone, he told her, "Stay put. I can handle this."

Long minutes passed. Diana could hear the determined man scaling the rough boards of the cabin wall, pulling his considerable bulk onto the top. His footsteps, though muffled by the snow, echoed inside the tiny room. A vision of the brave pilot struggling to keep his footing on the wet, icy tin flashed in her mind's eye. A shrill screech, like fingernails against a blackboard, followed, as Sean dragged the offending limbs across the metal roof.

Howling wind battered the front of the small building, making the worried woman cringe and shiver. She knew her stalwart rescuer would be all but freezing up there on his high perch. Finally, a muffled plop near the back of the cabin, signaled that Sean had dropped off the roof at its lowest point, and she let out the breath she didn't realize she'd been holding.

Several moments later, he popped through the rough wooden portal, covered head to toe with white powder, his breath wreathing his head. "Damn, it's cold!" he complained, his teeth chattering. "We're lucky. Roof's okay. S... some of the limbs were blocking the chimney pipe, but I was able to m... move them." He tossed the knife into the sink.

"That's good," she replied softly.

"Sn... snow's just about stopped." He went on, brushing off his jacket. "I was s…standing under the overhang when a b…big ledge let go of its load, d…dumping it right d…down my neck. I think I g…got enough of the stuff inside my jacket to make a good s…sized snowman."

Picking up his pack, he laid it on the table and dug around inside until he found his heavyweight sweatpants. He pulled off the cap and gloves, wiggled out of his soggy jacket, and hung it over the back of a chair near the stove. Then, with blue fingers, he clumsily unlaced his boots and kicked them off. Next, he unfastened his belt and started peeling off his jeans.

"What are you doing?" Diana shrieked, her voice shrill with panic.

"M…my clothes are soaking wet." He shivered again. "I'm not going to s…sit around here f…freezing my backside off just to protect your delicate sensibilities. If you d…don't want to watch, look the other way." She saw him suppress a laugh, when she deliberately scrunched down under the covers and turned her face away from him. She also caught a glimpse of the mischievous grin he made no effort to disguise.

Thankfully though, she'd taken refuge beneath the covers before he could notice the deep flush of color rising in her cheeks. She tried to sink as deeply as possible into the soft mattress, pulling the sleeping bag up around her face. Forcing her eyes away, she stared at the darkened window, beyond which an occasional flake of white flashed. Then she gasped, as she realized that Sean's movements were clearly visible, reflected in the mirror-like surface of the glass.

Despite the impropriety of her actions, and the embarrassment she felt at her audacity, she couldn't force her gaze elsewhere. She watched intently as he shucked out of his jeans and draped them over a chair. His legs were long, lean and muscular. Feeling the tail of his shirt for traces of dampness, he drew it off over his head and placed it beside the denim pants. He stood before her in nothing but a T-shirt and boxer shorts, and when it became obvious that he intended to remove those as well, she choked back a sigh.

He's as beautiful as a bronze statue, she thought, fascinated. Impossibly broad shoulders capped his v-shaped back, which tapered to a narrow waist and well-rounded derrière. When he bent down to step into the sweatpants, she could see the sinews of his arms rippling in the flickering lamplight. Her heart thudded in her chest and she bit her lip to keep it from quivering.

Once the lower half of his body was covered again, he took his time searching through the knapsack for the matching gray sweatshirt, then he crossed the room to retrieve his blanket. When he reached the sofa, the darkened surface of the window glass caught his attention. He raised one eyebrow as he stared directly into his reflection.

Flashing a lopsided smirk, he slowly turned toward the woman, peering into the shadows at the back of the cabin.

Diana's eyes slammed shut. *Oh, my goodness,* she prayed, *I hope he didn't catch me staring.* The thought mortified her. When he turned back, she cracked her eyelids just wide enough to see that he was trying to suppress the widening grin that tugged at the corners of his full mouth.

She squeezed her eyes tightly shut again until a strange creaking sparked her curiosity. Peeking out over the covers, she located Sean, slouching uncomfortably in one of the wooden ladder-back chairs, pulled up close to the stove, the blanket wrapped, mummy-like, around him. He was still shivering.

"What are you're doing?"

"Trying to get w…warm. It's c…cold as blue blazes over there." He nodded his damp head in the general direction of the sagging couch.

"Sean, you're exhausted. You can't sleep sitting up," she complained.

"Oh, I agree, b…but I don't have m…much choice, do I?" His dark eyes snapped.

After a moment's hesitation, she swallowed hard, took a deep breath to ratchet up her courage and suggested, "Look. We're both adults. This bed is large enough for two, and it's nice and warm. It's silly for me to hog it and leave you out there freezing. It doesn't make sense for you to sit up all night, probably making yourself sick, just for the sake of propriety."

"Thanks for the offer, but I c…couldn't," he

declined.

"I don't bite. I promise," she teased, prodding him. "Just pretend you're a kid again, sleeping with one of your big sisters. Come on... I dare you."

"You win," he agreed with a groan, unable to ignore the gauntlet she'd thrown down. "It sure will beat trying to s…sleep in this rickety old thing." Abandoning his perch, he blew out the lamp. The sky had cleared, and the full moon's bright, silver glow streamed in through the window, lighting his path. When he reached the bed, he spread his worn blanket over the sleeping bag and crawled in beside Diana.

Sliding to the far edge to make room for him, she pouted, "It doesn't say much for me, if sharing my bed is only slightly more appealing to you than spending the night balancing in a straight-backed chair."

"T…that's not how it is and you know it. Don't p…pretend to take offense." Rolling to his right side and putting his back to her, he added, "I'm a restless sleeper. I'll do my b…best to keep to my side, but I'm used to sleeping alone."

"I'll consider myself forewarned," she whispered, smiling.

Despite the addition of the heavy cover, he was still shivering so hard that he shook the mattress. "Goodness, you're a chunk of ice." Without thinking of the potential consequences, Diana scooted up close behind him, cupping her knees under his thighs and hugging him tightly. When her breasts made contact with his chilled back, her nipples hardened. She panicked and almost pulled

away, but forced herself to remain there, lending
him her body heat, and praying he wouldn't notice
her condition through his thick sweatshirt.

"W…what the hell are you doing?" he croaked
at her through chattering teeth.

"Hush up," she ordered. "I'm just helping
warm you up. Don't worry. My intentions are
completely pure."

"T…thanks," was his only response. The press
of her soft thighs against his backside and the gentle
brush of her breath across his ear made her motives
seem far less wholesome than she claimed. Sean's
shaking stopped abruptly.

Diana quickly realized that her impulse, though
well-meaning, had been extremely rash.
Everywhere her skin touched him, she burned. Soon
she was trembling too, so she beat a judicious
retreat, rolling to the back half of the mattress.
"Good night, Sean, sleep well."

"'Nite, Diana," he sighed, with obvious relief,
when she moved away.

As he'd predicted, Sean slept fitfully, his
dreams full of disturbing images. Interjected into his
recurring nightmare of an important mission gone
sour, were garbled visions of the helicopter
explosion and flashes of Diana's striking face,
wide-eyed in fear. His thrashing and moaning
awakened his bedmate, who propped herself on one
elbow and studied him. Though she couldn't make
out the words he muttered, his furrowed brow, tight-
lipped frown, and tortured movements, told her that
his dreams were not pleasant ones.

Attempting to calm him, she laid her fingers on his forehead, gently stroking away the deep creases of suppressed pain, while she whispered soft, soothing words of comfort. Her touch seemed to reach into the subconscious of the sleeping man. The feverous jerking of his limbs lessened, and his handsome face relaxed.

From somewhere deep inside his dream, Sean responded to her tender appeal. The image of the woman floating before him transformed. Instead of staring at him in terror, the cool blue eyes softened and warmed. Her echoing screams melted into seductive whispers. "Shhh…be calm. Everything's fine. You're safe here with me, my sweet Sean. Rest now. Shhh…."

Once his breathing had deepened and she could tell that he was sleeping more peacefully, Diana slipped back, tucking her arm under her head, so she could watch his profile until she drifted off.

When she awoke again, the room was ablaze with bright, golden sunlight. An unaccustomed pressure had her pinned to the mattress. As she struggled against the restricting weight, she realized that it was Sean's body, lying halfway across her own, which was confining her. *If I move*, she thought, *I'll wake him and embarrass us both.* She kept very still, and tried to think of other things.

Despite her efforts, she could focus on nothing except the large man sharing her bed. His knee was thrown over her leg, resting intimately between her thighs. His palm cupped her breast, and his deep, regular breaths tickled the tiny hairs at her temple.

The entire length of him was pressed tightly against her side, firm, and unyielding. His muscles twitched involuntarily, each time eliciting a jolt of heat from her enflamed nerves.

The hand on her chest contracted and relaxed. Her nipple immediately tightened beneath his touch. *Oh, my!* she silently screamed, panic rising. Reacting on an instinctive level to the natural biological invitation, the pressure of his body on hers increased, his morning erection thrust against her hip. *What are you going to do now, girl?* Her thoughts whirled.

Before she could decide upon an action, the man began to stir. Diana feigned sleep, struggling to keep her body relaxed and her respiration regular. As Sean's breathing became shallower, his movements increased. Once he was awake enough to recognize his surroundings, and to realize that he was draped possessively across her, he groaned. In one swift, cat-like motion, he rolled off of Diana and out from under the covers. As soon as his feet hit the floor, he bolted for his clothes.

Continuing to play possum for a long moment after he'd risen, Diana went through the motions generally associated with waking up. She sighed deeply and faked a yawn, stretched, and sat up. "Morning," she chimed merrily.

He grunted at her and continued tying his boots.

"What time it is?" she asked. When he reached for his jacket with a shrug, she added. "I'll check." Sliding out of the tall bed, Diana pulled her watch from the bottom of her suitcase. "It's after eleven.

You must be famished. I'll see what I can dig up for breakfast." She spoke casually, hoping her tone would reassure him that he'd escaped the embarrassing situation unscathed.

He showed her his back, Marine straight, and headed for the door, calling behind him as he went out, "I'm gonna look around some, so take your time." Only the blush creeping up his neck to the roots of his dark hair, gave evidence that the accidental intimacy had shaken him, too.

As soon as the door behind him, Diana let the fit of giggles she'd been holding in bubble out. The all-out effort he'd made to avoid facing her, and his stiff, self-conscious departure, had truly been comical. While she threw a couple of logs into the stove, put on the coffeepot and a large kettle of water, she let her thoughts tumble out unfettered.

Poor man. She told herself. *He's probably worried that you might think he's attracted to you. How silly. You're not some foolish romantic, imagining that a young, desirable man, like Sean, could possibly have any interest in you. Too bad you can't say the same about your feelings for him, old girl. He's a fascinating, and exciting man, for sure. But get a hold on yourself, she scolded. You can't afford to indulge in useless fantasies. You know how he sees you – just a frosty old bitch, a spoiled, rich, pain in the ass.*

Her rebellious imagination subdued, she turned her attention to searching the compartment under the sink. She found several small towels, a tattered washcloth, and a large, flat-bottomed tub. When the water she'd already placed on the stove boiled, she set the pan in the sink and poured it full of the steaming liquid, adding cold from the pump until the temperature was comfortable.

Using a small bar of scented soap she'd brought along with her, she indulged in a satisfactory sponge bath. Then she emptied the tub over her head and lathered her hair with shampoo from a sample bottle. The hot water supply depleted, a cold rinse was all she could manage. It left her chilled but much refreshed.

Donning her wool slacks and sweater, she took a few minutes to smooth on some moisturizer and a little makeup. "There, that's better," she told the reflection in the tiny hand mirror she always carried in her travel bag. A dusting of powder helped cover the dark circles under her eyes, and a smudge of eyebrow pencil, along with some hastily daubed mascara, brightened the shining blue orbs considerably.

The call of nature was becoming quite intense, and despite her still damp hair, she was forced to answer it. Drawing on her long coat, she trekked off down the hill to the outhouse, scanning the area for Sean. A trail of large footprints, marring the pristine whiteness of the snow, wound around the cliffside and out of sight.

She made the trip a quick one. Soon she was back in the cabin, combing through the cupboard, hoping to find something tasty for their morning repast. Locating tins of spiced apples, corned beef, and potatoes, she used the old opener and severed their lids. Then she dumped the first into a small saucepan, added some sugar she'd found earlier, and set it on the back of the stove. The corned beef and potatoes, she chopped together in a large cast-iron skillet.

Wish we had some onions, she complained to herself. *Corned beef hash just isn't the same without a few onions.* She poured herself a cup of coffee, sipping it while she worked.

"Whatever that is, it smells wonderful," Sean remarked as he came in the door.

Removing the pots from the heat and placing them in the middle of the table, she gestured for him to take a seat. She filled his mug with the hot, aromatic liquid, while he spooned out man-sized helpings of the hash and apples. "Sorry I couldn't conjure up any fresh eggs or biscuits," she told him. "Still, this should fill you up."

"Um…It's great. Thanks," he mumbled, his mouth half full.

"Well?" she began. "How do things look outside? Can we get going right away?" Anxiousness prickled her, yet this place was so peaceful and so far-removed from the demands and unhappiness of her life, that she almost wished his answer would be "no."

Sean hesitated but made no comment. He looked at her for a long moment, his dark eyes piercing and disturbingly serious, then he took another bite of his breakfast.

His lack of response, combined with that ominous glare, set Diana's intuition screaming. Her pulse pounded in her ears. She heard herself rattling on, but couldn't stop the flow. "As much as I'm enjoying it here, roughing it in the wilderness with you, I need to get back – right away. Best case scenario, my supporter on the board successfully proceeded with the incomplete plan he had in his possession, so my proposal could still have legs. Worst case, without having the full prospectus available for board review, James was able to step in to block me entirely. He's certainly had enough time."

Suddenly her nervous dialogue turned into a shrill cry of desperation. "Oh no! What am I thinking?! I must be a raving idiot. My briefcase! My computer! They were in the helicopter! Everything – my prospectus, my market analysis, my budget justification – was on that hard drive. It's gone, all gone! What am I going to do now?"

Watching one lone tear roll silently down her alabaster cheek, Sean swallowed the lump that had risen in his throat, and attempted to calm and reassure her. "You must have a backup copy hidden away somewhere safe."

"No, I don't. I couldn't take the chance. James and I live and work together. Nothing is private – not the office and certainly not the house." Her proud shoulders sagging, she concluded, "I'll just have to start over again, that's all."

A tortured look of defeat settled over her fair features, and Sean's stomach soured with hatred for James W. North III. "It's not a total loss, Diana. You still have your ideas in your head. It's just a matter of putting them on paper again."

"I guess, but that's all the more reason for me to get home. As soon as you're finished, I'll clean up. Then we can pack a few things, leave our gracious host some money to compensate him for what we've taken, and be on our way." Fidgeting restlessly, she urged, "I bet we could make it to a real road before dark, if we hurry."

The former Marine couldn't disguise the worried frown that crept across his face, and he sensed that the preoccupied way he dug his fingers through his short dark hair increased her apprehension. She was much too intuitive to suit him, and he was being way too transparent.

As if she couldn't stand the inaction a second longer, she jumped up and started collecting the dirty dishes. He grabbed her wrist and held it until she stilled, looking her squarely in the eye. "There's no rush, Diana. The damage is done; your proposal is lost. Working yourself 'into a tizzy,' as my dear old mom says, won't change a thing.

"Now sit down and eat," he insisted. "I'm not taking you anywhere on an empty stomach. Sit, I said. Finish your breakfast like a good girl." The stern look he shot her dared her to disobey. She sat and forced in a few bites, washing them down with gulps of strong coffee.

"That's better," he said. Laying his silverware across his empty plate, he propped his elbows on the table and interlaced his fingers. Giving her time to regain her composure, he waited until the frantic, driven look disappeared from her eyes. "Okay, if you're calm and ready to listen, I have something important to tell you, and I don't know a delicate way to say it."

"It's bad, isn't it?" she gasped, her eyes wide

with fear. "I don't know how I know it. I just do."

Sean ignored her dire prediction and spoke softly, "We won't be able to leave today. It's already after noon. We'd have four hours of good traveling time, at the most, and there's still a lot of snow on the ground."

She took a breath, clearly relieved. "Is that all? Well, I can deal with a little delay, I guess. We'll take the afternoon to pack up essentials, get ourselves a good night's sleep, and leave at dawn. It might be a good idea to go before the snow melts entirely, because we'll leave footprints that will be easy to follow. An air search might pick up our trail. Someone's bound to be looking for us by now."

"That's exactly what troubles me." He stared at her, his face set and grim, the bitter taste of dread burning his tongue. This was the disclosure that he'd been putting off revealing for the last day and a half. He wanted to protect Diana from what he was about to tell her; but that wasn't a viable option. Her life was on the line. Promising himself that he'd do anything in his power to keep her safe, he took her hand in his. It was trembling.

"What do you mean?" she whispered.

"We have to be careful, Diana. There's probably a search going on, that's true. But we can't be sure that whoever's looking wants to find us alive and safe."

"What? Why not?" She shot him an exasperated glance. "Stop being obtuse, Sean. Say what you mean. I'm not some fragile, porcelain doll. I won't go to pieces over bad news."

Taking a deep breath, and giving her a you-asked-for-it look, he disclosed, "The helicopter explosion was no accident."

"Why would you say such a thing? Of course, it was an accident! There was an electrical short, or computer glitch, or something that caused a fire and ignited the fuel." Eyes wide with fear and unbelief, she grasped at more appealing straws, rather than accept his terrifying conclusion.

"I said it, because it's true. When I reached under the control panel to check out the connections of the onboard computer, after the instrumentation went haywire, I touched an explosive device attached to the underside. It was probably set to detonate over the most remote section of the mountains, where there wouldn't be witnesses to the explosion and crash."

He spoke softly and deliberately, hoping that the sincerity of his words would convey his conviction. Years of experience told him that his deductions were accurate, and he didn't have the heart to argue the point with her.

"You're sure. You know about such things — like how a bomb feels." Obviously finding that thought disturbing, she pulled her fingers out of his grasp and slid away from him.

He nodded, understanding her need to put a little space between them. "One of the many skills I learned in my long government service. If I'd found it sooner, I might have been able to land and disarm it, but with the computer crashing and systems failing, there were more pressing things screaming for my attention."

"I guess that was plain bad luck."

"Actually, it was good luck. The electrical short was not part of the would-be assassin's plan, but it saved our lives. It was an amateur job. The timer on the device interfered with the helicopter's computer system. When the trouble started, I decreased our altitude while I tried to figure out what was going on. When I discovered the bomb, I was already low enough to set the bird down safely. If that glitch hadn't happened, I would have kept on flying high, none the wiser, until BOOM! We'd have been toast."

"Horrible," she breathed, shaking her head, clearly trying to get her mind around the possibilities. "Who would do such a thing? And why?"

Shrugging his big shoulders, he told her, his voice low, "This isn't going to be easy to hear, Diana, but I have my suspicions."

"Go on," she prompted, steeling herself with a shake of her head. "Tell me the rest."

"I think you were the intended target." The stricken look of terror and betrayal that crossed her face, tore at Sean's heart. He made a silent vow to find the culprit, the one responsible for causing her such horrifying grief, and make him pay. "Can you think of anyone who might want you out of the picture?"

Dealing with the unbelievable fear and horror she was feeling, in the only way that she knew how, Diana gave him a flip answer. "Only the scores of scorned women my husband seduced with his empty promises. Most of them would like to see me dead, so they could get their salon-perfect claws on his money." Sliding her chair back from the table, she paced the room, nervously chewing her short nails.

Sean sighed in frustration. Though he understood her reaction, he didn't appreciate her black humor. "Not helpful, Diana."

She huffed loudly, puffing out her cheeks in frustration. "No, I don't know of anyone who would want to hurt me, Sean." The "Sean" was stressed annoyingly. "I can name dozens who have been angry enough at James, at one time or another, to do him in, but not in such a calculated way.

"I can easily imagine someone shooting him in the heat of the moment, or throwing him down a flight of stairs. You know – someone he's cheated, legally of course, or a jealous husband. But me? Who could hate me enough to blow me out of the sky, and you along with me?"

Grasping at straws, she added, "Why are you so sure that I'm the target? Does it have to be me? You've been pretty tight-lipped about your career, but I get the feeling that you might have made some enemies along the way. Maybe it's someone from your past looking for revenge or trying to tie up loose ends."

Shaking his head, he explained, "Not likely. My job wasn't pretty or glamorous – and most of the time, it was downright awful, but no one has cause to want me dead because of it."

Sensing that the determined woman required more than a simple denial, he expounded, "I was the Captain of a special team of highly-trained, covert operations Marines. We were just a bunch of well-trained muscle, sent all over the world to do things our government won't admit to doing – strategic enforcement, assassinations, unofficial recognizance, all sorts of dirty, underhanded stuff."

"So, you must be keeping secrets that could cause trouble for important men in high places. Isn't it possible that our would-be explosives expert was after you, to prevent you from going public with something politically volatile, and ruining someone's career?" Apparently, the idea seemed reasonable to Diana, because she visibly relaxed, her dilated pupils returning to normal size and her respiration slowing.

Sean wished he could agree, but knew he had to make her face the truth, for both their sakes. "Your theory would be a good one, except for the fact is that I don't know anything damning. When we were on assignment, I didn't even know our location, for sure. The top brass went to great lengths to guarantee our ignorance, deliberately keeping us in the dark. We were nothing more to them than loaded weapons to be handled with extreme caution.

"My unit was a tightly knit team of talented, dangerous men, men you want on your side in a crisis. The military leadership took no chances with our loyalty. My orders came from an anonymous source. We were sent in to do what we were told to do, and immediately extracted. Even if I wanted to point a finger at someone – to make someone take responsibility for ordering the terrible missions we were assigned, I couldn't. Going public with anything I know would serve no purpose, because I can't prove a thing."

Her back was to him, but he could tell she was crying silently. He rose and went to her, taking her by the shoulders. Forcing her to face him, he spoke very softly. "I'm sorry, Diana. This shouldn't be happening to you. I wish I was the intended target. The violent acts I've committed deserve violent retribution, but you're innocent and totally unworthy of such a cowardly attack.

"The fact is, though, whoever set those explosives had no knowledge of my special ops background. Otherwise, he would have been afraid that I'd find the device and deactivate it. He wasn't after me. I was simply expendable – an acceptable casualty."

Tears streamed down her cheeks as she choked out her words. "Oh, Sean, I'm the one who's sorry. Sorry for putting you in such danger, and sorry I haven't told you before how very grateful I am – grateful for your skill as a pilot, and grateful for the consideration you've shown me. Even when I was acting like a perfect bitch, foolishly making demands, you put my safety first and did everything you could to protect me. Thank you."

Sending her a reassuring grin, he released her and dropped his hands to his side, his palms tingling. "So, from now on you'll trust me?"

"Yes, sir." She shot him a sharp salute before wiping her nose with the back of her hand. "Do you think we're safe here? What if someone found the crash site and followed us?"

He shook his dark head. "I searched the area this morning, even went up on the ridge above us.

There's no sign of any pursuit and the snow covered our tracks."

"I guess good fortune's been shining on us," she observed.

"I guess," he agreed. "We have to consider the possibility that there could be two search parties on our tail, one hoping to find us alive, and another wanting to make sure we're not."

"How will we know which is which?"

"There's no way to know, so we've got to elude both. If our luck holds, we'll be well out of these mountains before we run into any unexpected company. We'll have to stay on our toes and anticipate the worst. When we do encounter pursuit, and I'm sure we will eventually, it'll be on our terms, not theirs."

He went on, trying to reassure her, "It should be safe here for one more night. The way this cabin is set back into the cliff, it's almost invisible from above. If the sun shines, and the temperature continues to climb today, most of the snow will be melted by nightfall. Tomorrow we should be able to travel the road, fast and easy, without leaving any footprints to follow."

The defensive way she had folded her arms around herself made him want to soothe away her fears. He struggled against an impulse to pull her into his protective embrace and kiss away the demons that were chasing her. Afraid of what would happen if he touched her again, he whispered encouragement. "It's going to be all right, Diana. I'm going to get you out of this. Don't worry."

FOUR

The afternoon was spent, as Diana had suggested, packing up some of the meager supplies the cabin's owner had left, and getting ready for an early morning departure. Around three, Sean felt his restless night catching up with him, so he stoked the fire and stretched out on the old sofa to nap. Soon, he was snoring softly. Diana dug a new paperback out of the side pocket of her luggage and curled up on the bed. Despite her efforts to keep her mind on the story line of the suspense novel, her thoughts kept drifting. Unable to relax and enjoy the peaceful solitude, she worried.

How can he fall asleep, like that? He must be used to catching a nap whenever or wherever he needs to. She studied the handsome man's face, and asked herself. *Can he really protect you? I know he'll try, but how will he defend against an enemy he can't identify? Who could it be? Who in the world wants you dead? What have you done to make someone want to kill you, Diana?* The unanswered questions plagued her. They rolled over and over in her head, each one appearing and then receding, again and again, until she thought she'd scream in utter frustration.

When she decided she couldn't sit around any longer, she shook off the dark depression that she felt falling over her, and busied herself preparing an evening meal. Except for some instant oatmeal, the only food items left in the cabinet were canned vegetables – primarily beans and tomatoes. *Well, I hope he likes meatless chili,* she thought, filling a large kettle with the contents of several cans. Then she added dried spices and hoped for the best. *Well, I can't vouch for its palatability, but it should be filling.*

She washed up the dishes they'd used earlier and set them out again, noticing for the first time that there was a small drawer in the table skirt, hidden beneath the thin oilcloth cover. Quietly sliding it open, she discovered a deck of cards, a small note pad and pencil, and an ancient transistor radio inside. When Sean was awakened by the enticing smell of the simmering soup, he caught her entertaining herself with a game of solitaire.

"Hey, where'd you find those?" he asked, indicating the cards.

Tapping the table with a long index finger, she said, "There's a drawer we didn't see before." Holding up the radio, she beamed at him. "And look what else I found."

"Does it work?"

"I don't know. I didn't turn it on. Didn't want to wake you."

"Here," he offered, reaching out for the turquoise plastic box. "Let me try." Flipping the knob, he grinned when a static burst emitted from the tiny speaker. "Maybe we can get some news."

He ran his thumb over the dial, sliding the tuner, until a man's voice became audible above the interference, reading the weather forecast.

"The warming trend continues through the evening with zero percent chance of precipitation. Overnight lows in the upper thirties. Stay tuned for more news and a complete rundown of the latest sports highlights." A Pepsi commercial blasted out, loud and irritating. Sean turned the volume down.

"Do you think he'll report anything about us? If the remains of the helicopter have been found, it would make the news, wouldn't it?" Diana asked hopefully.

"Who knows? Guess we'll have to wait and see."

The announcer came back on the air a few seconds later. He did not, however, mention the disappearance of businesswoman and entrepreneur, Diana North, or give any information about a helicopter crash in the mountains of West Virginia. Sean shrugged noncommittally when the report ended, and tinny, pop music emitted from the miniature radio. Clearly, he didn't know if their failure to make news was a good omen or a bad one. Diana wasn't nearly so objective. The astute pilot could read the disappointment on her fair face.

"It doesn't mean anything, you know," he cautioned her. "That's a small, local station. They probably take their reports from a wire service. It's not an indication that we haven't been reported missing. Someone could still be out there looking for us."

"But whom? That's the question, isn't it?

Who's looking for us – a potential rescuer or a potential assassin?" Tears welled in Diana's eyes and her bottom lip trembled. "We're lost on this mountain, who knows how far from a safe haven.

"It was hard enough before, uh…before I knew about the bomb, thinking of all the things that could happen to us – lost in the woods, without provisions – and wondering if we'll make it out safely. But now I can hardly bear the thought of it. We'll have to look over our shoulder every second – afraid for our very lives, alert to every sound – and constantly searching for a place to hide should we need it. Because it's quite possible that we're being stalked by a cold-blooded killer."

Sean watched helplessly as she battled to gain control over her rising fear. Finally abandoning his rigid, hands-off posture, he drew her close, squeezing her tightly. She seemed to melt into his arms.

Sniffing back tears, she listened to the reverberating beat of his heart within the solid wall of his chest and told him, "You should go alone and save yourself, Sean. You'll travel faster, and be more likely to make it out without me holding you back. It's me they want. You'll be safe without me."

"That's not going to happen, Diana. I'm not leaving you alone." After a long moment, he added, "I'm in just as much danger, now, as you. Our would-be assassin won't stop to ask questions. He'll simply eliminate any witness – that's me – along with his primary target – that's you."

He held her at arm's length and looked directly into her cool, blue eyes. "We've found a road, of sorts, and we know someone comes here regularly. It'll probably be a long walk, but we'll make it out. If we're being trailed, we'll deal with it, together. We'll be prepared. Trust me. I'm a very handy man to have around. I know how to handle myself in the woods, remember?"

His calm, self-assured boast tickled her funny bone, and she giggled, lowering her lids and turning away from his disturbing gaze. *I'll just bet you do,* she thought to herself.

With one hand, he tilted her chin up so that her eyes met his again. Wiping away one lone tear from her cheek with the tip of his little finger, he teased her gently. "Laughing and crying simultaneously. That takes talent."

His intense, maple-syrup gaze held her transfixed. She couldn't break free even if she'd wanted to do so. His knuckles traced her jaw line. Suddenly, it didn't matter to Diana that she was lost, hundreds of miles from home, or that someone was out there, somewhere, searching for her, someone who wanted to kill her. It should matter, but it didn't, not at all. Not when Sean looked at her the way he was looking at her now.

Her heart leapt. She trembled. Laying her fingers over the hand that still rested lightly on her face, she pressed his palm against her lips. Then, flushing with embarrassment, her throat constricted with fear, she jerked away from him, knowing her eyes would reveal too much.

Understandably irritated by her ambivalence, he grabbed her arms and forced her to face him. "What's wrong, Diana? What did I do?"

"Nothing," she breathed, still refusing to meet his gaze. "It's not you; it's me. Please, let me go." Every second that his hands touched her was exquisite torture. She tried to twist free but he held her shoulders tightly. Desperate, she ordered him, "Take your paws off me!"

He freed her immediately, his arms dropping helplessly to his sides. He shrugged in confusion and defeat. For a second Diana was afraid she'd hurt him, but when the warm sparkle in his brown eyes was replaced by a cool, defensive hardness, she realized that he wasn't hurt; he was angry.

Sean snapped at her through clenched teeth. "No problem. Serves me right for trying to be a nice guy. Should've known better. I won't make that mistake again, Mrs. North." Grabbing his jacket off the hook, he stormed out of the small cabin, slamming the door hard enough to rattle the window.

Biting down hard on her knuckle, Diana choked back her tears until she thought he was out of earshot, then she let them flow unabated. *He despises you;* her tortured mind accused. *You've made him feel nothing but contempt for you.*

It had been years since she'd indulged in such a cathartic release, always preferring to stay in control, to ignore the emptiness of her life – the utter void left by a convenient marriage to a cold and calculating man. She'd never shed one tear for the love her husband had denied her, but Sean's rejection unleashed a flood of them. Her limp body, wracked by sobs, crumpled to the floor. She sat cross-legged on the rough boards, her face in her hands, and cried herself out.

Somewhere in the midst of the onslaught, Diana realized that, for the first time in her life, she'd given in to her rebellious heart. She uttered a prayer, thick with pain, "I know Sean could never really care for me, not in the way that I'm beginning to care for him; but please, oh please, don't let him hate me. I couldn't bear it if he hated me."

When the pilot stormed out of the tiny shack, he intended to walk off his frustration but a nagging apprehension brought him back. Instead of stomping off, he waited on the narrow porch of the structure and listened. Diana's tortured weeping could easily be heard from his vantage point. It made him feel empty and helpless. It tore at his heart. But when her whispered words, intermixed with deep, longing sighs, reached his eavesdropping ears, hope bloomed. His anger was forgotten. He decided to take that stroll, after all, thinking that a short respite would give her some privacy to pull herself together, and him an opportunity to mull over what he'd overheard. He wasn't exactly sure what to make of it and he needed time to process.

When Sean returned to the cabin an hour or so later, he found Diana curled up on the bed, reading. She laid her novel aside and addressed him sweetly, and as if nothing of importance had passed between them. "The chili's ready. Do you want to give it a try?"

He couldn't tell that she'd been pretending to read, hoping to appear unconcerned about him, when in reality, she was waiting impatiently for his return, afraid he would change his mind and abandon her. Nor did he detect the relief in her eyes, or hear the way that her heart thudded against her ribcage, when his dark head reappeared through the door.

"Sure," he said, smiling. While she served the food, he pulled out his chair and waited nervously, wanting to say something to her but unsure how to begin. Once she was seated, he jumped in, his words coming out in a rush. "I'm sorry, Diana, for being a jerk. I was out of line. You were upset and I had no right to get angry. I want to help you, to comfort you, be sympathetic, you know. But I'm not very good at it. Anger's easier."

Interrupting his apology, she stopped him. "Don't worry about it. I was sending mixed signals, grabbing onto you for support like some weak, clinging female, and then pushing you away in my usual ice-queen fashion. I confused you. Don't beat yourself up about it. It was nothing, really."

He shook his head, more frustrated than ever. She'd put on her invulnerable-bitch armor, covering up the pain he knew she was feeling. The sad, defeated smile was clearly in residence once more. How could he break through her defensive wall to the warm, caring woman he knew was inside? He wrestled with the question. *Maybe you should tell her how you're starting to feel about her?* A sudden, sharp stab of conscience said "no – absolutely not." *She's a sophisticated, wealthy woman. She'd see it as a come-on from a bum who's looking for a free ride. She'd figure you're just hoping to get your hands on her money. Forget it, Cody. She's married, and even if the marriage isn't a happy one, home-wrecking isn't your style.*

Each deeply involved in their own private thoughts, they enjoyed a comfortable silence while they ate. The chili was bland but filling. When they had finished, Sean pitched in to help Diana tidy the room and added some more wood to the fire.

"You up for a game of Gin Rummy?" he proposed.

"You bet," she agreed, her bright blue eyes avoiding his inquiring glance.

He slid his chair up under the table and started dealing out the cards. "We'll play a couple of hands and then turn in. We've got a long day ahead of us tomorrow. We'll need sleep."

After four games, each winning two apiece, they decided to call it a draw and retire. Sean could tell that Diana was about to offer, graciously but against her better judgment, to share the bed with him, so before she could suggest otherwise, he grabbed his blanket, kicked off his boots, and stretched out on the sofa. Though he knew he was dooming himself to a sleepless night, he didn't dare take a chance on what might happen if he crawled into that bed beside her.

Drained by the emotional roller coaster she'd been riding for the past couple of days, Diana fell asleep quickly and slept soundly. She was awakened early by the slurping and gurgling of water spewing out of the hand pump. Sean was filling the small kettle to make coffee. "It's my turn to cook this morning," he announced as he set out cups and bowls and opened several packages of instant oatmeal.

"Hey, that's not fair," she pouted, sitting up and yawning widely. "You get the easy stuff."

"That's the breaks." He shrugged. "There's nothing left except the few provisions we're taking with us for the trip." Grabbing up a couple of the smallish towels and a bar of soap from his bag, he crossed to the door. "There's a fairly good-sized creek running down the back side of this knoll. I'm going to go wash up while the water heats. You'll have plenty of time to get dressed and finish packing-up while I'm gone."

"Heavens, Sean, that stream will be freezing. Just wait, we can heat water for you to bathe after breakfast."

"No, that'll take too long, and I don't mind roughing it. The chill will wake me up," he insisted. One glance in Diana's direction sent him scurrying. Her shining platinum locks curled around her shoulders, tossed and wild, her eyes were still droopy and slightly unfocused from sleep, and the silk pajamas lay on her soft, full body like a gentle caress. She heard him groan as he retreated through the rough portal, and something about that tortured sound made her smile.

By the time Sean returned, Diana was ready to depart. They quickly downed the oatmeal, washed up the last of the dishes, and made one last sweep around the room. Taking out the hundred-dollar bill that she always kept stashed in the lining of her suitcase, in case of an emergency, the tall women laid it on the table beside a note she'd written on the pad she found in the drawer.

It read, *"Thanks so much for the use of your cabin and supplies. You saved the lives of two lost, cold, and hungry travelers. We hope this will cover the cost and inconvenience of restocking."* She left it unsigned.

"Here," Sean offered, reaching for her overnight bag. "Let me carry that."

She started to protest, but realized the foolishness of such an expression of pride. Instead, she handed him the case with a murmured, "Thanks."

He swung the strap of her suitcase over one shoulder, to balance the knapsack he carried on the other, leaving his hands relatively free. Moving his arm in a wide arc toward the exit, he said, "After you."

Diana preceded him, waiting while he made sure the door was tightly closed. Then they struck out, following the narrow dirt road, sticky with mud left by the melting snow, walking briskly. Several hours passed silently.

Tense and anxious, Diana was startled by every noise. She envied the former soldier his relaxed ease, though she wasn't completely fooled by his apparent composure. *He's like a tightly wound spring,* she thought, *still and deceptively unthreatening, but ready to burst into immediate action if released.* Her theory was proven correct when the distant whir of helicopter blades cut through the silence.

"Come on!" he ordered, grabbing her arm.

"We've got to get under cover." He dragged her through the underbrush and into a stand of small evergreens, bisected by several fallen deadwoods. Dropping the bags, he told her, "Stay here. I'm going to see if I can get a bead on that bird."

Settling herself onto a cushion of pine straw, Diana propped her back against one of the downed trunks and got comfortable. The sharp, pungent odor of crushed needles filled her head. Impatiently she waited, wishing he'd hurry back. The ominous sound of the copter got steadily louder as it approached her position. Though she couldn't tell for sure, the craft seemed to pause above the narrow ribbon of roadway they'd been traveling, before swinging right and heading in the general direction of the cabin.

Fidgeting restlessly, apprehension making it difficult for her to sit still, Diana had almost decided to abandon her safe haven to go in search of her companion, when his handsome head popped through a break in the trees. He moved stealthily. She was amazed that she hadn't heard him coming, not even the snap of a twig or the crunch of dried leaves had given away his approach.

"Did you see it? Could you tell anything about it?" Her eyes were wide with alarm, and her words poured out in a nervous rush.

"Whoa there. Calm down," he urged, crouching beside her on the fragrant needles. "Yes, I was able to find a clear break in the canopy. It's definitely not Search and Rescue. Their transports are brightly colored, easy to spot. This was a dark lady with no identifying markings, designed to be inconspicuous, as inconspicuous as a helicopter can be anyway."

"It was headed toward the dead end and the bluff," Diana noted, her voice still shaky. "What if they find our hideout?"

He laughed. "Our hideout? You make us sound like Bonnie and Clyde." The tense, almost desperate, look in her frosty blue eyes shot straight into him. He stopped teasing and tried to reassure her. "They won't spot the cabin from the air. And there's no good place to land up there, so relax."

Reaching into his backpack, he retrieved a plastic bag of trail mix and a bottle of water, and offered her some of each. "We'll rest here awhile, just to make sure they don't double back, and then we'll hit the road again."

Taking a handful of the dried fruit and nut mixture, she asked him, "Where'd you get this?"

"Brought it with me," he bragged. "I thought I might do some hiking at the resort while I was waiting for you to finish your business."

"Well, I'm certainly glad that one of us hasn't had to abandon his weekend plans entirely. You're definitely getting in plenty of hiking." Diana attempted a sad smile, but it lacked conviction. "Sean, I'm really frightened," she admitted reluctantly. "Do you think that helicopter was looking for us?"

"Most likely. By the way that bird was moving, I'd say they were definitely searching for something or someone."

"What if it comes back? They might decide to follow the road, and then what would we do? She wanted Sean to enfold her in his arms and whisper reassurances in her ear, but she didn't dare ask, and he didn't offer.

Instead, he lightened his tone and resumed his teasing. "They've covered this area so they'll probably move on. If they return, we'll deal with it. Choppers are pretty noisy, Diana, they won't be able to sneak up on us, if that's what you're worried about."

An image of a cartoon helicopter, tiptoeing up the trail behind them slid through her mind, striking her funny bone. She started giggling.

"You really are quite a changeling, aren't you?" he remarked, lowering the water bottle he'd raised to his full lips. "Just when I think I've got you pegged, you go and transform yourself into someone entirely new."

"What do you mean?"

"Well, when I first met you, I thought Sheila's assessment of you was right on target, but then you lost that cool veneer and seemed to be more real, still aloof and used to getting your own way, but not quite so demanding, and more natural."

"From ice-queen to spoiled princess, huh? Well I guess that's some progress." Her words were sarcastic, but the twinkle in her eye told him she wasn't taking offense.

"Once we reached the cabin, you changed again, doing everything you could to make us both as comfortable as possible."

"That's me," she quipped, "a regular Martha Stewart."

"When I told you my suspicions about the explosion, you showed me a vulnerable side I hadn't seen before. And just now, you looked and sounded like a giggly teenager. So, tell me, Diana North, who are you really?" Warm brown eyes regarded her inquisitively, sending a shiver up and down the length of her.

She swallowed the lump that had suddenly appeared in her throat. "All of the above. None of the above. I don't know," she croaked, shrugging, her mouth as dry as dust. "Do you honestly care who I am, Sean?"

"Yes, I do," he responded firmly.

"Why?"

"Because I think you're a fascinating woman and I want to understand you."

Feeling the hot flush of color rising up her long neck and across her prominent cheekbones, Diana lowered her face, hoping to hide her embarrassment from him. She knew her attempt had failed when he asked, lifting her chin with his forefinger, "Are you blushing?"

She pushed his hand away. "It's been a long time since anyone has taken an interest in me, personally. I was just surprised by your question."

"Time we got moving." Rising and gathering up the bags, he helped her to her feet. "We can talk about this as we walk." He led the way back to the road, grinning widely.

"I'd rather not." This topic was one she definitely did not want to continue discussing, so she said. "Tell me more about your family. What was it like growing up with all those sisters?"

"No way! You aren't changing the subject on me that easily." Sean pressed her. "Considering the nature of your marriage, and your husband's open and apparently calculated philandering, I'm sure you've had your share of involvements, too. You can't tell me you don't have several men on the string right now."

"No, not a one. And since you insist on continuing this embarrassing discussion, I'll admit it. There's never ever been anyone but James." Fighting back the tears that threatened, she added, "He gave his permission and even encouraged it, probably to ease his own conscience, but I've never slept around."

"Why not?" he asked, plainly perplexed by this complex and utterly frustrating woman. "You deserve some warmth and human comfort in your life, too."

"Well..." she began, then paused to consider her words before continuing. "For an affair to take place, one must have both inclination and opportunity. While I have to admit that there have been times in my life when I would have been amenable to a liaison, I've been unable to find a suitable, willing partner."

Though she sensed that he was irritated by the cold, high-handed phrasing which had crept back into her speech pattern, she clung to it like a suit of comfortable, protective armor. "It seems that men don't care much for me, as a woman that is. I'm not sure why. Perhaps they're somewhat intimidated by my husband, or my wealth, or my drive to succeed, but I tend to believe that none of those things is the primary problem."

"What is the problem?" Sean teased.

"I should think that would be perfectly obvious, but since you seem determined to force me to humiliate myself, I'll tell you." She cut her eyes at him, hard, and sighed. "I've never had a real proposition, much less a lover, because men don't find me attractive. Are you satisfied?"

"Diana, I...," the pilot stuttered apologetically. "I didn't mean to..."

She interrupted him, spurred on by painful memories. "It's difficult to get a man to see you in a romantic light when you look down on the top of his head, outweigh him by more than a pound or two, and outsmart him at every turn. James has me pegged. He says I'm too tall, totally unapproachable, and terribly difficult. "Fat, frigid, and fractious," were his exact words."

"But you're not," he argued, his dark eyes snapping.

"Not what?" she asked, choking back tears.

"Not any of those things!" he exclaimed, an unexpected edge to his voice. "That husband of yours needs a good shot in the mouth for what he's done to you. You may not have had many proposals but it's not because men aren't attracted to you."

"Then why?" she asked, giving him an imploring look.

"Few men are secure enough to come on to a woman with your combination of beauty, self-confidence, and power. But I bet if you'd make the first move, quite a few guys would jump at the chance to spend some time with you, unless they're blind, crazy, or both. Take it from me; you're a stunningly attractive woman, Diana."

She couldn't believe her ears. This young, virile man, with an irresistible, magnetic appeal, was saying things about her that she'd never heard from any other male, not even the one who had promised to love, honor, and cherish her. Blushing again, she responded shyly. "It's nice of you to say so, but if I have to make the first move then I'm doomed to a lonely life."

"Why's that? You don't seem like a shrinking violet to me," he quizzed.

"Chasing men is just not in my nature." She laughed at the ridiculousness of the idea. "I wasn't brought up that way. My mother told me that good girls wait for the boys to call, and I've always taken my mother's advice seriously.

"As a teenager, I was shy and insecure – a too-tall, too-smart girl from the wrong side of the tracks. Needless to say, the boys didn't call. College years weren't much kinder to me, until James came along. I jumped at his proposal and gave up my romantic fantasies."

"Really?" he teased again, one eyebrow raised.

"Well...no," she admitted with a shy grin. "It seems like I've been waiting around for the right man to notice me all of my life." She laughed softly. "I've never learned how to flirt. To be politically correct, you could say I'm coquettishly challenged."

He groaned. "What advice did your mother give you about making bad puns?" Obviously not expecting an answer to his rhetorical question, he added, "If you'd like to develop that particular skill, you can practice on me. I'm always up for a good flirtation."

"I'll keep that in mind," she said, flashing him an honest smile, one of the few she'd allowed to linger for more than a few seconds. Unlike those plastic, sad manifestations she usually used to hide her true feelings, this one was open and sincere. It didn't occupy her bow-shaped lips only, as the customary ones did, but lit up her entire face, making her blue eyes sparkle. "Considering the drastic step I'm about to take, learning to flirt might be a good idea."

"Drastic step?"

"Not only was I preparing for a fight with James over presenting my proposal to the board, I had one other little surprise up my sleeve. "Still do, I guess."

"What surprise?"

"Divorce," she stated flatly. "My mother passed away earlier this year. Her death was a turning-point for me. I finally realized that life's too short to waste one second of it."

"I'm sorry for your loss, Diana," Sean offered sincerely.

"Thanks, but it's okay. The last twenty years of her life were good ones. She had a great home, wonderful friends, plus a church she loved and volunteer work she was devoted to. I think she was really happy."

"Thanks to you."

"I guess." She shrugged. "James always used threats against Mom as a trump card, to bring me to heel whenever I tried to assert my ideas or stray from his agenda. So now that I don't have to worry about her welfare, I have no reason to stay married.

It seems ridiculous to go on living a lie.

"So, I've had two sets of divorce papers drawn up and I intend to use one or the other, depending upon how things go, in regard to the future of NSE. If James is willing to capitulate and throw in his vote with the board members who support my ideas, I'm going to offer him a very favorable settlement, asking for only a small portion of our joint property. But if he chooses to fight me and thwart my efforts, I'm going to demand half of everything, including North Star's assets and our personal holdings. My attorney has assured me it's my due, and that I'd have little trouble getting it."

Hope swelled in the pilot's chest. *She's divorcing him.* The thought warmed his heart. The words he'd overheard Diana pray while he stood on the porch of the tiny cabin flooded back. *Maybe, just maybe, there could be a future for us,* he decided, grinning inside. A muttered epithet broke his reverie and brought him back to reality.

"Oh, shit!" The unexpected curse sounded strange, coming as it did from her usually very proper mouth.

"What is it?" he asked, the grin moving to the outside of his ruggedly handsome face.

"The divorce papers were in my briefcase, along with my wallet and cell phone."

"I'm sure your lawyer kept a copy. Once you get home, you can find out what went on at the board meeting and if your proposal still has legs. Then you'll know which set of papers you need." His pragmatic thinking did little to calm her agitation.

"I can already guess which one it will be. I'm sure Mr. No-one-tells-me-what-to-do North sabotaged my plans very successfully. I expect that we're going to be in for a very long, and very unpleasant, fight. The mere thought of having to give up any of his precious stuff will kill James. But that's not what really concerns me right now. I'm ticked at myself. I could have saved us so much trouble if I had my phone."

She shook her head in frustration. "You risked your life to save my underwear and I didn't even think to grab my briefcase. How stupid!"

"Hey, stop berating yourself. It's never stupid to listen to your instincts in an emergency." A vision of her lovely face consumed by the fiery explosion shook him to the core. He slowed his pace a bit and assured her. "You followed my orders, on the double, jumped out of the helicopter and moved safely out of harm's way – just as you should have. There was no time for either of us to think."

Seeing the determined glint in her cool blue eyes, he knew she was unconvinced, so he added, "Your cell would have been useless anyway. Even if you could get a clear signal in these mountains, you couldn't have used it."

"Why not?!"

"GPS location. We couldn't have taken the chance that they, whoever they are, would ping your phone."

"Maybe not, but we'd have money. My wallet was in the briefcase, too. I had a hundred-dollar bill in my suitcase but I left that for the cabin owner. Assuming we make it to a town, what are we going to use for cash? I have nothing left. Nothing!" Her tone was beginning to take on a desperate edge. "Not even a credit ca...!" Suddenly, she grabbed at the baggage he carried, pulling it off his shoulder and letting it thud onto the ground.

Jerking open the zipper, she fumbled through the contents until she located her blazer. Her hand slid into the front pocket and pulled out a small rectangle of plastic, waving it around like a valuable prize. "Yes! We're in luck. I bought gas on the way to Baldwin Aviation and didn't take the time to dig my wallet out of my bag to put this away. James always criticizes me for my lack of organization – a place for everything and everything in its place – you know. Well, for once I'm glad I'm not one for structure and routine."

FIVE

They walked, and walked, and walked, stopping only for food and water. Twice, they had to run for cover under overhanging branches when a distant roar alerted them to potential danger. To their mutual relief, both instances proved to be false alarms and they were free to move on again. As the day wore on, the shadows of the trees marched across the road like distorted soldiers, growing steadily taller, darker, and more sinister.

Eventually, the dusk overcame the shadows entirely, making them indistinguishable from the grayish hues of the dirt. Yet the trail wound on, moving consistently downward with no end in sight. Based on the pace he'd set for them, and allowing for the time they'd lost along the way, Sean estimated that they had come nine or ten miles. The road had no forks or cross roads, so far, and that worried him. He was sure Diana was worried, too.

To ease the apprehension that was growing exponentially as darkness fell, the pilot tried to get his companion talking again. One nagging concern had been plaguing him since their earlier conversation, so he questioned her. "Are you sure James knew nothing about your plans to divorce him?"

"Yes, I'm sure," she answered, clearly annoyed

by his suggestion. "What are you implying?"

"Nothing," he declared, with a quick shake of the head. "I just can't help wondering if there's any way he could've found out. Who's your lawyer? Does he know Mr. North?"

Sean was sure Diana didn't like the direction his reasoning was taking him, but he hoped she understood the necessity of proceeding down that path. He was relieved when she elaborated voluntarily. "My attorney is an old buddy from college. He and James were in the same fraternity but they were never friends. In fact, Curtis Sloan was the only one who tried to talk me out of marrying James. He warned me that I was setting myself up for misery – spending my life trying to live up to the North family's standards."

Though he couldn't see it in the increasing twilight, Diana's eyes misty with suppressed pain, and she chewed her lower lip. "I know what you're thinking and the answer is 'No.' Curtis never worked for James or NSE. He's always been my personal counsel – exclusively. Curtis isn't cutthroat enough to suit James's taste in lawyers."

"What about your ally on the Board of Directors? Can you trust him?"

"I think so." Diana mulled that around a while before responding. "I haven't known Ralph Parker for long. He's a recent appointment but he seems to be an honorable man. James doesn't like him, says he's too much of an idealist, so that's good enough for me."

"Then…I guess that's that."

"Yes, I guess it is." Her face drawn, her brow

furrowed with dread, she asked the question Sean knew she didn't want him to answer. "Why did you ask?"

"Just making the obvious conclusions. If your husband had received information about your plans to divorce him, then he would have had even more reason to make sure you missed that board meeting, to insist that you visit the resort instead, and to keep you away as long as possible." He wanted to add – to have you eliminated – but he dared not.

Unfortunately, her quick, intuitive mind made the leap without his help. Placing a comforting arm around her shoulders, Sean could feel her shivering like she'd been chilled to the depths of her soul. She was unable to voice her fear but her companion sensed in his bones that she had drawn the same conclusion as he. Stoically, she pulled away, shaking off his support and straightened her spine.

Diana fell into a brooding silence while the pilot silently cursed himself for adding to her miseries. They were both walking along woodenly through the cloying darkness, staring morosely at the ground, so caught up in their individual thoughts that they were almost oblivious to their surroundings. If the woman hadn't lost her footing on some loose rocks, they would have passed by a wider road, forking off to the left, without noticing it.

Massaging her trim ankle, the pilot asked, "Are you okay? Do you want to rest a while?"

"No, let's go on," she urged. "I'm fine." Taking a couple of tentative steps to test the limb, she hobbled off.

"Wait!" Sean called after her. When made her way back to him, looking puzzled, he pointed toward the connecting road. "Look!" Squinting against the deepening gloom, he suggested, "We should go this way. It's too dark to see much, but it seems right."

"Whatever you say. Wherever you lead, I'll follow – since you're the big, strong man who knows how to handle himself in the woods," she teased, her mood lightened by the discovery of the new road. Even in the dim light, he could see that she was grinning at him.

She waited for him to lead the way and fell into step. "Ever since you made that boast, I've been wondering about other circumstances in which you've proven yourself worthy and able." Her deeply sensuous voice, and suggestive tone, slid down his spine like liquid fire, igniting every nerve.

"I thought you didn't know how to flirt," he countered. "Seems to me you've sold yourself a bit short."

"I'm just taking you up on your offer to let me practice on you. How am I doing so far?"

Before he could answer, the dirt road gave way to gravel, urging them on. Conversation forgotten, they broke into a slow jog. About a hundred yards down, the road dumped out onto a paved secondary. "Yes!" Sean cried, grabbing Diana in a bear hug and swinging her around. "Look out civilization, here we come!"

When he set her down, laughing, she asked, "What do we do now?"

"Keep heading that-a-way." He pointed to his

left. "Someone's bound to come along soon. Maybe we can catch a ride. Here," he offered, pulling out the trail mix. "We can munch on this as we go."

As if on cue, headlights flashed behind them. An eighteen-wheeler, heavily loaded with huge logs, crept around a bend in the road. Dropping the luggage and the baggie of trail mix, Sean waved his arms to get the driver's attention. Brakes screeched and dust flew as the rig slowed to a stop. A scraggly-bearded face leaned out the window, spat a black stream of tobacco juice onto the pavement, and drawled, "Where'n the world'd you folks come from? Y'all must be lost."

"We are," the pilot confirmed. "We could use a ride to town, if you don't mind."

"Cain't say as I'd mind a tall," the wiry little man said, lifting his greasy cap and digging dirty fingers through his longish hair. "I'm haulin' this here load down to the paper mill. It's still a pretty fur piece, so I could use the comp'ny. Hop in."

Sean boosted Diana into the cab. "We sure appreciate your help. We were out sightseeing when our vehicle broke down. Been walking all day."

His quickly concocted explanation seemed to satisfy the driver. "The lil lady can flop up in the sleeper." He pulled back the drape to give her better access, while Sean helped her inside the back compartment and handed her their bags. Once she was settled, he added, "Looks like she could use a rest."

"Yes, thanks," the former soldier said, taking his seat and buckling up.

"Well, hold on ta yer horses, here we go!"

Jamming gears, the man jerked the truck forward, slowly groaning into motion. "By the way, name's Riley, Pete Riley." He took his callused hand off the big steering wheel and offered it to Sean.

"Nice to meet you, Pete, I'm Sean, Sean Cody, and this is uh…my friend, Diana."

"It's very kind of you to help us, Mr. Riley," she offered.

"Oh, it's my pleasure, ma'am. Talkin' to you good folks'll keep me from fallin' asleep on these here dark old roads." The driver seemed content to chatter on while his passengers listened. "Got my own sawmill up on the mountain, ya know. Cut the timber, mill it, an' haul it all by myself. No middle man. Sell most o' the good stuff by the board foot, but the crooked, knotty leavin's well, I jest cut 'em inta lengths, load 'em up, an' take 'em to the Westvaco paper plant over ta Covington."

Sean urged him on with an occasional comment and offered him some trail mix.

"Naw thanks, won't mix too good with this here chaw," he said, declining the snack. "Yep, that's whar I'm aheaded t'nite. I like travelin' on Sund'y nite, cause thar's not too many other folks on the roads. I use'ly pull up by the gate and clime up into that sleeper thar, and saw logs 'til the plant opens up for deliveries on Mond'y mornin'."

Pete seemed very contented with his life as an independent logger. "They's a purty nice motel jest over by the river, near the mill. I could drop you and yer lady thar if'n you like. I 'spect ya'll won't have no trouble gittin' some hep to go after yer car in the mornin'."

"Oh, that old heap isn't worth much. I'll just see if I can get a wrecker service willing to go pick it up and sell it for junk," Sean improvised. "I guess we'll need to find another way home. Maybe we can catch the bus from Covington to Roanoke. There's an airport in Roanoke." The information Pete had given him about the nearby city had helped him get his bearings. He now knew that they were coming down out of the West Virginia mountains and into the Alleghany Highlands of Virginia.

"Yep, thar is," Pete announced. "Thar's also a lil biddy one over to the Mountaintop Meadow, ya know, for them real small planes. Well-ta-do folks likes to fly in to golf, an ski, an fill their bellies with rich food. If it's a plane yer after, I could take ya'll thar, but that'd be outa my way fer sure."

Since the resort was the last place Sean intended to go, he wasn't disappointed when the talkative man went off on a tangent. "Wonder what it'd be like to stay in one of them fancy, la-de-da re-sorts? You ever been ta a place like that?"

"Actually, no," the pilot admitted, growing fonder of the verbose driver by the second. "I was headed to one once, but never made it. Something else came up."

"Um-hmm," Pete sighed. "That's a pity." Nodding toward Diana, who was already sound asleep, he voiced an observation. "Now yer lady there, she looks like a woman who's been ta one o' them fancy re-sorts. Hell fire, prob'ly more'n one."

"I'm sure you're right about that," Sean agreed.

"You seem like a purty reg'lar feller. How'd ya git mixed up wit a so-ciety lady like her?" The pilot concluded that Pete Riley was much more astute than he appeared.

"Long story," he hedged.

Luckily, the driver didn't demand any further explanation but quickly went on with his observations. "Well, she's a looker, she is. I'd say yer a purty lucky man."

Diana's earlier words came back to Sean in a rush. It was still hard for him to believe that she saw herself as unattractive and unappealing to men. Pete's reaction to her confirmed the pilot's feelings. "Yes, she is, but I'm not… I mean, we're not…uh…We're just friends."

Pete cackled. "So, she wouldn't give ya the time a day, huh?" The driver shot his passenger a mocking sideways glance.

"Why do you say that?" Sean fidgeted uncomfortably in his seat.

"I could tell right off that ya cotton to her, and I cain't 'magine a big, strappin' fella like you, gitin' a purty gal way out in the woods without puttin' the move on her. So, I'm guessin' ya did but she warn't too co-oper'tive. Now if'n it wuz me, I wouldn't o' been surprised, but I bet you don't git too many no-thank-ye's. Do ya?"

Completely flustered by the driver's speculation, Sean pondered an answer, his mind in turmoil. *How can I explain my feelings for Diana when I don't even understand them myself?* Finally, he decided that Pete should keep his mistaken conclusions. "Even the best of us lose out sometimes."

That statement seemed to please the talkative

logger. He cackled. "I had meself an older woman oncet, an man, oh man, was she sweet. But older women take a bit o' extry care, ya know. Ya have ta tread lightly cause they tend to be more sens'tive about the age difference than us fellers. Worth the time, tho. Yep, def'nitly worth the time."

"Thanks, I'll keep that in mind," the pilot said, grinning at the man's attempt to impart sage advice.

Pete nodded his tattered cap toward the sleeping form behind him. "Say, she must be plumb wore out. How long y'all been out here anyways?"

Sean cautiously kept his answer ambiguous, "Most of the day."

"Poor gal," the driver sighed. "Guess she's not used to that kinda exercise. Didn't seem to bother ye none. You must be in purty good shape. Whadda ya do fer a livin'?"

Deciding another partial truth would suffice, the pilot answered, "I just got out of the Marine Corps."

"Hey, thas cool," Pete exclaimed. "Bet you've seen yerself a bunch a this ol' world. Me, I never hankered to stray too far from home."

For the next three-quarters of an hour, Sean described his travels while the driver listened attentively. Before either of them knew it, the distinctive rotten-egg, paper mill odor had permeated the cab of the tractor. Soon white plumes of steam were visible in the night sky.

The grinding of brakes and decrease in velocity woke Diana. Once Pete had the big rig safely parked, she crawled out of the sleeper compartment, still groggy, pausing to thank the logger for his help. "I'd like to compensate you for your trouble, Mr. Riley. If you'd be kind enough to give me your address, I'll see that you're well rewarded."

"No ma'am, wouldn't hear a it," he declined her offer firmly. "I don't want no re-ward for doin' what a body ought, helpin' out folks in trouble. You jest do the same for somebody else when the need arises, and we'll call it even."

"You're a very special man, sir," she replied, kissing his rough cheek. "I wish you well."

"Thank ya, ma'am," he said, blushing. "The motel's right over thar." He pointed to a small two-story structure. "It's late but the owner's prob'ly still up, so's ya can git yerselves a room and a good nite's rest. Good luck to ya."

"Thanks Pete," Sean said, grabbing their bags. "For the ride and the good advice."

"Anytime," Pete answered with one final handshake and a tip of his greasy ball cap. Gears groaning, the trucker pulled the huge semi off the shoulder and back onto the road.

Pete was right; the office of Johnson's Budget Inn was still open. A portly man with a fringe of white hair accepted Diana's credit card and ran it through the scanner, apologizing that he only had one vacant room. To the woman's relief, it was a double. "There's a big sub-contractor's meeting up at the paper mill tomorrow mornin,' so we're almost full up."

"That's okay, we'll manage," Sean assured him. "Do you know where we could get something to eat this late?"

The elderly, balding man looked at his watch. "Most o' the restaurants are already closed, but I reckon you could order some carry-out pizza. They'll deliver until 'leven." He handed the pilot a paper Pizza Hut menu.

"That's perfect, thanks."

"You bet. Now you folks have a good night, ya hear?"

With that, the tired travelers headed to their room. Diana was grateful that it was on the ground floor, because she wasn't sure she had the energy to climb the stairs. The curtains were drab and the bedspread was worn, but the bathroom was spotlessly clean.

Sean dropped the bags on the floor and crossed to the phone. "What kind of pizza do you want? My treat."

"Anything's fine, you choose. I'm dying for a shower." She pulled off her coat, threw it on one of the beds, and started rummaging through her suitcase. Pajamas and toiletry bag in hand, she made for the bathroom.

Moments later, warm water flowed over her tired body, soothing away the aches, relaxing over-taxed muscles. She sighed with pleasure. Indulging herself, she soaked a long time. When Diana finally climbed out of the tub, she was greeted by the tantalizing aroma of fresh, hot pizza. Realizing she was famished, she wrapped a towel around her wet hair, slid into her pajamas, and she pulled open the door.

The big pilot sat cross-legged on the middle of one bed, the huge pizza box open in front of him.

"Hey! Why didn't you wait for me?" she teased the man as he folded a huge slice into his mouth.

"Let me warn you, sweetheart, when I'm this hungry it's every man for himself. You can dig in whenever you like, but just watch out for flying elbows!" Sean mumbled as he tried to chew the huge bite.

The endearment took her by surprise, knocking her off balance. Diana covered her stunned reaction by joining him on the bed and scooping up a piece of pizza for herself. The sauce was tangy, the cheese creamy, and the crust almost melted in her mouth. "Um, this is great. Good choice," she praised appreciatively.

"Here." Sean handed her an ice-cold soft drink can. "You'll need this to wash it down."

"Thanks." She smiled at him and popped the tab.

They devoured every bite of the pizza before turning on the TV to catch the eleven o'clock news. There still was no mention of the missing helicopter. Diana tried to appear unaffected, but couldn't disguise the defeated look that flashed across her face.

Sean saw it and attempted to reassure her. "I'll use the room phone and call Vic first thing in the morning. He usually gets to the office well before Sheila."

Diana didn't ask why he wanted to talk with his employer without the office manager around to overhear. She didn't have to ask, because she already knew the answer. Sean was concerned about the perky Miss Stewart's relationship to her husband. "Maybe I should call home; one of the servants always picks up."

"NO!" was the definitive, firm response. The tears welling in Diana's frosty blue eyes softened his tone. "I don't think that's a very good idea, Diana. Let's get some sleep and ring up old Vic in the AM. Then, based on what he tells us, we'll figure out what to do next. We can't be too careful. You shouldn't trust anyone until you know for sure that they're not involved."

She knew he was still holding something back from her but she let it pass without comment. "You're probably right."

"Go on to bed. You need your rest. Things'll look better in the morning," he urged. "I'm going to take my turn in the shower, and when I get back, you'd better be asleep."

Laying her things off the bed, she turned back the covers and slid between the cool sheets. As she reached up to click off the light, Sean leaned over and kissed her softly on the forehead. "Sweet dreams, my lovely Diana." She dozed off almost immediately, those gentle words echoing in her head, a contented smile teasing the corners of her mouth.

When he returned from his bath, Sean was glad to see that she'd followed orders. Slipping back into his grubby jeans, he grabbed his cellphone and battery out of his knapsack and tiptoed out of the room. A few minutes later, the lock snicked, the door creaked, and the pilot crept back inside, stripped down to his underwear and crawled into the vacant bed. Then he too, drifted quickly into the welcoming arms of Morpheus.

Sunlight, streaming in through a break in the threadbare draperies, tickled the big man into consciousness. He groaned and rolled over, drawing the blanket over his head. Despite his desire to reclaim the last shreds of blissful slumber, a bothersome, nagging apprehension prodded him into full wakefulness. His eyelids cracked opened.

"Morning, sleepyhead," Diana chirped cheerfully. "There's hot coffee." She waved a large cup under his nose, enticing him to rise.

Swinging his long legs out of the bed, he sat up, snatching the sheet over his bare midsection. "Thanks," he told her, grabbing the proffered paper cup. He took a couple of reviving sips before asking, "Where did you get this?"

"Mrs. J keeps a pot brewing all the time. When I got up, I went to the office to see if I could get a cash advance on my credit card. I commented on how wonderful the coffee smelled, so she told me to help myself. I got you some, too."

The tall woman seemed very proud of herself. There was a childlike playfulness about her that Sean hadn't seen before. "We met Mr. Johnson last night when we checked in. He and the Mrs. just got back from a second honeymoon trip to Hawaii. She told me all about it. They had a wonderful time."

"Sounds like you got her life history," Sean growled, in no mood for her chattiness.

"Not at all. She's simply a friendly, kind woman, that's all. Not a grouch like some people I know."

"We can't all wake up like Little Miss Sunshine. What's gotten into you anyway?"

She shrugged her elegant shoulders. "Just happy to be alive, I guess."

A dark grimace passed over his handsome features. He rubbed his closely cropped head with his wide palms. "Now let me get this straight. You got up, dressed, went out, visited with Mrs. What's-her-name, poured coffee, and came back without disturbing me?"

"Yes, I did, but you forgot one thing. I managed to convince her to advance me fifty dollars," she boasted. The troubled frown he shot her alerted her to his displeasure. "Why? What's the problem? You can't be upset with me for being too quiet."

Unable to hide his irritation, he snapped, "Dammit all! If you'd stop being proud of yourself for one second, Miss Sweet Disposition, you'd figure it out. If you can leave this room and come back in again, without alerting me, then I'm not doing a very good job of protecting you, am I?"

He was so angry with himself that he jumped up, grabbed her by the shoulders and shook her hard. "What were you thinking, going outside alone? There's no telling who could have been waiting for you."

"I'm, I'm sorry, Sean," she whispered, her lip quivering. "You're right, I didn't think." She lowered her face to avoid his scathing stare. That, however, proved to be another mistake, for it focused her gaze on the lower half of his body, which was naked except for a tight-fitting pair of gray cotton boxers. "Oh, my," she choked, jerking out of his grasp, her cheeks crimson.

He pressed his point, stepping yet closer. "Look at me Diana," he ordered.

She slowly forced her eyes back up to his face and suppressed a giggle, a devilish grin tugging at her lips.

"Promise me you won't do anything that foolish again," he demanded, still angry and totally oblivious to the effect his state of undress was having on her.

"I promise," she agreed solemnly, before allowing the mirth to squeeze out. "If you'll put your pants on. I'm not up to dealing with you practically naked. My old heart won't take it."

Blushing from the roots of his dark hair to a point halfway down his broad, lightly furred chest, he grabbed the sheet off his bed, wrapped it dramatically around his waist, snatched up his knapsack, and stormed into the bathroom.

"That woman is going to be the death of me yet," he complained to his reflection in the mirror over the sink. A splash of cold water on his face cooled his temper a bit. "You asked for it, big guy," he told himself, "when you said you enjoyed flirtation. You might as well get used to it." His good humor somewhat restored, he wiggled into his jeans and T-shirt, dug his toothbrush out of his backpack, scrubbed his teeth, and headed back out to face her.

Diana was sitting on the bed, head down, trying to look repentant. Tilting her face up just enough to get a quick glance at him, she measured his mood before she spoke. "I must apologize again, Sean. I shouldn't have been teasing when you were trying to point out the danger we're in here. Please don't misunderstand; I didn't take your warning lightly. I know you're honestly concerned for my safety and I won't act so thoughtlessly again."

She looks so angelic, so innocent, he thought, watching her study her hands, while her platinum hair tumbled forward in shimmering waves. He did his best to wrestle down the lecherous grin that threatened and to put a smugly disapproving frown in its place. He tore his eyes away from her face, clearing his throat. "I'd better make that call to Vic. What time is it?"

Diana checked her watch. "Just after eight."

"He should be in the office by now." Sean punched the buttons on the bedside phone and waited.

"Baldwin Aviation," the whiskey and cigarettes voice on the other end of the line announced. "What can I do you for?"

"Hey, Vic."

"Well, well, well, if it isn't the wayward Mr. Cody. It's about time you checked in." The older man's tone was playfully scolding. "The old' Ice Queen' been keeping you on a short leash? Having a good time?"

"What are you talking about?" the pilot snapped. "How could I be having a good time? Someone sabotaged your chopper and almost killed Mrs. North and me. We're damned lucky to be alive. Why are you talking like we haven't been

MIA for days?"

"Sabotaged? Did you say sabotaged?"

"Yeah, your bird went up like a Fourth of July rocket. We barely escaped with our hides. We were snowed-in and had to hike out of the mountains on foot. Now you act like you weren't surprised when I didn't get in on schedule. What's going on?"

"I, uh, well…When you didn't get back by noon on Saturday, I was worried, so I called Mr. North," Vic admitted, his voice uncharacteristically shaky. "He told me to relax. Claimed his wife has a habit of sneaking away with willing younger men. Told me she probably tricked you into hanging out with her for a couple of days for some extracurricular activities, if you know what I mean. He convinced me not to report your flight missing, till the end of the week."

"Holy shit, Vic! You believed him?"

"Sure. Why not? Even if she is a cold bitch, that Diana North is quite a looker, and I figured you'd be up for a little fling at her expense. I'm real sorry, Cody. Whada you want me to do now?" Vic sounded distraught, his words pleading. "Should I contact North again?"

"No!" the pilot declared. "Just pretend you never heard from me. I'll get back to you. In the meantime, see if you can find out who had access to that helicopter, prior to take-off. Talk to the mechanics, but don't be too obvious about it."

"Sure, okay, I can do that," Vic agreed, anxious to make amends.

"And don't let Sheila get wind of this." Sean added.

"No problem. You can count on me," his employer assured him.

"I hope so. Talk to you soon." When he hung up, he turned to Diana. He could see the question in her eyes but wasn't ready to tell her what Vic had said.

"Pack up. I'm going to buy a newspaper. Then we'll get some breakfast and look for the bus station."

"Yes sir, whatever you say, sir." She threw him a mock salute.

Deliberately ignoring the irritating gesture, Sean pulled on his boots and jacket and tromped out, leaving the door ajar. He walked across the parking lot, toward the tiny office in the front corner of the building, slowing his pace as he approached the door. Just as his hand gripped the knob, his sharp ears detected a serious, gravelly voice, conversing with the woman inside.

Peering through the small, streaked window in the top half of the door, Sean could see an average-sized man, clad in a khaki trench coat, standing just inside. He was leaning across the counter toward a white-haired, grandmotherly type, holding something out for her to examine. The hairs on the back of Sean's neck stood up. He retreated a step, flattening his body against the building, and listened intently. The ancient office door stood on sagging hinges that didn't close properly, making every word easily distinguishable from outside.

"So, you have seen this woman?" the man asked, "and she's still here?"

"Why yes, I 'spect she is." Mrs. Johnson smiled

sweetly. "She was in here this mornin' early. 'Peered to be a nice young woman. Is she in some kind of trouble?"

"It's possible," he confirmed. "We have reason to believe she may have been kidnapped."

"Kidnapped?! Ooh, that's just awful. Poor thing." The elderly woman's voice dripped concern, then she hesitated, "That don't seem right, tho. Why would she be in here by herself if she'd been kidnapped? Never heard of a kidnapper sendin' his victim out for coffee."

"You say she was alone?" the raspy voice pressed her, ignoring her confusion.

"Well…She was when I talked to her, but she musta had someone else with her in her room, cause she took two cups of coffee. My husband was workin' last night when she checked in. Here, I'll check the register."

Pages flipped. Sean guess that Mrs. Johnson was leafing through the old-fashioned, ledger-style guest book Diana had been asked to sign. "Nope, can't tell by this. All it says is Diana North. There's no mention of anyone else. Mr. Johnson's not too good about making sure all our guests sign in, especially if one of them is as pretty as that young lady.

"He's just gone down to Hardee's to get us some biscuits and gravy for our breakfast. They make the best biscuits, you know, and my husband's right partial to their gravy. He'll be right back, directly, and then you can ask him about Ms. North and her companion. If'n you'd care to wait."

Sean heard the man shifting from foot to foot,

clearly impatient with the old woman and her long-winded attempt to be helpful. "That won't be necessary. Just tell me which room the woman is in," he demanded, flashing her an ID and adding, "I'm special agent Larry Stark, FBI."

SIX

While Sean was gone, Diana touched up her makeup and finished packing her few belongings. She placed her case by the door next to Sean's backpack, her mind whirling with fear and doubt. Baldwin had told Sean something that disturbed him greatly. Of that she was certain. The dark expression that crossed his handsome face, and his deliberate haste to leave without discussing the conversation with her, convinced her absolutely. Unfortunately, she had no choice but to wait, impatiently, for her companion to return. She didn't, however, expect his reappearance to be so dramatic.

He burst through the door at a run, shouting. "Let's go. Now!" Slinging the bags over one shoulder, he grabbed her hand and pulled her along behind him, barely giving her a chance to pick up her coat. "No time to explain. Just follow me and be quiet."

The deadly glance he shot her told her that now was not the time to disobey. Diana crept out behind him, following closely. Sean urged her across the parking lot at a brisk jog, constantly eyeing the motel office. When a khaki-clad arm pushed open the sagging door, Sean jerked her down behind a huge four-wheel drive pickup truck. "Keep out of sight," he warned ominously.

The frightened woman could hear Mrs. Johnson's animated chatter, with gruff interjections by a male stranger. "This is highly irregular, you know," the elderly woman told the man, obviously flustered. "Even the FBI is supposed to have a warrant to go into any of our rooms without the permission of our guests. I'll knock on the door and ask Miz North if'n it's okay for you to come in, but I won't unlock it without the legal papers."

"You just get them to open up and I'll take it from there," the man growled impatiently.

Shaking her white head as she struggled with the moral dilemma facing her, the kindly older woman tapped lightly on the door of the room Diana and Sean had just vacated. "Miz North, it's Elsie Johnson. Can I speak with you, please?"

"Come on," Sean urged his companion, "before he realizes we're not in there." The pilot led the way out of the lot and across the street, glancing back at the trench-coated figure, who was still shifting from foot to foot as he waited to see if Mrs. Johnson's summons brought a response. Just as the fleeing couple ducked into a narrow alley between two large buildings, they heard the crack of splintering wood, followed by a dull thud. "Looks like our mystery-man decided to take charge. We'd better keep moving."

Diana was frantic. It was all she could do to keep up with the former Marine's ground-eating strides. He pulled her along in his wake, racing between storefronts and down dim alleyways. She fought the urge to look behind her, fearing a backward glance would confirm that the terrifying man in the tan coat was only steps away, and gaining ground. When Sean was comfortable with the distance they'd put between them and the motel, he slowed to a walk. Diana asked him, breathlessly, "Did I hear Mrs. Johnson say that man was FBI?"

"That's what he claims."

"But who is he? Why would the FBI be after us?" Fear blazed from her cool blue eyes, bright and intense.

"I overheard them through the office door. He showed the old lady an ID and called himself Larry Stark." Though Sean seemed reluctant to tell her the rest, the determined set of her jaw told him that she wouldn't be satisfied until she'd heard the entire story, so he elaborated. "He said that he, or they – the FBI that is – believe you've been kidnapped."

"Kidnapped? That's ridiculous. Who do they think kidnapped me?"

"Yours truly," he concluded with some hesitation.

"Then let's go back, find that Stark fellow, and set things straight. I just don't understand how a mistake like this could have been made. It's preposterous."

"No, Diana. We're not going back," he declared firmly, gesturing for her to keep moving down the sidewalk.

The businesswoman stubbornly planted her feet and studied the pilot's face for a long moment before demanding, "What's really going on here, Sean? Tell me."

Tugging her sleeve, he backed into another alley, out of sight of passersby. "If you're going to insist on discussing this now, we'd better not stand around in plain view." Sean growled through clenched jaws.

One hand splayed over her chest, as if trying to slow the beating of her heart, Diana seemed determined to force the man to tell her everything he knew, or suspected. She waited, challenging him. "Why can't we go back and explain things, straighten it all out?"

"Because it will likely to be the last thing either of us does, Diana. Is that plain enough for you?" She didn't answer, but tears welled in her eyes. He softened his tone. "Agent Stark's manner is too brusque and his technique's too heavy-handed. He's not trying to rescue you from a kidnapper. You're his target."

"Why would he tell Mrs. Johnson that I'd been kidnapped if he wants to kill me? It doesn't make any sense."

"Because, Diana, it gives him the perfect excuse to kill you. The guy's sharp. It's a great idea actually. He played on that sweet old woman's sympathy and she led him right to our room. If he'd taken me by surprise, he'd have us in custody right now and then, who knows? He could drive us to a remote location and shoot us both, claiming that he fired at me to save you and that you were accidentally hit in the crossfire. We wouldn't be alive to contradict his story."

Trying her best to get her mind around his conclusions, Diana shook her fair head. "Do you think he's really FBI?"

"It's possible." Swallowing hard, he added the

next, difficult question. "Does your husband have any connections in the Bureau?'

"I don't think so. Why, Sean?" Her desperate voice rose shrilly. "You think James is behind this, don't you? You've been hinting at it for some time."

"It's likely," he told her grimly.

The harsh, almost unbearable pain of betrayal dragged her down, and she slumped against him, lacking the power to stand on her own. He wrapped his arms tightly around her, willing his strength into her. "I'm so sorry, Diana. It's the only logical conclusion." He set her on her feet, steadied her, and told her about his earlier telephone exchange with Vic.

"Evidence is piling up against your husband. He forced you to make this trip against your wishes. And he insisted that you go by helicopter, didn't he?" Diana's affirmative nod was almost imperceptible, but it was enough to confirm to the pilot that he was on the right track.

"After the explosion, an unidentifiable bird scours the mountainside, not Search and Rescue. There's no mention of your disappearance in the news, so the guy hasn't filed a missing persons report or the wire services would have picked it up. The kidnapping of a woman of your status is newsworthy stuff. The press would have been all over it.

"When Vic gets concerned because we haven't come in on schedule, your husband tells him that you have a habit of running off with younger men and not to worry. And now we have a man on our tail, claiming to be FBI, who operates like a bounty hunter hot on a scent.

"Who would have the right connections and pockets deep enough to keep a federal agent on retainer? Who would benefit the most from your death?" Sean shoved his fists into the pockets of his jeans and dropped his chin toward his chest. "Maybe I'm way off target, Diana, but the only single thread that I can see, tying this all together, is Mr. North himself."

"You don't believe him, do you?"

"Who?" Sean asked her, obviously puzzled by her dazed, unfocused expression.

"James. You don't believe what James said about me. Do you? Th…that I make a habit of carrying on with younger men? Because it's a lie. I've never…," her voice tapered off to a tortured silence.

"No, Diana. I recognize your husband for what he is, a lying, self-serving manipulator. He'll say or do anything that gets him what he wants." The haunted look in the woman's eyes told Sean that his approval was very important to her and prodded him to try another tack. "Look. Don't I have first-hand proof that you're a proper lady?

"We've spent several nights together and you've yet to lay a hand on me. I'd say that's hard evidence of your trustworthy restraint," he teased, adding, "Unless you're just not attracted to me. Is that it? You haven't put the move on me because I don't turn you on?"

"Hardly," she blurted out without hesitation, then blushed scarlet. When she noticed the broad, mocking grin on his full lips, she punched him, hard, on the shoulder. "What are you trying to do, get me to embarrass myself?"

"Maybe."

"Well, all right, then. I admit it, though I'm sure you already know it perfectly well. I find you very handsome and desirable, Mr. Cody. But since I am quite a few years older than you, still legally married, and not inclined to chase men of any age, I've fought my natural urges and resisted your charms. Does that satisfy you?" Mild annoyance had replaced the fear in her eyes, but her prominent cheekbones still sported high color.

Giving her a brotherly hug, he whispered into her hair, "I'll accept that, for now." Slapping on a smug, lop-sided smirk, he slipped a long arm around her waist. "Glad to see you haven't had all the spunk scared out of you." With that tidbit of encouragement, he urged her forward. When they passed an open door on the alleyway, he stopped.

A small sign over the lintel read *Second Time Around- Consignments*. A heavy-set woman was carrying trash out of the shop and stacking it next to a big green Dumpster. "Excuse me, ma'am," Sean drawled. "Could you help us? My friend and I need a change of clothes."

"OOOH!" she squealed. "You're not supposed to be back here." Her large, bulging eyes swept the alley nervously. "Cain't help you now cause the shop's closed. Don't open till ten o'clock. Come back then. Use the front door." The woman's tone was brusque and insistent, but the pilot sensed that

she wasn't being deliberately rude; she was just
frightened.

"Please, Ms....?" He hesitated, waiting for her
to fill in the blank.

"It's Mrs., Mrs. Moore," she informed him,
sharply.

"Please, Mrs. Moore, don't be afraid. We're
harmless." His mother, always full of platitudes,
had assured him that honesty was the best policy.
He prayed she was right. "My friend and I are in a
bit of trouble. We could really use your help."

The portly woman looked him up and down,
assessing his sincerity. "What kind o' trouble?"

He didn't hesitate but told her, "There's a man
looking for us, a very dangerous man. We've been
running for several days and desperately need fresh
clothing. If you'd be kind enough to help us out,
we'd pay you for your trouble."

"Yes," Diana chimed in, clearly anxious for the
feel of clean garments against her recently-scrubbed
skin. "You won't regret it, Mrs. Moore. We'll make
it worth your time." She waved her VISA Platinum
Card under the woman's bulbous nose.

"Well...okay," the shopkeeper reluctantly
agreed. "Come on in and look around. Bring
whatever you want up to the register at the front and
I'll ring it up."

Following her inside through a dusty, dimly-lit
storage room, they searched the tightly-packed
racks. Diana found some tattered blue jeans, a faded
sweatshirt and coordinating turtleneck, and a pair of
worn hiking boots in her size. To her delight, the
shop stocked new underwear and socks, so she

quickly snatched up the necessities.

Sean met her at the front counter. Mrs. Moore stood guard behind the cash register, watching them cautiously, her arms folded over her generous chest.

The big man's arms were loaded with a pair of camouflage fatigues and a dark green Henley shirt, along with the expected T-shirts and boxer shorts. He also had two maroon baseball caps, each emblazoned with a Virginia Tech logo. Laying them on the counter, he turned to Diana. "I'll pay you back when we get home."

"Don't worry about it," she insisted, handing the credit card to the shopkeeper. "It's my fault you're in this mess and I intend to cover all the expenses."

Just as Mrs. Moore was about to swipe the card through the sensor, Sean grabbed her hand and stopped her. The old woman squealed again. "Hold it a second," he ordered.

"What's wrong?" Diana asked.

"We can't use your card."

"Why not?"

"How could I be so stupid?" The former Marine smacked his palm against his forehead. "That's how he found us. How he tracked us to the motel. He had a watch on your credit card. When you used it last night, he got our exact location." Sean mentally berated himself for allowing this costly mistake. "We'll have to dig into that cash advance unless Mrs. Moore is willing to make a trade."

The large woman studied the enormous diamond glistening on the third finger of Diana's left hand, her huge eyes sparkling with greed. She licked her thick lips in anticipation. "I might consider a barter, if'n the goods is somethin' I can find a market for."

Shrugging out of the cashmere topcoat, and dragging her suitcase off Sean's arm, Diana laid all of her belongings in front of the woman. "This luggage, suit, and coat are all exclusive designs. Together they're worth over five thousand dollars. I'll throw in the boots I'm wearing and everything in the suitcase, except for my toiletries. That should me more than enough to cover the value of the things we want."

"Yeah, and you can have my old stuff, too," Sean offered, looking longingly at the brown leather bomber. "I really hate to give up this jacket. It was a gift from my mom."

"I don't know," the shopkeeper hedged. "I don't get much call for that designer stuff. The clothes he's wearing aren't worth much, not even that beat-up old jacket. And I'd have to have it all cleaned and foot the bill."

"Here." Diana tugged off the ring the woman was eyeing and tossed it across the counter. "Take this. It should buy us anything we want."

"Hell, that rock's worth a lot more than this whole damned store. Maybe more than this whole damn town," Sean groaned. "No, Diana. You can't."

"It's okay, Sean." She smiled her sad smile. "The ring has no sentimental value to me anymore. If it will help get us out of this mess, the sacrifice will be a small one."

"You got yourself a deal," Mrs. Moore agreed before the younger woman had time to change her mind, and snatched up the ring. "Pick out anything you want, dearie, and it's yours."

"Thanks. Is there someplace we can change?"

"Sure. Behind those curtains in the back." The shopkeeper waved a beefy arm toward a bank of partitioned dressing rooms.

A few minutes later, the couple returned to the front of the store outfitted in their semi-new attire. Diana grabbed a fabric-covered elastic band out of a box in front of the cash register, and secured her hair into a sleek ponytail before donning the ball cap. She tucked her toiletry bag, another set of underwear, and two pair of socks into his knapsack, picked a fleece hoodie from one of the racks, and shoved her old clothes and suitcase across the counter to Mrs. Moore. "Here, you can still have these. Lugging them around will just slow us down."

When Sean followed suit, hesitating slightly as he laid the jacket on top of the pile, Diana turned to him. "You should keep that. It means too much to you to let it go."

"We can't take any chances. I'd be too easy to spot in that jacket. It has to go."

"Well, I've changed my look entirely. It will be very difficult for anyone to identify me like this," she asserted with a quick twirl.

"That's true," he agreed, studying her closely. The casual outfit and hairstyle, topped by the baseball cap, had taken years off her age. At a distance, she could easily pass for a college student.

"Wait." Her eyes lit up as a thought struck her. She crossed to a rack of military-green field jackets and picked out an extra large one. "Try this," she instructed, holding it up for him. Then she laid aside the hoodie, reached for his leather bomber and slid it on. "I'll return it once we're home safely," she promised him.

The jacket swallowed her, and the cuffs that fell down well past her fingertips, but it felt wonderful, like she was enfolding herself in his protective embrace. It was still warm from the heat of Sean's body and smelled pleasantly of him. She buried her face in the collar and inhaled deeply.

He smiled at her, his maple syrup eyes melting her heart. Forcing her gaze away from his face, she told the shopkeeper how much she appreciated her help. "Thanks again, Mrs. Moore."

"You're very welcome," the woman chirped, holding the diamond up to catch the light.

"Enjoy the ring," Diana said, sincerely. "It's quite valuable, you know, a perfect emerald-cut stone, just over three carats."

"So, can we assume it will buy your silence as well as the things we're taking with us?" Sean asked her, his tone seriously insistent.

"Why, of course," the portly woman assured him. "Ask anyone. They'll tell you Mabel Moore knows when to keep her mouth shut." Then she leaned across the counter and lowered her high-pitched voice conspiratorially. "You don't have to worry, dearie. If your husband sends someone by here looking for you, they'll not get any help out of me. I wouldn't want to have to explain how I came by this little bauble." She admired the ring once more. "He might just want it back."

"My husband?" Diana was puzzled by the shopkeeper's conclusion. "What makes you think my husband is looking for us?"

"Now, now, I'm just an old romantic. It's easy to tell that you two're lovers, runnin' off together. I'm guessing the man you say is chasing you has got something to do with your husband. Well, I say good for you – leavin' the old man for this here handsome young fellow. More power to you. It usually works t'other way round you know. My Melvin walked out on me fifteen years ago for a no-good slut half his age. It's nice to see a woman like yourself, turnin' the tables on the lyin', cheatin' men for a change."

Shocked and embarrassed, Diana immediately refuted, "Oh, but we're not..."

"...Not going to be able to spend anymore time chatting with you," Sean finished for her, stepping up beside the flustered woman and encircling her waist with his arm. "We need to be on our way. Again, thank you, Mrs. Moore, for your help and your discretion."

"Oh, call me Mabel. Everyone does," she said, winking at him.

Taking advantage of the woman's well-compensated kindness, he asked her to direct them to the bus station. She happily supplied the information and escorted them to the back door, where they slipped out without being seen from the street. When they were about half-way down the alley, Sean turned and waved to the shopkeeper.

"My, my, aren't we getting chummy all of a sudden?" Diana complained, jerking her elbow out of his grip. "What's gotten into you? Why did you let her believe that we're lovers running off together?"

"It seemed the safest course," Sean explained. "Stark might get lucky. If he shows up at her shop, and she believes we're on the lamb from a jealous husband, she won't take a chance on losing that diamond to him. Miz Mable Moore will keep mum." He grinned at his own clever alliteration. "Why do you care what that woman thinks?"

"I don't. It's just...just," she stuttered. "It just bothers me that she jumped to the conclusion that we're having an illicit affair. I know I come across as an icy bitch with a thick skin; but despite what you think, it hurts me when people believe bad things – untrue things – about me."

"What if it was true? Would that be so terrible?" he questioned, his dark eyes flashing. "I can think of lots of things I don't want people to believe about me, Diana, but a false assumption that I'm having a love affair with you isn't one of them. Fact is, I'd put that on the things-I-hope-people-do-believe-about-me list."

She blew out a breath and turned that sad, hopeless smile on him. "I didn't mean that the way it sounded. No, it wouldn't be terrible if it were true, but it's not." Silently, her heart added a wistful, *"Though I can hope that maybe one day..."* Aloud she concluded, "Nor is it likely to be."

Looking at her like she'd just flung a bucket of

cold water in his face, Sean made a retaliatory strike. "Yes ma'am, Mrs. North, I've got it! From now on I'll correct anyone who falsely assumes that there's anything going on between us. I'll make it clear that you're the boss and I'm just your hired muscle." His full, sensuous mouth was drawn into a thin, hard line and a deep furrow bisected his thick brows. "I'm sorry you were insulted by the suggestion that you would lower yourself to take a man like me as a lover."

His warm brown eyes, shining with indignant fury, met her cool blue ones, demanding a response, daring her to deny the truth of his accusations. The force of his words struck her speechless. She reeled from the impact. Tears threatened, but she fought them back, managing a whispered denial, "It's not like that."

"Couldn't prove it by me." Sean continued to stare at her, but when she dropped her eyes, avoiding his piercing gaze and refusing the challenge, he relented. "Let's go find that bus station."

Diana forced her stubborn limbs to follow along behind him, moving woodenly, her strength suddenly gone. The constant fear plaguing her, that Stark would step around the next corner and fire a bullet into her brain, paled in comparison to the debilitating anguish she felt now, from the blow Sean had struck at her heart. She was sure the rift she'd created between them was irreparable, and the thought almost paralyzed her, making her wish that the FBI agent would appear, pistol blazing, and put her out of her misery.

A small part of her wondered why she was more deeply wounded by this simple misunderstanding with Sean than by the almost unimaginable betrayal by her husband. She had accepted James's desperate, driven desire to be rid of her but she couldn't bear the thought of losing Sean's respect. It was a paradox she didn't understand.

She'd only known the pilot for a few days but he'd become essential to her, as essential as water, or air, or any of the other life-sustaining nutrients. *Could it be? Is it possible? Is this what love feels like?* Those questions flooded her numbed brain. She'd never been in love before, so how could she know the answers?

Love was something that happened to other people, not to Diana Grayson North, the great "Ice Queen." She was incapable of love, or so her husband had told her, many times. Lust yes, there was no doubt she felt desire – swift, sure, and white-hot – when she looked at the big man striding ahead of her, but love? That was something else entirely.

James's frequent claims of her frigidity, her inability to feel passion, flooded her thoughts. *He's wrong about that,* she realized, *so maybe he's wrong about his other assessments.* That thought buoyed her spirits. If she could feel love at a time like this, when she was scared out of her wits, then maybe there was still hope for her. The dreadful, constricting pressure that was twisting her heart and turning her stomach inside out, lessened just a bit.

When they reached a tiny brick storefront with

Greyhound Bus Lines painted on the window, Sean held the door open for her, while he scanned the street for any signs of their pursuer. He purchased two, one-way passages to Roanoke and asked the ticket agent if there was a comfortable place nearby where they could wait for the coach.

The red-faced man directed them to a small restaurant across the street. "Bus leaves promptly at eleven. If you keep an eye out, you'll see the driver pull in, probably around ten-fifty. He won't wait aroun' mor'n ten minutes, so don't be late," he warned. "You can board as soon as the bus stops and unloads, if there's anythin' to unload that is."

"Great. That gives us over an hour for breakfast," the big pilot acknowledged, taking Diana's elbow and urging her toward the exit. They quickly crossed to the café. The savory odor of frying bacon wafted out the door as they entered.

Sean chose a cozy booth near the back and slid into the far side, facing the huge, plate-glass window. Diana took the place across from him, her mouth watering. He motioned for her to move all the way to her left so that he would have an unobstructed view of the entrance.

When she started to remove her hat, he told her, "Leave it on. It hides that all too recognizable hair of yours."

A long-legged waitress in a very short skirt approached their table, smiling brightly when she saw the booth's handsome occupant. "Mornin' folks. Coffee?" she asked, holding out a glass pot and flipping her luxurious chestnut mane.

"Sure, thanks," Sean said, doffing his cap with

a flirtatious wink.

There was a thick mug on the tabletop in front of him, which she poured full of the steaming liquid. Then she turned to Diana and asked, "How about you, ma'am?" She made a point of stressing the ma'am.

Diana cringed. Though the implied insult beneath the young woman's overt politeness was clearly delivered, she bit back a sharp retort and nodded in the affirmative.

After filling Diana's mug, the pretty waitress shifted her position and edged closer to Sean, leaning over just enough to make sure he had an unobstructed view of the generous cleavage she displayed above her low-cut uniform. "I'm Nora. What can I get you?"

"Well, Nora, I don't know. What's good here, besides the scenery?" Sean gave her another wink, this one bordering on lecherous.

Pretending to study the menu printed on her paper place mat, Diana seethed. The way the shameless woman was throwing herself at the pilot infuriated her, and his obvious encouragement of her advances was almost too much to bear. Struggling to keep down the bitter bile rising in her throat, she gritted her teeth and waited for him to place his order.

Sean settled on a western omelet and biscuits. Nora made a note on her pad; but then, instead of turning to Diana and asking for her selection, the audacious waitress ignored her entirely and inquired of the man, "And for your mother?"

The calculated pettiness of the deliberate attack took the man off guard. His pride stinging from the imagined slight he'd suffered at Diana's hand, he'd made the most of the suggestive exchange with the comely waitress, playing along and enjoying his companion's discomfort, but this was too much. Despite her painful rejection of him, Diana didn't deserve this sort of calculated mistreatment. He knew Nora didn't really think the older woman was his mother. She was just making a not-too-subtle point about the difference in their ages.

Sean's anger flared. He had every intention of coming to Diana's defense, but before he could open his mouth to set the sharp-tongued female straight, the cool-headed businesswoman had already done so.

"Just order me something soft, son, and easy to chew," she said, smiling sweetly. "And not too spicy. The old stomach's not what she used to be." Scooting out of the booth, she patted his hand. "I'll be right back. Got to visit the ladies' room. Weak bladder, you know. Nora, honey, you just wait. In a very few years you'll know exactly what I mean."

The stunned waitress watched her straight, aristocratic back as she strode across the room and disappeared into a small alcove. "What's her problem?" she asked the man who was doing his best to keep the laughter he was suppressing from bursting out in the waitress' face.

"I think you insulted her. She's not my mother and you know it."

Nora tilted her head saucily and raised one shoulder, making her generous bosom bounce. "Just call 'em as I see 'em. What in the world are you doin' with an old broad like that anyway, a good-looking guy like you? Man, what a waste."

"Oh, it's not wasted, I assure you," Sean snapped, tiring of the game. "Just bring us two omelets, biscuits, and more coffee," he said, cutting off the exchange and hoping Nora could sense his annoyance.

She dipped her head and whirled away, swaying her hips seductively as she moved across the floor. Though it was clear that she wanted to show the man what he was passing up, he ignored her completely.

When Diana returned, his expression was penitent. "Sorry."

She seemed to shrink into his beat-up jacket. "Doesn't matter. Actually, she's not far off base. It's a bit of a stretch but it's not inconceivable that I could be your mother."

"No, you couldn't," he retorted.

"How old do you think I am, Sean?"

"I don't know and I don't care. What does it matter, anyway?" He was trying to be as honest and sincere with her as possible. The difference in their ages meant nothing to him, but he knew that she couldn't say the same. To Diana, it mattered. It mattered a lot. The way she looked at him, her brilliantly blue eyes coolly appraising him, reflecting the icy veneer she used to mask her true emotions told him so.

"If you don't already know the answer to that question, there's no way I can explain it to you. But ask Nora. I'm sure she can, if she hasn't already."

Folding her hands on the table, Diana informed him, "I'm forty-five. Using what little brain power I have left to make the calculation, that makes me at least twelve years your senior. I would have been one of those shocking teen-pregnancy statistics, but it is possible for me to have a child almost as old as you, hypothetically."

He grimaced, hating the change in her, wanting the real Diana back, the soft, teasing, warm-hearted, loving woman he knew her to be. But that woman was gone again, frozen back into her ice-queen hardness, and it was his fault.

SEVEN

Just before Nora returned with their breakfast, a young woman barely out of her teens, holding the tiny palm of an active toddler in one hand, while balancing an infant carrier and several large bags in the other, took the booth behind Diana. She was very busy getting her belongings and her fussy children settled, when the waitress reappeared.

Sighing and rolling her false-eyelash framed eyes at the commotion revolving around the distracted mother, Nora slapped the plates she was carrying down in front of Sean and Diana. The guest check followed immediately, placed under the edge of Diana's plate without so much as a "Hope you enjoy it," or "Let me know if you need anything." Her attitude made it clear that she had no intention of providing any additional service to the couple. Deliberately ignoring the young family, she flounced back into the kitchen.

"Well, I guess we can forget coffee refills," Sean observed, grinning crookedly.

"What did you say to her?" Diana asked between bites of the tasty omelet.

"Nothing she didn't deserve," he admitted, refusing to clarify his answer. When the waitress reluctantly returned to the booth behind them, impatiently tapping a pen against her order pad, he reached across the table toward his companion. "Give me your hands," he whispered.

Diana's blue eyes widened with surprise.

"Just do it," he insisted. Hesitantly, she slipped her fingers into his outstretched palms. He squeezed them gently and leaned in, bringing his face as close to hers as the table between them would allow. Before releasing them, he brought her hands together in front of his mouth and placed a soft kiss on her knuckles.

"What was that all about?" Diana asked him, thoroughly confused.

Nodding at the waitress who was stomping away, dark hair swinging furiously, he smiled a pleased smile. "Oh, just putting our sweet, sensitive Nora in her place. I was afraid your witty sarcasm was lost on her so I thought I'd take a more direct approach."

Though Diana rewarded his gallantry with a disapproving frown, inwardly she was grateful. The thoughtfulness of his gesture struck a chord, igniting the spark of hope she'd felt earlier. Maybe some of her fantasies weren't as improbable as they seemed.

The delicious meal was finished in silence. Diana retrieved a coffeepot from the warming tray on the counter and poured them both seconds while they watched for the bus. The restaurant wasn't busy, but the young mother's haphazard attempts to feed her children proved to be entertaining. It wasn't Diana's intention to eavesdrop but she couldn't help overhearing the frazzled woman talking to her little boy. Based on the tot's repeated pleas of "wanna wide de bus," followed by his mother's assurances that they would do so very soon, and several choruses of "The Wheels on the Bus, "she concluded that the young family would be joining them on the coach to Roanoke.

"There's our ride," Sean announced when the big Greyhound Bus pulled up across the street. He unfolded his long legs, dropped two ones on the table, picked up the check and his backpack and headed toward the cash register. Instead of following, Diana stopped to speak to the young mother who was hurriedly gathering up her things and her children.

"Hi. It looks like you could use a hand. Is there anything I can do to help?"

The petite brunette grinned up at her, gratitude shining in her huge green eyes. "Hey, thanks. I'd be much obliged. I'm Trixie and that's little Jesse." She indicated the toddler. "This here's baby Tiffany. We're trying to get on that bus over there."

My goodness, the older woman thought, examining the girl's flawless complexion, *she's not much more than a baby herself.* "Yes, I heard you telling your son. So are we. Here, let me take that," Diana said, throwing one large bag over her shoulder. "I'm Diana and that's my friend, Sean."

When the man finished paying for their meal and looked back, he offered his assistance as well. Smiling widely, her green eyes brightening considerably when they latched onto the attractive man, the young mother greeted him warmly.

"Well, Sean, am I happy to meet you. Wow! This is really good of you folks." She stared at the big man for a long moment, looking him over carefully. Then she bent down to address the toddler. "Jesse, honey, will you hold the nice lady's hand for Mama?"

Obediently, the adorable, tow-headed lad slipped his sticky fingers into Diana's proffered palm. He looked up at her with a tentative smile. "Hi, Jesse, I'm Diana," she said smiling back and hoping to reassure him.

Jesse's mom took charge quickly, giving the rest of her luggage to Sean and maneuvering herself and her baby to a position between him and his companion. Thus encumbered, the small group made their way out of the café and across the street to the bus station.

The excited mother chatted away, directing her conversation to the man at her side. "We're goin' to live with my sister over in Roanoke. She's got a real nice apartment and a good job at the hospital. Since Jesse's dad left me, things has been real rough round here. We've had a hard time makin' ends meet, you know, but I think we'll have a better chance in a bigger city." Trixie's attention was totally focused on Sean. She seemed to have dismissed her tiny son and the woman in whose care she'd left him.

As they neared the coach, the former soldier felt a familiar prickling down the back of his neck. Scanning the street, his keen eyes caught a glimpse of a khaki trench coat approaching from several block away. Hustling the women and their burdens up the steps, he pushed them toward the back of the bus. As Diana got little Jesse settled in a window seat, Sean stepped up and urged her, "You sit there, with the boy. The girl and I'll take the one behind you."

"Yes, sir," she snapped sarcastically, clearly biting back annoyance.

"Please, Diana," he whispered. "Trust me. Stark's here."

Fear rushing through her veins like liquid fire, Diana sat down obediently, bending her fair head toward the tiny boy who was showing her a colorful picture book he'd removed from one of the bags. Her senses tingling and alert, she pretended to be paying close attention to the tot while she watched the front of the bus out of the corner of her eye, expecting to see the FBI agent appear at any moment.

Larry Stark did not disappoint her. He mounted the steps of the bus and addressed the driver in low tones. Then he turned to examine the bus's passengers. Diana bent closer to her tiny seatmate, tucking stray strands of platinum hair under her cap. She kept her face averted but continued to regard him surreptitiously.

Stark was a man on a quest, determined and intense. His long, sharp nose and beady, dark eyes, flitting from side to side as he made his way down the aisle, reminded her of a hawk searching for prey. She held her breath as he passed her seat, feeling like a mouse hiding from the shadow of the hunting bird as it circled overhead.

Once his circuit of the coach was completed, Stark left with a nod to the driver, but Diana didn't relax until the door closed and the bus pulled away from the curb. Only then did she allow herself a backward glance.

Trixie had taken the aisle seat, pinning Sean against the window, his large frame folded uncomfortably into the cramped space. He held baby Tiffany in his lap. The young mother's hand lay possessively on his knee. A casual observer would assume that they were a happy couple making over the newest addition to their family.

Smiling again at the tow-headed tyke in the seat next to her, she was thankful Sean's quick-thinking ploy had worked to their advantage. It was no wonder Stark hadn't spotted them. The fair boy could easily pass for her son – or grandson. Diana sighed heavily, grateful the misdirection had been successful but despising the need for the charade.

When Diana glanced behind her again, the pilot caught her eye and offered a silent plea. He was desperate to extricate himself, but he didn't know how to do so without raising the young mother's protests. Deciding it would be best to endure Trixie's inane prattle for the duration of the trip, he settled in and tried to relax. Her questions irritated him all the more because he knew Diana could hear every embarrassing word.

"So, what did you do to git Nora in such a snit? She usually goes out o' her way to be nice to the good-lookin' men, but she was really peeved at you. What did you say to her?"

"She made a snide comment to my friend and I let her know I didn't appreciate it," he explained, hoping she'd let it drop.

Not one to be put off a quest for juicy gossip, Trixie demanded, "Wha'd she say?"

"She assumed Diana was my mother," Sean told her, cringing inwardly. "But I set her straight."

"That's a big joke," the pretty young woman chirped brightly. "Old Nora's not a spring chicken herself. Why, she's thirty if she's a day."

Sean couldn't suppress a chuckle.

"What's so funny?"

"You think thirty's getting on up there, huh?" he teased her.

Flipping her hair indignantly, she quipped, "Yeah, don't you?"

"No," he answered, smiling indulgently. "How old are you, Trixie?"

"Just turned twenty," she boasted proudly.

"I guess thirty does seem ancient to you, then. I thought the same thing when I was your age," he affirmed.

"How old are you?" she asked, her green eyes sparkling with curiosity.

"Thirty-three."

Pausing a moment to think it over, she tapped her fingers against her lower lip before flashing him a killer smile, "Oh, that's okay. Men hold their age better'n women do. An you don't look it nohow. Plus, my mama always told me that I should find myself an older man cause he'd take better care o' me than a fella my own age."

"Is that right?" Sean asked, more than a little

amused by the obvious girl.

"Are you from Roanoke?" she asked.

"Near enough," he supplied.

"Then you can call me when we git to my sister's, if you want. We could go out for drinks, or dancing,' or somethin'. You'd have yourself a good time." She batted her mascara encrusted eyelashes at him and crossed her legs to show off a creamy thigh. "Unless you and that Diana lady have somethin' goin' that is."

"No, we don't have anything going," he imitated. "We're just business associates."

"That's good, cause I agree with Nora. She's too old for you," the petite mother declared, leaning toward Sean and whispering.

"But I'm not too old for you?" he asked her, puzzled by her deduction.

"Hell, no. It's fine for the man to be older than the woman. It's maybe even better. But it don't work the other way round." A quick, definitive nod punctuated her statement. "An older woman with a younger man just ain't natural. Unless the woman has money o'course."

"What's money got to do with it?"

Staring at him wide-eyed and incredulous, she explained patiently, "Well, if the lady has a lot of money, then it don't matter how old she is cause she can have any man she wants."

"And this man would be with her for what she can give him?" he asked feigning ignorance.

"O'course," Trixie assured him. "I cain't imagine a younger, good-lookin' man really goin' for an old woman. If he's with her, then you can bet it's cause she's loaded."

"That would make him a gigolo," Sean concluded.

"What's that?" Her tiny, upturned nose wrinkled in confusion.

"A paid escort, a kept man – a male prostitute."

She seemed to be considering his conclusion before answering. After a moment or two, she shook her head. "Nope. He wouldn't be that no more'n a woman who marries a man cause he's well-off. I don't see nothin' wrong with it myself, if a woman, or a man, is lucky enough to find theirselves someone who can take care of 'em. But you don't have to worry about it, cause I don't think that's why you're with that lady."

"Oh, you don't?" He grinned. "Then why do you think Diana and I are together?"

"I know it ain't for her money. She don't look like she's got more'n a dollar or two to her name. You cain't be expectin' to git any cash outa her," Trixie concluded. After a moment's pause, she added," I watched you two in the diner. I saw the way you looked at her."

"So?" he asked, wondering where the silly girl was headed with her observations.

"I think you like her."

"Why would you think that? You said you'd never heard of a younger man liking an older woman" Sean tried to point out the inaccuracies in her logic.

"No, I said I never heard of a young man goin' for an old woman. There's a difference, you know." Trixie lowered her voice and pressed closer to him.

"You said that you and Diana are business 'sociates. I'm only sayin' that I think you're more'n that. It seems to me that you care about her. But I'm not sayin' I think you want to sleep with her. I reckon a man like you'd be more likely to have eyes for a gal like me."

Surprised at her unexpected insight, the pilot didn't respond immediately. The girl was right about one thing, he cared for Diana, cared deeply, but she was way off target with her second conclusion. Though Trixie seemed convinced that the power of her youth provided her with a distinct advantage over the more mature woman, his true feelings would amaze and confound the naive girl. Luckily, tiny Tiffany picked that moment to pucker up her pixie face, squirm, and cry, giving Sean an excuse to hand her back to her mother.

The distraction temporarily occupied Trixie, who seemed to lose the thread of the conversation as she struggled to quiet her baby. After unsuccessfully trying a pacifier, a finger, and an assortment of jiggles and shakes, she started unbuttoning her shirt. "She's hungry. I'm goin' to have to feed her. Hope you don't mind."

Realizing what she was about to do, Sean flushed hotly. "Why don't I switch seats with your son, so you can have some privacy?"

"That's all right. It don't bother me none," she bragged, baring her breast and bringing the baby girl close. "My mama always says I ain't got no shame, but I think nursin' a baby's special and beautiful, and we oughtn't to be embarrassed by somethin' so wonderful and natural. Don't you think I'm right?"

"Uh, sure," he stuttered, averting his face and staring out the window at the passing scenery, silently cursing his inability to extricate himself from this ridiculous predicament.

Diana sat in the seat in front of the young mother, holding Jesse's golden head on her lap as he slept and smiling at Sean's obvious dilemma. *Serves him right,* she mused. Thankful for the peaceful silence that had descended on the talkative girl as she relaxed and enjoyed the experience of feeding her baby, Diana mulled over the conversation between the two behind her. *Maybe he has some tender feelings for me after all,* she hoped, *if that simple, unsophisticated young girl was able to discern it.* That possibility buoyed her spirits.

But the discussion about kept men worried her. *What if Sean does have some affection for me, but he's afraid to show it because he thinks I'll question his motives?* she conjectured.

She wished she were a better judge of men and their interactions with women, but she didn't have the experience she needed to tell her what she wanted to know. She wished she had half of Trixie's confidence in her innate ability to appeal to and attract the opposite sex. Most of all, she wished she could trust her instincts where Sean was concerned, because her instincts told her there was something tangible, something important, developing between them.

Her gut knew. She felt it when he held her in his arms, when he looked into her eyes, but she didn't trust her gut, or her feelings. Her romance-deprived past, her years of cold, North-family conditioning, and her tendency to analyze everything in light of logic and reason, made that trust impossible.

Sixty minutes later, following one short stopover, the Greyhound pulled into the Roanoke terminal. Diana was still lost in her thoughts when the bus jerked to a stop. Little Jesse raised his sweet, sleepy face and rubbed his eyes with his fists.

Sean whispered a brief, "Thank you, God," under his breath, and quickly began helping the young mother gather up her children and belongings. With Diana's help, they got the girl and her entourage off the bus without delay, crossed between the rows of busses, through the lobby, and out onto the street, where Trixie said her sister would be waiting.

Just as they reached the sidewalk, another pretty brunette ran toward them, squealing in delight. Hugs and kisses were swapped all around, then Trixie introduced her traveling companions, making sure her sister knew that she had dibs on Sean.

"Trudy, these nice folks helped me with the kids – gettin' my stuff on the bus and all. I don't know what I woulda done without them. Little Jesse's really taken to Miz Diana, haven't you, honey?" She smiled down at the lad without expecting an answer.

"And this gorgeous hunk o' man was a perfect gentleman." She wrapped her arm around Sean's bicep possessively, marking her territory." He even held the baby for me so I could rest my arms, and he promised to take me out sometime."

Sean wondered how she'd drawn that conclusion but he let it go. She'd get the point soon enough, when the expected contact never came. Encouraged by his silence, she urged him, "Look me up on Facebook – Trixie Nicely – and message me. I'll send you my cell number so we can talk."

"Come on, Trixie," her sister urged. "The car's over there." She pointed to an old gray Dodge parked a few spaces down. "Let's get the kids strapped in so your friends can be on their way. I'm sure they're tired of luggin' your stuff around."

Smiling her thanks, Diana followed the older sister to her automobile. She secured the boy into a car seat, kissing him on his silky cheek, while Sean loaded Trixie's bags into the trunk. Once the little family was inside and buckled up, the relieved couple waved good-bye. As the car pulled out into traffic, Trixie's head popped out of the passenger's window, making one final appeal. "You won't forget, will you? Trixie Nicely. That's N-I-C-E-L-Y."

The pilot answered her with a dismissive wave.

Diana smirked. "You know, Sean, if you play your cards right, you might have a chance with that girl."

"Humph," he grunted. "She's trouble. That's T-R-O-U-B-L-E ! Can't say I blame Jesse Senior for running off."

"Be nice," she teased. "She's a sweet girl. Just a little bit needy."

"Yeah, but I don't have anything she needs!" he said with conviction.

"That's not what she thinks." The tall woman squeezed his arm playfully. "She thinks a big, strong fellow like you is just what she needs."

"Too bad she'll never get the chance to find out for sure," he growled.

"She won't?"

The big man refused to answer, shooting her a sideways glance that said, "Drop it!" as clearly as if he'd spoken the words aloud.

So, she did. "What now?" she asked him. "What do we do for transportation? Call a taxi?"

"No need for that," announced a husky voice from directly behind Sean. "The FBI is at your service. I've got a car waiting."

The former Marine whirled around to face Stark, his well-trained muscles coiled to strike out at the imminent threat, but the man's next words stopped him in mid-stride. "Take it easy, big boy. I have a 9mm Beretta in my pocket, aimed right at the lady's chest. Lay one finger on me and she gets it."

"What do you want from us?" Diana breathed, her eyes bright with desperation.

"Your cooperation," Stark informed her, grinning wickedly, his balding pate shining in the mid-afternoon sun. "Now step this way, slow and easy." He gestured toward a blue sedan parked next to the curb, about thirty feet down the street. "Keep your hands where I can see them."

Deliberately stalling, Diana tested the limits of the man's patience. "I'm not going anywhere with you until you tell me who you are and why you're here. If you were a real federal agent, you'd be trying to help us, not treating us like criminals."

"Shut up!" Stark growled. "Don't worry, my dear Mrs. North, I am a 'real' agent, and I'll explain everything to you and your large playmate, as soon as I have you safely in the car. Discussion-time is over. Move it! Or I'll shoot you where you stand."

"You wouldn't dare," she gasped.

"Try me," he challenged, meeting her frosty gaze with a dark, feral glare. Her open defiance clearly infuriated him. Determined to force her compliance, he grabbed for her arm.

The momentary distraction gave the former Force Recon Marine the opening he needed. Aiming a swift, almost undetectable thrust to the agent's midsection, he struck hard, the entire weight of his upper body in the blow. Stark doubled over. The air left his lungs in an agonizing whoosh, the gun in his coat pocket suddenly forgotten. A second, lightning-fast punch took him squarely on the chin, dropping him to the sidewalk.

As soon as Stark hit the concrete, Sean went down to his knees, screening the agent's body from view as he retrieved the weapon from his trench coat pocket. He called out, "Someone get help! This man collapsed. I think he might be having a heart attack!" He pushed the pistol across the sidewalk toward Diana, whispering, "Get rid of that."

She watched the pistol skitter over the edge of the curb and out into the street, coming to rest between two parked cars. Stepping down, she kicked the gun into a storm drain. Then she quickly returned to the fallen man's side, where several pedestrians had gathered to observe Sean's feigned attempts to revive the prone agent. The pilot surveyed the gawking bystanders and asked, "Does anyone know CPR?"

A middle-aged man in a three-piece suit, who looked like he was used to giving orders, volunteered. "I do."

"Good!" Sean jumped up and clapped him on the shoulder. "You take over because I have no idea what to do." He encouraged the would-be Good Samaritan to kneel next to the prostrate man. "We'll make sure the paramedics are on the way."

Grabbing Diana's elbow, he urged her, "Let's go." They took off down the street at a jog. Sean glanced back once to assure himself that no one had noted their departure. As he expected, all eyes were glued to the motionless agent and his well-intentioned rescuer, who was attempting mouth-to-mouth breathing.

"Stark's going to be surprised when he comes to," Sean chuckled, struggling to laugh and run, simultaneously.

When they'd covered several blocks, the pilot slowed their flight and angled toward a small coffee shop. "We have an hour before we can pick up our wheels. Let's hide out in here. I could use some caffeine. How about you?"

Diana nodded. Sean held the heavy wood and glass door for her and waited for her to precede him inside. The heavenly aroma of roasting beans washed over them. "Sit over there." He pointed to a small table in the very back corner of the long, narrow room. "My treat."

Grateful for his thoughtfulness, the tall woman let her trembling knees buckle and collapsed into the cane-bottomed chair, her heart still pounding a jackhammer staccato. She took several calming breaths and tried to force her tense muscles to relax. Tears threatened, stinging her eyes. Watching the handsome man approach through a watery haze, she wiped her nose on her sleeve and smiled at him.

He set two large cups of foamy latte on the small table top, returning to the counter to retrieve a couple of thick slices of cheesecake, topped with creamy brown curls. "Thought you could use some chocolate."

Diana didn't trust her voice, but wrapped her long fingers around the huge porcelain mug and lifted it to her lips, taking a cautious sip of the steaming liquid. She sighed with pleasure.

"Good, huh?" Sean asked. She nodded in the affirmative, swiping at one final tear, inching its way down her soft face. His brow furrowed with concern. "You okay?"

"Yeah," she croaked, clearing her throat. "I think so."

He returned her sad smile with a matching one of his own. Then he leaned his head close to hers and said, "Look, Diana, I know this is hard and I don't want to scare you, but things are gonna get worse, here, before they get better. Stark won't give up easily."

"How did he find us?"

"I guess we weren't as cleverly disguised as we

thought. He must have identified us on the bus after all." The big man took a bite of the rich dessert.

"Then why didn't he just pull us off the coach in Covington or take us at the stopover?" Diana wondered aloud.

"Too many witnesses," Sean concluded. "The passengers would have seen him remove us – by force. Hell, Diana, he probably got on the bus to make sure we were aboard so he could tail the coach and jump us when our guard was down.

"Shit! I can't believe I was so quick to believe we were safe. I should've known better. A seasoned special agent wouldn't be fooled by such a superficial bluff. I should've been ready."

"It's all right, Sean," the woman offered sincerely. "You redeemed yourself quite well when the need arose. What else could you have done, anyway?"

He shrugged deeper into his field coat. "The question now is what do we do next? Stark will have the airport staked out so that's not an option. We need to find a safe place to hide out and think. Any suggestions?"

"Well, since we can't use my credit card, a hotel is definitely out of the question."

"I've got enough dough left to rent an inexpensive room for one night, but after that we're flat busted," he admitted. "My mom always told me to carry a bankcard but I never bothered. Now I wish I'd listened to her."

"Don't worry," Diana encouraged him, energized by the intake of caffeine and chocolate. "We'll come up with something."

"Speaking of my mom, the farm's not too far from here, over the mountain in Franklin County. I'm sure the folks would be happy to put us up for a while."

"No, Sean, it's too dangerous. I won't involve your family in this mess." Her tone was insistent, telling him an argument was useless, but he tried anyway.

"My dad and my brothers-in-law are all good old country boys. They know how to protect themselves. Some branches of the family have been fighting the government for years." The man grinned sheepishly. "A measly FBI agent wouldn't stand a chance against my kin. They're used to going up against real G-men – Revenuers."

"Revenuers?"

"Tax collectors – from the Department of Alcohol, Tobacco, and Firearms."

When she just looked at him, wide-eyed and confused, he elaborated, "Franklin County, Virginia is famous for the production and sale of illegal whiskey. They don't call it 'The Moonshine Capital of the World' for nothing. Believe me, my kinfolk can smell a government man a mile away and they know how to protect themselves."

"Maybe so, but we can't take a chance with their lives. It's out of the question," the tall, woman insisted.

"That's what I thought you'd say but I had to give it a try."

"Thanks for the offer, though. I really would like to meet your family." Her sad, longing smile slipped back into place. "Maybe after this is over, you'll take me to me to visit them."

"Sure," he agreed, squeezing her hand. "It's a deal. My sisters are always after me to bring a woman home. They'd be tickled to meet you."

"They would?" Diana remarked, a bit surprised by his statement. Before he could respond, however, an idea struck her. "Oh, my goodness, I don't know why I didn't think of this sooner. I know where we can go but I need a phone."

Sean scanned the room. Several of the patrons were engrossed in conversations, cell phones plastered to their ears. Others were tapping away on tablets or smart phones. Choosing his target, a chubby woman with fuzzy brown hair, wearing a navy, polyester suit one size too small, the clever pilot approached. She flipped her phone closed with a snap and took a big bite of the gooey brownie on the plate in front of her.

"Excuse me," he drawled, flashing a killer smile, which she returned with obvious delight, a huge chunk of chocolate icing stuck to her left front tooth. "I know it's a terrible imposition but could we possibly use your phone? My friend misplaced hers and she needs to make a very important call."

"Uh…I don't know," she mumbled, sucking at the icing glob as she eyed the handsome man. "I guess it would be okay." Hesitantly handing over the phone, she ordered, "Make it quick."

While Diana made the call, Sean kept the reluctant woman occupied. He asked her name, complimented her hair, and even patted her arm flirtatiously. Minutes later, when Diana returned the phone, he finished with a vigorous handshake, a big

"Thank you," and a devilish wink.

As they navigated toward the door, Diana teased, "Well, aren't you just a regular ladies' man? I had no idea you were such a charmer."

"Aw, shucks, ma'am, t'weren't nothin'," he twanged, wagging his eyebrows suggestively before dropping the country-boy façade and getting serious. "What did you find out?"

"It's all arranged. We have a place to stay. If you can find a way to get us there, that is."

"What time is it?"

Checking her watch, she replied, "Two-fourty."

"Perfect. Our chariot awaits us, my dear. Right this way, please."

EIGHT

Bright sunshine and a warm, spring-like breeze greeted them when they stepped back out onto the sidewalk. The overcast sky had shed its covering of leaden-gray clouds, allowing golden rays to shower the people below. Sean led Diana down the street, away from the tall buildings of the business district, across parking lots, under bridges, and into an area crisscrossed by railroad tracks and tall, metal poles and overhead wires.

Following her companion's example, Diana peeled off her jacket and folded it carefully over her arm, then she asked him, her apprehension growing, "Where are you taking me?"

"To get our ride," he answered cryptically, flashing her a heart-wrenching smile.

"Which would be...?" she prompted, probing for more information.

"A surprise!" he beamed at her. "Be patient. We'll be there in a minute."

Surveying her surroundings skeptically, the woman could find nothing except a few Bus Stop signs which might indicate that they were about to come upon a viable means of transportation. Private vehicles were parked along the side of the road, adjacent to a knee-high rock wall, but no taxis or rental car establishments were anywhere in sight.

Just as she was beginning to suspect that he was playing some sort of cruel joke on her, the big Marine waved his arm over his head. A block or so further on, a man waved back from the bed of a battered pick-up. "There he is." Sean noted. "Right on schedule." Picking up the pace, they were soon alongside the dusty truck.

"Hey, little brother, long time no see," the lanky stranger called, jumping down from his perch and slapping Sean on both shoulders. "Whatcha been up to?"

"You don't wanna know," the pilot told him, grimacing and returning the friendly blows.

"So, who's this lovely lady, and how'd a scoundrel like you get yourself mixed up with such a comely woman?" The stick-thin, scarecrow of a man flashed Diana a wide grin, removing a green, John Deere cap and scratching his head through a thick thatch of light brown hair.

"J.D., this is Diana North." Sean told him, adding, "She hired me to fly her up to a resort in West Virginia but we ran into a bit of trouble on the way."

"I'd say," J.D.'s thin-lipped grin grew even wider. "You're a few miles off course." Tipping his hat again, he addressed the woman. "Pleased to meet you, ma'am, I'm this roughneck's brother-in-law, J.D. Craddock."

"Ellen's husband," Sean clarified.

She offered him her hand. "The pleasure is mine, Mr. Craddock."

Wiping his callused palm on the dark blue coverall he wore over his clothing, he slipped it into hers, shaking it firmly. "Sean says you're in need of wheels so I brought you some." He gestured with his head toward the bed of the mud-encrusted truck. Lashed down tightly between the side rails was a shiny black Harley Davidson motorcycle. "I was just gettin' 'er out when I caught sight of you."

"I'll do it," the bigger man offered, springing up effortlessly onto the open tailgate, and removing the restraints from the front fork of the huge motorcycle. "If you'll put the ramps in place so I can roll her down, I can handle the rest."

J.D. did as he was asked, affixing long wooden boards to the tailgate. That accomplished, he retrieved two helmets from the truck's cab and handed one to Diana. Reluctantly taking the heavy headgear from him, she stared at it in disbelief. "Don't worry," he said, "I give him a hard time, but Sean's a good man. He'll take care of you. You'll be safer on that Harley with him, than with most any other man around. He knows how to handle himself."

"So he tells me," she quipped, returning his sincere smile with her usual sad one. Noting the quizzical look on the man's narrow but pleasantly featured face, she told him, "I'm sure you're right. He has protected me very well so far. And thank you for your assistance, too. It was kind of you to go to the trouble."

"Wasn't no trouble a tall," he denied. "When Sean called me last night and told me about the fix you're in, I was anxious to help out. It's his bike anyway. I've been after him to get it outa my shed for months now."

Just then an earsplitting whistle blew. Throwing the ramps up into the truck bed and slamming the tailgate shut, Sean urged, "You better go, J.D. We've made you late for work as it is. Thanks, buddy. I'll be in touch."

"You'd better," J.D. warned sprinting away. "Ellen and the girls said they'd split my skull if I didn't get you to promise to call them right soon."

"I promise!" Sean called after him, waving a good-bye.

While the man was giving the cycle a once over, Diana fumed. "You talked to J.D. last night?" Her question sounded like an accusation.

"I did. I went out after you were asleep and called him," Sean explained calmly, ignoring the unconcealed suspicion in her tone. "He works the three-to-eleven shift at the Norfolk Southern locomotive shop. Over there." He pointed to a long row of brick buildings that Diana had assumed was a factory.

"It didn't put him out much to load up this old hog and bring it with him. I knew the bus station was within walking distance and figured it would save us cab fare."

"You called him? How did you manage that feat in the middle of the night?" she asked suspiciously.

Sean blew out a breath and admitted. "I used my cell."

"You said you don't carry a cell phone,"

"I lied."

Diana's frosty blue eyes shot darts. "You've had a phone all this time, lied about having it, and refused to use it. Why, Sean?"

"Same reason you couldn't have used yours, Diana. GPS tracking, like I told you before," Sean offered calmly. "My phone was turned off to save charge so I thought it would be safe, but I pulled the battery out the first chance I got, just to be sure. I lied to you because I didn't want to tell you that I thought someone was trying to kill you."

"Why did you risk using it last night?" she asked reasonably.

"No other choice. Everything was closed up tight and I couldn't find a pay phone, of course, so I went a ways from the motel and took a chance."

Accepting his explanation with a relieved sigh, she watched Sean stuff his arms into his coat and zip it up tight. "You'd better put that jacket on," he encouraged her. "The weather's warmed up some but it'll still be cold as hell with the wind whipping at you."

She did as he suggested. He flipped the cap off her bright head, crammed it into the backpack along with his own, and helped her fasten her helmet securely. "Where are we going?"

"My college roommate and her husband have a small summer place about twenty miles from here, at Smith Mountain Lake. Do you know the area?"

"Like the back of my hand," he boasted, throwing one muscular thigh over the massive cycle. Holding out an upturned palm, he helped her onto the seat behind him and handed her the knapsack. "You'll have to take charge of that while

I steer."

When she tried to secure it on the seat between them, he objected. "That's not gonna work. It'll be in the way. You'll need both hands free to hold on."

Realizing he was right, she slipped her arms through the backpack's shoulder straps and pulled them up snugly. Then, she laid her palms gently against his waist. Grabbing her fingers, he brought her hands around in front of his body, forcing her chest against his broad back. "Hold on tight," he demanded. "The closer you sit to me, the warmer we'll both be."

Retrieving his gloves from the pocket of his coat, he pulled them on. "If the arms on that jacket are long enough, tuck your hands into the opposite sleeve, so your fingers won't freeze."

Her heart pounding, Diana complied. When the motor growled to life, an exhilarating tingle rushed throughout her body. She choked down a surprised shriek.

Ignoring her involuntary cry, Sean wheeled the huge bike around and headed east. The ride was cold but not unbearably so. Diana shouted their destination's address over the hum of the engine and they rolled into a wide concrete drive less than three-quarters of an hour later. The pilot stopped the bike in front of an over-sized garage, which was attached to a rambling, contemporary ranch. A covered porch ran down the front of the impressively large house, sheltering a row of sparkling, floor-to-ceiling windows. The grounds around the dwelling were lavishly tended.

"Whew!" Sean exclaimed. "I thought you said

this place was a small. It looks like you understated it a bit. Might be just a little summer home to you and yours, but to me and mine, it's a mansion. Are you sure it's all right for us to stay here?"

Prying her cold fingers apart, she struggled to detach herself from the seat of the motorcycle. It took a few moments to regain the feeling in her buzzing toes. Tugging off the helmet and tossing her hair, she reassured him. "Yes, it's okay. Eleanor said the place is already set up for the summer season. There's plenty of food in the pantry and freezer."

Hobbling on numb feet, she crossed to the keypad mounted on the wall to the right of the automatic garage door. "She gave me the opener and alarm codes."

Seconds later, they were inside. Sean rolled the Harley into one of the empty bays. "Do you think they'll mind my hog in their fancy digs?"

"Not at all," Diana admitted, helping him with his helmet. "Dick, Elly's husband, has always wanted a motorcycle. She calls it his 'born-to-be-wild' fantasy. But she refuses to allow it. As a trauma nurse, she's seen too many accident victims in the emergency department.

"He's a doctor – cardiologist. If you ever need heart surgery, call Dick. He's one of the best. But when it comes to operating any type of machinery, look out! Dick Randall is an accident waiting to happen. I can't tell you how many fender-benders he's had since college. Elly's afraid he's going to kill himself one of these days.

"So, she puts her foot down," Sean concluded.

"Repeatedly." The tall woman grinned at him. "But he'd be delighted to find such a beautiful bike in his garage."

"You like it?"

"I do," she admitted, surprised at herself. The way he looked at her, his dark eyes searching her pale ones, probing and intense, shook her composure. She turned away and urged him, "Let's get inside and warm up."

Taking the backpack, he followed her into a spacious utility room slash pantry. Diana removed her coat and reached for Sean's, hanging them on hooks behind the door.

"I could give the good doctor a few motorcycle-safety lessons," Sean offered. "With practice, he could become a careful rider. Maybe that would convince his wife that he's not going to crash and burn. Or, I could just take him out with me sometime. A couple of butt-numbing hours on the back of my Harley might cure him of the bug for good."

"It's considerate of you to offer," Diana remarked, leading the way into the great room. "Next time I speak with him I'll see if he's interested."

"It'd be fun – and partial payment for their hospitality." Looking around the luxurious interior, Sean whistled appreciatively.

What had appeared to be a one-story ranch from the front, proved to be a multi-level structure that followed the contour of the hillside, as it sloped down to meet the lakeshore. The couple stood in the middle of a huge, gourmet kitchen, facing a massive window with a spectacular view of the private cove. A half-turn to the right revealed a granite-topped bar, dividing the kitchen from an enormous, sumptuously appointed living and dining area. On the far end of the great room, a massive stone fireplace covered the entire wall.

"Why don't you start a fire while I see what I can whip up for supper?" Diana suggested, untying her boots and setting them inside the pantry door. "There's a wood box next to the hearth. I'm sure you'll find plenty of dry logs and tinder inside."

"Be happy to, after I clean up."

Gesturing toward a polished mahogany staircase separating the living area from the entry foyer, she told him, "Bedrooms are downstairs. Take your pick. Each one has its own ensuite." Shrugging out of her sweatshirt, she tossed it at him. "Here, put this in whichever room you choose for me."

He grabbed his knapsack and headed for the stairs. "I won't be long."

Sean reappeared, clad in a fresh T-shirt and a pair of comfortable blue jeans, while Diana was chopping a variety of vegetables she'd found in the pantry and refrigerator.

"That looks interesting," he commented, standing close behind her, leaning over her shoulder to watch her work.

"Oh, you shaved," Diana remarked, noting that the removal of the three-day growth had taken years off his face. *He looks so young,* she thought, involuntarily reaching out to touch the smooth planes of his cheek. Before her fingers made contact, her better-judgment alarm went off. She jerked her hand back and quickly resuming her task. The clean, masculine scent of him filled her head. She had to force herself to concentrate on her cooking and to pretend to ignore his presence.

Taking her feigned disinterest as a rebuff, Sean snorted and turned away. "Guess I'd better start that fire now."

"That would be nice," she encouraged him, thankful when he moved away and focused on the task across the room.

Muttering to himself, Sean worked quickly. Minutes later, a cheerful blaze snapped away inside the huge fireplace. As he added logs to the flames, he agonized over Diana's ambiguous reactions. Every time she seemed about to show him a small gesture of affection, something stopped her. *She's admitted that she's attracted to me, so why can't she bear to touch me?* Tormented by that question, he decided it was time to confront her.

While he waited for dinner, he examined the contents of a built-in shelving unit, nestled into the corner beside the fireplace. Finding a receiver for satellite radio, Sean switched it on. Soon the strains of soft, instrumental classics filled the air, emitted from state-or-the-art speakers mounted inconspicuously around the circumference of the room.

"It's ready," the woman chimed from the kitchen.

"Why don't we eat it in here, next to the fire,

where it's warm and cozy?" Sean suggested. *And romantic,* he silently added. He dragged the glass-topped coffee table a little closer to the hearth, and gathered an assortment of pillows and throws off the sofa, scattering them around on the thick wool rug. Then he crossed the long expanse of polished boards to assist Diana as she carried in their plates and silverware.

When she went back to retrieve the wine and glasses, he moved a pair of candlesticks from the mantle, placed them in the middle of the table, and lit them. Finally, he turned off the artificial light, leaving only the warm glow of the fire and candle flames to illuminate the area.

Once his companion was seated on a comfortable pile of cushions, Sean joined her, folding his long legs under him, and pouring their glasses full of the sparkling burgundy. He took a long sip before breathing in the delicious aromas wafting up from the heaping plate she'd placed in front of him. "Smells wonderful."

Diana had prepared thick rib-eye steaks and steamed rice, accompanied by stir-fried vegetables. Hungrier than he thought, the former soldier focused his attention on the food until only a bite or two remained. When his appetite was sated, he praised her cooking. "My dear Mrs. North, that was a mighty fine meal. You are an excellent chef."

Blushing at the compliment, she disagreed, laying her fork aside, her food barely touched, "Good cook, maybe, when I have the chance, but never a chef. I haven't the right sort of imagination or creativity. My talents lie in other directions."

Smiling at him, her cool eyes sparkling with sincerity, she remarked, "This is the first time I've seen you clean-shaven. It changes you."

"Yeah?" he asked, curiously.

"It makes you seem more vulnerable," she concluded.

"Vulnerable, huh? That's not a good trait to see in the man who's supposed to be protecting you from a killer." His playful tone didn't minimize the truth of his statement.

"Not the best choice of words, I guess" Diana admitted. "It just makes you seem less intimidating, less dangerous."

"Scruff makes me look dangerous?" His bright brown eyes flashed his approval. He tilted his head to an arrogant angle, raised his eyebrows, and threw her a cocky grin.

She nodded. "A little. Those scars. The one there," she said, pointing to the eyebrow he'd raised quizzically. "And the one just under your chin, say that you don't back down from a fight. You meet trouble head-on. But clean-shaven, the one on your chin almost disappears, so you look a bit less like a devil-may-care rogue."

"Just temporarily, of course," he added. "Which do you like better, the dangerous rogue, complete with beard stubble and battle scars, or the clean-shaven, safe version?"

"Oh, I'd never classify you as safe, clean-shaven or not," she quipped, avoiding his question. "It's not polite to ask, but how did you get those scars? Were you wounded on a mission?"

"It's not something I like to talk about." He

studied his hands, and struggled to keep a brooding, reluctant look in place on his handsome features

Taken in by his sham, she apologized, "I'm sorry, Sean. It's none of my business. Forgive me for prying."

"It's okay," he told her, raising one shoulder. "I understand your curiosity. I'm just not ready to talk about it, yet. Maybe I'll tell you…" He swallowed hard, pretending to be shutting out an unpleasant memory. "…when I know you better."

Diana laughed. The sad smile tickled the corners of her lips.

"What's so funny?"

She laughed again. "It's strange that you say you need to get to know me better. I've shared more about myself in the past four days than I have in the last decade or more. You asked me sincere questions and listened to the honest answers. Frankly, I don't think there's too much about me that you don't know already. And that's a first, for me."

"There's one thing I can think of, right off," he noted.

"What's that?" she asked, her eyebrows raised quizzically.

"I don't know why you start to reach out to me but pull back like your fingers are on fire. Why do you avoid touching me, Diana?" His dark eyes bore into hers, imploring her to answer truthfully.

Diana cleared her throat nervously. "You really want to know?"

"Yes. Give me the truth. I'm a big boy. I can handle it."

"Once it's out there I won't be able to take it back, you know," she cautioned. "We'll just have to deal with the consequences."

"That's enough stalling. Out with it," he demanded. "What are you afraid of?"

She met the challenge of his gaze with a cool, direct stare, her blue eyes brimming with unshed tears. "Afraid doesn't begin to describe what I'm feeling," she admitted. "The truth is…I'm terrified. I'm terrified to touch you, because I want to touch you so badly. I'm terrified to touch you, because I can't be sure what will happen if I do."

Sean absorbed each word, cherishing it, but saying nothing and forcing her to go on.

"Admitting that I find you attractive was an understatement." She tore her eyes away from his face. "The truth is, I find you more desirable than any man I've ever met and it frightens me senseless. I'm terrified of what I feel when I look at you, Sean. I'm terrified that my fingers ache to touch you."

Now that her pent-up feelings had been released, she couldn't seem to stop the outpouring flood. "My hands itch to smooth away the tiny lines that cross your forehead when you're angry or worried. Those scars on your eyebrow and chin cry out to be kissed. I want to bury my face in the depression at the base of your throat where your pulse beats." With one long finger, she reached across the table and laid her fingertip on the spot.

A jolt like liquid fire shot through Sean when her touch contacted his bare skin. He inhaled sharply, tingling with an exquisite burst of sensation, his heart singing.

"I want to do all of those things, desperately, but I can't take the risk," Diana whispered.

"Wh... why not?" he croaked, his deep voice echoing in his chest.

"Two huge reasons." Studying the plain gold wedding-band she wore on the third finger of her left hand, she told him, "My marriage is not a real one, in any true sense of the word, but until I'm legally divorced, I'm still bound to James. I made promises." She seemed to be fighting to overcome the shame of her heart's disloyalty.

"You don't love him. You never did," Sean prompted, desperation trickling into the spaces in his heart where the joy was retreating. "He's never been faithful to you so why do you feel obligated to be faithful to him?"

Diana shrugged. "Faithfulness to James is not the primary reason I can't reach out to you, Sean." "Then, what?" He asked, though he'd already guessed the answer.

"I work hard to come across as confident and self-assured but I have a deep-seated fear of rejection that I've never been able shake. I couldn't bear it if I reached out to you and you turned away." Pausing to study his face, she added, "Despite what my heart is telling me, my head knows that a young, powerful, passionate man like you could never look at an old, hopeless, ice-queen like me and feel anything but contempt and disgust."

Sean opened his mouth to object, but she stopped him by placing two fingers across his lips.

"You say sweet things to me. You make me feel feminine and desirable. I want to believe that you mean what you say, but I know you can't, not really. And so, every time I'm tempted to touch you, I remind myself that, just because I want something to be true, doesn't make it so, and I pull back. I'm a coward, terrified to take a chance on love."

Diana said nothing more, but dropped her face into her hands. Several agonizing moments dragged by before she raised her head, wiped at a tear, and told him, "I'd like to forget you ever asked me that question and you can pretend you never heard the answer. That way we can go on as we were, as friends."

"Not possible," he replied, his sensuous voice low.

"Then I'm sorry, Sean. I was afraid the truth would come between us. I just hope that knowing how I feel about you doesn't make you too uncomfortable."

"Not uncomfortable at all," he told her, grinning, "at least not in the way you mean." He could tell she didn't grasp his insinuation but made no effort to explain, wondering how to convince her that her assumptions were completely wrong. Abandoning words in favor of action, he unfolded his legs, stood over her, and reached out his hand.

"Dance with me," he pleaded.

"What?" she questioned, still avoiding his eyes.

"May I have the pleasure of this dance?" he replied, with deliberate formality.

"Here? Now?"

"Right here. Right now." His outstretched hand was insistent, unwilling to accept a refusal.

The woman hesitantly placed her fingers in his palm and allowed him to help her to her feet. As an interesting instrumental arrangement of "Stand by Me" whirled around the room, Sean pulled her into his arms, drawing her tightly against the firm wall of his chest, and began to sway to the music. He moved with a fluid grace uncommon in a man of his size. Diana lost herself in the music, the movement, and the man.

Placing his strong fingers under her chin, he tilted her face up to meet his eyes, then he smiled. With the other arm, he pulled her closer and dropped a soft kiss on the side of her neck just below her earlobe. Diana's breath caught in her throat. He tightened his embrace, yet again, and she responded, clinging to him fiercely, her arms encircling his neck.

When the song ended, his feet stopped moving but he didn't release her. He took a half-step backward, his eyes searching hers, and whispered, "I'll never be able to forget what you told me, Diana, because it's what I wanted to hear."

"I don't understand… You can't possibly mean that you..." Hope beyond all reason swelled inside her heart.

"I've wanted you since the first moment I saw you, striding across the tarmac toward me like you owned the world. I didn't want to want you because I believed the unflattering things I'd heard about you, but I couldn't help myself. A look of sincere regret crossed his handsome features, striking Diana like a well-aimed punch.

"It didn't take me long to figure out that you use that icy veneer to protect the warm, soft woman inside and that made me want you even more. But I didn't show you because I was afraid too – afraid you'd think I was coming on to you because of…well, because of your wealth. I convinced myself that a smart, sophisticated, beautiful woman like you couldn't be attracted to a rough-edged knockabout like me. I pretended that the only thing between us was a casual flirtation because I didn't dare hope for more.

"You've been the brave one, opening your heart to me. Now it's my turn. The truth is, Diana, I wasn't just flirting. I meant every compliment, every endearment. Believe it. The age thing is a non-issue. The money thing still chafes but we'll deal with it.

"My precious, Diana, don't be afraid of wanting me. I'll never reject you. I will never turn you away because I want you desperately." Before she could respond, he lowered his lips to hers.

NINE

The kiss left her breathless and weak-kneed. Without the support of his arms around her, Diana was sure she would have collapsed onto the floor. She clung to him tightly, her thoughts reeling. He quickly followed the first soft, teasing exchange with another, this one more intense and demanding, which she answered fully, urgently. The room faded into the background. Nothing existed except the feel of Sean's lips on hers, the taste of his tongue in her mouth, and the demands of his hands upon her flesh.

He held her fiercely against him. She could feel his arousal pressing hard, bold and impudent, through the thick fabric of her jeans. When he grabbed the hem of her turtleneck and drew it off over her head, she didn't think to protest but responded by sliding her fingers under his T-shirt. Then, almost before she realized what was happening, they were lying together amidst the heap of pillows, naked, her alabaster skin glowing in the warm light of the fireplace. Sean covered her body with his, whispering her name, his voice husky and deeply thrilling.

Just when she couldn't bear to wait a second longer to fill the urgent, aching need melting her bones, he slid into her. She welcomed him with a breathless, longing sigh. Long, delicate fingers caressed the planes and angles of his back, urging him on. He moved against her with a practiced deliberation and she met every thrust enthusiastically.

In the act of love their bodies fit together perfectly. Even thus intertwined, her face was almost level with his, allowing Sean to shower her face and neck with fiery kisses and to whisper words of devotion into her ear. As Diana's body tensed he instinctively increased his pace, watching her face intently, until a deep tremor ran the length of her, and a soul-wrenching moan of release escaped her lips. She held him even tighter than before, digging her fingertips into his muscles.

The force of her climax pushed him to follow. As he poured himself into her, Sean knew that what they'd experienced was not simply the culmination of mutual sexual desire. It was something more. No woman had ever made him feel the way Diana made him feel. He relaxed into her and tucked his face into the hollow of her neck, inhaling deeply.

A long moment later he drew back, needing to see the satisfied glow left in the aftermath of their lovemaking on her beautiful face. The sweet, rosy hue that slashed across her cheekbones and the sincere smile on her bow-shaped mouth pleased him, as did the look of sated longing in her sapphire eyes. But the tears that twinkled in her long eyelashes were like daggers stabbing straight at his chest.

"I was too rough," he breathed. "I just wanted

you so badly that I got carried away. Can you forgive me?" He tried to roll off of her, but she held him tightly.

"Be still," she ordered softly, "or you'll slip out."

Obeying, but shaking his head in confusion, he whispered, "But you're crying."

"Only tears of joy," she whispered, grinning suggestively. "You didn't hurt me." Sighing again, she added, "It was wonderful! You were wonderful! We were wonderful together! I had no idea it could be like that. I'm just so happy that I can't help crying a little." She laid her palm on his cheek.

"There you go again, changing right before my eyes," he teased, "from a mature seductress to a wide-eyed teenager experimenting with sex for the first time. You are fascinating my lovely Diana." To show her he meant what he said, he dropped another kiss on her lips. That one turned into another and yet another. It was a long time before he raised his head to look at her once more.

"Why don't I clean up the kitchen and the remains of our dinner," he suggested, "while you go downstairs and freshen up? Then we can start all over again, this time in a nice, comfortable bed."

"That sounds like a wonderful idea," she agreed, giving him one final, fierce hug.

Rolling to his knees, Sean searched for his jeans. He located his shirt and underwear, under the coffee table and tossed the bundle in Diana's general direction. "Take those with you, please. I don't think I'll need them again tonight."

"Not a chance," she promised with a wink,

watching him wiggle into the tight denim. Pulling on her turtleneck and panties, she asked him, "Where'd you leave your backpack? I want my toiletries."

"In the master bedroom," he admitted, wagging his eyebrows.

"Taking the best room for yourself, huh?" Diana teased. "Were you being presumptuous or just sure you'd persuade me to share that huge bed with you?"

"Not presumptuous or sure. Just hopeful." Reaching out one long finger, he tilted her chin up so he could look into her sparkling blue eyes. What he saw reflected there delighted him. The frosty veneer was gone completely. Her gaze was warm and open. A wide, genuine smile graced her lips.

Just as the promise of spring had melted the winter snow from the mountainside, the heat of his love had melted the icy glaze from her heart. He uttered a silent prayer that should the wintry chill ever come between them again, he would have the power to invoke an immediate and lasting spring thaw.

With a playful swat on her thinly clad derriere, he teased, "Off with you, then. And prepare yourself for my pleasure, wench!" With a suggestive grin, he added a tender kiss, full of promise.

Diana's response thrilled him. She willingly played along with his game and took it a step further. "Of course, my lord, as you wish," she retorted, sliding her palms down his back to the seat of his jeans and squeezing. "You do realize that this poor wench has been deprived of her liege's love for so long, that her demands might prove too much for a pampered lord like you to bear."

"Never!" he denied vehemently. After kissing her again, he pushed her toward the stairs. "I'll be down as soon as I clean up and check all the windows and doors."

Sean's reminder of the need to secure the house brought Diana's suppressed fears bubbling back to the surface. "What are we going to do?"

"I told you," he said, crossing the distance between them and enfolding her in his embrace. "You're going to get a nice, hot bath while I put everything back in order and make sure the house is locked up tight. Then we're going to make love until we fall asleep, completely exhausted."

"No, no, I mean what are we going to do about this mess we're in? What are we going to do about that special agent?" Sean could almost feel the anxiety clawing its way up her spine.

"We're going to do our damnedest to forget about it tonight." His tone was firm and left no room for disagreement. "In the morning, we'll check in with Vic and call your husband to find out what he has to say. Then we'll decide how to proceed. Trust me, Diana. I'll get us out of this, yet. Don't worry."

Reassured by his words and the intense heat flashing in his maple-syrup eyes, gazing down on her, the woman nodded, accepting his proposal. "Don't be long."

Easily locating his knapsack, flung in the

middle of the king-sized bed in the largest suite, Diana dug out her plastic travel kit, clean panties, and one of Sean's cotton undershirts. She showered quickly, toweled off, and dried her wet locks with a blow drier she found in the vanity drawer. Then she applied perfumed body lotion to her glowing skin and brushed her teeth. She coated her lips, swollen and pink, with a moisturizing balm, remembering the feel of Sean's mouth on hers and eagerly anticipating his arrival.

When she heard Sean's footsteps approaching, she threw back the covers on the big bed and climbed in, calling out to him. "I borrowed one of your undershirts. I hope you don't mind."

The pilot's large frame filled the doorway. A gravelly voice announced from behind him, "Don't mind a bit." Before the surprised woman could react, Larry Stark shoved Sean into the room and waved a huge pistol toward her.

"Now isn't this cozy? Won't old James be happy to know he's been replaced? Can't wait to see the look on his face, when I tell him the lies he's been fabricating are actually true. How ironic. The old 'Ice Queen' had gotten herself a hot, young stud to fill her bed."

Diana tore her gaze from Stark's malicious grin, wondering what was wrong with Sean. *Why is he just standing there?* A rush of adrenaline hit her bloodstream, bringing the pilot's face into sharper focus. A bright line of crimson trickled from a deep gash on his forehead, his eyes were glazed, and he swayed slightly, unsteady on his feet. His hands were clasped behind him, his wrists clearly bound.

Fury flashed through her, bright and hot, leaving no room for fear.

She flew to Sean's side, ignoring the threatening glare Stark shot her and the blue steel barrel he had pointed at her head. "You bastard! What did you do to him?"

"Sean! Look at me," she urged, breathlessly, trying to get him to meet her eyes. "Are you all right?" His body sagged back against Stark and he seemed to be having trouble maintaining his balance.

The agent answered for him. "It's only a little bump on the head. He's a big, tough guy. He can take it."

Ignoring Stark, who indulged her by stepping back so he could train the pistol on both of them at once, Diana steadied Sean and gently examined the wound on his temple. The pilot groaned, then whispered, almost inaudibly, "Knife, left-hand pocket." When she hesitated, he insisted, "Kiss me! And make it look good."

Pulling his head down to meet her, she kissed him, long and deeply. Slowly, as if coming up out of a heavy fog, he began to respond. Stark was intrigued by the exchange. He watched the entwined couple with amused interest. "Yeah, that's the ticket," he urged. "If that won't put the starch back in him, nothing will. I can't wait to talk to your husband. It's about time someone turned the tables on that filthy son-of-a-bitch."

Tuning out Stark's taunts, Diana followed Sean's lead, rotating their bodies slightly so her right hand was hidden from the agent's line of sight.

Moving carefully, the woman slid her palm into the pilot's pocket and down his thigh until her finger touched on a heavy, metal object. She drew it out, maneuvered it around to the pilot's back, and dropped it into his open hand.

"That's enough!" Stark snarled, grabbing the tail of Diana's shirt and dragging her away from Sean. "Get over there," he ordered, pointing the barrel of his handgun toward the far corner of the large room. "Do exactly as I say and your lover will live a little while longer. Make one stupid move and I'll empty a clip into him."

When the woman complied, he gave Sean a violent push that sent him careening. A second blow followed the first, squarely on the solar plexus, knocking the wind out of the former soldier and forcing him backward onto the bed. Once the large man was prone, and apparently harmless, Stark pulled a plastic zip strip out of his coat pocket and secured his ankles.

"That should hold you until I get back to finish you off." Dismissing the younger man for the moment, he whirled to face Diana. "Get dressed. We're going out."

Stalling for time, the woman moved as slowly as she could without raising the agent's ire. "Why are you treating us like criminals? Why are you threatening us instead of trying to find out who blew up the helicopter, who wants us – wants me – dead?"

Stark refused to answer, so she pressed harder. "We're innocent citizens. You should be trying to help, offering us protection, not harassing us and making up lies about us."

"That's a laugh. 'Innocent citizen' doesn't describe you or your eager lover, my dear Mrs. North. The games you two have been playing are most certainly not innocent." He offered her a sly wink. "I can see no harm in answering your questions. I wouldn't want you to die curious and ignorant. Of course, the information won't do you much good, because you won't be around long enough to share it with anyone."

He grinned at her maliciously, his beady eyes watching every move she made as she dressed. "As for the attempt to blow up your helicopter, frankly, I'm quite vexed that it failed. I don't like having to do something more than once. You see, my dear, I planted the explosive device myself."

Obviously enjoying the look of shock and fear his announcement elicited, he thrust the knife deeper into her heart, "Your husband paid me to do it."

Pleased with himself, he chuckled arrogantly and boasted, "James got wind of your plans to divorce him and take half of his fortune, so he hired me to run interference. I rigged the helicopter to look like an electrical malfunction caused the crash. If you had died, like you were supposed to, I'd already be a rich man. But somehow you escaped and now I have to tie up the loose ends." Drawing a nickel-plated .357 out of his waistband, Stark tossed the weapon on the bed where it bounced dangerously.

Sean's dark eyes widened at the sight of the revolver and his reaction did not go unnoticed.

"You recognize that piece. Good. This situation is becoming more and more ironic by the moment, don't you think? I can see the headlines now." Stark gestured theatrically, writing the banner in the air. "North Star VP's Kidnapper Killed with His Own Weapon," he cackled, obviously pleased with his cleverness.

"Sean's not a kidnapper and you know it," Diana objected sharply.

"That's not what the media will say," the agent countered.

Changing tactics to gain time and information, Sean abandoned his semi-conscious pretense and prodded him, "Since we're the major players in this little melodrama you're creating, shouldn't we know what type of performance we're expected to give?"

"Our would-be hero is more alert than he wanted me to believe," Stark smirked, beaming with confidence. "Curiosity getting the better of you, huh? Well…I guess you do deserve to know the whole story…before you die. So, it would be my pleasure to explain."

He threw a hip up onto the dresser as he began his monologue. "Here's how it goes: Rich businesswoman, Diana North, is kidnapped and held for ransom by her helicopter pilot, Sean Cody, a former Marine suffering from Post-Traumatic Stress Disorder. While he has her at his mercy, Cody decides to take something more from Mrs. North than the ten million-dollar ransom he's put on her head. Add rape to his long list of transgressions."

Diana was appalled by the malicious lie. "How dare you suggest such a thing? I haven't been raped."

"You weren't kidnapped, either." Flashing her an arrogant smirk, he insisted, "This is my story. I'll tell it any way I choose. And from what I heard while I was hiding in the mudroom, your eager lover provided me with all the DNA evidence I'll need to substantiate my accusation. Now if you'll quit interrupting, I'll continue."

Diana bit her tongue and waited. "During the brutal attack, the brave woman is somehow able to gain possession of her rapist's gun. She shoots him. She tries to call for help, only to find that the phone line is dead. Frantic now, she flees the house, but she's not familiar with the area. In her panic, she falls, hitting her head and knocking herself unconscious. She slides over the embankment, into the lake, and drowns."

Pausing for impact, he concluded with a flourish, "Tah Dah! That's when I come in. Agent Larry Stark to the rescue! I've been on Cody's trail for days, tracing him to this location by means of a phone call he forced Mrs. North to make to an old college chum, whose cell I'd had monitored, just in case.

"I arrive just in time to catch a glimpse of her fleeing through the woods. I radio for backup and pursue, but I'm too late. I see her tumble down the embankment, but it's steep and rugged, and the rip rap makes it impossible to maneuver quickly. By the time I get to the shoreline, she's disappeared. With no regard for my personal safety, I dive into the frigid water. After several attempts, I pull out her lifeless body."

Grinning evilly, he added, "It's a sad tale, is it not?"

"Very creative," Sean agreed. "You'll get free publicity, a big promotion, and impress North to boot. You'll make a fortune on the book."

"My thoughts exactly." Stark beamed.

"If you ignore a couple of great big holes." Sean's challenge was an obvious ruse to keep Stark distracted while he sawed away at the plastic cord tying his wrists.

The agent cut his eyes sharply in the pilot's direction. "Such as?"

"Even if you get folks to believe that drivel you're spouting about my mental state, you'll never convince anyone that I'm stupid. You'll need more than a manufactured ransom note to link me to this concocted crime."

"Not to worry. We already have all the evidence we need. Your spurned lover, the darling Miss Stewart, is more than a little obsessed with you. She's kept every message you ever left on her voice mail. The new man in her life convinced her to share those messages with him. In addition, we have your voice tracks from the recordings James made on the occasions when he flew with you. James records all of his business conversations. Says it helps him remember what he agreed to and reminds him of what others promised.

"With the wealth of resources at the command of NSE, it was a simple task to create a very believable tape. We have a ransom demand, in your own words, that will pass any voice recognition test available." The balding agent smirked. "That's one hole plugged very nicely; don't you think?"

"Maybe," Sean mused, still stalling, "How are you going to explain the severed telephone line? Cutting off a kidnap victim's primary means of calling for help isn't standard operating procedure."

"That was just an unfortunate accident. I was so intent on rescuing poor Mrs. North, that I failed to notice the phone pedestal in the dark and ran right over it. Quite a shame, really. Could've happened to anyone." His thin lips were curled into a very smug smile. "See, no more holes." He smacked his palms together, brushing off all objections.

Sensing that it was time to draw Stark's attention away from the supposedly incapacitated pilot, Diana countered. "I can think of one."

He turned to her, incredulously, "Oh, yeah? Let's hear it."

"How will you explain that huge gash on Sean's head? No one will believe I have the strength to do that."

Stark laughed indulgently. "You are naïve." Crossing to her, he brushed a stray lock of hair off her forehead. She cringed from his touch and he laughed again. "The answer is quite a simple one, my dear Mrs. North. A well-placed bullet will erase all signs of that wound."

The horrifying picture his words elicited stabbed through her mind like a fiery brand, shaking her to the very core of her being. She couldn't let the conniving agent bring his vicious plan to fruition. "No!" she screamed, lunging at him, tearing at his face with her fingernails. A quick, jabbing punch to her jaw rocked her back but not before her attack caused some damage. Two long, deep scratches marred Stark's well-lined cheek.

Furious now, he slapped her again. Sean raged in protest but Stark ignored him, keeping his attention focused entirely on Diana. "You bitch! Just look what you've done."

Facing the challenge head-on, she looked him straight in the eye, pointed at the reddened whelps on his cheek, and asked, "How will you make those fit into your tidy little story?"

Shaking his head dismissively, he chuckled. "When one runs through the woods at night, one is likely to be struck by stray tree branches. See, all tidy again."

He took a step toward her, pressing his body close. "It's about time you realized that I'm in complete control of this situation. I underestimated that big brute Marine of yours once, but I won't do it again. If you don't want to witness his immediate demise, you'll do everything I tell you, with no further argument. I'm losing patience with your childish games." He leveled his Ruger at Sean's chest and grinned again.

"It's a damned shame you had to go and shower after you spread those long legs for your hot-blooded stud. You washed away some of the most convincing evidence supporting my rape story. It would be much easier for me if you hadn't done that. I could have killed you both right here and rigged the scene to make it look like you'd offed each other fighting over the gun. But now I have to drag you down to the lake, bash you over the head, and throw you down the embankment and into the water, just because you have a penchant for cleanliness."

As he talked, he casually crossed to the bed, picked up the .357, pulled a handkerchief out of his pocket, and wiped the gun down. "Then I have to come back here and pump a few rounds into your would-be hero, before I call in the troops and run back to the lake. If I've planned it right, my backup will arrive just as I'm dragging your limp carcass out of the water. I sure hope the payoff 's worth the trouble you're putting me through."

Still calm and focused despite Stark's graphic complaints, Sean conjectured, "How'd you get my pistol? Sheila?"

"As a matter of fact. A very handy woman to have around, that Sheila. Conveniently enough, she'd made an extra key made to your apartment. I used it to secure this piece and several other items that I'll use to enhance my kidnapping story."

Waving to Diana, he ordered, "Take this. Hold it like you're going to pull the trigger. I want to make sure your finger prints are retrievable."

When she hesitated, he leveled the barrel of his gun at Sean's head. "His death is inevitable but your obedience will gain him a few more minutes. I'm trying to be considerate of your feelings for him, but if you want to watch him die, keep defying me."

Realizing that she had to do whatever she could to buy time, Diana complied slowly, timidly taking the shiny revolver from him. Then, as the notion struck her, she turned the heavy piece on Stark and tried to hold it steady.

He crowed with delight. "Do you think I'm totally stupid? It's not loaded."

Hope drained away. The hand holding the gun fell limply to her side. When Stark reached out to take the weapon from her, Sean sat up, slipped his knifepoint under the strip binding his ankles and bolted from the bed, launching his considerable bulk at the older man.

The agent fired off one round before the pilot brought him down, hard. His semi-automatic flew across the room. Stark came to rest, back to the floor, gasping for air, the blade of the former soldier's knife pressed against his carotid artery.

"I'd love to slit your worthless throat," Sean growled in his ear. "Give me a reason, please. Any reason will do."

Stark swallowed hard and tried to take in a full breath but Sean's knee, planted firmly in the middle of his chest, made that impossible. Patting the agent's pockets, the pilot found several more of the tough plastic cuffs. He rolled the agent over and secured his hands behind him. He did the same with his feet, then took a third band and bound his wrists and ankles together. "That should keep you busy for awhile."

Seconds later, Sean was on his feet with Diana in his arms. Gently, he examined the side of her face and jawline where Stark had struck her. A dark bruise was already forming under her fair skin. "I should make him pay for hurting you."

"No, Sean, please," she said. "Stark's just the hired muscle. James is the real villain. I've got to talk to him and put an end to this violence." Pulling away from his embrace, she lifted the handset of the telephone that sat on the bedside table. Silence greeted her ear. "Line's already dead. What do we do now?"

Kneeling beside the downed agent, Sean went through the man's pockets again to retrieve his cell phone. "Make it snappy," he urged, tossing her the unit. "We need to get out of here. There's no telling how much help Stark has standing by, waiting for his call. As soon as I'm dressed, we're hitting the road." Backpack in hand, he disappeared into the bathroom.

Punching the numbers to their luxury condominium near Washington, D.C., Diana waited mere seconds before James answered. His voice was thick with irritation. "It's about time, Stark. I hope you've finally cleaned up those loose ends."

"Sorry to disappoint you," Diana said. "Your FBI lapdog failed in his mission once again, and is currently indisposed."

"Diana? What...How?" her husband stuttered.

"Calm down, James," she urged. "You're going to give yourself a heart attack. And then how would you spend all your money?"

True to form, the arrogant Mr. North, entrepreneur extraordinaire, composed himself quickly. "You and your pet Marine might have bested Stark but this isn't the end, Diana. Next time, and there will be a next time, you won't be so lucky."

"I have no doubt of that. You're nothing if not persistent. That's why I have a proposal for you. A proposal I believe you'll find very interesting, and beneficial to your financial future."

"You have my attention. Go on."

She took a deep breath, blowing it out in a puff. "I don't know how you managed to get a federal agent to do your dirty work for you, but if you'll call off your dogs, clear up the lies, and make sure Sean is protected, I'll sign over my interest in North Star Enterprises to you."

A shrill whistle sounded from the other end of the line. "So, you've fallen for that meat-headed bastard. I would never have believed it. The 'Ice Queen' melts. Wish I could have been there to see it happen." When Diana failed to respond, he pressed her, "What did you have to promise him to get him to take you to bed?"

Refusing to rise to the bait, she insisted, "What do you say, James? Do we have a deal?"

"Sure. Why not?" He sounded pleased and relieved. "There's just one more thing."

"What's that?"

"I want a divorce, Diana. An immediate, no-fault, I-never-have-to-lay-eyes-on-you-again divorce. That and complete control of NSE will get you your life back and ensure the safety of your boy-toy."

"Agreed," she told him. "I'll call you later to set up a meeting. In the meantime, have the necessary documents prepared. I'll sign them after I have the fake ransom tapes and any other evidence you've fabricated to implicate Sean in this kidnapping plot, in my possession."

"Yes, ma'am," he mocked, chuckling. "I'll

eagerly await your call. Oh, by the way, I have one final question."

"What is it?" she snapped, infuriated by his gloating.

"How will you hold onto that handsome young stud of yours once he finds out you're penniless? Won't that be funny? Poor old Diana sacrifices her fortune to protect his worthless life, then he dumps her because she's broke!"

With his laughter ringing in her ears, she pushed the END button.

TEN

Sean reappeared, two butterfly bandages neatly placed over the deep gash above his temple. "Your doctor friend keeps a well-stocked medicine cabinet. Antibiotic ointment and a couple of Band-Aids, chased with some extra-strength pain reliever, and I'm good as new."

Taking her chin in his fingers, he examined her jaw again. "That bruise needs ice." Noting the distant, distracted look in her eyes, he asked, "What did that greedy bastard you call a husband have to say?"

Shaking her head to clear away a fog of doubt, she told him, "I think I convinced him to call off his dogs."

"How'd you manage that?" the pilot asked, incredulous.

From his place, face-down on the floor, Stark chortled with glee. "Just wait till you hear what your fancy meal ticket has done to save your hide. It'll just kill you. Oh, this is priceless. Truly priceless!"

"Shut up!" Sean growled at him. "One more word and I'll kick your teeth in." Turning back to the woman, he asked, "What is it, Diana? What did you do? What did you promise him?" A disturbing foreboding clawed at his belly.

"We should be safe now but it's probably a good idea to get going anyway. I'll explain everything once we're away."

Realizing it would do no good to press her, Sean relented. "I know where we can stay the night. I have our stuff packed up. Where're your boots?"

"In the utility room with our coats."

"Then let's go," he urged.

"What about him?" she asked, nodding toward Stark. "We can't just leave him like that."

Sean reassured her. "He'll work his way loose or help will arrive eventually." He followed her through the door, pausing to toss the agent's cell phone down the hallway. "There. How's that?"

She nodded in approval.

"I don't know why you care what happens to the black-hearted skunk. He tried to kill you. Remember?"

"I won't stoop to his level." Her blue eyes were bright with conviction.

Sean called back to the bound man. "Good-bye, Stark, and good riddance. Your phone is out here. Come and get it if you can."

Snarling in fury, the agent threatened, "This isn't the end of it, you sneaky bastard. You and your frosty bitch haven't seen the last of me!"

Ignoring the taunts he screamed at them, the pilot urged his companion up the stairs, across the living area, and into the kitchen. Retrieving some ice cubes from the freezer, he wrapped them in the cotton towel he'd used to dry the dishes and placed them gingerly against Diana's cheek. "Hold that on there for a few minutes. I'll get our jackets."

When he returned, he made her sit down on one of the tall barstools while he slipped her boots on her feet. She tried to protest his ministrations but he insisted. "I told you to ice that bruise. I'll do this."

As he worked, she asked him, "How long do you think Stark was here, hiding in the mud room?"

"No idea," Sean admitted. "I could kick myself for letting him get the drop on me again."

"I was wondering how that happened," she teased, smiling indulgently.

"I was preoccupied," he snapped.

"Preoccupied?"

"I was thinking of you – instead of keeping my mind on what I was supposed to be doing, securing the house. When I went through the utility room to check the garage door, he nailed me with a wrench the size of a sledgehammer. Your doctor pal might not know much about machinery but he sure has some monster tools."

"Oh, those aren't Dick's, they're Eleanor's," Diana informed him with an airy chuckle. "She worked her way through college as a plumber's assistant. I used to tease her and call her a 'plumber's helper,' you know, toilet plunger – 'TP' for short. She didn't like it very much."

"Can't imagine why," he quipped. Touching the bandage on his forehead, he told her, "That very big wrench left a very big dent in my hard head – knocked me senseless for a few seconds. I played up the disorientation bit, hoping to take Stark off guard."

"Your ruse worked."

"It didn't win me any golden statues," he

admitted grinning, "but it bought us some time. So, let's not waste it. Stark could have back-up." He secured the final knot in her shoelace and patted her thigh. Then he threw the icepack in the sink and enfolded her in his arms for one lingering kiss.

A few moments later, Sean rolled the sleek black bike out of the garage, while Diana punched the buttons to lower the door. She slung the backpack over her shoulders and threw her leg across the seat. Her reluctance to touch the man had evaporated. She slid up close against his back and wrapped her arms tightly around his lean waist.

Kicking the powerful motor to life, the former soldier guided the bike down the drive. As he turned out onto the narrow lane, he pointed toward a weirdly shaped shadow looming ominously on the right side of the road. Squinting into the darkness, Diana recognized the outline of the telephone pedestal, crumpled back against a tree trunk. Next to the tree, a dark-colored sedan had been abandoned.

The pilot flew down the winding country roads, guiding the motorcycle with effortless ease, laying into curves with consummate skill. The night air was cool and invigorating against Diana's skin, and despite the thrill of the ride, she relaxed and began to hope they were actually safe from pursuit. Just as her hands were becoming uncomfortably numb, Sean turned onto a gravel side road. A mile or so further on, he made another turn onto a lane which was little more than a narrow path through the woods. Soon, he rolled to a stop and shut off the engine.

"Hop off," he instructed, offering her a helping hand. The woman complied, wondering why he'd brought them to the middle of nowhere. Once the headlight winked out, nothing but a blanket of darkness, the trilling of tree frogs, and the heavy scent of decaying leaves surrounded them. The pilot dismounted and pushed the big cycle into a thicket.

"Too bad the spring foliage hasn't sprouted yet," he complained, pulling off his helmet. "It would provide more cover. We'll just have to hope those sassafras bushes will hide the old gal from prying eyes."

Following his lead, she removed her helmet and asked him, "Where are we?"

"On my family's farm. Not too far from the house," he admitted.

"Sean, we can't take the risk," she warned. "It's too dangerous."

"There's no risk in staying here, at least for the night."

"Here?" She shrugged in confusion, looking around a bit as her eyes adjusted to the dimness. "Out in the open – on the cold, hard ground?"

Pointing skyward, Sean grinned, his teeth flashing in the darkness. "Look up."

Diana tilted her head back and peered above her, into the branches of an ancient oak tree. As her eyes adjusted to the dimness, an amazing, and totally unexpected structure came into focus.

"It's a tree house," the young man explained, beaming with pride.

"That much is obvious, even to a city girl." Handing him the backpack, she moved closer to the broad trunk of the enormous oak. "You expect us to sleep up there."

"No one will ever find us."

"That's for sure," she admitted. "Okay. At this point I'm willing to try almost anything."

"Glad to hear it," he leered suggestively. "Since we'll have all night to experiment."

Swatting him playfully, she huffed, "That wasn't what I meant and you know it."

Searching the far side of the tree, Sean found a knotted rope secured over a low branch. Slipping on the knapsack, he climbed the rope effortlessly, hand over hand, and disappeared into a dark recess in the wooden construct above. A few seconds later, the rope was pulled up and a ladder made of nylon cord dropped down in front of Diana.

"Your turn," he called to her. "Come on up, but take your time and be careful."

Managing the turning, twisting ladder proved much more difficult than expected. With Sean's help, Diana pulled herself into the tree house and collapsed, panting for breath. While she rested, the pilot hauled in the ladder and closed the trap door, which was set squarely in the middle of the floor. Once the exit was secured, the room was almost completely dark. Inky blackness surrounding her, she listened intently as Sean ruffled through his backpack.

"Here we go," he announced, flicking his thumb against the ON button of the flashlight he'd confiscated from the garage at the lake house. Suddenly, the tiny structure was ablaze with illumination. The room was shaped like a large slice

of pie with the tree trunk embedded in the point.
The curved front wall was the longest of the three.
In the middle of it was a large, tightly shuttered
window. The ceiling was too low for Sean to stand
erect. "Hold this for me," he instructed, handing her
the light. "Point it in that corner."

Diana did as he directed, keeping the beam on
him, as he unfolded a thin mattress and covered it
with a pile of quilts and blankets he retrieved from
an old, battered footlocker. "My dad and I built this
place when I was just a kid. I haven't been up here
in years but my nephews keep it well supplied." He
tossed her a plastic bottle of spring water.
"Dessert!" he crowed, waving an unopened bag of
Oreos cookies.

Then he sat down, Indian-style, in the middle
of the pallet and patted the place beside him.
"You're too far away. Come closer. I won't bite
you," he teased, "at least not too hard."

"You said 'nephews'," she noted as she slowly
scooted across the floor toward him. "Don't you
have any nieces?"

"Sure, several, but they're not allowed up here.
This place is off limits to girls. You are, in fact, the
only person of the female persuasion who has ever
been allowed in old Fort Cody, a stronghold of male
superiority." Impatient with the pace of her
approach, he grabbed her hand and tugged. "Come
hither, wench. Your liege grows tired of your
tarrying."

Giggling childishly, then feeling foolish, Diana
crawled into his arms. When he began to undress
her she suggested timidly, "It's cool in here. Maybe

we should sleep in our clothes."

"We'll be plenty warm without them," he countered, folding the covers around her.

Entranced, she watched him shuck off his jeans. For a brief moment before he switched off the flashlight, he knelt over her, his powerful form gleaming in the golden glow. Despite the cold, he was fully erect, his arousal impressive and intimidating. She couldn't stop the sigh that escaped her parted lips. *He's absolutely magnificent, she thought, her body aching for his touch. What did I do to deserve a man like this? What will I have to do to keep him?*

Crawling under the blankets and snuggling close, Sean's kisses and caresses stirred her in ways she'd never imagined, and soon drove away the night's chill, and with it the nagging doubts filling her min. Once more he carried them to that lofty pinnacle and beyond.

Exhaustion overtook Diana and she dozed fitfully, plagued by uncertain dreams that awakened her with a start, her heart pounding. She lay still, hoping her restlessness wouldn't disturb the pilot. The moon had risen. Silvery beams snuck in between the cracks in the walls and around the shuttered window, illuminating the room.

Hoping to make out Sean's features, she turned her face toward him. To her surprise, he was awake, too, watching her intently. "What's wrong, sweetheart? Can't you sleep?" he whispered, planting a soft kiss on her forehead.

She shook her head. "Too much on my mind, I

guess," she admitted, the small endearment twisting her heart.

"What is it, Diana? Tell me," he urged her, his voice low and deeply sexy.

Shivering at the sound of it, she pushed down the feelings his close proximity aroused and answered, "Just thinking of James. He agreed to call off his men. He says he'll give me all the evidence they've concocted against you. And he promised to leave you…uh, us…alone."

"I see. And what did you promise him?"
"A no-fault divorce plus my interest in North Star Enterprises."

"No, Diana. You can't do it!" Sean raised himself onto one elbow and gazed at her, clearly incensed. "I won't let you sacrifice everything for me. I'm flattered that you'd make such a crazy deal to protect me but that dirty bastard shouldn't get off scot-free. He has to pay for the terrible things he's done. He hired someone to kill you. Damn, woman! You can't just forgive the son-of-a-bitch, hand over everything you have to him and forget it! I won't let you."

"It's already been decided. There's nothing you can do about it." Her tone was firm, despite the abject sorrow tearing at her throat. "Once I talk with James again, arrange a place to meet him and sign the papers, you'll be completely out of danger. Then you'll be free to go on your way."

"Why would I do that?" he asked, eyes flashing with anger.

"You're a bright boy, I'm sure you've figured it out already; otherwise you wouldn't be trying so hard to talk me out of this. I'll be broke, flat busted, 'without two cents to rub together,' as they say." She couldn't know that the defeated way she was withdrawing from him was like a knife twisting in his heart.

"I'm sure you'll want to cut your losse and I understand completely. We had a great fling, an exciting adventure, a couple of equally wonderful and terrible days, that I'll remember for the rest of my life. I can't ask for anything more from you."

"Ahh…the money thing. I knew we'd have to deal with it eventually. I'd just hoped to postpone it a while." Even in the pale moonlight, she could see his dark eyes flashing dangerously. "You listen to me. Believe every word I say. I am not interested in your money, Diana. I'm interested in you in spite of it."

She tried to turn away but he caught her chin and held it, forcing her to meet his gaze. "Hell, woman, I don't need your money. If I wanted to be rich, I could be. Do you know how many greedy politicians the world over, offer former operatives, like me, a sizable payoff to do their dirty work? Well…the list is long and distinguished. I could have millions piled up in a Swiss bank account if I wanted it."

The bold truth of his statements touched her. "As a mercenary soldier?"

"That's right. As a paid assassin – selling my services to the highest bidder. But that's not how I want to live my life. I don't need their blood money.

"Keep that in mind when you try to convince yourself that I'm playing you. Diana, you know that

I'm not the sort of man who'd ever be happy living off a woman. I make my own way in the world."

"I'm sorry, Sean," she whispered, ashamed to meet his eyes. "I shouldn't have doubted you. You've done nothing to make me distrust you. James just said something…uh, something that pushed my buttons. He knows how to play on my insecurities," she admitted, with a shrug. "And I'm having a difficult time believing that you really want me."

"Well, I do." He kissed her hard. "I wanted you the first moment I saw you. You were cool and distant but I still wanted you. When you let me see the warm, vulnerable woman underneath the ice, I wanted you even more."

Sniffing back tears, she answered his declaration with joyful kisses. "I want you, too."

"And that's a miracle," he breathed in her ear. "It means a lot, that you're willing to sacrifice so much to protect me, but I can't let you just give up. Surrender is not in my vocabulary. I'd rather go down fighting."

"It's not your battle," she noted. "You weren't the intended target. It's my fight and I choose to surrender."

"Stark brought me into it when he made me expendable, then he added insult to injury by accusing me of kidnapping and rape. You'll have to make me understand why I should stand by, twiddling my thumbs, while you meekly accept defeat."

"Please, Sean, please. It's got to end. I can't take any more chances with your life." In her desperation she opened herself to him completely. "I've been happier the past few days with you, living in run-down cabins, tree houses, and budget motels, riding buses and motorcycles, and wearing second-hand clothing, than I ever was with James, living in mansions, penthouses, and four-star hotels, riding in private jets and limousines, and wearing the latest designer fashions.

"I'm not the person I was four days ago, Sean. The 'Ice Queen' is gone and in her place is the real me, a woman in love for the first time in her life."

"Did you say in love?" he asked, shaking his head like his ears were playing tricks.

"Yes. I love you, Sean," she admitted. "And I want to be with you for as long as you'll have me."

Hugging her to his chest he whispered against her hair, "Oh, my darling Diana. I love you, too, and I want you with me for as long as you want to stay. Forever has a nice ring." Answering his invitation with fervent kisses, she led the way to an intensely satisfying union of body and spirit.

Much later, physically and emotionally spent, they lay entwined, blissfully planning their future. "I hate to keep beating a dead horse," Sean murmured. "But…are you sure you've considered every angle of this deal you've agreed to? What about your plans to re-vamp NSE?" he reminded her. "Are you willing to give up your dreams along with your stock options?"

"My plans went up in flames along with your helicopter," she sighed. "It would take months to reconstruct them and I don't have the heart for it. I want something else now, something more."

"Like what?"

"I want to get back to the goals I had for myself when I was younger. I want to see if I can make those dreams come true, if it's not too late."

"It's never too late," he urged.

"I hope not." She smiled at him. "I just keep envisioning a little office with a sign over the door reading, Diana Grayson, Licensed Professional Counselor."

"Not Diana North? You might get some mileage out of the name." he teased.

"No, way! I want that name and everything it stands for, out of my life for good," she protested vehemently.

"Would you consider another name then?"

"Grayson's my maiden name. What other one would I use?" she wondered innocently.

"Mine."

"Yours?"

"Unless you don't like the sound of Diana Cody."

"Hmmm…. Let me see…Diana… Cody," she rolled the name around slowly, considering. "It does have a nice ring," she told him. "Are you suggesting a legal name change?"

"Actually, I would recommend marriage over the expense of a legal name change. It'd be the simpler way to go."

"What are you saying, exactly?" she queried, afraid to breathe.

He raised himself on an elbow and asked, "When this mess is over and you're finally rid of that bastard husband of yours, will you consider letting me make an honest woman of you? Marry me, Diana."

"Yes. Definitely yes," she declared, holding him fiercely. "I don't even have to think about it. We've only known one another for about five minutes, relatively, but I've never been so certain of anything in my life. My heart belongs to you."

"I'm glad we got that settled," he quipped, enfolding her in his arms once more "Now, it's time to sleep."

Giggling, she said, "In the immortal words of Scarlet O'Hara, 'Let's think about that tomorrow'."

"Fiddle de de," he chirped in a cheesy falsetto, throwing Diana into a fit of laughter.

When she could finally breathe again, she wiped her eyes and told him, "You're a hoot, Cody."

"I aim to please, ma'am," he drawled.

"So, where's that comfortable bed you promised me?"

"Tomorrow," was his whispered response. She could feel the tension leaving his body as he drifted into the welcoming arms of Morpheus. Moments later, she joined him there.

They slept soundly, well into the morning. Even the former soldier slumbered peacefully, his rest undisturbed by the usual nightmares. As the temperature outside climbed to a warmer, decidedly more spring-like mark, the heavy covers became unbearably warm. The big man threw them aside and went on sleeping. Too soon however, the raucous caws of a determined crow roused him. He peered around the small room through slitted eyelids, momentarily confused by his surroundings. A quick shake of his head brought his sharp mind into focus and his short-term memory flooding back. Unfortunately, the movement also sent him reeling from the blow he'd suffered the previous evening. He groaned. The woman beside him stirred.

"Good morning, my love." he said, greeting her with a soft kiss.

"Good morning yourself," she answered, her devotion shining clear in her bright, blue eyes. "Are you okay?

"Just a little headache," he admitted. "I'll be better after I've dosed myself with some more of your doctor friend's pain relievers." Reaching for his jeans, he pulled a white bottle out of the pocket. "Now, what did you do with that water?"

"Here," she said, retrieving the plastic container from the corner where it had rolled.

Tossing down a couple of pills and following them with a huge gulp of the water, Sean crawled back in beside her. The preoccupied look on her lovely face alerted him to trouble. "What's up? You look like you've thought up another problem."

"Not a problem really, just a funny feeling."

"I trust your intuition, so please, elaborate," he prompted her.

"It's hard for me to believe that James masterminded this plot to get rid of me, that he hired Stark and set it all in motion. He's self-centered and greedy but he's not blood-thirsty."

Tears threatened, and her voice was thick with emotion. "When we talked yesterday, he almost sounded relieved by my proposal."

"I'm sure he's relieved. You gave him everything he wants, free and clear, and he didn't have to kill you to get it." Sean was irritated by her compassion for a man he considered beyond all hope of redemption. "Don't waste your time worrying about him. He isn't worth it."

"I know, I know. But my instinct tells me that there's more here than it seems."

"It's gotta be hard for you. You've lived with the man for twenty years, supported him and cared for him, but don't let your heart override your head. Your husband is your enemy. Make no mistake. Don't trust him or anything he tells you."

"I won't," she agreed. "It's probably just wishful thinking. I know you're right. We have to proceed under the assumption that James is in charge, that he's the one pulling the strings."

"And make sure we're prepared in case he isn't," Sean added with a sly, suggestive grin. "Right now, I want to kiss you. Then we're going to get some breakfast. We can't live on love, you know."

"It would be fun trying and a great way to go, you have to admit." Her eyes sparkled playfully and the sunny smile she offered him warmed him thoroughly.

"Shut up and come here," he ordered.

The good morning kiss consumed them. They were both oblivious to the insistent voice calling out from below until it sounded for the third time.

"Hey! Wake up! You thick-headed jerk! I know you're up there, so stop pretending you don't hear me!"

Reluctantly pulling away from Diana, the pilot slipped on his pants and rolled back the makeshift bed to uncover the trap door. Unlatching the heavy wooden panel, he lifted it a crack and peered out. Standing below, tapping her foot in annoyance, was a tall, dark-haired female.

"Hi, Bridgett," he called to her, trying on his most beguiling smile.

"Stop grinning at me like a fool and get down here!" she demanded. "You've got a lot of explaining to do. The whole family has been worried sick about you."

"Give me a minute," he told her, pulling his head back through the hatch. Huffing out a frustrated breath he warned Diana, "Shit! That's Bridgett. Trust her to make a pest of herself. Ready or not, you're about to meet the rest of the Cody clan."

ELEVEN

Ignoring Diana's protests, Sean rolled up the mattress, returned the blankets to the footlocker, and tossed his backpack through the trap door. Then he held the rope ladder for her to climb down. Stubbornly refusing to exit, the woman pleaded, her voice taut with tension, "We can't risk it. Stark has too many connections and too much information at his disposal. He tracked us to Eleanor's lake house so he might find us here. I can't endanger your family."

"Don't worry," he said, calmly trying to allay her fears. "The Codys can take care of themselves. I promise." Realizing that his assurances were having little effect, he thought for a moment, scratching the beard stubble on the point of his chin. "Okay. Here's what we're gonna do. We'll keep them in the dark – at least as much as possible. We'll hit the high points but won't tell them the whole story."

"What if they won't accept that?"

"They will." He sounded very sure of himself. "My family learned long ago not to press me for information. They'll believe whatever I tell them. Then we'll keep our eyes open just in case Stark comes snooping around. Whatever happens, my folks won't know anything that would put them in harm's way."

"I'd never forgive myself if..."

"Stop borrowing trouble," he urged. "Since you struck that ridiculous deal, there's no reason to think anyone will bother looking for us here, or anywhere else. Your soon-to-be ex and his FBI lapdog are smart. You promised to come to them so they'll wait for you. They won't bother continuing a costly search or take the risk of exposing their illegal behavior to additional witnesses.

"If Stark has researched my background, he already knows that our farmhouse is always full of my relatives so he won't chance it. The next move's yours. It won't cost him anything to be patient." Seeing the wide-eyed way she looked at him, he knew she wasn't convinced. "Trust me, Diana. Do you think I'd risk the lives of my family?"

"No, of course not, but..."

"What in the hell's taking you so long? I'm freezing my ass off. Shake a leg! Will ya, Sean?" Bridgett's exasperated voice called up to them again.

"Except for hers," he quipped, nodding toward the woman on the ground. "I could wring her scrawny neck myself. She'd definitely give Stark a run for his money."

Finally acquiescing with a grim chuckle, Diana began her descent. When her feet were planted firmly on the earth once more, she found herself facing a surprised, feminine version of Sean. Bridgett Cody was tall and broad shouldered, with the same dark hair, warm brown eyes, and angular face as her younger brother. Only the streaks of silver, peppered through her almost black tresses, gave away the difference in their ages.

The women studied each other speechlessly, while Sean pulled up the ladder, dropped out the knotted rope, shinnied down, and tossed it back over the low branch where he'd found it. Grinning sheepishly, he faced his sister. "Bridge, I'd like you to meet Diana North. Diana, this is my youngest sister, Bridgett."

Offering her hand, the graceful blonde smiled her most friendly smile. "It's very nice to meet you. Sean has told me a lot about you."

Eyeing the unexpected and clearly unwelcome visitor suspiciously, Bridgett returned the handshake cautiously, refusing to return the greeting.

Sensing trouble, Sean asked her, "How'd you find us?"

"You're not nearly clever as you think you are," she smirked, pointing at the black motorcycle which was partially sheltered beneath the bare branches of the sassafras bush.

"I had a layover in Roanoke so I drove out to check on the folks. On my way in, I noticed fresh tire tracks but figured it was one of the boys out here turkey hunting. When I got to the house, Mom and Missy were all aflutter about you disappearing, into the blue on your Harley, which got me thinking. So, I walked back to check things out. It was pretty clear that the tracks were made by something larger than a dirt bike so I figured it had to be you."

Bridgett seemed very pleased with her amateur

sleuthing. "You didn't do a very good job of hiding that hog." He shrugged, noncommittally.

"So why in blazes did you sleep out here in that drafty old tree house when you have a perfectly good bed at home?" She jammed her fists into her hips, demanding a response.

Before he could form one, she speculated, "I'd lay odds it has something to do with your pretty lady friend." Nodding her head toward Diana, she added, "The boys are gonna shit when they find out you let her into the inner sanctum of Fort Cody."

Shooting his sister a warning frown, Sean defended. "Diana and I had plans for the night that didn't work out. It was really late when we got here. I didn't want to wake everyone, so we used the fort. It was comfortable enough for a few hours."

"Yeah, I bet," the dark-haired woman didn't bother to disguise the disgust in her voice. "Guess it was more private than a house full of kinfolk. I hope you got it out of your system," she warned, 'cause Mom and Dad won't allow any shenanigans under their roof."

"Get off your high horse, Bridgett," Sean snapped, his dark eyes flashing angrily. "I'm not a horny teenager sneaking my girlfriend out to the tree house for a little nooky."

"Okay, sure," she cooed, not even pretending to accept his implied denial. "Whatever you say, Sean. But I'm not a damned fool and I know what I see. Unless you shake off that you-caught-me-red-handed look before you get to the house, everyone else is gonna know too. You and Ms. North have been playing house and nothin' you say will convince me otherwise."

"It's Mrs.," Diana broke in. "Mrs. James North."

"Well, well. That explains it," the sister concluded, shaking her head. "An older woman and married to boot. What in heaven's name are you thinking? What has happened to the good sense God gave you?"

"Don't preach to me," her brother parried. "You've had at least one lapse in common sense yourself." They glared at one another like two boxers waiting for the bell.

Diana stepped in to referee. "Sean, you don't have to defend my honor." He tore his eyes from his sister's determined face and stared at her in confusion. "Bridgett has obviously guessed the truth and she deserves an explanation."

"Humph...," he mumbled, still furious with his sister's condemnation.

Ignoring him, Diana took Bridgett's arm and leaned in. "You see, my husband and I are estranged and soon to be divorced. Your brother has, quite by accident, found himself in the middle of our dispute. He's been very gallant in his efforts to help me. In the past few of days, we've run afoul of an unusual string of bad luck. Any sensible man would have beaten a hasty retreat but Sean has stuck by me through it all. Somewhere along the way we have come to care for one another, very deeply."

Diana leveled her frostiest gaze at Bridgett. "Your assessment is correct. I'm twelve years older than your brother. If that bothers you, I'm sorry. But then, it's really no business of yours, is it?"

When Bridgett failed to respond, she added, her tone dripping honey, "Let me assure you that I understand your concern. If I had a brother, I would be just as protective of him as you are of yours; however, there's no need for you to worry. I won't hurt him. I couldn't."

Diana's reassuring smile turned to one of utter devotion as her eyes met Sean's. Bridgett's ire melted a bit. "No, I guess it's not any of my business, really. He's old enough to know his own mind."

"Well, thank you for that," he teased, not taking his eyes off Diana.

"You'd just better be ready to explain yourself to Mom and Dad," she warned. "They might be okay with the age thing but you know how they feel about the sanctity of wedding vows. When they find out your woman's married, they're gonna hit the ceiling. You'll have a lot more to explain than that bump on your head."

Taking a deep breath, Diana suggested, "It would make things simpler if we kept our feelings for each other private until after my divorce is final."

"Listen to her, Sean," Bridgett prompted, wheels turning. "She's making sense."
The determined jut of his sister's jaw told him that she intended to use every tool available to undermine his relationship with Diana. Delaying a public commitment would play right into her hand and that worried him. Needlessly upsetting his parents worried him more, though, so he agreed

reluctantly. "I'll try, but they know me too well. My feelings will be written all over my face."

"It'll be hard for me too." Diana smiled sadly. I want the world to know how much I love you but the time's not right."

"Yeah, okay. It's the smart thing to do. But my heart's not in it." He hugged her tightly and sealed the deal with a fierce, longing kiss.

"Uh-hem…," Bridgett interrupted. "My ass is still freezing. I'm not dressed to spend all day out here jawin'." She flapped the sleeves of her lightweight gabardine jacket for emphasis. "Let's get back to the house."

Sean pulled the big bike out of the bushes and held it for Diana to mount but she refused. "I'll walk with your sister."

He nodded, thankful for her consideration. "Bridge will show you the way. It's not far. Can you carry these?" He handed her the backpack and helmet. "I'll have some hot tea waiting to warm you up."

Offering him a grateful smile, she threw the pack over her shoulder. Then she watched him kick the big motorcycle to life and ride off, dreading the short trek in the company of her disapproving companion.

To her surprise, Bridgett had apparently decided that Diana's relationship with Sean was none of her business. She didn't bring it up again, but made small talk instead. By the time they reached the sprawling two-story farmhouse, Diana believed she'd heard the younger woman's entire life story.

Bridgett worked as a flight attendant for American Airlines. Most of the time, she flew out of Dulles International Airport, sharing Sean's small apartment in Fairfax during layovers. She'd never been married but had one son, Colin, who'd just turned twenty-four.

When she'd found out she was pregnant, at seventeen, by a very appealing teen-aged boy with little ambition and less promise, she'd been devastated, and ashamed. She'd worried more about letting her parents down than about how the baby would change her life. They were hurt and angry, of course, but still determined that their youngest daughter should have her dreams fulfilled, so they sent her off to college and raised her son as their own. Colin had grown up in the family farmhouse, complete with five older "sisters" and one big "brother." Bridgett told Diana that Colin worshipped Sean.

"I can see why," the blonde woman commented. "He's pretty special."

"Yep, he is," the sister agreed, her voice tapering off slowly, as if she wanted to add a warning but thought better of it. Then she took Diana's elbow and held it. "What's up with you and your husband? I think I've heard of him. He has a few bucks in the bank, doesn't he?"

"You could say that." Diana chuckled at the younger woman's flair for understatement.

"Then why in the hell would you dump a rich guy like that for Sean? He's my brother and I love him, but the poor guy barely has two nickels to rub together. Money's not an issue for you I take it."

"Right again. Having piles of money means nothing to me, but James doesn't share my point of view. We're splitting up because we have very different ideas about how our company should do business. His goal is to keep on increasing profits."

"And yours isn't."

"No, I want North Star Enterprises to start giving back to the communities where we've profited in the past. James is totally against that, of course." Diana was surprised that she was able to explain her situation to this relative stranger with such ease. "Combine that with twenty years of marital infidelity, and an inability to produce an heir to the North fortune, and we're both ready to call it quits."

"Who did the fooling around, you or him?" Bridgett asked frankly.

"Considering the way we met, you'll find this difficult to believe, but it was James. Until your brother, I'd never been unfaithful." The steady, forthright tone conveyed the honesty of her words.

"Which one of you is to blame for the empty cradle?"

"James again," Diana sighed. "But that doesn't mean I haven't paid for it. James hated his inability to father a child. It messed up his silver-spoon entitlement, pseudo-royalty image of himself – the infallible corporate magnate from an old-money, New England family. He never ceased to punish me because I knew of his imperfection."

"So, what you're saying is that your fairytale marriage hasn't ended happily ever after," Bridgett quipped.

"Hardly," was the terse reply. "It has been pretty brutal. I wouldn't have survived if it hadn't been for Sean. Literally."

"What are your plans for my brother, once your divorce is final?" Bridgett tilted her head and raised one eyebrow.

"Well...," Diana hesitated. "Again, this is hard to believe, since we've only known one another a few days, but it's true. I love your brother. He thinks we might have a future together. I hope he's right."

Finding the chink in Diana's well-constructed armor, Bridgett stuck in a knife and twisted it. "Do you regret not having children?"

"I...uh...Yes, I do," the tall blonde stuttered nervously. Bridgett's sudden shift in tactics took her by surprise. "I wanted to adopt but James refused. Now it's too late. Even after my divorce is finalized, I'm too old to realistically consider motherhood."

"It's not too late for Sean." Diana's face went white, telling Bridgett that her well-aimed barb had found soft tissue, so she pressed her attack.

"You're tied to a selfish husband who's forced you to give up your chance to have a family. Can you do the same to the man you claim to love? Think about that, Mrs. North, long and hard, before you make a commitment to my brother. Doesn't Sean deserve a wife who can give him children? You promised you'd never hurt him. Are you going to keep that promise?"

Desperate tears stung her eyes. Diana could

feel her heart ripping in two as she struggled to draw a breath through the tight knot squeezing her chest. *Bridgett's right. Sean deserves a family.* Though it went against her deepest desires, she knew it wouldn't be fair to hold him to the proposal he'd made.

Letting the older woman to stew, Bridgett stood by silently, smiling. After a few moments, she said, "Let's get inside. My reckless brother should have that tea ready by now."

Diana followed her across the wide back porch and into the bright, cheerful kitchen, where the comforting smell of baking bread swirled around her. "Finally!" Sean tossed her a reassuring wink. "What kept you? My big sis been chewing your ear off?"

Crossing the room in two long strides, he took the pack and helmet from her, set the latter on the floor by the door, and heaved the former into an empty chair. "I want you to meet my mom."

Placing a guiding palm in the middle of her back, he urged her toward a short, stocky, gray-haired woman, who was leaning over the sink, busily scrubbing potatoes. "Mom, this is Diana North."

The Cody family matriarch turned to greet her guest with a sincere, welcoming smile, and dried her hands on her apron. Sarah Cody's face was round, her skin youthfully smooth, and her cheekbones flushed with color. Blue-gray eyes twinkling, she offered Diana her palm and squeezed her fingers tightly.

"My poor dear, it's good to meet you. My boy

told me about the awful time you've had the last couple of days. You must be plumb wore out. Now you can just relax and let us take care of you. Please, set yerself down." She pulled a ladder-back chair from under the polished oak table.

"Sean, didn't you say you were fixin' something hot to drink?" she prompted. "What are you waitin' for, boy? Get this woman a cup to warm her up. Her hands are like ice."

"Thanks," Diana whispered, guessing that everyone in this huge house obeyed the diminutive woman without question. "I appreciate your hospitality. It is very generous of you to take me in like this."

"Nonsense," Sarah huffed. "There's always a crowd around here. What's one more? Besides, we're accustomed to Sean bringing in strays, in one form or another. Just make yourself ta home and speak up if you need anything."

Sarah nodded her approval when Sean handed his sister a steaming mug, placed two more on the tabletop along with several thick slices of buttered toast and a jar of homemade strawberry jam, and slid into the chair next to Diana. "When you're done, Bridgett will take you upstairs so you can clean up and rest a spell before dinner. Now you'll have to excuse me, I've got to get back to it. Missy'll be here any minute with chicken to fry."

"Dinner?" Diana remarked quizzically, helping herself to a slice of thick toast. "It must be later than I thought. I've lost my watch somewhere. What time is it?"

Sean laughed. "A little before eleven, I think."

When she looked at him with a quizzical tilt of her head, he explained. "On the farm, we have two regular meals. Breakfast, which is ready around seven, after the milking's done, and dinner. Mom and Missy always lay out a big spread every afternoon, between two and three. It's not fancy mind you but it'll stick to your ribs. The food stays on the table until the kids come in from school. When they've eaten, everything's put away and the kitchen's closed for the day. If anyone wants supper, as we call it, they're on their own. There's always plenty of leftovers and makings for sandwiches."

Fumbling around until he located the hand she'd tucked under the table, out of sight, he gave her knuckles a reassuring squeeze. Diana turned her adoring gaze on him, leaving no doubt about the depth of her love for him, but when the familiar half-hearted, sad smile touched her lips, Sean felt like she'd deliberately knocked the wind out of him. *Something's wrong!* His heart screamed. *Bridgett, it has to be Bridgett. She said something awful to Diana,* he concluded to himself. *I'll wring her meddling neck.*

"Sean, would it be okay if I used your cell phone? I need to call James and make the final arrangements."

Diana's whispered request tore him out of his silent reverie. "Sure, it's in my bag, but it'll probably need charging." Lowering his voice so only she could here, he added, "It should be safe since he already knows you're with me."

"That won't be necessary," Sarah Cody chimed in. "Use the phone in the front hall. I'll make sure you have all the privacy you need."

"It's not that," the visitor protested, her intuition cautioning her against placing a call from the farmhouse landline. "It's long distance and might take a while. I wouldn't think of imposing."

Bridgett, obviously offended, fumed, "I know my folks aren't rich by your standards, Mrs. North, but I assure you they can afford a toll call."

"I... I'm sorry. I didn't mean to imply...," Diana stuttered. "I was just trying to...."

Sean's dark eyes shot daggers at his sister, but before he could give voice to his complaint, their mother intervened. "Bridgett, that's quite enough," she snapped, clearly embarrassed by her youngest daughter's rudeness. "Our guest was just being considerate not tryin' to insult us. You're not use'ly so sensitive. What's gotten into you?"

The ingrained obedience to her mother's orders backed the outraged woman down from her aggressive posture. Sighing in defeat, she offered, "You can use my cell. I have unlimited nationwide and international calling. The airline pays for it."

Looking to Sean for an approving nod, Diana said, "That's very kind of you."

"Humph," the dark-haired woman huffed. "It's in my briefcase in the front room."

Diana followed her through a wide foyer and into a comfortable living area, appointed with overstuffed furniture upholstered in cool blues and greens, and sturdy, functional tables in an attractive knotty-pine. The neutral walls were covered with an assortment of family portraits.

"Here." Bridgett handed Diana the phone, whirled about, and left her alone.

James answered on the first ring. He said he was eager to have things settled, speaking civilly for the most part. His anger flared briefly when Diana refused his offer to send the company jet for her, insisting that the meeting take place in Roanoke and not at NSE headquarters. He whined about her lack of consideration for his enormous obligations and the distressing inconvenience of her demands, but when she stood her ground unflinchingly, he agreed. He'd have his lawyers make the necessary arrangements. Someone would meet her in the lobby of the Wells Fargo Tower, at 8:45 a.m. sharp.

Diana returned to the kitchen to find that Sean's oldest sister, Missy, had arrived. There was no mistaking the eldest daughter's relationship to her younger siblings. She had the same body type and dark coloring as Sean and Bridgett, though at forty-nine, her white hairs were beginning to outnumber the sable ones, the laugh lines around her eyes were deeper, and her waistline had a more mature contour.

Not waiting for a formal introduction, she approached their visitor offering a friendly welcome. "Hi, Diana, I'm Missy. Glad you're here. You must be a very special lady because you've impressed my little brother, and that's not an easy thing to do."

Blushing brightly, Diana thanked her for the kind words, her eyes darting nervously between

Missy and Sean.

Unable to contain his curiosity any longer Sean asked her, "What did he say? Where are you going to meet him?"

"He didn't like it much but he agreed to set up the meeting in the city. His attorneys will arrange for a conference room in the Wells Fargo Tower.

"Good. It's better for us to meet him on neutral turf."

"Us?" Diana quizzed him. "What do you mean, us? I can handle this – alone."

"You are not going in there without me, Diana," he insisted. In a whispered hiss, he warned, "It's too dangerous."

Fighting back tears of frustration, she nodded. "Okay. I could use a ride into town."

"So what time is this big pow-wow scheduled to convene?" he asked.

"Uh…ten," she told him, almost choking on the lie. "Now, I'd like to take your mother up on that bath and nap."

"Sure." He touched her cheek gently before retrieving her toiletries from his backpack. "Bridge will show you upstairs." Turning to his sister he added, "Find her some clean clothes to wear, will ya?"

"No problem. There's plenty of stuff stored up in the attic. Something's bound to fit." Unable to resist the opportunity for a cheap shot, the indignant airline hostess added, "If she's not too picky." Sean sent her a warning glance that she shrugged off with a wry grin and jaunty tilt of her head.

Accustomed to the squabbling of her siblings,

Missy ignored them and called after the retreating women. "When you're fresh and rested, I want to hear all about your adventures. I haven't been able to get details out of Sean. He's so close-mouthed." She punched him playfully.

Diana turned to Missy and smiled shyly. Her body ached with fatigue and her mind whirled with so many conflicting thoughts that she had trouble settling on a response. She opened her mouth to speak but nothing came out.

Thankfully, the youngest sister's impatience saved her. "Come on," she ordered. "I don't have all day. Let's get you settled."

Breathing a deep sigh of relief, Diana trotted after her. Upstairs, Bridgett pointed out the bathroom and indicated one of the bedrooms. "You can bunk in there with me. The room belongs to Amanda and Allison, Missy's twins, but they're away at college. I'll bring some things down from the attic and leave them on the bed for you to try after your bath."

"Thanks, Bridgett," Diana said, sincerely. "I know we didn't get off on the right foot but I want you to know that I really appreciate what you're doing for me."

"Like Mom said, Sean's always bringing in strays. When he was a kid it was wounded animals of every sort. As he grew up, it was the kids everyone else ridiculed and bullied. You know, the ones who had no other friends. Sean collected them. When he left home, we thought it would stop. We were wrong. Then he started bringing home his Marine buddies – guys who didn't have family to visit on furlough. Now he brings you. Just another stray. We're used to it."

"I get the picture. I'm no one special, but thanks anyway." Through sheer will, fired by a deep determination not to let Bridgett know how much her words hurt, Diana offered her a sincere smile.

TWELVE

The murmur of voices and the enticing aroma of fried chicken, wafting up from below, roused Diana from her nap. A clock radio on the nightstand that stood between her bed and its twin, announced that it was almost two. Stretching, she slipped out from under the crocheted bedspread and reached for the clothing Bridgett had retrieved from the attic and draped over the footboard. To her delight, the youngest Cody sister had chosen well.

Wiggling out of the T-shirt she'd borrowed from Sean, the graceful blonde replaced it with a v-neck cashmere sweater, in a shade of blue that matched her eyes, and black pants made of soft, cotton knit. The flight attendant had also provided a pair of leather slippers which fit her quite well.

Grabbing her toiletry bag, Diana returned to the bathroom, brushed her pale locks to a lustrous shine, and applied some mascara and lip-gloss. "Well, old girl," she told her reflection. "That will have to do." Taking a fortifying breath, she made her way downstairs, following the hubbub emitting from the kitchen.

"Great! You're up." Sean jumped to his feet, beaming a welcome. He introduced her to several more of his kinfolk, who had arrived while she was resting and were now busily helping out with the meal preparations, or sitting around the table chatting with one another.

Kathleen greeted her politely but coolly, leaving Diana to wonder if Bridgett had been sharing her prejudices. By contrast, Ellen was warm, outgoing, and friendly. Neither woman bore a strong resemblance to their other siblings. They were small-boned and shorter, with medium brown hair and light eyes, like their mother's. Life as a stay-at-home mother of four had left Ellen pleasingly plump; whereas childless, career-minded Kathleen had maintained her youthful figure.

Offering her a large, callused palm, Kathleen's husband, Dwight Young, took her measure through the smudged lenses of thick, dark-framed glasses. The powerfully built man was made for heavy work. Sean confirmed her intuition about him, explaining that Dwight owned and operated a livestock transport business.

"Got to pick up a load of hogs late this afternoon and head out for Chicago," the soft-spoken man told her. "Thought I'd get me a belly full of Miz Sarah's fried chicken first, though."

"It's very nice to meet you, Mr. Young," Diana said, smiling at the way he rubbed his generous abdomen in anticipation of the meal.

"You, too, ma'am. Call me Dwight, ever'body else does."

"And you already know J.D." Sean concluded, gesturing toward Ellen's spouse.

"Hello, again," the thin man grinned at her.

"How'd you like ridin' that big old bike?"

"It was exhilarating," she admitted. "And a little scary."

"That's enough small talk," Missy broke in. "Dinner's almost ready, and I want to hear all about Diana's adventures before Colin and Page get here and monopolize the conversation with wedding trivia."

"Colin's coming to dinner?" Sean asked, obviously surprised and pleased.

"Yeah," the eldest sister sighed with a shake of her head. "They've been here since the weekend. Those Martin girls and their social-climbing mother have been draggin' the poor boy all over creation, worrying the stuffin's out of him, fussin' over this ridiculous spectacle they're putting on – just to show off. You'd think Page Martin was the first girl to ever catch herself a husband. Colin's gotta be sick of it by now. I bet he wishes they could just run off and forget the whole blame mess."

"Now, Missy," Bridgett scolded. "There's absolutely nothing wrong with wanting your wedding to be special, and it doesn't hurt Colin to help out. Years from now, they'll look back at the pictures and remember their special day with pride."

"They'll remember it all right," the eldest sister huffed, "because they'll still be payin' for it!"

Bridgett shot Missy a disapproving look, which Missy ignored. Despite the lack of compassion that the woman had shown her so far, Diana's heart went out to the youngest Cody sister. This wedding was very important to her. That much was clear. Perhaps Bridgett had always dreamed of a fairy-tale wedding of her own, and a lavish marriage celebration for her son and his bride would fulfill her dream vicariously. If she couldn't have one of her own, she'd do everything in her power to see that her son did.

"Speaking of the wedding," Bridgett interjected. "You guys know we're responsible for the rehearsal dinner so you need to make some decisions pretty soon, or it'll be too late to reserve a nice banquet room somewhere in Roanoke."

Grandma Cody chimed in. "Why do we need to go to Roanoke? The church social hall is free and I'm used to cookin' for an army. Don't you worry about it, Bridgett. Your sisters and I will take care of everything."

"No, Mom. I won't think of it." Bridgett laid a long arm around her mother's shoulders. "Colin and Page deserve something more elegant than a country-style buffet in that dinky old fellowship hall. The Martins are putting a lot of money into this wedding so we have to plan a dinner that will live up to their standards. We can't serve them ham biscuits, baked beans, and potato salad on paper plates, while they sit on cold, metal folding chairs in a tacky, cinderblock hall. It would be humiliating!"

Sarah seemed to sag under the weight of her daughter's disapproval. "It's a sad day when a child of mine tells me she's ashamed of her church and her family." She shrugged off Bridgett's arm. "Well, my dear girl, maybe you should take your high and mighty airs upstairs right now, instead of pulling yourself up underneath my dinner table."

"I'm sorry, Mom," Bridgett told her, sighing in

exasperation. "That's not what I meant. Sure, I want this done right. But I'm also thinking of you. I don't want you, Missy, and Ellen working your fingers to the bone, cooking, serving, and waiting on everyone else, when you should be enjoying yourselves."

"Can we discuss this later, please?" Missy broke in. "There's no need sharing our disagreements in front of company. And I still want to hear how Diana managed to get our wandering brother home for a visit. He's not been willing to tell us anything, Diana, so you'll have to do it."

"There's not much to tell, really," she began, hesitantly. "Just a series of misfortunes, I'm afraid." Trying to be as vague as possible, the nervous woman smiled woodenly and feigned a nonchalant posture. To her relief, her story was interrupted before it could begin when the back door swung open and a man burst through, beaming a wide grin, his longish, sun-streaked curls swirling around his tanned face like a golden cloud.

"Surprise, surprise!" he shouted, smoothing his rebellious locks with his fingers. Before he could take three steps into the kitchen, the Cody women surrounded him, squealing. Fierce hugs were doled out all around. When the crowd finally parted, Sean grabbed the newcomer by the shoulders and shook him soundly.

"Skip, you son-of-a gun. It's great to see you."

"You too, Amigo," the visitor responded, pounding Sean's broad back. As the two men stood side by side, it was easy for Diana to make comparisons between them. The newcomer was the shorter of the two, with a more compact physique.

Though his muscles were less bulky and well-defined there was definitely power in them. His wiry, athletic build suggested that he used those muscles regularly, and with great strength, skill, and ability.

"Someone take the boy's bag and coat," Sarah ordered. Any male under forty-five was still a boy to the Cody matriarch. "And get him something to drink." Her son complied, tossing the green duffel into the corner behind the door and laying the man's bright orange windbreaker on top.

The newcomer nodded a greeting to the other men and made himself comfortable, choosing an empty chair, and rearing it back to balance on two legs. When his bright green gaze encountered Diana, he whistled appreciatively. "Who have we here? Where've you been keeping this beauty, you old dog?" he asked Sean, who was pouring him an iced tea.

Sean set the glass on the table and offered an introduction, "Diana, this is Skip Taylor, a Marine buddy of mine. Skip, meet, Diana North, my, uh… my client."

"It's a real pleasure." The blonde man grinned crookedly, revealing two rows of large, white teeth. The beguiling, devil-may-care smile was quickly followed by a flirtatious wink.

Unaccustomed to the overt compliments the attractive man offered her, Diana smiled shyly. She could feel her cheeks flaming with embarrassment.

"What have you been doing with yourself, Skip?" Bridgett asked him, hovering close.

"Following the big waves, as usual," he

quipped, nonchalantly.

"You're as bad as Sean," she complained. "Always keeping secrets. So, what brings you to our back door this time?"

He shrugged and gave his golden locks another shake. "Thought I could use a home-cooked meal for a change. And where else can I be sure to see five," he hesitated, tossed a glance in Diana's direction and added, "make that six, gorgeous women, all in the same room at the same time?"

"Oh, you!" The youngest Cody sister mussed his hair playfully. "You're an awful flirt. Should be ashamed of yourself."

"Yeah, but you love me for it," he teased her.

Doggedly moving the conversation back to the previous topic, Missy interjected, "Before you came in, Diana was telling us about her recent adventures. Wouldn't you like to hear the story, Skip?"

"Sure would," he chirped, cutting his eyes in his buddy's direction and giving him a mischievous smirk. "I'd love to know how a scoundrel like your brother got himself mixed up with such a stunner. He always has been the lucky one." Taking a long pull on the glass of tea, he waved a palm toward Diana.

"As I said, it was just a series of unusual circumstances, really," she began softly, taking her time and struggling for the right words, enough to satisfy their curiosity and nothing more. "We left D.C. on Friday, headed to a resort in West Virginia, on business. As we reached the mountains, Sean noticed a problem with the electrical system and set the helicopter down. We barely got out before it exploded."

"Oh my," Sarah Cody sighed. "How horrible. Guess that explains the nasty bruise on your chin. Weren't you scared to death?"

"I was extremely frightened. But your son kept his wits about him. Before we could make it out of the mountains, it started to snow. Thankfully, Sean found an empty hunting cabin so we stayed there until the weather cleared. Then we walked out and caught a ride to Covington."

"Sounds dangerous," Missy commented. "Hitchhiking isn't safe."

"It's not, of course, but we were cold and exhausted so we didn't think much about it at the time. Luckily, the driver was very accommodating. He dropped us at a small motel where we spent the night."

Diana paused briefly, afraid that Bridgett would ask about their sleeping arrangements, but when she let it pass without comment, the tall blonde went on. "My wallet was in my briefcase, which was destroyed in the explosion, so we didn't have much cash."

"That's so typical," Kathleen fumed. "We've always urged Sean to carry plastic for emergencies but he's too darned independent."

"So, how'd you rent the room, then?" Bridgett asked, suspiciously.

Swallowing hard, Diana fidgeted in her seat, deciding how to continue. "I... I found a credit card in my jacket pocket."

"Then you should have been able to get all the cash you needed," Bridgett snapped back. "Haven't you ever used an ATM?"

Knowing she couldn't reveal the real reason she hadn't used her credit card to make a withdrawal, Diana's thoughts congealed in her head. She looked to Sean for help. As soon as her eyes touched his handsome face, she could see that he was furious.

"Are you going to let the woman finish her story or keep badgering her with asinine questions?" he growled. "Not that's it's any of your business, but Diana is in the middle of a nasty divorce. Her husband put a watch on her card. When she used it to rent the room, the company notified him and blocked further charges. Does that satisfy you, Miss Nosy?" He glared at Bridgett, daring her to speak again.

"You poor thing," Ellen crooned. "It's terrible when a marriage fails. I'm so sorry. I know you must be awfully unhappy."

"I appreciate your concern," Diana told her, "but I'm okay, really. All things considered, James and I will both be better off when this divorce business is finished."

"Yeah, I bet you'll make the best of it," Bridgett interjected sarcastically, giving Diana an openly hostile, accusatory stare.

Sean jumped to her defense, "What is that crack supposed to mean?"

"Yes, Bridgett," Kathleen began, eyeing her brother hesitantly. "What are you insinuating?"

Sensing the room turning against her, Bridgett backed down, "Nothing. Forget it. Please, Mrs. North, go on with your little tale."

Clearing her throat nervously, Diana resumed. "The next morning, we found a second-hand store and bartered a few things for a change of clothing. Then we caught the bus to Roanoke, met J.D., and picked up Sean's motorcycle. We rode down to a friend's place on the lake, planning to spend the night. But an unexpected guest arrived so we decided to leave and come here. Since it was so late, we spent the night in the tree house rather than waking the household. That's where we were when Bridgett discovered us."

"I can't believe Sean made you sleep out there in that drafty old treehouse," Sarah said, shaking her gray head. "Especially with warm, soft beds only a few hundred yards away. My boy, what were you thinking?"

His youngest sister couldn't resist the opening her mother had given her, or the urge to stick the needle through it. "That's what I asked him but he insisted they were quite cozy and comfortable."

Shooting her another warning frown, Sean headed off that line of thinking before anyone else could take it up. "Like Diana said, Mom, it was really late. You all have to get up so early that we didn't want to disturb your rest. You know there's no way to get into this house without waking everyone."

When Missy raised a dark brow at him, he added, "Don't fret over it. We managed well enough for a few hours, and we're here now, so you can pamper us all you want."

"The boys are gonna have a fit when they find out you let a female into Fort Cody, you know,"

Ellen warned him.

"Then let's not tell them," he taunted.

Brushing off her third daughter's concern as unimportant, Sarah asked Diana, "So what's next, dear? I heard you say you have a meeting with your husband tomorrow. Was he upset when he found out you almost died in a helicopter explosion? Wasn't his heart softened, just a little bit?"

"I wish I could say it was," Diana lowered her face and studied her hands. "James is very anxious to have me out of his life."

Unable to resist the urge to comfort her, Sean laid a hand on her shoulder and squeezed. She looked up at him with grateful, sad eyes.

Witnessing her brother's obvious sympathy for the older woman seemed to incense Bridgett. Unable to hold her sharp tongue any longer, she quizzed, "What on earth did you do to make your husband despise you so?"

Sean whirled to face her, his eyes shooting sparks, his fists clenched and ready to strike out against her intentional cruelty. She glared back at him in an unspoken challenge.

Before either could speak, Ellen recoiled, aghast at her sister's insensitivity. "Bridgett! That's horrible! Why would you ask such a thing? What's gotten into you?"

Sarah stared at her daughter, shocked and appalled by her deliberate attempt to inflict pain. "I warned you earlier, my girl. You've always been willful but I've never seen this mean streak in you before. Miz North is a guest in this house and I will not have you treatin' her with anything less than the most gracious hospitality. Now, apologize!"

"No apology is necessary," Diana defended. "Bridgett has every right to question me. I am a complete stranger, imposing myself upon the good will of your family. She wants to know what sort of person I am, and I don't blame her for that. In fact, I admire her directness. She deserves an answer."

"You don't have to do this," Sean whispered, close to her ear.

"Yes, Sean, I do. I need to put an end to the animosity, if I can." She gave him an icy, determined look.

"My relationship with James is more of a business partnership than a marriage, a partnership he wants dissolved because our goals for our company, North Star Enterprises, have taken divergent paths. James has never cared for me as a husband should care for a wife, so his lack of concern for me is not as unusual as it might seem."

"That's so sad," Ellen sniffed into a tissue she'd pulled out of her apron pocket. "I can't imagine marrying for any reason except love."

"You've always been a silly romantic," J.D. teased her softly. She circled the table, wrapped her arms around his neck and kissed his whiskered cheek.

"Look at that," he quipped, elbowing Dwight. "Married over twenty years, with four kids to brag on, and she still can't get enough of me."

"Ohhhh!" Ellen whined, slugging him playfully. "What am I going to do with you?" Turning to Diana, she said sincerely, "I hope you find true love someday."

It was all Diana could do to keep her eyes from seeking Sean's beloved face. "Thank you, Ellen. So do I."

Bridgett mumbled something unintelligible under her breath, then she stomped across the room and took a stack of plates out of the cupboard. "I'm going to set the table. Colin and Page will be here any minute."

"I'll help," Diana offered, following the volatile woman through a swinging door and into the huge dining room.

"Flatware's in there." Bridgett nodded her dark head toward an oak sideboard.

Diana retrieved a handful of stainless-steel utensils from the top drawer, and placed each piece on the tablecloth in its proper place, next to the white stoneware plates. After the table appointments were complete, she smiled at her hostess expectantly, but to her chagrin, Bridgett's chilly attitude had not warmed.

The youngest Cody sister threw her adversary a warning grimace and hissed at her through clenched teeth. "I do not need you to defend me to my family. Do you understand?" Not giving Diana a second to respond, Bridgett spun around and stormed out.

Biting back tears, Diana took a few moments to compose her raw emotions before rejoining the group in the kitchen. *Buck up,* she ordered herself. *You only have to endure this torture for one day, then you're out of here.* The thought of spending the entire night sharing a room with Sean's belligerent sister made her shiver.

Running her fingers through her hair and taking a deep, bracing breath, she reached for the door, only to have it swing in toward her. Skip's classic, California-surfer face peeked through the opening, followed immediately by his lean, athletic body. "Hey, you okay?" he asked hesitantly, grinning foolishly.

"Just a little overwhelmed." She smiled back at him, thankful for the temporary reprieve from the well-meaning attentions of the Cody family.

"I know exactly how you feel." His grin grew impossibly wider. "The first time Sean brought me home to meet his folks, I thought I was going to suffocate under the pressure of all that devoted attention. It didn't take long for me to fall in love with them, though, one and all. Even bitchy Bridgett has her finer qualities, if you can survive her barbed tongue long enough to see them."

"I take it you don't come from a large family."

"It's just me and my dad, and he spends most of his days in a drunken stupor." Shrugging off the pain in an off-handed manner that suggested he'd done it often, Skip took a step closer.

Telltale laugh lines, crinkling around his eyes, told her that he was a bit older than he'd first appeared. Diana guessed his age at a hair over forty. "So how about you? Not accustomed to a house full of relatives, huh?"

She shook her fair head.

"Give 'em time, Diana. They'll grow on you," he reassured her. "Before you know it, you'll love all the Codys as much as I do.

She sighed and smiled at him. It was one of the

saddest smiles imaginable. "The real question is…Will they ever love me?"

"One of them already does."

Skip's declaration surprised her. "How...uh…Why do you say that?"

"I've been real close to the Captain since I was assigned to his unit. We've been through a scrape of two together and I know him as well as I know myself, maybe better. I'm more screwed up than he is, by the way." Skip offered her another aw-shucks grin. "Anyhow, truth is, he can't keep secrets from me. The first time I saw him look at you, I could tell that he's crazy about you."

"You could?" She was incredulous.

"Oh yeah, and you're pretty gone on him, too."

"You might say that," she admitted.

"I thought I just did," he teased playfully.

His encouraging optimism uplifting her spirits, she giggled.

"That's better." He touched her mouth with the tip of his finger. "Finally! I was wondering if I'd ever see a real smile on that beautiful mouth." A long, uncomfortable moment passed before he spoke again. "Come on. We'd better jump back into the fray. There are more members of the Cody clan yet to meet."

"Oh boy," she sighed joylessly, adding, "Thanks, Skip."

"For what?"

"The pep-talk and ...everything. You're very sweet."

"Yeah, well. Don't spread that around, hear?" he urged her, flashing a roguish grin. "It would ruin my reputation as a self-centered hedonist."

With a flourish and an overplayed bow, he waved her through the swinging door. He stepped in behind her, silently offering her support. As he'd warned, several additional people were milling around in the already crowded kitchen.

First, she met Mike Cody, the family patriarch, who greeted her with an enthusiastic bear hug. It was easy for Diana to see where Sean got his above-average size and striking good looks. Next, Melissa's husband, Nelson Angle, offered her his hand. The round-faced, balding man seemed a good match for Sean's eldest sister. Something about the pair gave the immediate impression that they fit together better than most couples.

"This is Colin," Sean said, guiding her toward a slender young man who stood near the back door with his arm around the waist of a stunningly attractive young woman. "And his fiancée, Page Martin."

"It's nice to meet you," Colin said, tossing his head to throw a tawny curl out of his twinkling hazel eyes.

"The pleasure is mine," Diana responded, thinking that the boy looked nothing like his mother or any of the other members of the Cody family.

Page put out her hand politely. Colin's girl was petite, delicately formed, and exceedingly lovely. Diana took her fine-boned fingers into her palm and squeezed them gently. Just as she was about to offer a greeting, the door flew open once more.

"Patti! There you are. It's about time. Where have you been?" Page asked the entering woman, who Diana concluded must to be related to the bride-to-be, an older sister perhaps. "Everyone, everyone!" Page announced, forgetting the introduction. "Look who's here!"

All eyes flew to the newcomer as she made her grand entrance. Her self-assured manner indicated that she'd been in the Cody home many times before, and that she knew she'd be welcomed. "Sean, aren't you going to give your old girlfriend a hug?" Page prompted. "Patti's divorced from Ron Sanderson now, you know. She's just Patti Martin again."

Reluctantly stepping away from Diana's side, Sean wrapped his long arms around the tall, slim woman. "Hi, Patti."

"Sean," the Cindy Crawford look alike crooned in his ear. "It's sooo good to see you." She held onto him even after he started to pull away and planted a loud kiss on his cheek.

Diana felt her stomach twist. This woman was the personification of her worst nightmare. Though she wasn't quite as tall as the older women, Patti's svelte figure had to be twenty pounds lighter. Her bones were long and thin, and her skin was ivory perfection. Cinnamon hair, streaked with honey-gold, fell in shimmering waves to her delicate shoulders, and the fashionably tight jeans she wore, topped with a low-cut ruffled blouse, set off her obvious assets marvelously.

Oh no, Diana thought. *She even has a beauty mark, right by her mouth, calling attention to her artificially plumped lips and begging for a kiss. It's no wonder Sean was in love with her once. She's every teenaged boy's dream girl.*

THIRTEEN

For Diana, the nightmare seemed to just get worse and worse. Dinner was served shortly after Colin and the Martin sisters arrived. Sarah insisted that the Cody men-folk and their guests dine first, while she and her daughters waited on the table. Grandpa Mike took his usual place at one end with Nelson occupying his customary one at the other. Diana was seated on her host's right hand, next to Skip and directly across from Sean. The former dentist's wife grabbed the chair on Sean's left before anyone else could claim it, taking every opportunity to lean her elegantly coifed head close to his, or to press her ample bosom against him.

Despite the delicious food, Diana couldn't muster up an appetite when the passing of each succulent dish provided Patti with another excuse to touch Sean's hand or brush his arm. To make circumstances even more miserable for the humiliated woman, the man who'd so recently declared his love for her appeared to be enjoying every moment of his former girlfriend's clinging, saccharin-coated attention. He smiled into Patti's adoring face, while deliberately avoiding eye contact with the woman across the table.

The dinner conversation, as Melissa had predicted, revolved around the excited young couple's wedding plans. Animated, charming Page recounted the weekend's activities, which included visits to bridal gift registries and the selection of a caterer, florist, and tuxedos. Every time Mike or Nelson brought up a business question, the Martin girls adeptly steered the discussion back to things that interested them more than the day-to-day operations of a dairy farm. The only other topic allowed any airtime was Patti's reminiscence about the "good old days" when she and Sean were "going steady."

Diana filtered out the majority of their inane chattering, concentrating instead on the ordeal she'd be facing in the morning. When it became impossible for her to withstand Patti's obvious advances for one second longer, she studied the fried chicken and mashed potatoes she was pushing around on her plate, while she formulated a firm plan for dealing with the ultimatum she expected James to make. Engrossed in her thoughts, she didn't hear the one comment that was directed at her when it was spoken.

"Diana," Skip prompted her, his pale green eyes darkening with concern. "Kathleen was talking to you."

"I'm sorry." She looked up and scanned the room for Sean's sister. "I'm afraid I was lost in my thoughts. What did you say?"

Placing refilled bowls of steaming gravy and hot biscuits on the table, Kathleen repeated her inquiry. "You mentioned that you were planning to stay down on the lake last night, at the home of a friend. I was just wondering who they were."

Taken off guard by the question, Diana responded, "Why?"

"Just curious," Kathleen admitted. "I might know them."

Jumping at the opportunity to show off her superior knowledge of the Cody family, Patti chimed in. "Kath's a real estate agent, you know, so she's familiar with every piece of property on Smith Mountain Lake and practically every property owner."

"I didn't realize," the older woman admitted softly. "The house belongs to my college roommate, Eleanor, and her husband, Dick Randall. It's a summer place, really, though they use it on weekends year-round. Their primary residence is in Northern Virginia."

"Oh yes, I know them," Kathleen chirped proudly. "Probably met them at some homeowner's association function or another. Dick's a heart surgeon."

"That's right," Diana confirmed, taking a quick glance at the prim woman's truck-driver husband, as he shoveled his mouth full of creamed corn, and thinking that he didn't seem the sort who would fit in very well in his wife's pretentious social circle. Ignoring her completely, his attention was focused entirely on the delicious meal.

"Small world, isn't it?" the haughty realtor observed. "Who would've dreamed that we would have mutual friends?" She placed an unusual emphasis on the word we.

Diana remained silent, hoping the conversation would return to its original path and turn the attention away from her. Unfortunately, Patti's curiosity had been piqued. "Say, Diana," she began, waving one long, red-lacquered nail for emphasis, "Page and I would like to know something about you. Wouldn't we, sweetie?" She paused for her sister to add a few words of encouragement.

"Why, yes, we would. Where're you from, and what brings you to Franklin County?" The younger Martin girl seemed sincere in her questioning, unlike her sister, who appeared to be feigning interest in hopes of impressing Sean with her concern for the visiting stranger.

Not wanting to repeat the entire tale, Diana spoke briefly. "I'm from the D.C. area. Sean was flying me to West Virginia on company business. Helicopter trouble stranded us in the mountains, then we ran into a series of unexpected problems, and eventually ended up here."

"I'd call that an understatement," Skip teased. "Diana and Sean have been through quite an ordeal since they left Northern Virginia on Friday."

"So…you and Sean have been alone together for days," Patti noted, apparently bothered by her conclusion and its potential implications. Now genuinely interested, she added, "Where'd you stay?"

"Anywhere we could," Sean said, smirking mischievously, "A hunting cabin, a cheap motel, and even the treehouse. We've had ourselves an adventure. Wouldn't you say so, Diana?" He turned his warm, maple-syrup eyes on her and her heart melted.

She smiled back. "Yes, a true adventure. One I'll never forget."

As Patti watched the exchange between Sean and Diana, jealousy seeped through her veins like liquid fire. That woman had been allowed inside Fort Cody, a coup she'd never been able to pull off. She'd used of all her considerable wiles, shamelessly, in her pursuit of that privilege, but Sean had adamantly refused her. Immediately she knew, deep in the core of her self-centered heart, that her plan to rekindle the romance with her high-school sweetheart was in imminent danger. Pursing her plumped lips together in barely concealed ire, she prodded, hoping to discover a tidbit of information that she could use to undermine this mysterious, and threatening older woman, "So, Mrs. North, where do you work?"

"North Star Enterprises."

"And what do you do there?" the model-like beauty demanded, pressing on in her quest.

"I'm one of the vice-presidents."

"One of the vice-presidents, I see," Patti said, glaring at Diana like a viper curled to strike. "What, pray tell, are you a vice-president of?"

"Of development." Diana's answer was short and circumspect.

Her impatience stretched, Patti's perfect face reddened to an unbecoming shade that clashed with her blouse. "What does that mean, exactly?"

The younger woman's needling brought out the

worst in Diana. The comfortable, reassuring armor settled over her. The "Ice Queen" spoke. "If you must know, Mrs. Sanderson, my husband, James, is the President and CEO of NSE. As VP of Development, I'm an equal partner, and responsible for finding new enterprises of potential investment interest. In other words, my job is to find unique and innovative ways to help the company grow. And, I'm very good at my job. I produce millions in profits every year."

Skip, who'd always disliked his buddy's former girlfriend, laughed aloud. He draped his arm casually over Diana's shoulders and leaned close to her ear, "That's tellin' her. Now, maybe she'll shut up and give someone else a chance to talk."

Patti stared at her, open-mouthed and speechless, shocked at how Diana had transformed before her very eyes, from soft-spoken and vulnerable to tough-minded and self-assured. *Sean could never be interested in this cold, calculating bitch,* she decided, much relieved.

His nerves raw from Patti's determined and irritating pursuit, Sean sighed inwardly. *That's enough of that,* he told himself. Grabbing the opening her momentary silence presented, he deftly shifted the discussion. "How's the computer business, Colin?"

"Good," the young man answered, grinning his relief that the conversation had moved onto more comfortable ground. "The company's doing well. In fact, we're so busy it's going to be hard for me to get time off for our honeymoon." Turning soulful eyes on his fiancée, he added an assurance, "But I'll manage somehow."

When Nelson asked Skip about his most recent pursuits, a long discussion of surfing and snowboarding and the relative attributes of each, ensued. Mike Cody admonished the free-spirited man for his continued avoidance of respectable employment, saying that any man his age should be "settled down with a good woman at his side, working to be a productive member of society." Obviously, this was a pronouncement that the Cody family had heard more than once before, for it sparked a roar of cheering laughter from Colin, Sean, and the sisters.

When most had eaten their fill, Diana politely excused herself and slipped away. Carrying her plate with her into the kitchen, she depositing it on the battered, but well-scrubbed countertop. For a long moment, she stared out of the long window above the sink.

Far in the distance, the Blue Ridge Mountains rose, serene and majestic, their topmost peaks still touched with a few splotches of white. Closer by, a bright red cardinal picked seeds from a small feeder that hung from the branches of a dogwood tree. Though it was still bare of leaves, tiny buds at the end of each wooden finger held the promise of spring. The place was altogether idyllic. She wondered if Sean's family realized how lucky they were to have this peaceful, nurturing environment, and the devotion and loving support of one another.

A soft voice behind her startled her. "You feelin' all right? You didn't hardly eat a bite. That's a bad bruise you got on your chin. Is it botherin' you?"

"Oh, Mrs. Cody," Diana turned toward the older woman, unconsciously rubbing her injured jaw. "I'm fine, really, and the food was delicious. I just wasn't hungry."

"Call me Sarah," the aging matriarch said. "I understand, dear. That crowd can be a little upsettin' to the appetite for anyone not accustomed to such prying ways. I hope you'll forgive us for bein' so pushy. It's only because we're interested in you, you know."

"I do," Diana assured her. "But your family is not the problem."

"I see. You're worried about this nasty divorce business you're in the middle of, aren't you?" Sarah Cody was an astute woman and a good judge of character. "Well, you shouldn't fret yourself over it. You hear? Things have a way of workin' themselves out for the best."

"I'm sure you're right," the graceful blonde replied, smiling sadly. "You should go eat something yourself," she urged. "You've been on your feet all day. My place is empty. Please, get a plate, sit with your loved ones, and enjoy your meal. I'll start cleaning up."

"Why, thank you. That's very kind. I believe I'll take you up on that offer. I'd like to set a spell with Sean. I don't git to see him very often."

As Diana worked in the kitchen, the older men wandered through, one-by-one, on their way to work or back to the fields, and the sisters filled the vacated seats at the table. By the time everyone had finished eating, she had the pots and pans washed and the surfaces wiped clean. The kitchen sparkled. Sarah thanked her graciously, poured her a fresh cup of coffee, and shooed her into the front room.

The Martin sisters had already staked out their respective territories, each one possessively claiming the position closest to her chosen man. Colin and Page sat side-by-side on the love seat, their heads bowed together in a private discussion, totally absorbed in one another. Sean had chosen a big, overstuffed chair that sat off by itself in one corner of the room, but his attempt to put a little distance between himself and his former girlfriend had failed miserably. Her designer blue-jean clad bottom was perched on the matching ottoman, facing him. She was leaning forward, resting her elbows on his knees.

The pilot was the only one in the room to acknowledge Diana's arrival. He grinned sheepishly. His eyes followed her, as she set her cup and saucer down on the coffee table and settled back into the soft cushions of the sofa. Then he shrugged helplessly, while Patti continued her constant stream of chatter, oblivious to the fact that her intended audience was not listening to a word she was saying.

Reaching out a red-tipped finger, she gently touched the small bandage on his forehead. "My poor baby," she whined. "That must have hurt something awful. What in the world happened?"

With a backhanded swipe, he brushed off her attention. "It's nothing, really, just a scratch."

Giving up her shallow efforts to appear concerned for him, she got on with her determined pursuit. "You're so lucky that you never married, Sean. Looking back on things, now, I know I really made a mistake by not waiting for you. I was just so hurt when you left. I felt abandoned and rejected. So, I had to prove I was desirable. When a professional man, with real earning potential and good prospects for the future, said he wanted me, I couldn't refuse. But Ron and I weren't meant to be together. I never really loved him the way I loved you, the way I still do."

"Patti, please." he implored her. "Let's discuss it later, in private." Though he was not moved by the emotional appeal of the young woman casually caressing his thigh, the cool, aloof acceptance of the older one across the room disturbed him deeply. Diana had withdrawn into her frigid shell and he was to blame. He and his family had driven her back into that awful, cold, lonely place where she hid when she felt threatened. He'd witnessed her retreat and had done nothing to stop it. Even the knowledge that he was following her wishes, by keeping their relationship secret until her divorce was finalized, did nothing to assuage the guilt he was feeling.

"If that's meant to be a sneaky way to arrange to spend some time alone with me, I accept." Patti flashed him a brilliant, seductive smile. "When?"

Taken aback by her determined forwardness, he stuttered, "I... I don't know. Later...sometime later." Then, he added, "Diana's my guest and I haven't been a very good host. I should be entertaining her.

Showing her around."

Shifting his attention away from the unwanted beauty who was practically climbing into in his lap, to the one he really desired who was sitting across the room from him, he asked, "I bet you'd like to see the baby calves. Nelson said we have a new foal, too."

Before the visitor could respond, Patti did so for her. "I'm sure a sophisticated woman like Mrs. North would have no interest in dirty, smelly old animals out in a dirty, smelly old barn."

"You're wrong about that Mrs. Sanderson," Diana interjected quickly. "I'm very interested in a tour of the Cody farm, but you and Sean are having such a wonderful reunion. I wouldn't want to intrude."

"It's no intrusion," Sean declared immediately, ignoring the look of shocked disapproval that crossed Patti's perfect face, as well as her indignant huff. Pushing out of his chair, he held out a hand to Diana. "Come on. Let's find you a wrap."

Trotting along behind them, Patti insisted, "I'm going, too."

"Suit yourself." Then he warned her, "But I'd better not hear any griping about mud on your shoes or dirt under your fingernails."

Huffing again, she insinuated herself between Sean and Diana, latching onto his elbow and leaving Diana to fall in behind. In the kitchen, Sean retrieved his field coat and grabbed a colorfully embroidered shawl from a hat rack by the back door. Placing it around Diana's shoulders, his hands lingered, gently tracing her collarbones.

Annoyed that the man seemed to enjoy the thoughtful service he was providing for the older woman, Patti held out her tailored wool jacket and pouted prettily, waiting for him to extend the same courtesy to her.

With barely concealed irritation, Sean took the coat from her and held it as she slid her arms in. *Damned, single-minded woman,* he fumed to himself, his frustration growing. *Why won't she give up and go home?* Patti had always been extremely determined. He'd never been able to dissuade her when she was in pursuit of something she wanted, and it looked like she'd decided she wanted him. Gritting his teeth, he snapped, "Let's go."

For the next half-hour, he led them through the barn and sheds, offering a running commentary of interesting details about dairy farming. Patti shifted from foot to foot restlessly, still huffing, making little effort to hide her boredom. Nor did she squelch the numerous complaints that erupted every time something pricked her delicate sensibilities.

While the younger woman fumed and fussed, the elder was relaxed and calm, thoroughly enjoying the tour. She lingered over the fuzzy, yellow chicks, peeping at her from the incubator, knelt on the straw beside the black and white calves and let them lick her fingers, and sighed in awe at the wobbly newborn colt, as he awoke from a nap and painstakingly propped himself up on his toothpick legs.

"Oh, he's soooo cute." The bright glow of pleasure in her frosty blue eyes made Sean's stomach do an unexpected flip. The foal lurched his way to his mother's side and nuzzled around in search of his dinner. Within seconds, he was sucking noisily. Diana laughed. "He's a hungry little fellow."

"Awww, gross," Patti whined. "I can't watch this. Can we go now, pul-lease?" She tugged on Sean's coat sleeve and huffed again.

"You two can go back to the house if you want," Diana offered. "I'd like to watch this little fellow a bit longer."

"Come on, Sean." Patti jerked on his jacket again, this time with more insistence. "Let's go find a private place. To talk. We have a lot of catching up to do."

"No, Patti," he said firmly, removing her hand from his arm. "Go on back inside. I'm staying out here with Diana. Then I'm gonna change the oil in the dump truck."

"Oh, Sean..." she whined. He'd forgotten how much the nasal, petulant tone of her voice irritated him. "Why do you have to do that now, when we could be alone together, getting things settled between us?"

"Because I promised Dad I'd take care of it."

"But you'll get all dirty and grea-sy," she complained, drawing out the last word.

"Yes, I expect I will," he admitted.

Huffing her irritation yet again, Patti trudged toward the house, coat-tail flapping. Calling behind her, she insisted, "Come inside as soon as you get showered and cleaned up. We are gonna talk."

As soon as she was out of earshot, Sean sighed in relief. "Jeez, I thought she'd never leave! Can't believe I'd forgotten what a pain in the ass she is."

A tiny, rueful smile touched Diana's lips. "She's very beautiful. I can see why you were in love with her once."

"Was I?" he asked with a shrug. "It's so weird. There was a time when I really thought I loved her – the dream girlfriend everyone wanted and I had. I was all broken-up when she dumped me for the good Dr. Ron. Felt betrayed and rejected and angry. I even blocked out the fact that one of the major reasons I joined-up in the first place, was to get away from her."

"It was?" Diana asked, her tone skeptical.

"I wanted to break things off with her, but I was chicken. My sisters were already planning our wedding. And, I didn't think I could stand up to the ribbing I'd get from my buddies, if I threw away the trophy girlfriend they were all hot for. She'd earned me a pile of stud points, and I didn't want to admit that she wasn't the prize everyone thought."

"So, you ran off instead."

"Coward that I am," he admitted with a foolish grin. "Today I finally realized that when she dumped me, Patti was giving me exactly what I wanted most, my freedom. I romanticized our relationship and mourned its death, on the outside, but inside I was relieved."

"She wants you back, you know," Diana warned.

He nodded. "She's not subtle about her intentions."

"If you're serious about not wanting her, you're not going to be able to dodge that final confrontation this time."

"I'm up to the task now." Sean leveled his clear, determined gaze at her. "I'm not a horny teenager anymore – that she could wrap around her little finger with a sexy come on and a push up bra."

"Was she good in bed?"

"What?" Sean barked, startled by the question.

"You heard me. Was she a good lover?" Diana smiled at him playfully.

"Not that I'm obligated to answer that nosy question, but no, she wasn't." He grinned back at her. "Patti puts on a good show. She flirts like a champ, flaunts her assets, and teases shamelessly, but she has no follow-through. She makes a guy work for every second of her attention and expects him to reward her, repeatedly, for allowing him the privilege of touching her precious body."

"We only had sex a couple of times. It was all I wanted of her. She was cold and unresponsive. She found sex distasteful and whined for me to 'get it over with.' Patti has no warmth in her and her sexuality is just for show. Love isn't something she gives to others, but a precious commodity she receives from them. Patti loves to be adored." Diana concluded, "So you're saying that it wouldn't have been a marriage made in heaven."

"We'd have been divorced in about thirty seconds flat," he said with conviction. "And if she thinks she's going to maneuver me back into a relationship with her, after all these years, she's even more self-centered and deluded than before."

"I guess time will tell about that," the tall woman teased him. "She seems pretty persistent to me, and I'm not convinced that you, even with specialized Marine training, will be able to stand up under the barrage of her well-aimed guns."

"Ha, ha, very funny," he quipped. "We've wasted enough time talking about Patti. Let's take a closer look at that little guy." He indicated the chestnut-colored foal. "Seems like he's finished his supper."

"Could we?" Diana pleaded.

"Sure. His mom is placid and well-mannered. She'll be proud to show off her offspring." Sliding back the stall door, he ushered Diana inside. "Sit over there." He pointed to a bale of straw in the corner.

As soon as the excited woman complied, the tiny colt skipped toward her on trembling legs. When he reached her, he gently laid his soft, fuzzy muzzle, still wet with his mother's milk, against her cheek and sniffed loudly.

"He likes you," Sean observed. Sensing her hesitation, he prompted, "Go ahead. Touch him. It's okay."

The colt's coat was as soft as silk. He smelled of fresh hay. Diana rubbed his neck and tickled his ears, her face glowing with delight. When she stopped, he flopped his head from side to side and punched her with his nose, begging for more."

Diana laughed.

Pleased to see her sincerely happy, her troubles behind her for a while, Sean watched the two for a few more seconds before pulling himself away. "I'd better get to that truck before Dad comes looking for me. Stay as long as you want. I'll meet you back at the house."

Diana nodded her agreement without taking her eyes off the tiny foal. His mother nickered softly when Sean exited the stable, and took a hesitant step closer to her visitor. Apparently deciding that the woman was no threat, she allowed Diana to caress her muzzle.

Later, when Diana reluctantly took her leave of the barn and made her way back to the farm house, she noted another car in the gravel driveway. Missy's youngest daughter, Ashley, a seventeen-year-old high school senior, and Ellen's four children, John Jr., Rachel, Matthew, and Mark, who ranged in age from eight to fourteen, were noisily clearing the dinner table. As soon as they were finished, the boys conned their cousin, Colin, into playing a video game with them, while Page and Patti entertained the girls with a complete re-telling of their wedding-extravaganza plans.

The afternoon went by in a whirl of activity. Unaccustomed as she was to living in such a crowd of people, Diana found herself searching for a quiet corner, where she could escape the sensory overload created by the joyous hum of humanity. To her disappointment, it seemed impossible to be alone in the Cody household.

When Sean came back in, fresh from the shower as Patti had commanded, the emotionally exhausted guest sighed thankfully and shot him a welcoming smile. Unfortunately, Patti's reflexes were too quick. The determined divorcee jumped up from her seat and maneuvered herself between the big man and his intended target, before Diana could move from the chair she'd retreated to, at the back of the room.

Sean's efforts to avoid Patti's attentions were futile. She steered him out of the living area with a practiced expertise, giving him no option but to comply or to risk embarrassment. Diana's fears were confirmed when she overheard Patti beg him, "Take me for a ride. Please, Sean. I really need to talk with you, alone."

Though she couldn't make out the man's lower tones, Diana guessed that he'd refused when the demanding woman pressed her breasts against his chest and whined. "It'll be fun, I promise. I'll let you drive my new convertible." Her suggestive plea gave new meaning to the words, insistent and manipulative. "If you're a good boy I'll let you..." She bent her cinnamon and gold head close to his dark one and whispered in his ear.

His face blazing, Sean pushed Patti away self-consciously and grabbed her wrist, every eye in the room on them. Shoving her toward the door, he growled, "So let's go." Snapping an angry bow to his audience, he stomped after her retreating back.

As they stepped out, Skip sauntered into the living room where everyone was sitting in shocked silence. Stuffing in a huge chunk of cherry pie, he mumbled, "What did I miss?"

FOURTEEN

The evening crawled on at a snail's pace. Kathleen breezed through, blowing kisses to everyone, and announcing that she had a house to show. In her wake came Ellen, who rounded up her crew and shooed them home. Soon afterward, Colin and Page prepared to depart. Colin had waited for Sean to return from his outing with Patti, but their trip back to Richmond would take them the better part of three hours, so the young man decided that they'd better not delay any longer.

Diana watched silently as Sarah, Missy, and Bridgett waved to the young couple from the back porch. Colin called to his mother, "Tell Sean goodbye for me, will ya? I was hoping to see that big lug one more time, but I guess he and Patti are busy getting reacquainted."

"Will do," Bridgett assured him. "Now, you drive safely. Hear?"

"Love ya!" He waved again before ducking inside his shiny Volvo sedan. The engine roared to life and the car rolled away, stone crunching under the tires. As they reached the end of the drive, a red Corvette convertible wheeled in, stirring up a cloud of orange dust. The sports car skidded to a halt. Sean vaulted from the driver's seat and sprinted to the other vehicle. His broad shoulders filled the window as he leaned inside to give Colin a farewell hug.

Moments later, he pulled the convertible up near the porch. He hopped out and circled the vehicle to open the passenger door, then he waited while Patti slid out. Tossing him a dazzling smile, she touched his scowling face with her fingertips before rounding the automobile, her eyes gleaming with smug satisfaction. With an agonizing leisureliness, she reclaimed the driver's seat and allowed Sean to close the door behind her.

Before he could escape, she grabbed the front of his shirt, pulling his face down toward hers. Then she planted a deep, sensuous kiss on his unsuspecting mouth. Sean tried to draw back from her embrace, but his heavy shoulders were fully inside the car and weighed down by Patti's encircling arms. Instead of retreating, he toppled forward, making it seem that he was trying to prolong and intensify the kiss.

When the woman released him with a shove, he lurched backward, apparently stunned by the exchange. His sisters giggled with pleasure at the flush of color rising up his neck. Patti dropped the sports car into gear and sped away, gravel flying, throwing him an exaggeratedly theatrical kiss.

Bridgett couldn't resist teasing her brother, knowing that she was driving a wedge firmly between him and Diana. "Well, well, well, seems like you and the enticing Miss Martin are still going at it as hot and heavy as ever. The old spark only needed a little fanning, huh? Where've you guys been, at some secluded spot making out?"

Sean grunted noncommittally.

"Admit it, lover boy. Patti still does it for you, doesn't she?" Bridgett's dark eyes twinkled with mischief.

"Shut-up, Bridge!" Sean growled, searching Diana's face. His gut twisted. Her expression was totally blank, an unreadable mask. There was no light in her pale blue eyes. Furious, he lashed out at his meddlesome sibling, "You don't know what the hell you're talking about, so mind your own damned business!"

"That's enough! Both of you," Sarah ordered. She turned her back on them, standing toe-to-toe, eyes flashing dangerously. "Let's me and you go get ourselves a cup of coffee and a piece of pie." She took Diana's arm. "And let those two stubborn fools work out their problems without an audience."

As they savored large slices of the tart cherry filling and flaky pastry, Diana tried to ignore the angry voices battling it out on the back porch. Sarah shook her head sadly. "I'm real sorry about that. Bridgett and Sean are like oil and water. They've always been able to find something to fight about."

"This time it's my fault," the visitor admitted. Realizing too late that she'd spoken without thinking, Diana cringed but forged ahead, choosing her words carefully. "Bridgett and I got off to a bad start, I'm afraid, and she doesn't think much of me. She loves her brother very much and is trying her best to protect him from me."

"By throwing Patti Martin at his head," Sarah concluded astutely. "Well, that certainly explains why she was so intent on callin' her up and gettin' her over here. This mornin', after she got you settled, Bridgett paced around like a dervish till I looked up the Martin's number. She called that conceited little twit and told her to get herself over here as soon as possible."

"She did?" Diana replied, encouraged by the older woman's candid criticism of the glamorous Mrs. Sanderson.

"I'm ashamed to say she did." Taking a long sip from her steaming cup, Sarah added thoughtfully, 'But what I cain't figure out is why she thinks that feather-brained gold-digger could make a good wife for my boy. It wasn't about to work before. And it ain't gonna work now. That's why he left and went into the Marines, you know."

"He told me."

"Did he now?" Sarah looked surprised.

"Well then, that explains a lot," the Cody matriarch stated cryptically. "It's no wonder Bridgett is havin' herself a hissy-fit."

"What do you mean?"

"If Sean's tellin' you personal things about himself, then he trusts you more than a mite. Bridgett has always been able to see right through the boy, which frets him somethin' awful, I might add. Makes sense now. She could tell, right off, that he's head-over-heels in love with you, and she set right out to put a stop to it."

"Wh... what? Why would you think such a

thing?" Diana stuttered, amazed. "I'm still married, and I'm much older than your son."

Before Sarah could answer, the door swung open, admitting the subjects of their conversation. Patting Diana's fingers indulgently, Mrs. Cody leaned her gray head close to her ear and whispered, "It's okay, dear, not to worry. Your secret's safe with me."

Shifting her attention to her children, she prompted, "I hope you two got things settled between you. I'm tired of your bickerin. I don't know how you manage to live together, up there in the big city."

The daughter opened her mouth to raise another objection, but her mother cut her off before she could speak. "Bridgett, why don't you take Diana into the front room and show her the family scrapbook? I'm sure she'd like to see some o' Sean's old baby pictures. He's gonna stay with me a spell and have a little talk."

Obeying the commanding woman's instructions without protest, Sean took the chair Diana vacated as she rose and followed his youngest sister. Bridgett pulled a dusty photo album out of a large bookshelf and retreated to a seat on the end of the sofa.

"Here, sit over by me where you can see," she instructed Diana. "This'll probably bore you silly, but when Mom gets like this, there's no use trying to defy her. She'll be in here in a minute to make sure we're doing as she said."

"It's fine, really," the graceful woman responded. "I'd like to see it." Diana offered the younger woman a friendly smile, receiving a determined frown in return.

For the next few minutes, they bent their heads over the old album, while Bridgett gave a running narration of each picture. Skip came in, started a fire, and switched on a lamp, as the pale rays of the setting sun waned into darkness. Then he pulled a chair up close to the hearth and propped his feet on the bricks.

Diana looked at pictures of Sean as a pink-cheeked, roly-poly infant, a bare-footed boy with scraped knees, and a handsome teen in the first blush of manhood, all hands and feet and Adam's apple. In almost every one, he was surrounded by one or more of his sisters, smiling brightly. She couldn't help laughing at the clever tales Bridgett proudly told her about her brother's daredevil escapades. When the last page was turned, the lonely woman suddenly felt the room closing in on her. The warmth of the fire was stifling and she gasped for breath. Her chest tightened painfully and her head throbbed.

"Thank you for sharing the album with me," she told Bridgett sincerely. "You have a lovely family." Almost choking on the thick knot of sadness, she added, "Excuse me, please."

A few desperate steps took her out through the front door, where Diana found herself on another porch, this one wider and more expansive that the one on the rear of the house. The bright beams cast down by the full moon fell on her. She bypassed a row of inviting rocking chairs, crossing to the front edge, where she leaned against the protective railing and drew in huge gulps of cool, fresh air. The evening breeze stung her flushed cheeks, but she welcomed the distraction from her tumultuous thoughts.

The Codys were special. What wouldn't she give to have such precious memories? More than anything, she wished she could accept Sean's proposal and become a valued member of this loving and supportive family, but deep in her heart, she knew that dream would never come true. It was impossible. Though they might pretend otherwise, his folks would resent her for forcing childlessness upon their only son. Sean deserved much more than she would ever be able to give him. He'd be an exceptional father. He should have children of his own – children with his maple syrup eyes, children to carry on the Cody name.

She took another deep breath to shore up her flagging courage. *I'll get away from here in the morning, without Sean,* she promised herself. *Bridgett will help me. If she wants me out of her brother's life as badly as she seems to, she'll do whatever it takes to be rid of me.* The thought of deceiving him tortured her but she didn't know what else to do. He'd probably never forgive her for leaving without saying goodbye. He might even hate her for it, but what did that matter? His ultimate happiness was more important. Of that she was convinced.

The screen door creaked behind her, breaking her concentration, but she didn't turn around. A pair of gentle hands placed the colorful shawl over her shoulders and remained there, softly caressing her collarbones. She smiled warmly and let her body relax against her visitor.

When her back contacted the wiry, hard-sinewed frame, she knew immediately that the man standing behind her was not the one she'd expected. She stiffened and drew away. The smile slowly disappeared from her lips as she whirled to face Skip, who shrugged and gave her a roguish grin, his teeth flashing in the moonlight.

"Sorry to disappoint," he breathed, his voice low and husky. "I sure do wish that look had been for me, though. It was a heart-pounder, I tell you." When she made no comment, he went on. "I was afraid you might be a little chilly out here, in the night air."

"Thanks." She tried to muster up a sad smile for him, too.

"So, does that thick-headed bastard have any idea what a lucky man he is?"

"Sean?"

"Who else?" Skip grinned again. "I guess he's just about the luckiest son-of-a-bitch I know."

She pulled the ends of the shawl around her arms. "You're very sweet."

"But...?"

"The feelings that Sean and I have, or don't have, are immaterial. There's no future for us." Despite her efforts to fight them, bitter tears filled her eyes.

"Uh...huh," he noted thoughtfully. "You might be able to sell yourself that line of horse shit, but I'm not buying it. Sean loves you and you love him. And you should be giving this thing between you your best shot."

Shaking her head determinedly, she whispered, "A week ago, I didn't believe in love at first sight. I was convinced that it wasn't possible to meet a man and know immediately that he's the one, but it happened, and I do. You'll have to trust me, Skip. It might not seem like it, but I know that what I'm going to do is the right thing for Sean, in the long run."

"And what's that?" he asked skeptically.

"I can't explain. Just promise me you'll be there for him." She swallowed hard. "It's okay if he despises me, because one day he'll realize that I only want him to be happy."

"What about your happiness?"

She lowered her face to hide the deep sorrow reflected there. "Doesn't matter. I've made so many bad choices in my life that I've stopped counting, but I refuse to pull Sean into the misery along with me. Don't misunderstand, I want nothing more than to spend the rest of my life with Sean, loving him and being loved by him, but it's simply not possible. He might not see that immediately, but he will."

"You play the martyr very well," Skip observed snidely. "Sacrificing yourself for others is a recurring theme in your life I take it."

His words struck a raw nerve. "How dare you say such a thing? You don't know anything about me."

"I know you're planning on dumping my good friend because you think that's what's best for him, even though you're sick in love with him." Skip's anger flared too. He gripped her shoulders firmly and shook her gently. "And you're making a huge mistake."

"You're entitled to your opinion, but you're wrong." Her face was a frosty mask of grim determination. "I refuse to let Sean ruin his life because he cares for me."

"The man's old enough to know what he wants, Diana. Have you even considered the possibility that you're the one woman for him, and that his future will be empty without you? Of course, you haven't," he warned.

She shook her head slowly. "I'm too old to give him the family he deserves."

"So?" Skip asked, incredulous. "From where I stand, he already has a pretty swell one of those. Seems to me the only thing he's missing is the right woman by his side."

"And children."

"There is that," he admitted softly. "But you should talk with Sean before you go jumping to the wrong conclusion." Raising her chin with his forefinger, he forced her to meet his gaze. "Promise me you will, Diana."

Sniffing back tears, she sighed deeply and nodded.

"Good." Then he chuckled playfully. "If you still decide to give that big meathead the boot, remember me, will ya? I'm a lot of fun to have around."

"What's this?" Sean's deep, booming baritone startled them both. "Are you moving in on my gal, Taylor? Man! Can't turn my back on you for one second."

"I'm not the one who's been sniffing after Miss Perfect, the dentist's wife, all afternoon," Skip countered. "I couldn't leave this lovely lady feeling neglected, now could I? It's not my fault you can't keep up with your women."

Ignoring his friend's jabs, Sean forced out a half-hearted apology. "Sorry, Diana. Skip's always been able to read me. Didn't take him long to figure out how I feel about you, so I quit pretending." Slipping a long arm around Diana's waist, he hugged her tightly. "Ahh, just what I've been waiting for all day – time alone with you."

He shot his buddy a sideways glance, and jerked his head toward the house. "Hint, hint. Time to split."

"Okay, okay, you don't have to hit me upside the head with a two-by-four." Before he left, he leaned close to Diana and whispered, "Don't forget your promise."

When Skip was safely inside, Sean asked her, "What was that all about?"

"Skip offered me his services, should I ever decide that you're not the man for me," she improvised.

"He did, did he?"

"Yep."

"And what did you promise him?" Sean's dark eyes were wide with amused curiosity.

"I said I would remember what he told me, that's all."

"Well, I didn't expect to have to duel for your favors quite this soon," he teased.

She punched him. "You don't have to worry. Skip's not my type." Struggling to keep the despair out of her voice, she told him, "I need for you to promise me something too, Sean."

"Anything."

"Promise me that no matter what happens tomorrow, you'll always know, in your heart, that I love you."

"Why the gloom and doom?" he quipped, sensing her dark mood and trying to lighten it.

Promise me," she insisted.

"Okay. I promise," he agreed, sealing it with a long, deeply stirring kiss, which Diana returned with equal ardor. When he finally pulled away, he smiled into her eyes. "Would you like to take another look at that frisky little colt before you turn in?"

"Oh yes," Diana answered, enthusiasm bubbling.

While the woman got reacquainted with the chestnut mare and her tiny foal, Sean refilled the mangers with fresh hay, and topped off the water tanks in each of the large barn's ten stalls. When he had finished, he leaned over the gate of the enclosure, where Diana sat with the colt's fuzzy head in her lap, and whistled softly. She looked up and smiled a contented smile that made his heart do an excited somersault. He motioned for her to join him.

She stood and waited for him to open the stall door. "What is it?" she asked.

"Shh...," he hushed her, index finger to his lips.

Repeating the beckoning gesture, he backed away, disappearing through a small door. Curious, Diana followed. Just as she cleared the opening, he flung the portal closed behind her, propped a saddle against it to prevent any unwanted intrusion, and swept her into his strong arms, lowering his lips to hers.

The kiss was hard and insistent, but she welcomed it and pressed her breasts firmly against the unyielding wall of his broad chest, telegraphing her desire. Pushing her down into a thick pile of straw, over which several horse blankets had been thrown, he covered her soft, supple body with his firm, muscular frame. They made frenzied, feverish love, each demanding and giving more than either had thought possible before. They drank their fill, driven by some inexplicable sense of desperation, by an unspoken, yet intuitive understanding that this time might be the last.

Even after their passion was spent, they lay entwined, whispering mutual declarations of undying love. Diana's limbs trembled. "Are you cold?" Sean asked, alert to her every movement.

She shook her head and brushed away his half-hearted attempts to draw some of her scattered clothing over her. "Just overwhelmed. Give me a second. I'll be okay."

He dropped a tender kiss on the tip of her nose. "That was pretty remarkable. It's like we're connected on some weird, subconscious level. Don't understand it, but... one thing's for sure; I didn't know making love could be like that. It was like I was feeling your body and your heart at the same time."

One lone tear slid down her fair cheek. "It was special and wonderful. When we're together I feel complete, like we make each other whole."

"That's it exactly."

Reluctantly, she wiggled out of his embrace and started retrieving her clothing.

"Where do you think you're going?" he teased, pulling her back for another deep kiss.

"It's late. I should get back before your sister comes looking for me," she insisted, drawing away again.

"You're right, unfortunately," he groaned, blowing out his breath in a frustrated whoosh. "Let me help you."

With his aid she was dressed quickly, kissing him once more and breathing "I love you" into his ear. She retreated on leaden feet, glancing back. Sean's strong, golden body sprawled in the middle of the pile of blankets, his muscular torso bare and his eyes closed, a satisfied smile on his full mouth.

"I'll see you at breakfast," he called without opening his eyes. She didn't respond.

When she entered the kitchen, she found Nelson and Missy sitting at the table, enjoying big slices of succulent pie. Bridgett was standing, her hip propped against the counter, her arms folded across her chest, her foot tapping impatiently. "It's about time you decided to come in. I have an early flight. I'm tired and need my sleep. Dad and Mom have already gone up. Where the hell have you been anyway? What were you doing?"

"I... uh, I was in the barn, visiting with the new foal, while Sean put out hay and watered the animals," Diana explained hesitantly.

Plucking a long piece of straw out of the older woman's flaxen locks, Bridgett sneered at her, waving the object in front of her nose like a prize. "Humph…you and Sean were taking a roll in that hay." Her older sister and brother-in-law looked up from their plates and stared at her in surprise. Bridgett relented cautiously, "Since you're finally here, I'm going to bed. Don't be long. I'm a light sleeper."

A bit intimidated by her intensity, Diana nodded. "I'll be right up."

Once Bridgett was out of earshot, Missy jumped to apologize. "Don't pay her any mind, Diana. She's always a grouch. Her job takes too much out of her. She has to be so nice to everyone, you know, and Bridgett has only so much niceness in her. The job uses it all up, so when she gets home there's none left over. Unfortunately for you, she's treating you just like one of the family."

Nelson issued an indistinguishable grunt. Diana wasn't sure if he was trying to offer support, or if his opinion of Bridgett differed from his wife's.

Diana chuckled. "I guess."

"Please don't hold it against her," Missy asked. "She doesn't mean anything by her gruff ways."

"I know," the tall blonde woman assured her. "She loves her family and has your best interests at heart."

Missy smiled at her, and patted her arm. "You sleep well, now."

"Yep," Nelson mumbled through another bite pie.

"Thanks…for everything," Diana added. "Please tell your mother, father, and sisters that I appreciate their hospitality. I've enjoyed meeting them all very much."

"You talk like you're leaving this very minute. You'll get to see most everyone at breakfast. You can tell them yourself." Missy winked encouragement at her. "We're up at the crack of dawn."

Not knowing what else to say, Diana smiled once more before pushing open the swinging door, crossing the foyer, and heading up the stairs. She stopped by the bathroom to wash her face, brush her teeth, and steel her nerves for another confrontation with the strong-willed Bridgett Cody.

Once inside the bedroom, she slipped out of her borrowed clothing and into Sean's T-shirt. Her recalcitrant roommate was already in bed, the bedside light turned down low. Diana hesitated to disturb her but knew she had no choice.

Whispering, she asked, "Bridgett, are you asleep?"

"No," the younger woman barked. "What do you want?"

Ignoring the belligerent tone, Diana told her, "I just want you to know that we don't have to be adversaries. You win."

"What do you mean?" Bridgett asked her, sitting up and plumping her pillows to support her back.

"I've thought a lot about what you said, and

you're right." Diana's words were stones weighting down her heart. "Sean deserves more than I can give him, so, if you'll help me get away from here in the morning, without his knowledge, I'll disappear from his life, and yours, for good."

Her dark eyes bright with pleasure, Bridgett argued, "It's a good idea, in theory, but I'm not sure how we'll make it work. Sean intends to go with you, so even if you leave without him, he'll follow you."

"If he does, he'll be too late."

"Huh?" The determined flight attendant grunted in confusion.

"Come on, Bridgett. You're a bright girl. Figure it out," Diana snapped, letting irritation seep in to cover her sorrow. "If your brother refuses to take such an obvious hint, and stubbornly trails me into Roanoke for the meeting, he'll be too late. I lied to Sean about the time. He thinks it's at ten, but I told James I'd meet him at 8:45 sharp. Given his usual efficiency, our business will be concluded well before Sean arrives. I'll be long gone – and out of his life forever."

"Aren't you a clever girl?" Bridgett chirped, her face alight with a satisfied glow. "Frankly, I'm surprised you've come to your senses, but since you're being so reasonable, I'll be glad to help you. I was planning to leave before seven anyway.

"Sean and Skip will be helping out with the milking, so we should be able to slip away while they're occupied. If we're lucky, no one will know you're gone until you don't come down for breakfast."

"Sounds good," Diana agreed. "Thanks."

"No, thank you." Smacking her pillow, Bridgett slid down and pulled up the covers. "Now get some sleep. You have a big day ahead of you, Mrs. North."

FIFTEEN

Bridgett had her rental car packed and ready to go well before the milking was finished. Then, she distracted the family, keeping them in the kitchen saying their farewells, while Diana slipped out the front door and into the waiting vehicle. She breathed a sigh of relief when the younger woman pulled the rental car out of the gravel road and onto the hard surface. "We made it!"

"Told you, didn't I?" Bridgett boasted. "I know my folks. They'll be surprised to find your bed empty when they go up to fetch you for breakfast."

"I guess." Diana's voice was sad and filled with regret. "I hate leaving like that, though. It seems so thoughtless and inconsiderate. You will express my thanks to them for me, won't you? I appreciate their kindness more than I can say."

"Sure, sure," she agreed impatiently. She watched the older woman surreptitiously and she drove. Diana sat quietly with her face lowered, staring at her hands. Though she couldn't be certain, Bridgett thought she saw a tear slide down the other woman's fair cheek, and drop onto the sleeve of the battered leather jacket she was wearing.

Diana's deeply resigned sadness moved her. Her heart softened a little. "You're traveling light," she observed, hoping to brighten the mood. "Made our getaway a lot easier."

Obviously surprised by Bridgett's uncharacteristic small talk, Diana responded hesitantly, "I guess so." Then she smiled sadly and held up her toiletry bag. "You know, it's funny. In little more than an hour from now this will be just about all I have left in the world."

"What are you talking about?" Bridgett quipped, skeptically. "I'm sure you'll get a big, fat settlement out of your old man."

Diana laughed derisively. "You'd think so, wouldn't you? But that's not the arrangement I've made with him. I get my freedom. James gets everything else."

Mulling over her words, Bridgett concluded. "You're going to give up everything you have, just so you can get a divorce?"

"More or less."

"And you're doing that why? – Because you're in love with my brother?"

"It's not quite that simple." When Bridgett looked at her askance, still unconvinced, Diana explained, "I was planning to leave James, even before I met Sean, and to use the divorce settlement as a negotiating tool. Unfortunately, the last few days have caused me to change my plans drastically. Now I just want to be free."

Her voice almost a whisper, she added, "I'll have a fresh start. It's all I want. James is welcome to all of our earthly possessions, as long as he keeps his word."

"His word about what?" Bridgett asked, curiously.

"Your brother."

"Sean? What does your dispute with your soon-to-be ex have to do with Sean? I thought this thing between you two had only been going on for a few days. How could he be involved in your marital problems."

"That's a question I'm not going to answer." Diana's face was set with grim determination. "I'm sorry. I've said too much already. Forget it, please. I'll be out of your life very soon. You won't have to see, or even think of me, ever again."

"Suits me fine," the dark-haired woman growled in irritation, squelching the sympathetic feelings that were beginning to blossom. Bridgett refused to let Diana see that she was moved by her display of courage and apparent strength of character. They rode on in silence. Three quarters of an hour later, Bridgett steered her rental car around the corner, adjacent to the Wells Fargo Tower, pulling onto a narrow side street. Easing the automobile up to the curb, she waited for her passenger to exit.

Diana opened the door and slid out. Then she hesitated, removed the leather bomber she was wearing over her worn sweatshirt and faded blue jeans, and tossed it onto the seat. "That's Sean's. See that he gets it, please, and tell him I said goodbye." Leaning her fair head inside, she added, "Thanks, Bridgett…for everything."

"No problem," the other woman snapped with

obvious relief.

"So long, then." Diana said, reaching for the car door.

"Yeah," Bridgett responded thoughtfully. Suddenly overcome with a sense of foreboding, and with it, unwanted feelings of concern for the older woman's welfare, she called out to her, "Hey, you gonna be okay?"

Diana nodded, but couldn't hide the tears filling her bright blue eyes. "Don't worry about me," the proud woman declared, slamming the door. She whirled around and marched away, back straight, shoulders proudly squared. Crossing the street, she waited until Bridgett's car was out of sight before she headed up the sidewalk and into the lobby of the huge building.

Once inside, Diana scanned the area for a clock, wishing she had her watch. Her eyes swept the almost deserted lobby as she moved toward the bank of elevators. She was quite surprised when she spotted her attorney, Curtis Sloan, standing off to one side, nervously running his fingers through his thinning hair.

Her boot heels clomping loudly on the polished marble floor, Diana crossed to him. "Hello, Curtis. What are you doing here?" she asked him, her face a mask of unreadable calm.

"Goodness sakes, Diana," he gasped, hugging her awkwardly. "I didn't recognize you. What's happened to you?" He held her at arm's length and looked her over from head to toe. "Why are you dressed like that? How did you get that terrible bruise on your face?"

"It's a long story," she evaded. Her suspicions aroused by his uncharacteristic fidgeting, she asked, "When did James contact you?" Looking him over carefully, too, she noted that he'd dropped more than a few pounds off his rotund frame, and had aged, years, almost overnight.

"Well...uh...he called yesterday and insisted that I drop everything and fly down here with him. Said it was urgent." A splotchy, crimson flush started at the top of his starched collar and spread upward until it reached his balding dome.

Something was definitely fishy. A warning scream coursed through Diana's body like an electric current. *This is bad, very bad,* she thought.

"James asked me to wait for you and escort you upstairs. They have a nice conference room reserved. Ready?" Curtis tried to take her elbow but she pulled away.

"Do I have any choice?" she smiled grimly.

He pushed the elevator button alight. The door to their left slid open immediately, and the lawyer gestured for her to precede him inside. Once the car was moving, she asked him, "So how long have you been doing business with my husband?"

"I... uh...I don't know what you mean, Diana. I'm your counsel, not James'. He just asked me to come along to protect your interests in the divorce agreement." Though it seemed impossible, his face reddened to an even deeper hue. Diana could almost see his nose growing.

"Be careful there, Curtis, a few more whoppers like that and your head is going to explode."

"Wha...huh?...uh..." he huffed, shamefaced and completely bereft of words. The elevator dinged open, and he breathed a huge sigh of relief. "Here we are!"

Diana let him guide her across the elegantly carpeted hallway and through an enormous set of polished mahogany doors. James was alone in the room, comfortably seated in a big swivel chair at the head of a huge conference table, behind an imposing stack of papers. He didn't rise to offer her a welcome, but grinned smugly at her as she crossed the floor. "Good God, Diana. You look like shit! Where'd you come by that get-up, a rag bag?"

She knew his assessment of her appearance was accurate, and despite her efforts to ignore his jabs, she cringed at his words. The expensive three-piece suit and designer shirt he was wearing, only served to intensify her discomfort. *The bastard,* she thought. *He'll go to any lengths to humiliate me.*

Launching a counter-attack, she lashed out at him. "My attire is from a second-hand shop, actually. I traded my engagement ring for it. I thought it wise to change my appearance, since I was running for my life. To complete the look, your buddy, Larry Stark, used my face as a punching bag. Of course, you probably know that already."

James wasn't at all surprised. Curtis Sloan was appalled. He drew in a shocked, rasping breath the woman could hear across the wide table. "What does she mean, James, running for her life? Who is this Stark person and why did he hit Diana? Why does she think you know anything about it?"

Waving off his questions as inconsequential,

James shook his perfectly coifed head, a practiced expression of benign innocence on his handsome face. "Apparently, the helicopter Diana chartered for her weekend flight had some sort of electrical malfunction. It blew up, quite by accident, and it's made her rather paranoid."

Turning his attention to Diana, he crooned, "You've been through quite an ordeal, my dear, but there's no need to exaggerate, or accuse. No one is trying to kill you. Calm yourself. Sit down." He pointed toward the chair on his left hand. "Curtis, get her a glass of water."

The heavy-set man rose from the seat he'd taken on the far side of the table, and moved to a long credenza where a large pitcher of ice water and several glasses had been placed. James leaned across the corner of the table toward his wife, playing the caring spouse role with supreme confidence. "Unless you'd rather have coffee. I could have some brought in."

"No, thank you," she snapped. "Can we just forego the social pleasantries and get down to it?"

"Fine, fine." He grinned at her again. "Forget the water, Curtis. It seems Mrs. North is all business today. Why don't you show her the divorce agreement I had you draw up?"

Sloan returned to the table and began shuffling through the pile of papers before him. His hands were shaking, making the task difficult. After several moments, he produced two identical folders, handed one to James and the other to Diana.

"Why did you involve him in this, James?" she asked. "Couldn't your lawyers have handled it?"

"My attorneys would make short work of a simple no-fault divorce, but Curtis brought himself into it when he schemed with you to rob me of my company. I thought it only fair that he see it through to the end. He'll not be getting much in the way of a fee; though, because he seems to have breached attorney-client privilege where this negotiation is concerned. Your trusted counsel has a problem keeping secrets. A good woman can pry almost anything out of him, if she knows the right way to do it. Isn't that right, Sloan?"

The portly man was sweating profusely, his face an alarming shade of purple. "I... uh...I'm sorry, Diana, but he has me by the short hairs."

James reached across the table and punched a button on the telephone that had been conveniently placed at his elbow. "You may come in, now," he announced into the speaker.

Seconds later, a small door, tucked neatly into the wall behind James, swung open. Sheila Stewart flounced in. She flashed Diana a victorious grin, her pixie face surrounded by a glowing cloud of curly red hair that crackled with warmth and cried out to be touched. Diana imagined Sean running his fingers through those crimson locks and her stomach heaved. She wondered how the petite secretary kept her balance in the unnaturally high heels she wore, but with practiced precision, Sheila sashayed to an empty chair, swinging her hips seductively.

"Hel-lo Curtis," she purred, tossing James a conspiratorial wink. "You see, my dear Diana. Uh… may I call you Diana?" Sheila paused briefly.

Since it was apparent that she'd been using the intercom to listen in on the conversation, and equally clear that she wasn't expecting a response, Diana didn't bother to give her one.

"You see, Diana, your lawyer here has a tendency to get carried away with his pillow talk. Show him a good time and he'll tell you anything. I don't think I've ever seen a man so desperate for some action." Reaching out, she patted Sloan's pudgy hand indulgently.

"Except for that jar-head helicopter pilot of yours, of course. It amazes me that he was so hard-up that he screwed you – the old, ice-queen, bitch herself. He's a good-looking bastard. I'll give him that. Not as handsome or classy as my Jamie, of course, but if you like the tough-guy, roughneck sort, he'll do. Could have done much better than you if he'd tried at all.

"On second thought," she grinned wickedly and winked at James again, "It probably wasn't desperation at all. Pity, that's what it was. The poor jerk felt so sorry for you that he gave you a little poke out of the kindness of his heart."

The usually proper, James W. North, III, laughed nervously, his eyes darting around the room, clearly embarrassed by Sheila's crudeness. Diana couldn't resist throwing out a sarcastic barb. "Bet you can't wait to take her home to meet dear old Mom and Dad. Her eloquent choice of words will make quite an impression on your folks and their high-society friends when you show her off at the country club."

Flashing Diana a look of pure hatred, he

refused to rise to the challenge, but directed his comments to his mistress instead. "Not pity, my dear Sheila. Our clever Mr. Cody is motivated by cold, hard cash. His absence today proves the self-righteous bastard's no better than the rest of us, willing to screw anyone for money. He knows payday's not coming, as he'd hoped, so he's abandoned his cash cow, leaving her to face us alone."

"Yeah. That should bring you down a peg or two," Sheila chimed in, reveling in the humiliation being heaped onto Diana, repaying the older woman for the painful jab she'd just scored. "You poor thing, dumped by your young stud even before you're officially penniless. I thought he'd come along, to try one more time to change your mind about the settlement. I didn't figure he'd give up so easily."

Her husband added. "I expected more out of the guy myself. Where is the son-of-a-bitch, by the way?"

"Right here!" snarled a raspy voice from the hallway. As if on cue, Sean's huge frame was shoved into the room, the force of the blow throwing him to one knee. Stark entered behind him, closing the portal, his automatic weapon leveled at the middle of Cody's back.

Diana sprang from her chair and ran to Sean. "Are you all right?"

He shook his dark head and slowly rose to his feet. "I'm fine, just furious with myself for letting that sneaky bastard get the drop on me again."

"Why did you follow me?" she asked him, her

eyes filling with tears of regret, her voice edgy with apprehension.

"I couldn't let you go through this alone, Diana. We're a team, now." Ignoring their audience, who were watching with intense interest, he took her hand and squeezed.

"How did you figure out I was gone?" The rest of the people in the room melted into the walls. For Diana, there was no one present but Sean.

"After your little discussion with Skip, he warned me that you were gonna pull something. I heard Bridgett leave, so I went to check on you and found your bed empty. I grabbed Nelson's Jeep and headed after you. I was almost here when Bridgett rang my cell to tell me you'd mislead me about the meeting time."

"Bridgett called you?" Diana could hardly believe her ears.

"She was worried about you. She phoned the house first, and Missy told her I was already on the way. But this damned building has too many lawyers' offices. I had to check every one, from the ground-floor up. That slowed me down and gave Stark time to intercept me. As soon as I poked my fat head out of the elevator, he stuck that damned pistol in my face." Staring into her crystal blue eyes, he silently conveyed encouragement.

"I've had all of this tearful reunion I can stand," the FBI agent growled, as he waved his weapon in the general direction of the long table. "Get over there, both of you."

His voice shaking, Curtis Sloan asked James, "Who are these men? Why does that one have a gun?"

"All will be explained in good time," the NSE Chairman replied. "Don't you worry."

"Now, Diana, sit down and sign!" he ordered.

"Not until you hand over everything you promised, James. Every last shred of your concocted evidence." Her frosty blue eyes flashed with determination.

"As you wish." Grinning arrogantly, he slid a pile of documents and flash drives across the table toward her.

"Is this all of it?"

"Every bit. Now sign."

Pulling her chair up under the table, Diana briefly scanned the document as she flipped the sheets. When she reached the last page, she took the pen Sheila was holding out to her and touched the point to the paper, hesitating when she noticed that the date was already printed under the signature line. "This is dated last week, James. What are you up to?"

"It's simply a precaution, Diana," he explained, "in case you renege on our deal, and go to the authorities with your little helicopter-explosion conspiracy theory. It removes any motive I might have had for trying to eliminate you, because the date on this document proves you had already signed everything over to me. So, I can't be implicated in any accusations you might make because I'd have no motive."

"Stop asking stupid questions and sign the damn thing," Sheila hissed, crossing behind James and hugging his neck possessively. "Unless you'd rather have your lover cooling his heels in a federal prison." She picked up one of the flash drives and waved it around threateningly.

"Don't do it, Diana. Their evidence is manufactured. I'll never stand up in court. Call his bluff," Sean urged her.

"Just as I expected, "James interjected. "What's the matter, Cody? Watching your gravy train pull out of the station giving you a queasy stomach?"

Leaning his elegant head toward Diana's, he warned, "All he wants is your money. He's going to dump you when you do, but since you're head over heels in love with the bastard, I know you can't stand to see him hurt. So, sign!"

Stark took a step closer, placing the muzzle of his semi-automatic against the back of Sean's head. "Give me an excuse. Please," he taunted. "At this range, one shot would leave a hole the size of a softball where his pretty face used to be."

While her attorney shifted nervously, Diana took up the pen and scratched her signature. "Now, tell your pit-bull to back off."

Sighing with satisfaction, James stretched backward, smiled smugly, and laced his fingers together over his vest. "Stark, that's enough. We have what we want. Put that thing away."

The special agent made no move to comply with the North Star CEO's order. Instead, he crowed, "No, I don't think so, James. I expected you'd wimp out on us in the end. You might have everything you want but my little sister's desires are not so easily satisfied."

"Your sister?" Sean's dark eyebrows were

drawn together in surprise.

"Yes, you stupid fool. I'm Sheila's big brother, and I always see that she has her fondest wishes fulfilled."

"What more could you possibly want, my dear?" James asked her, his face suddenly pale. "We have complete control of North Star and more money than you'll ever be able to spend. As soon as the divorce papers are recorded, we can get married. Isn't that enough?"

"Don't be obtuse, darling." Sheila's pouty lower lip stuck out petulantly. An abrupt change came over her pixie face as she explained, "Marriage to you and a full partnership in your company are only a fraction of my demands. I want revenge. I deserve it." She tossed Sean a scathing glance, full of fury bordering on madness.

"That hard-hearted son-of-a-bitch rejected my affections and I want him to pay, and pay dearly. No man tosses Sheila Stark Stewart out of his bed without consequences. I want to see him beg for his worthless life."

"Sheila, my sweet, you should try to put your need for vengeance behind you," James pleaded, and Diana detected a note of desperation in his usually controlled voice. "You've won We've won. There's no need for more violence."

"You spineless jellyfish," the fiery redhead hissed at him. Giving up all pretense of compliance, she let her viscous narcissism show through. "You have no backbone at all, do you? If it weren't for dear old daddy's bankroll, and dependable wifey's creativity, you'd be nothing. NSE would be nothing."

Sheila stalked around the room like a tiny, deadly cat on the prowl. "I waited and waited for you to deal with your ice-queen bitch, waited until I was ready to pull my hair out. I'd still be waiting, too, if I hadn't taken matters into my own hands." Her voice rose shrilly as her tirade intensified.

"Thank goodness old Curtis was so pitifully needy. He was an easy mark. Cleverly manipulated." The portly attorney dropped his face into his beefy hands to hide the tears of shame that slid over his round cheeks.

"If it wasn't for me, you wouldn't have known anything about Diana's plans to divorce you and take half of your fortune, until it was too late. Without my help, she'd have gotten the best of you and you know it! Don't you remember how furious you were when you saw the copies I made of her two proposals? You wanted to punish the high and mighty bitch just as much as I wanted to get even with that conceited bastard." She jabbed an orange-tipped claw in Sean's face.

"I remember. I was angry. I wanted Diana out of my life for good, but I didn't want her dead," James claimed, his composure continuing to slip. Beads of sweat trickled down his temples. "I was appalled when you told me Larry had rigged their helicopter to explode."

"Yeah, well, you didn't object too loudly."

"What could I do?" he asked breathlessly. "It was too late to protest. The damage was already done. I had to try to make peace with the contribution I'd unknowingly made to the deaths of two people."

Turning to his wife, he added, "I know there's never been much affection between us, Diana, but believe me, I had nothing to do with the attempts on your life."

Though Diana failed to respond to his denial, Sheila was quick with her rebuttal. "That's bullshit, James. You're no innocent victim here. It might not have been your idea, since you have been conveniently void of any good ideas, but you're complicit. You were fully aware that your cheating wife, and my heartless lover, had somehow escaped the untimely death we'd planned for them, but you didn't raise a hand to stop Larry from pursuing them. You knew full well that he planned to finish the job he'd started.

"You provided us with Diana's credit card number and the cell number that got us the access codes to the Randall's lake house."

"I didn't have any choice," he countered, loosening his tie with a jerk.

"Sure, you did," Stark disagreed, grinning. "We all had choices. You could have gone to the authorities with your story at any time, James. But you weren't about to risk losing your position, power, or reputation, so you went along on the ride, and now you have to pay for the ticket. You get to watch your lovely ex and her handsome stud die." He raised the pistol again.

"Wait," James urged him. "Diana kept her end of the bargain. She signed the agreement. As soon as the divorce is finalized and recorded, NSE is ours. You said you'd let them leave safely if she signed."

"I lied." Reaching across the table to the stack of papers in front of North, Stark lifted up the divorce document and scanned it. Then to the surprise of everyone present, he tore the sheets in half. "So much for that!"

"What're you doing?" James screamed at him.

Ignoring his outburst, Stark pulled Sean's nickel-plated pistol out of the waistband of his pants. "Too bad you were in such a hurry the other night. You left this." Tossing the gun into Sean's lap, he ordered, "Pick it up!"

"And if he doesn't?" James asked, his eyes darting back and forth between the two men.

"He'll blow my brains out first and place it in my limp hand," the former Marine explained.

"Very good," Stark commented, grinning again.

"I don't understand, Larry," James' eyes were wide with terror. "Why did you let me go through this charade, forcing Diana to sign the divorce papers, if you had other plans all along?

"Goddammit, James. How can you be so stupid and blind? You had to play out your part so I could be assured of your compliance, and so I could see the queen of NSE, the royal ice-bitch humbled. I needed to witness it, as she fell to her knees and handed over everything to you, just to save her bastard lover's neck." Sheila shrieked in frustration.

"Now that it's done, we can get on with it. You might be dense as a post, James, but Sean isn't. He has it all figured out. Don't you, sweetie?" Sauntering around the table, she wrapped her arms around the pilot's neck and kissed him on the ear, pretending not to be bothered by his efforts to shake off her advances. "Please tell my fiancé what's about to happen."

"As you wish," he agreed, buying time. "Our friend Stark fancies himself a writer of cheesy detective stories. He likes to create dramatic scenarios for others to enjoy. He's setting the scene to make this meeting look like a ransom exchange. He probably has me, the crazed kidnapper, flying into a fit of rage when I realize that he, the brilliant FBI operative, has trapped me with no means of escape. He'll claim that I, in my fury, shot my poor victim and turned my weapon on the rest of you. Which is why he wants my prints on this gun. Of course, he's here to save the day by killing me and sparing the lives of everyone else. That about it?"

"Pretty close." Stark grinned devilishly.

"But why destroy the divorce papers?" James asked, clearly distressed beyond all ability to reason.

"Because a post-dated, signed divorce settlement, leaving everything to you, would weaken his story," Sean explained calmly. "Why would you pay a multi-million-dollar ransom for an ex who has no claim on your fortune, and no interest in your corporation? A wife you never loved and couldn't wait to be rid of?"

When James dropped his face into his hands, Sean added, "Don't fret. With your wife dead, the divorce settlement is unnecessary. You'll inherit everything anyway. And with me out of the way, there'll be no one left to link you to the helicopter explosion."

"Larry, please," James begged. "Here's another copy of the agreement." He waved the thick document at Stark. "Diana will sign it, and we can let them go. They won't accuse us of anything, and even if they did, there'll be no proof. You can't possibly be thinking of murdering them, right here before our eyes. It's just too horrible to consider."

He turned to Sheila and continued his plea. "Isn't it enough to see them humiliated, to know they'll live out their miserable little lives struggling to make ends meet, fully aware that we forced them to give up a fortune?"

Turning on his considerable charm, he approached her. "Sheila, darling. We've been lucky. No one has been hurt so far. Let's count our blessings, take the money, and run. Like we agreed. Talk to your brother before it's too late."

Tossing her fiery curls, she glared at him. "Larry and I brought us to this point, James, not you, and I refuse to be thwarted now. You wanted to back out the minute your ice-bitch melted over her hot-blooded stud and caved-in to your demands, but I'm not gonna let that happen. I still want it all, the whole enchilada – your name, your money, your company, and my revenge. No one treats me with disrespect and disregard and gets away with it. I want to see them begging for their worthless lives, just as brother-dear puts a couple of bullets in their brains."

"Two people have to die for you to feel avenged?" he asked her, his eyes shining with disbelief.

"Three, actually," Stark cut in.

"Three? Is there any end to your blood lust? Who else are you going to kill?" Though the agent refused to answer the question, he cut his eyes sharply toward at the portly attorney cringing behind the table. The dangerous flush had disappeared from Sloan's full cheeks, replaced by a deathly shade of gray.

Unable to keep his seat one second longer, James pushed his chair back from the table and stepped toward the federal man. Diana had never seen him so angry, or so frightened.

Stark warned him off with a flash of the pistol barrel. "I'd hate to use this on you, North, but a well-aimed shot would easily disable you without any permanent damage. And I'd have no trouble explaining how you got caught in the crossfire. Now sit down and shut up, so we can get on with it."

"Here, Sis, hold this." He handed her his gun while he removed a pair of latex gloves from his coat pocket and snapped them on. Then he took Sean's weapon, loaded it with several rounds, and aimed it at the chubby attorney. "Sorry, Sloan. I hate to do this, really. You're basically a good guy – just a little needy. But you know too much and we can't trust you to keep your mouth shut."

The barrister looked back at him unemotionally, as if he'd accepted his fate as his reward for his unintentional betrayal of Diana's confidence. He raised his eyes to her in apology.

"You can't do this," James rasped breathlessly. "How will you make murdering Curtis fit into your story?"

"That's an easy one. While they were dating, my dear sister overheard a phone conversation between Mr. Sloan and our over-eager, somewhat deranged kidnapper. She'll testify that they were working together. His partner shot him when their plan began to fall apart. I tried to stop Cody before he fired, but I was just too slow." Raising the nickel-plated revolver once more, he pointed it at the center of Curtis's chest.

SIXTEEN

Diana froze. Her mind screamed at her body to act, to do something to save the life of her long-time friend and associate, but her fingers encircled the arm of her chair like steel clamps, and her feet seemed buried in huge blocks of solid concrete. Liquid fear coursed through her veins, leaving her trembling helplessly.

A sharp report shattered the heavy silence of the boardroom. Her wide blue eyes snapped to the terrified man across the table from her. She watched Sloan's face intently, expecting to see the spark of life flicker out as his body slumped in his seat. Horrified by Stark's cold-blooded actions, seconds passed before she realized that the agent had not discharged the weapon. Instead, he'd whirled to face the door, the unfired weapon concealed behind his back.

Following the direction of his gaze, her numb brain slowly allowed the scene to creep into focus. A maintenance worker was trying to back a heavily loaded cart into the room, repeatedly flinging open the door so that it slammed against the metal stop behind it, causing the shot-like retorts. Dressed in a nondescript coverall, grimy John Deere cap, and dirty work boots, the man rattled his assortment of mops and buckets with abandon, oblivious to the din he created, and to those already occupying the conference room.

Slowing turning, the janitor started with surprise. Recovering quickly, he grinned sheepishly. "S'cuse me, folks. Didn't know ya'll was in here," he drawled, ripping off the earbuds he wore under his soiled hat. "Thought this room was empty. Your meetin' ain't on the schedule. With these here plugs in I cain't hear a blasted thing." He tugged at the earphones swinging around his neck. "Didn't mean to bother ya none."

Diana stared at the man, slack-jawed, as recognition dawned. It was Skip. Sean leaned toward her and whispered, "Close your mouth, love, and be ready to dive under the table."

"Well, you know now," Stark snapped at him. "So, get out!"

"Okay, man, be cool." Skip grinned even wider as he slid out of the country-bumpkin vernacular and back into his more comfortable surfer-dude banter. "Whatcher hurry? I'm a'goin'. Keep your pants on." Struggling with the unwieldy vehicle, he made it a production of trying to swing the contraption around and maneuver it back out the door. "Just give me a mo here, I'll get this baby movin' in a sec." He fumbled with the conveyance again, pushing it one way and pulling it another, grunting and groaning with the effort.

"Well, shit," he breathed, grinning again. "No wonder I was havin' such a problem. Damn brake's on." As he released an imaginary lever, Skip gave the cart a hard shove that send it barreling directly at Stark.

Like a stalking tiger intent on its prey, Skip crouched on his haunches, leveling the semiautomatic weapon, which had suddenly appeared in his hands, at the surprised federal agent, who tried too late, to dodge the careening cart. It struck him squarely in the solar plexus, knocking the wind out of him.

Sean shouted for Diana to take cover as he sprang from his chair, relieving Stark of the weapon which dangled from his limp fingers as he gasped for breath. In their haste to disarm the dangerous man, both ex-Marines overlooked and underestimated his vicious, vindictive, and heavily-armed sister. It was lucky for them all that Diana did not make the same mistake.

Instead of ducking under the table, as Sean had ordered her to do, the terrified woman remained frozen in her seat, her clear blue eyes locked on his broad back. The sigh of relief she was about to expel, when Sean grabbed his pistol from the disabled Stark, congealed in her throat. Another imminent threat – this one equally deadly, drew her gaze.

Driven by her lust for revenge, Sheila had reacted quickly, positioning herself for a clear shot at her former lover. She had the pistol raised and Sean in her sights. Fire in her eyes, her finger curled around the trigger.

Adrenaline surged. The muscles of Diana's long legs contracted involuntarily, propelling her out of her chair and directly at the smaller woman. Diana hit Sheila with the force of a linebacker attacking a tackling dummy, driving the tiny woman to the floor. Crying out in surprise and fury, the determined redhead repeatedly squeezed the trigger she was still gripping tightly. Shots rained indiscriminately around the room, until Diana wrestled her wiggling body into submission and grabbed her wrist, wrenching the weapon from her fingers.

Then Sean was there to take charge of the still smoking pistol. "You okay?" he asked her, his dark eyes smoldering with concern. When she nodded hesitantly, he let out a breath and smiled in relief. "Anyone hurt?" he asked.

Curtis Sloan, his ruddy face an ashen gray, patted himself, searching for injuries. Finding none, he exhaled deeply. "I'm okay, but James needs help." An agonized groan emanated from the corner of the room.

Leaving Sheila in Sean's competent hands, Diana rounded the table and knelt beside her husband. The threat Stark had issued moments before echoed in her head. James lay on his back, grasping his chest with both hands. A crimson stream gushed out despite his efforts to staunch the flow.

Ripping her sweatshirt over her head, the frantic woman pressed the makeshift compress over the gory wound. "Call 911!" she screamed.

"Already on the way," Skip reassured her. "Sean's wired. The FBI and local police have been monitoring us. The shots will bring 'em running."

Before his words were completely out of his mouth, the blue suits swarmed in. Seconds later, two EMT's crouched beside Diana. Pushing her aside, they began their triage procedure.

"Wait, Diana," the injured man groaned, reaching out a bloodstained hand. "I need…I need to tell you something."

"Later, James," she whispered, her voice thick with emotion. "Let these men help you. We'll talk later."

"No!" he protested with his remaining strength. "I need to say this now, in case I don't…"

Understanding his unspoken fear, she crouched beside him again, her ear close to his mouth.

Choking on the blood bubbling between his lips, James forced out the words he was determined to say. "Please forgive me…for…everything."

Her heart aching, Diana smiled down at him. "Of course, James," was all she could bring herself to say. It seemed to be enough to satisfy the dying man. Closing his eyes in acceptance, he resigned himself to the care of the efficient technicians. They worked furiously, but Diana knew their efforts would be futile.

"Come on, love." Sean tugged at the sleeve of her sweater. "Let's get you out of here. These guys will mop up." He indicated the efficient agents and officers who'd taken charge of the scene, two of whom were still struggling to handcuff the hissing, spitting redhead. "They know where to find us when they're ready for our statements."

Wrapping a long arm around her shoulders, he led her out of the plush boardroom and across the lobby. Skip and Curtis Sloan followed closely. Sheila hurled scathing curses at their retreating backs but her vindictive threats landed harmlessly.

When elevator doors slid open and they stepped inside, Diana let the flood of sorrow wash over her. By the time they reached the ground floor, she was sobbing uncontrollably. The world swam through a veil of tears. Sean had to guide her outside and into a waiting automobile.

He slipped his battered jacket around her shoulders and held her tenderly, while she cried herself out. A long time later, the wrenching sobs diminished and the flood of tears subsided.

Diana found herself in the backseat of Nelson's Jeep, squeezed between Sean and Skip. Bridgett was behind the wheel. Curtis Sloan rode shotgun, nervously eyeing the young woman, as she wheeled the vehicle through the curves of the winding country roads with practiced skill.

She wondered why Bridgett was driving the four-wheeler instead of her rental car, but her numb brain couldn't hold the thought long enough to ask. Sighing softly, she lifted her face to look at Sean. Noting the change in her, the pilot brushed a soft kiss against her hair. "Feeling better?" he asked hopefully. Slowly returning from the deep well of sorrow, Diana attempted a sad smile. "We'll be home soon."

Her strength gone, the woman mustered no protest but let the man take control, doing with her as he pleased. Resting her head against his wide, strong chest, she closed her eyes and let her mind go mercifully blank, until the crunch of gravel under the car tires brought her back. When the SUV rolled to a stop, Sean opened the door and helped her out.

"I'm taking Diana up to my room. She needs to rest," he informed his sister, his authoritative tone booking no disagreement. "We'll be in for dinner. Everyone can question us all they want – then. In the meantime, Skip can fill them in. And get Mr. Sloan a stiff drink. Looks like he could use it."

Nodding sharply to his former Captain, Skip clapped the heavy-set man on the back and urged him toward the back porch. "C'mon, Curt, my man. Mike Cody always has a quart or two of high-quality moonshine. If that doesn't put the roses back into your cheeks, nothing will. Uncharacteristically quiet, Bridgett led the men into the big, white house.

Supporting Diana with a muscular arm clamped tightly around her waist, Sean helped her across the yard, and up a wooden staircase to his apartment above the garage. He was worried. In the past week he'd seen her weather unexpected hardship, and terrifying danger, with unflagging courage and iron-willed determination. Now, she seemed totally drained. She'd reached her breaking point, and passed it. He wondered what it would take to bring her back.

He turned down the covers on his bed, helped her pull off her boots and jeans, and slipped her between the cool sheets. Throughout his ministrations, she made no sound, no gesture of gratitude, no response whatsoever, except for one sad, haunting smile. When she was settled in, he stretched out beside her, spooning his body against her back and lending her his warmth.

He felt her jerk as she fell into a restless slumber, and while she slept, he comforted her, whispering soothing encouragement in her ear when she whimpered and moaned. A blurry memory of the night when she'd performed the same service for him, touched his consciousness. *Seems like an eternity ago,* he thought.

Diana slept on until the distinctive roaring of a farm tractor roused her. Stretching and yawning, she rolled toward Sean. He was relieved to see that a faint sparkle had returned to her eyes and her timid smile was a bit brighter. Her resiliency amazed him.

"What will your family think?" she asked softly, her voice teasing. "Bringing me up here to your room?"

He shrugged noncommittally. "They've learned that there are times when it's best not to question me. And this is one of those times. If they dare complain, I'll remind them that I've done worse things than spend a couple of hours in bed with a beautiful woman."

"What about Bridgett? She's probably in the kitchen inciting your family to rally against me, the selfish cradle-robber that I am. I don't think I'm prepared to do battle with her again."

Her tone was light and mocking. Still, Sean felt compelled to reassure her. "I think you'll be pleasantly surprised by the change that has come over my very cynical sister. Bridgett's in your corner now."

Diana's eyes widened in amazement. "How in the world did that happen?"

"It's complicated, and a bit hard to explain, but to give you the 'Cliff Notes' version, Bridgett became the communications hub of our little rescue operation. She heard every word that was said inside that boardroom, after I arrived, and relayed the action to the cops."

Confused, Diana stuttered, "Bridgett had a plane to catch. Why was she still at the Wells Fargo building helping you? How did she hear what was going on? And what did she do with her car?"

His deep, sexy laugh vibrated through his body. "After she spoke with me, my stubborn sister figured we could use another hand, so she called the airline, told them she wouldn't make her flight, and asked them to send someone to pick up her rental. She was waiting on the corner when I got there, cell phone in hand.

"It's amazing how ingenious you can be, when you're truly desperate. Skip and I rigged up a makeshift relay system, using cell phones and a set of earbuds with a built-in microphone. It worked, thanks to Bridgett."

Diana fell silent, distracted. She looked away. It was several long moments before her gaze met his again. Her eyes were brimming with tears. Not wanting to pressure her, Sean waited patiently for her to put her thoughts, her fears, into words. "James is dead. Isn't he?"

Sean nodded grimly. "I think so. I warned the

family not to disturb us until dinnertime, on the threat of bodily harm, but I expect there'll be a message waiting for you."

She sighed. "And there'll be questions to answer and arrangements to make." Her body sagged against him. "I've postponed the inevitable long enough." She started to rise from the bed but he pulled her back.

"Are you sure you're ready? No one's rushing you, Diana. Take all the time you need." He cradled her in the crook of his elbow, his strong arms holding her secure. It was so very tempting to stay there, lost in his maple syrup eyes, but she resisted with considerable effort.

"I'm ready." She smiled warmly at him.

"Then we'd better go." Though his words echoed hers, he made no move to follow through on them.

Diana drew away from his embrace once more, only to have him resist yet again. "Wait," he whispered in her ear. "You need this for courage." Grinning suggestively, he lowered his mouth to hers.

Buoyed considerably by the kiss, Diana withdrew before the shared caresses led to something more intimate. Knowing she couldn't enjoy another romantic interlude with Sean and still maintain the strength to walk away from him, she left his bed using nature's call as a convenient excuse.

When she'd escaped to the tiny bathroom, she splashed her face with cold water and ran her fingers through her disheveled hair. She offered encouragement to the exhausted woman she saw gazing back at her in the mirror above the sink. "Chin up, girl. You can do this." Wishing she had a brush or some lip-gloss, she forced a smile and pushed the door open with a flourish.

"Better?" Sean asked her.

She chuckled ruefully. "A little, I guess, but I really feel silly. After you risked your neck to save it, and we carted the darned thing all over the countryside, I've gone and lost my toiletry kit."

He smiled at her indulgently. "So what? You can afford to replace it."

"Yeah," she agreed. "It's so weird. A few hours ago, I told Bridgett that after my meeting with James, the little bag would be just about all I'd have left in the world. Now, the bag's gone, and I have a multi-national corporation, and billions of dollars in assets. This's definitely not how I expected things to turn out."

"You'll make a good CEO, Diana. Don't doubt yourself," he encouraged.

"Maybe." She chewed a nail thoughtfully, a thoroughly disagreeable but possibly workable idea beginning to form. "Well, let's go. I'm anxious to see if there's been any word about James's condition."

Their worst suspicions were confirmed as soon as they entered the bright, cheery kitchen. Bridgett handed Diana a note, hugging her briefly. "I'm sorry. Your husband didn't make it. You're to phone the coroner to let him know what arrangements you want to make."

The rest of the Cody clan steered clear, but Sean stayed with Diana while she made the necessary calls. The first one she placed to James's nephew, Justin, who, in his usual classy style, offered to handle things at home. Then she made the second, empowering James' assistant to arrange for his body to be sent home to Northern Virginia. When that odious task was finished, she turned to the big man at her side, welcoming his embrace, hoping he could warm away the cold which had seeped into her bones and set her to shivering.

"It's gonna be okay, Diana," he assured her. Squeezing her tightly, he prompted. "Smells like dinner's ready. Do you think you can eat?"

"I'll try."

"That's my girl," he praised, leading the way.

"Oh good, there you are," Sarah Cody gushed, hugging Diana tightly. "You poor child. Come on over here and set yourself down. I made sure those gluttonous men saved you a chair."

All eyes on her, she took the proffered place, already hating herself for what she was about to do. She let Sean's mother wait on her, filling her plate from the brimming bowls without protest. The food did smell inviting but she had no appetite. Not wanting to offend her kind hostess, she forced down a few bites.

Once Diana and Sean were served, the rest went back to enjoying their meal. After a few minutes, Mike Cody breached the silence, asking the question that was on the tip of everyone's tongue. "What's happened, exactly? Tell us everything. Bridgett and Skip have been as close-mouthed as two monks, and I'm fed up with all this cloak and dagger nonsense."

Diana turned pleading eyes on Sean. Knowing she wasn't up to explaining, he wiped his mouth with his napkin and recounted, in depth, the events that had taken place since he and Diana lifted off from the Baldwin Aviation hangar on Friday morning. He even filled in some gaps for Diana about how the successful rescue had been orchestrated. It pleased her to know that Sean and Skip had planned for all contingencies.

Sean told them that he'd expected some sort of treachery from Stark, so the previous evening, after everyone else had gone to bed, he'd contacted a former platoon-mate who was now an employee of the Bureau. Calling in a favor, he arranged for a trustworthy operative to meet him outside the Wells Fargo Tower. The special agent was already on his way to the rendezvous when Sean phoned to tell him that he'd been misled about the time. So, in a matter of minutes, he and the local police were on the scene.

Diana noted gratefully, and with pleasure, that he told his family almost everything, omitting only the most private and personal details. They didn't interrupt and when he was finished, they all stared at him in amazement.

J.D. whistled appreciatively. "That's quite a tale."

His wife added, "You've had an even bigger adventure than you let on."

Missy wiped her eyes with her apron, sniffed, and said, "How horrible for you, Diana. I just can't imagine how you endured it all."

"Diana's a very brave and resourceful woman." The declaration shocked the entire clan, coming as it did from the businesswoman's most determined detractor. Her mother smiled knowingly when Bridgett expounded, "Unselfish, too. She tried to trick Sean about the time of the meeting to protect him, and agreed to give up her entire fortune, just to make sure he wouldn't be harmed."

"Thank goodness that wasn't necessary," Kathleen put in, always concerned about finances. "I'm sorry about your husband, of course. It's a terrible shame. I know it's no consolation, but at least you still have your company, and now you can make the changes you wanted to make."

Smiling at Kathleen's pragmatism, and thinking that she would gladly sacrifice it all for the impossible dream of a simple, peaceful life with Sean, Diana told her, "That's true, and I'm also extremely grateful no one else was hurt."

Curtis Sloan interjected, "I say AMEN to that." He patted his generous stomach. "It would have been hard to enjoy this fabulous spread with a belly full of lead."

The rotund attorney's droll delivery struck Bridgett's funny bone. Her family watched in amazement as the usually humorless sister doubled over in hysterical laughter.

"My goodness, Curtis. You're a hoot," she wheezed, her mirthful spasms subsiding. Her dark eyes twinkled at him suggestively. The look the man sent her in return was as obvious an invitation as anyone at the table had ever seen, bringing giggles and knowing smiles from Bridgett's sisters.

"I take it you and Mr. Sloan will be seeing a bit more of each other, once you get back to D.C.," Ellen noted.

Embarrassed by their transparency, Bridgett sported an uncharacteristic flush of high color. "I think so," she admitted. "Curtis and I have a lot in common. We enjoy one another's company." He covered her hand with his.

"About time," Sean prodded her. "I thought you'd never find a fellow who'd be willing to take you off my hands. Curtis, my man, do you have any idea what you're getting yourself into? The woman's an impossible old maid."

"OOOOH!" Bridgett screeched, swallowing the bait whole. "How dare you say such an insulting thing, you spoiled, conceited jackass! After all I did to save your worthless neck, you have the unmitigated gall to belittle me. Sean Cody, you're insufferable!" She stood over him threateningly, her fists propped on her hips, ready for action. Long seconds passed before she realized he was teasing her. and that she'd fallen headlong into his trap.

When his broad, guilty smirk finally pierced her fury, her ire evaporated. She returned his grin, and punched him hard on the upper arm.

"Ouch!" he complained loudly, rubbing the offended member.

"Serves you right for baiting me," she defended. "You know how angry I get."

"Yeah, and it's so much fun to watch," he countered still massaging his bruised muscle.

Taking the offensive, Bridgett sought her

revenge. "Maybe I should share some of your deep, dark secrets and very bad habits with Diana. I bet I could change her mind about you in a flash. How would you feel about that, Mr. Smarty Pants?"

"How's that a threat?" Ellen asked her younger sister, clearly confused. "Sean and Diana aren't…uh… they aren't involved, are they?" It took the quiet mother of four a bit longer to grasp the obvious than it had the rest of her family. She regarded her brother beseechingly.

"Don't be dense as well as blind, Ellen," Bridgett responded for him. "Of course, they're involved. Sean's been mooning over Diana for two stinking days. Everyone else already knows it, everyone except you and Patti Martin. We've all just pretended not to notice."

"Bridgett!" her mother reprimanded.

"It's okay, Mom," Sean broke in. "I started it. Bridge is just getting her licks in. Besides, it's time I came clean."

Diana reached out a tentative, restraining hand, trying to stop him as he rose to formally address the group, but he shrugged off her plea. "Trust me, babe. It'll be better to get it out in the open. I'm tired of pretending."

Feeling like she was on a speeding roller coaster, hurtling downward, Diana fought against the rising panic. As long as certain words hadn't been declared aloud, she could keep up the charade, hoping to make a graceful exit from Sean's life without causing him too much heartache or humiliation. But once their relationship was out in the open, there would be no way to spare his feelings. Gritting her teeth and biting back tears, she ordered herself to be strong. *He's forcing you to be cruel,* she told herself. *Now, there's no other way to do it.*

She held her breath as he rose from his chair and formally announced, "I love Diana, and I've asked her to be my wife. If she agrees, I'd like to be married as soon as we can arrange it. Six months should be long enough to wait, don't you think?"

The dining room was as silent as the proverbial tomb, and Diana felt as cold as a lifeless cadaver. "I don't know, Sean," she answered softly, her face a grim, unreadable mask. "So much has happened since we first discussed this. We should consider it more carefully."

"But why?" His warm brown eyes sparkled dangerously.

Slipping into her icy armor, she insisted, "This is not the time or place to make such an important decision, Sean. I'm sure your family would rather not be drawn into our discussion."

"Discussion? Is that what this is, Diana, a discussion?" His voice rose with indignation. "Funny, I thought it was a public declaration of mutual love and devotion. Now, I wonder where I got that ridiculous idea."

"There's no need to overreact. Let's go somewhere private and talk calmly." It took all of her strength to defy him.

"No!" he shouted. "Say whatever it is you have to say, right here, where the people who truly care about me can hear it. I have nothing to hide from my family." Taking an ominous step toward her, he asked, his face contorted in pain, "You told me you loved me, Diana. Was that a lie?"

Closing her eyes so she didn't have to see the look of utter betrayal marring the rugged planes of his beloved face, she shook her head. "It was the truth when I said it. But our circumstances have changed." Steeling herself for the final blow, she struck, hitting him where she would inflict the most grievous wound. "I was flattered by your attention, even carried away by the passion of the moment, but now I can see things more clearly.

"No matter how I feel about you, I would never be completely sure of your true feelings for me. I can't accept your proposal, because I would never really know your true motivation for making it. You claim to love me, Diana Grayson, the girl from the wrong side of the tracks, and I wish I could believe you. But there'd always be a nagging doubt in the back of my mind, that you really love Diana North, heir to North Star Enterprises."

Then she added another thrust, just to be certain he wouldn't rally. "Face it, Sean, if I marry you, I'll be the laughingstock of Washington society. I can hear the gossip now, 'Poor, needy Diana, trading her money and position to get a hot, young lover in her bed. I bet she gives him an enormous allowance and keeps him on a short leash.' And those would be the nicer things they'd say. You can't want that any more than I do.

"No one will ever believe that our marriage isn't a sham. How could they? The idea is simply ridiculous." Leaning back in her chair, she tapped her lips lightly with her napkin and regarded him coolly, her face expressionless and her manner convincingly haughty. She played her part so well that it was almost impossible to tell that her heart was breaking. *Oh, my dear Sean, my only love,* she cried to herself. *I'm so, so sorry.*

Struck speechless by the harsh cruelty of her words, Sean stared at her, unable to believe Diana could be capable of such a deliberate attack. All trace of the warm, sensitive, caring woman he'd dared to believe might be his soul mate, had disappeared. This woman was not the one he'd discovered underneath the frosty exterior, the one he'd loved. She was the "Ice Queen" incarnate, and he hated her – hated her spoiled selfishness, her cold calculation. So, she was just like every other wealthy woman he'd met after all, only worse.

"Sheila was right about you after all," he snarled, through a red haze. In his fury, he failed to see Diana flinch at the painful jab.

"You are the most cold-hearted bitch I've ever had the displeasure to meet. I hope I provided you with an amusing distraction, mooning after you like a lovesick schoolboy. You'll get plenty of chuckles telling your bored, rich friends all about it. You can brag about how you saw through my scheme to seduce you out of a few million. You can tell them how you outmatched me from the start. The problem is, Diana, compared to you, the consummate gold-digger, I'm a rank amateur.

"I risked my life, and the life of my friend, to save you from Stark and his sister, and you repay me with distrust and betrayal. I should have let them kill you." Knocking an empty chair against the wall with enough force to break it into several pieces, he fled the room.

"Hmm… well," Diana cleared her throat and affected a practiced, superior attitude. "Has a definite tendency to overstatement, hasn't he?"

"Skip, go after him," Sarah ordered her son's friend. "Make sure he doesn't do anything foolish." Then the concerned woman turned her tear-filled eyes on Diana. "You sure had me fooled, and that's not easily done. Please remove yourself from my table. You're no longer welcome here."

Knowing she deserved the dismissal did nothing to ease the intense pain, but despite the knife twisting in her heart, Diana continued to play her part with supreme confidence. Rising gracefully, she thanked them all for their hospitality, and offered a sincere apology for putting them in the middle of her misunderstanding with Sean. She almost lost it when her words were met with open hostility. Her knees buckled. By sheer dint of will, she braced herself against the table and said, "I know you all want me gone, but I'm afraid I must impose on you for a ride to the airport. Will someone drive me, please? You'll be well-compensated."

No one wanted to oblige her. Every set of eyes turned away, refusing to meet hers. Finally, Bridgett offered, "I'll take you. I should check in anyway. Come on."

"I'll ride along," Sloan said, giving his client a blistering glare that was meant to shame her unmercifully. "I flew in with James. Guess I'd best get back home the way I came."

"Good," Mike Cody snapped, his dark gaze scathing. "The sooner you get her out of my sight, the better."

Though she didn't know how she managed it, Diana led the way through the door of the dining room, her head regally high. She was stepping off the porch when she collapsed. Her sudden, unexpected weakness took Curtis completely by surprise. Fortunately, Bridgett was more prepared and did her best to cushion Diana's fall.

"Help me, Curtis. We've got to get her into the car before someone sees us." The flight attendant on one side, the lawyer on the other, they guided her toward Nelson's Jeep.

"What's wrong with her?" Curtis asked, totally confused. "She seemed just fine a few seconds ago."

"It was all an act. A superior performance, I must say. She even convinced me for a little bit."

"An act?"

"Diana thinks Sean will be better off without her. This was her way of running him off," Bridgett informed him as she struggled to help her passenger into the vehicle.

"Well, it looks like it worked."

"Yeah, too well."

From the point where he stood, high in the hayloft, staring out at the cornfields, Sean couldn't see his sister and the attorney struggling across the yard, half carrying, half dragging their incapacitated burden. He did, however, hear the engine roar to

life. Looking up, he turned to watch them drive
down the lane, taking Diana out of his life forever.

SEVENTEEN

Weeks later, Diana sat on the patio of her mother's house, watching the pontoon boats glide lazily across the glassy surface of Lake Barcroft. Her mind wandered aimlessly, reviewing the flurry of activity that had surrounded the tedious process of laying James to rest. The family visitation and funeral had been unbelievably trying. But it was finally over, and she'd walked away from the haughty North clan, deeply thankful that she wouldn't have to see them, ever again.

The day after the funeral, she and Curtis Sloan had met with Justin. Though he'd protested strongly, she signed over everything to him – including her interest in NSE, her luxury condominium in the city, and her company car. Her only condition was that Baldwin Aviation be returned to its original owner, providing Vic was willing to make Sean Cody a full partner.

Justin had begged her to reconsider, even suggesting that she come back to help him implement some of the changes she wanted to make in North Star operating procedure, but she refused. His kindness and concern had touched Diana deeply, and she'd prepared to leave the North Star board room for the very last time, knowing that she had done the right thing.

Before she could escape entirely, Justin had grabbed her hand and asked her, sincerely worried, "Are you going to be okay, Diana?" When she nodded, he probed, hesitantly, "It's none of my business, but where are you going to live, now that you've given me your condo?"

She remembered smiling at him. "You can use it. Wouldn't be right for the President and CEO of NSE to bunk at home with dear old mom and dad." Then she'd patted his hand indulgently. "You don't need to worry about me. I still have my mother's house."

"But what about your living expenses?" he had argued. "You'll need income from somewhere. Let me help you."

"That's not necessary. I'm not handing over my personal savings or investments, Justin. I might not be a jet-setter anymore, but I won't starve." She'd smiled at him again. "And it's going to feel great to be independent, and completely free of North Star Enterprises and the North family."

The determined young man had relented only after Diana's attorney assured him, "I wouldn't be going along with her on this if she hadn't thought it through completely. It's what she wants. Now accept her gift graciously, and say 'Thank you'."

Always obedient, Justin had said, "Thank you," punctuating his gratitude with a sincere hug.

Thinking back on that moment now warmed her heart, her very broken heart. She had many regrets, but one weighed heaviest. Every waking hour of every interminable day, Diana was filled with crushing grief – not for the husband she'd lost, but for the love she'd deliberately thrown away. She dreamed of what she'd dared to hope could be, but had realized that it could not.

Shaking off the longing for the impossible, she consciously shifted her thoughts to the previous day, when she'd had an unexpected visitor. The FBI agent, who was handling the case against Stark and his sister, had dropped by to give her an update. He told her that the Bureau had been suspicious of the crooked operative for some time.

The Internal Affairs Division had begun investigating Stark following a sting operation, eighteen months ago. The dubious procedure he'd employed to implicate the prominent businessman, who was his target, bordered on entrapment. There was also evidence that he'd used Sheila as bait for the trap, and that he'd taken bribes from the man before turning him over to the prosecutor. The I.A. agent had speculated that the pair was setting up her late husband in a similar manner. Had their scheme succeeded, the agent believed the Stark siblings would have manufactured evidence to frame James for crimes he hadn't committed, so they could extort millions from him. Then, once he'd been bled dry, they would have moved on to another target.

Diana felt sorry for James' family, and that surprised her. The Norths were not accustomed to scandal. They'd been incredulous and indignant when they were told that their fair-haired, do-no-wrong boy was not the perfect son they thought him to be. The sordid details had been cleverly glossed over with a cover-up story about an accidental shooting, linked to a federal investigation with which James had been cooperating. So far, the aristocratic family had been spared the intense scrutiny of the media, as well as the ridicule that was sure to come from their fickle society friends, when the true facts became public.

Though Diana expected the U.S. Attorney's office to stall as long as possible, it was inevitable that Sheila and her brother would eventually be brought to trial. When that happened, all of the dirt would come out – every ugly detail, and Justin would have his hands full, maintaining the company's good reputation.

Diana sighed, trying to force herself out of the pit. Regret had a way of turning to despair, and despair to hopelessness, but she was a fighter. She didn't give in, or give up, easily. One lone tear slid silently down an alabaster cheek.

"That's it! I've had it!" a pleasantly feminine voice called to her from inside the house. "I can hear you sighing from in here, and I'm sick and tired of it – and that pitiful face you're wearing." Eleanor Randall's curly head popped out through the French doors, followed immediately by her slender, graceful body.

As soon as she'd gotten word of James's death, Elly had dropped the kids at her mother's, and fought her way through beltway traffic to be with her friend. Since then, she'd been visiting Diana whenever her job and family obligations allowed.

This time, she'd been able to stay for a week while her kids were away at summer camp, but she had to leave soon, and Diana's deep depression worried her. Her former roommate had always been a bit moody, but this was different.

At first the efficient nurse had chalked it up to fatigue and stress, but the longer it went on, the more convinced she'd become that there was some deep emotional pain, a pain not associated with her husband's death, tormenting her friend. She was also worried that there was something physical ailing her. Plopping down on the foot of the chair where Diana lounged, Elly shot her friend a challenging gaze.

"You are going to tell me what's going on with you. I know you're not still grieving over James, so don't even pretend it's that. I've never seen you like this, Diana. Life has thrown shit at you since you were a kid, but you always threw it back. You didn't let it get you down. Hell, you put up with that bastard you called a husband for twenty years, so I thought you were indestructible!"

Pinching Diana's toes, playfully, she demanded, "I'm not budging from here until you come clean, dammit! Who is he?"

Not really surprised by Eleanor's astute assessment of her situation, Diana sighed again. "You know me too well, T.P."

"That I do. So 'fess up. I want all the juicy details." Elly's green eyes flashed with mischievous delight. "Is he a hunk?"

"Yep," Diana confirmed, flashing back to

college days when she and Elly would sit like this for hours, swapping secrets. "A serious hunk."

"So why are you mooning after him instead of swooning over him?" Eleanor Randall had never been one to mince words. "Where is he? Why isn't he here by your side in your time of need? Did he dump you?"

"Au contraire," the graceful blonde said, smiling her usual sad smile. "He told me he loved me and asked me to marry him."

"Wow! That really sounds terrible." Eleanor's tone was thick with sarcasm. "A handsome man says he loves you, and asks you to marry him, and it throws you into a blue funk for weeks on end. Diana, my girl, I always knew you were weird, but that takes the prize. I repeat…Why is he not here, now? And don't you dare try to tell me you don't love him, cause it's oh so obvious that you do."

"I kicked him in the gut as hard as I could and walked away."

"You did WHAT?!"

"You heard me. He offered me his love and devotion, and I refused him, claiming that I'd always be afraid that he was really after my money." Her eyes swimming with tears, she accused herself mercilessly, "Elly, I said the worst things I could possibly think of to say to him, things that were sure to make him hate me, and then I ran."

"You finally break free of a sterile marriage to a husband who used and demeaned you. Then you find the true love you really deserve, only to throw it away. Why in hell did you do such a thing?" Eleanor screeched.

"Because I knew he'd be better off without me," Diana explained, forcing down the sorrow that rose in her throat like fiery fingers, choking off her air. The pain in her chest was almost unbearable.

Shaking her curls, the doctor's wife probed deeper. "You're gonna have to do better than that. I know you like to play the martyr role, sacrificing yourself for others and crap like that, but this is carrying it just a bit too far."

Diana laughed.

"What's so funny?"

"Sean's friend, Skip, accused me of exactly the same thing. I guess you're both right, I am too comfortable playing the martyr."

"Sean, huh? So that's one mystery solved. His name is Sean." Eleanor's eyes burned with curiosity.

"Yes, it's Sean…Sean Cody. He's the helicopter pilot who saved my life, repeatedly. I told you a little about him." Diana's face brightened when she spoke his name.

"Conveniently leaving out the juicy parts," Elly complained.

Shrugging an apology, Diana continued, "If it hadn't been for Sean, I would have died in that explosion, just like Stark planned. He stuck with me through those terrible, wonderful days when we were running for our lives. Somewhere along the way, we fell in love."

"And that was a problem, because…? Your marriage to James was already over, for all practical purposes. You couldn't have been worried about cheating on him."

Diana giggled. Elly Randall had always had a way of putting things into perspective for her.

"HEL-LO, James had been screwing around on you for years, or hadn't you noticed?"

"I know that, T.P., And no, I didn't feel guilty about cheating on James," Diana admitted in exasperation.

"Oh, so you did cheat. Tell me more. Details, girl, details." Eleanor's eyes sparkled with mischief. Her ploy had worked, prying information she was dying to hear out of her tight-lipped friend. "Was this hunk of yours good in bed or did you ditch him because he was a disappointing lover?"

"Don't you ever think of anything but sex?" A deep flush spread from Diana's collarbones upward to the roots of her fair hair, but Eleanor's deliberately off-color approach was helping to buoy her spirits through the embarrassment. "If you must know, Miss Nosy, Sean didn't disappoint me in any way – in bed or otherwise. Come to think of it," she shot her friend a mischievous glance. "We never make love in a bed."

"This just gets better and better." Elly leaned closer. "Where did you do it?"

"I'm not going there. You can just forget it!"

"Spoil sport. You're no fun at all." Eleanor stuck out her lower lip in a feigned pout. "Well then, if you're determined to keep the best parts to yourself, you have to tell me why you gave the guy the bum's rush."

Sighing a resigned sigh, Diana whispered, "It was simply a matter of years."

"Years?"

"Twelve of them."

"I don't get it," Elly complained, scrunching her tiny, up-turned nose.

"Sean is thirty-three."

"Ohhhh...I see," the sensitive nurse responded.

"And that scared you shitless."

"I wouldn't put it quite so crudely," Diana said, folding her hands in her lap. "But yes, it did. But that's not the biggest reason. Sean is the only son of a large, tightly-knit family. His folks expect him to carry on the Cody name..."

"And you're too old for babies," Elly completed.

"Bingo! You got it. Tell the lady what she's won." Though her words were playful, Diana's tone was completely joyless.

"You gave him the heave-ho before he had time to realize what he'd be giving up for you, and have second thoughts. Shit, Diana, I'm sorry." Reaching out, she took her friend's hand and squeezed it. "I just have one more question."

"Shoot!"

"Are you sure he wants kids? Maybe he doesn't. It's possible, you know."

"I didn't discuss it with him," Diana admitted ruefully. "Because I knew what he'd say. He would have assured me that we were meant to be together, and that the baby business would work itself out. And I knew he'd mean it, too, when he said it. But I also knew that circumstances change, people change, and one day he'd look at me, the old woman who stole his chance at fatherhood, and he'd hate me for it.

"I've lived that nightmare, Elly, bound to a selfish husband who robbed me of my opportunity to be a mother. I couldn't do the same thing to the man I love."

"So, you made him hate you now instead of later." Eleanor's tone conveyed understanding, if not agreement.

"I drove him away because I want him to have a complete life, with a wife who is worthy of his love and devotion, and children to dote upon, if he wants them. Sean will make a wonderful father. I had to set him free, so he could find true happiness."

"Even when walking away from him made your life totally miserable?"

"Yes, even then. I've ruined my chances for happiness with the decisions I've made, and I have to live with that, but I was determined not to ruin Sean's life too. At least I have the memories of the time we had together. I know that, for a little while at least, I was deeply and truly loved by an honorable man. It will have to be enough."

"Hah!" Eleanor snorted. "You're full of it! But since you're determined to live in your little delusional world, there's nothing I can do about it. Let me tell you this, though. If I were you, I'd call the guy, tell him I had a serious brain fart, and beg him to forgive me."

"Well, I'm not you, am I?" Diana's irritation with her friend was growing.

"Thank God!" Eleanor proclaimed. "Okay, we've established that you're love-sick over a wonderful guy you pushed away because you're too stubborn and insecure to grab onto him with both hands. But that's not all that's going on with you, Diana."

It was clear that she'd put on her professional nurse hat when she added, "I'd bet my stethoscope, or even my monkey wrench, that you're sick – and not just in the head. You can't eat. Your stomach's upset all the time. You're dragging with fatigue, but you can't sleep. You need to see a doctor, to make sure it's not something more than your depression talking."

"I hate to admit it, but you're probably right. I do feel awful. I'm so tired I can barely put one foot in front of the other, and I can't look at food without throwing up." Diana hung her head in resigned acceptance.

"Then let me call Brian and make an appointment for you." Brian Wade, another college classmate, had a thriving internal medicine practice in Arlington. "I'm sure he'll work you into his schedule tomorrow."

"Okay," Diana nodded.

Flashing an encouraging smile, Eleanor went inside to make the phone call. The busy physician seemed genuinely pleased to hear from his old school chum, and readily agreed to squeeze an appointment for Diana into his schedule.

Less than twenty-four hours later, the nervous widow sat across the desk from the be-speckled doctor, admiring his spacious office. When he looked up from the report he was scanning on his computer screen, she asked, "What's the verdict?

Am I gonna live, Doc?"

"For a woman's who's on the high side of forty, you're in remarkably good shape, Diana," he observed, peering at her over his wire-framed glasses.

"You don't have to remind me of my age, Brian," she scolded him. "I know how old I am. I feel every year of it. Just spit it out. What's wrong with me?"

His very myopic eyes twinkled. "Oh, nothing too serious. And nothing that won't resolve itself in about five months."

"If you don't stop being so obtuse, I'm gonna sock you," she snapped back. "What kind of medical condition isn't too serious, but still takes months to get over?"

"Pregnancy."

"What!?"

"You heard me. You're expecting a baby, Diana."

It took a very long minute for his words to sink in. "It…it can't be. I'm too… old."

"Apparently not," Dr. Wade chuckled. "What makes you think you're too old? Had your cycles stopped coming regularly?"

"Well, no, not until recently," she answered thoughtfully.

"Didn't you suspect that you might be pregnant?"

Shaking her head a bit shamefully, she told him, "I just figured it was the stress I'd been under, or maybe pre-menopause sneaking up on me."

"Hardly. I'd say you've got several good years

in you yet, based on the lab results I have." He scrolled through the electronic files in front of him.

She was still incredulous. "What do we do now? Isn't it dangerous for a woman my age to have a baby?"

"Not necessarily." Sensing her concern, the kind doctor tried to reassure her. "We'll get you to in to see an obstetrician as soon as possible, of course. Some tests will need to be done right away. Do you have a particular OB you'd like to use?"

She shook her head again.

"Then let me recommend one. I'll have my nurse call her and see if she can see you this afternoon, if that's do-able."

"The sooner the better, I guess," the woman agreed, still trying to get her mind around this overwhelming and unexpected news.

Dr. Wade adjusted his glasses with his forefinger, looked at her through the smudged lenses, and blinked. "You have options here, Diana. You know that, don't you? Obviously, this is quite a surprise, a shock even. With your husband's recent death, I know you'll need time to think things over. I'm not trying to rush you. I just want you to have all the information you need to help with your decision." The dedicated physician folded his hands in front of his white coat, interlocking his fingers, and propped his elbows on the desktop.

"I appreciate your concern, Brian, but there's no decision to be made. I want this baby more than I've ever wanted anything in my life." The radiant, even joyful expression on her fair face told him that her words were truthful and sincere.

"Good." Sliding out of his chair, he circled to her and reached out an open palm. "Then let's go find Elly. She'll be beside herself, waiting for news."

Brian was right. Eleanor squealed with delight when Diana told her that she would soon be a Godmother. Then, she proudly drove her friend to the next appointment and anxiously paced the floor during the examination.

Though the obstetric physician Dr. Wade had recommended was enviously young, Diana liked her forthright manner. She was competent and efficient, and soon had her patient poked, prodded, plummeted with sound waves, and sent on her way with a prescription for pre-natal vitamins and an assurance that she was carrying a strong, viable fetus.

Eleanor chattered incessantly throughout the drive home, clearly overjoyed. "So how do you intend to tell the high and mighty North clan that there'll be an heir to their fortune after all?"

"This isn't James' baby and you know it," Diana protested with a shiver. "And thank goodness for that blessing."

"I didn't think so, but they're bound to assume…"

"Let them assume anything they want, but no member of James' family will ever lay claim to my child."

"It wasn't an immaculate conception, Diana," Eleanor warned. "How're you gonna break the news to Papa?"

"I'm not."

"What do you mean, you're not?" her friend screeched, waving her hands in frustration. "You force the guy out of your life because you think you're too old to give him a kid, but when you find out that, miraculously, you're going to make him a father after all, you don't plan to tell him about it?"

Diana's face was set with determination.

"You are one seriously screwed up gal."

"Who asked you?" her friend retorted. "It's been over four months since I walked out on Sean. I'm sure he's moved on, gotten his life back in order. And besides, he has every reason to hate me. "He said he wished I'd died in the helicopter explosion, Elly." She admitted through the thick lump in her throat. "If I did call him, he'd probably refuse to speak to me. I'm sure he wouldn't agree to see me."

"Well, hell! What did you expect him to say after you'd totally humiliated him? Give the guy some credit. If he ever cared for you, he'll give you another chance. But you'll never know unless you try." Steering Diana's Subaru wagon deftly into the garage, Eleanor shut off the engine and insisted, "Now, you're going inside, right this second, and telephone the man."

"And say what?" The color drained out of Diana's cheeks, as she considered the possible outcomes of that dubious course of action. "Hi, Sean, this is Diana. Surprise, surprise. I'm knocked up and you're responsible?"

Elly choked back a fit of giggles. "That would get his attention, but I'd recommend a more subtle approach. Make up an excuse for the call. Pretend you have something of his that you need to return." Giving her friend a reassuring hug, she encouraged, "Come on. Let's go do this before you have time to talk yourself out of it."

Diana crossed the polished tile floor, headed to the telephone or her execution, she wasn't sure which. *What if he hangs up on you?* she asked herself. *What will you do then?* Forcing her trembling fingers to punch the numbers, she waited through several rings.

"You've memorized his number?" Elly teased. "So, you've thought about calling him."

Diana stuck her tongue out at her irritatingly observant friend. Just when she'd decided there was no one home, a feminine voice sounded from the other end of the line.

"Hello." The disruptive squeals of children could be heard in the background.

Caught off guard by the din, Diana didn't respond immediately.

The voice snapped with irritation. "You called me, so speak up!"

"Uh, Bridgett?" Diana posed, her mind grasping at the only tolerable possibility.

"No, this is Patti. Bridgett doesn't live here anymore. She moved in with a friend, Curt something or other, I think. I could give you the number. Sean has it written down somewhere."

"Don't bother, I have it." Then she added, "Thanks."

The background noise intensified. "Hold on a second." Laying the receiver aside with a thud, Patti half-heartedly scolded her children. "Shut up that racket. Can't you see I'm on the phone?" A second later, she was back, apologizing, "Sorry, my kids are just full of themselves. We're waiting for their father to get home and take us out for dinner. If you'd like to leave a message, I'm sure I could get it to my sister-in-law."

Diana refused, her voice barely audible, "That's not necessary. Goodbye."

"Bye," Patti replied cheerfully. Covering the mouthpiece with her hand, she added, "and good riddance, Mrs. North," a victorious gleam in her mascara-encrusted eyes.

The stricken look on Diana's face as she dropped the receiver into its cradle, spoke volumes. Elly asked her, "Who was it?"

Forcing down the acidic lump of disappointment, sourly burning her tongue, Diana breathed, "Mrs. Sean Cody, apparently."

"What!? He's married? Why didn't you bother to mention that little tidbit?!" Eleanor's mouth was drawn into a thin line of disapproval.

"He wasn't – four months ago."

"Are you sure you didn't misunderstand?"

Diana shook her head, not trusting herself to speak.

"Shit, I'm sorry." Elly hugged her friend tightly. "Didn't take him long to move on," she spat. "Well, it's better that you know his true colors, Diana. Dumping him was the right decision. Why don't you make yourself comfortable outside on the patio? I'll bring us some tea."

"Thanks. Tea sounds great." She tried to put on

a brave smile, but failed miserably. When Eleanor disappeared into the kitchen, Diana wandered outside. Staring blindly at the lake, she was oblivious to the warm rays of light that flickered off the surface of the water, giving everything a rich, golden glow. The scene was beautiful, but the distraught woman didn't notice. Instead of enjoying the panorama, she scolded herself. *Serves you right. You wanted Sean to have, a wife and a family. Now he does.*

Then one bright thought occurred to her. *I might not have the man I love, but I have his baby. That'll be enough. It will have to be.*

EIGHTEEN

While Diana and Eleanor were getting ready for the appointment with Brian Wade, Sean stood on the tarmac outside the Baldwin Aviation hangar, awaiting the arrival of his next passenger. When the familiar maroon Jaguar rolled into sight, his stomach jumped into his throat and his pulse pounded recklessly in his ears. He didn't breathe normally again until the car glided to a stop and its young, male occupant stepped out.

Immediately struck by the man's resemblance to his uncle, Sean quickly guessed the identity of the fellow striding confidently toward him. Sticking out a hand, the new CEO of North Star Enterprises confirmed succinctly, "Mr. Cody. Justin North. Good to meet you."

"Same here," Sean responded, less than enthusiastically. "But it's just Sean."

"Great, Sean." Closer up, Justin's resemblance to James was only superficial. The nephew's eyes lacked the hard ruthlessness and cold, calculating gaze of his uncle. Instead, Justin appeared open, honest, forthright, and friendly. "Ready to go?"

"Right this way." Sean waved toward the

waiting helicopter. Soon they were airborne, en route to a perspective NSE property, east of Washington D.C. along the Potomac River.

"Thanks for arranging this trip on such short notice," Justin offered. "Balancing work and school, I'm really socked in. This real estate has potential, but the timetable's tight. I had to move fast or risk losing it."

"No problem," Sean grunted, warming to the charming young man despite his reservations.

"Aunt Diana said I could count on you. She thinks you're great."

Sean's derisive grunt conveyed his disbelief.

"She tries to play it cool, of course. She likes to keep up that ice-queen act, but I can see through her." Justin settled into the seat and added. "Her face lights up when she hears your name. That tells me how she really feels, not that I blame her. Any woman with one romantic bone in her body would worship the guy who saved her life."

"Don't know about that," Sean protested. "Last time we talked, I got the distinct impression that your aunt has a very low opinion of me."

"That's because you listened to what she said. You can't do that," Justin informed him.

"You can't?"

"Heck, no. To know what the lady's really thinking, you have to pay attention to what she does, not to what she says. I'd say her actions have proven that she cares about you, and cares a lot."

Sean's curiosity poked him hard. "What actions are you talking about?"

"The agreement with your boss," the young

man explained. "Returning Baldwin Aviation to Vic, and to you. How's that working out by the way?"

"Uh…fine," Sean stuttered in surprised. "You're saying Diana is responsible for…"

"I guess Vic didn't go into detail about it. Before Diana signed the agreement to relinquish her interest in NSE, she insisted that Vic's company be signed back over to him, provided he make you a full partner. Everything else she handed over to me, unconditionally, right down to her condo and company car."

Trying to get his brain around the far-reaching implications of that tidbit of information, Sean swallowed hard. "Explains why you're driving her Jag."

"Uh-huh. Washed her hands of North Star entirely, and left me in charge, with plenty of competent help, of course." The new exec beamed with deserved pride. "You should call her. She'd love to hear from you."

Curiosity needling him, Sean queried, "Where's she living?"

"At her mother's place, over in Arlington." Fumbling in his jacket for his cellphone, a scrap of paper, and a pen, Justin offered as he scribbled, "Here's her address. Stop by sometime.

"To be honest with you, Sean, I've been worried about Diana. Seeing you would cheer her up, and she could use some serious cheering up." The young man slipped the note into the pilot's shirt pocket and followed it with a slap of encouragement.

Saved from making a firm commitment by their opportune arrival at their destination, the pilot set the copter down in a grassy clearing, near a narrow road where a sleek, black limousine was parked. Then he waited, running a routine systems-check, while his passenger joined the occupants of the huge car and moved out for a tour of the area.

A little over an hour later, Justin returned. He hopped into the helicopter, giving Sean an enthusiastic thumb's up. On the return trip, the young CEO kept busy making phone calls to confirm the purchase of the valuable property. Sean was impressed by the young man's tact and skill.

When Justin disembarked, he shot the former Marine a friendly smile and urged him again. "Promise me you'll check in on Diana."

"Why not?" Sean agreed, with no intention of keeping that promise. *When hell freezes over,* was his honest, unspoken response.

When he finished going over his post-flight checklist, the big man went in search of his partner. He found him in the tiny office at the back of the hangar and barged in without knocking. "Why didn't you warn me that I was flying NSE's child prodigy this morning?"

Leaning back in his swivel chair, and interlocking his pudgy fingers behind his balding head, Vic grinned sheepishly. "I figured you'd refuse the hop if you knew the client. I didn't want your stubborn pride to get in the way. I wanted you to meet Justin. He's a good guy. Not like his old Uncle James."

"He's okay," Sean reluctantly agreed. "Since

we're on the subject of NSE and keeping secrets, I have another question for you."

"I'm all ears. Fire away."

"According to my passenger, offering me a partnership was a condition you had to meet to get your company back. I was wondering when you were planning to pass that important bit of information along." Sean's dark eyes snapped dangerously. He hovered over the desk like an eagle ready to swoop down on an unsuspecting rabbit.

Since honesty generally worked whenever there was a conflict with his top pilot and partner, he tried it. "Never," he admitted. "I deliberately withheld that morsel from you, for the same reason I didn't tell you who you were shuttling this morning. You would've refused the offer."

"You're damn right I would've refused. I don't want charity from the high and mighty Diana North."

"See. That's exactly what I mean. Your pride would've kept you from accepting what's rightfully yours." Lowering his chair and folding his hands on the desktop, Vic told him. "I was going to make you a full partner anyway, Sean, even without Diana's arm-twisting. In the past twelve months, you've put Baldwin back in the black. I've repaid NSE's original investment, plus a sizable profit. You earned that partnership with hard work and sweat."

"Yeah?" Sean was still skeptical.

"Yeah. So, you can cut the indignant crap and relax. That partnership was yours, with or without Diana North's edict, so you don't owe her anything."

"Good. I won't be in her debt," Sean snapped.

"You're not. So, drop it!" the aging pilot ordered with a laugh.

"What's so funny?"

"She gets you worked up, doesn't she?" Treading on unstable ground, Vic forged ahead nevertheless. "Why don't you swallow that shit-load of pride you're toting around? Call the woman and tell her you're still crazy about her!"

"You sound just like the nephew," Sean griped.

"Justin?"

Nodding, the big man explained, "He was pushing me at her, too."

"He was? Why?"

Sean shrugged. "Something about her spirits being down. Not that I care how she's feeling. He seemed to think I might cheer her up. But he's dead wrong, and so are you."

"Have it your way, but get your butt out of here. I mean it. You're going home this weekend, for a wedding or something, right?"

Sighing, Sean said, "Yeah. I've got Best Man duty for my nephew, Colin's, wedding. The rehearsal's Friday night."

"Take a few days off and make it a long visit. Things are pretty slow around here. I can hold down the fort till next week," Vic persisted. "You need a break, you jerk. Go!"

"Have it your way. I'm outta here. See you Monday."

Kicking his Harley to life, Sean sped out of the Baldwin Aviation compound. A few minutes later, he pulled up in front of his apartment building, shut off the bike, and sprinted up the stairs. When he unlocked the door and stepped inside, he was greeted by a very unwelcome surprise.

Patti Sanderson's overly indulged children had demolished the living area. Toys, shoes, and colorful assortment of cast-off soda containers and candy wrappers were strewn everywhere. The youngsters were so involved in a deafening battle over the control of a portable video game, that they failed to notice him. Their mother hung up the telephone, muttering something to herself. As she turned to yell at them, as ineffectually as always, her gaze touched on Sean and she broke into a broad, seductive smile.

"Welcome home, sweetheart." She glided toward him, arms extended in a warm greeting, but his disapproving frown warned her off.

"What in the hell are you doing here?" he growled.

"Sean, please, watch your language in front of the kids," she scolded him.

Noting that the din hadn't diminished in the slightest, he objected, "There's no way they could hear me. They're making too damned much noise. I'm sure they've heard worse from the lips of their own dear mother, so cut the crap, Patti. What you're doing here, taking over my home?"

The wily, manipulative woman lowered one hip suggestively and softened her voice. "The kids were bored, and we all needed a little vacation. We decided to visit with you for a couple of days and do some sightseeing. Then we can give you a ride back home, with us, for the wedding. I figured you'd be as happy to see me as I am to see you, particularly since Bridgett's moved out and left you all alone.

"You figured wrong. I told you months ago that I'm not interested. What part of 'No thanks' don't you understand?" Sean was furious. "How did you get in?"

"Bridgett stopped by to pick up some of her things, and we just happened to catch her as she was leaving. She said it would be alright for us to stay." Patti's beautiful eyes pleaded her case passionately. She licked her full, parted lips in a deliberate invitation.

She sure knows how to pour on the sex appeal, Sean silently observed, *thankful that he was immune to her charms. Too bad her follow-through isn't nearly as good as her serve.* "So, you made yourself at home, gave your kids the run of the place, and placed a few phone calls."

"I didn't make any calls," she denied, irritated by his sarcasm.

"Don't lie to me, Patti. I saw you hang up, just as I walked in."

"Oh, that." She shrugged, feigning innocence, and grinned at him again. "Some woman was looking for Bridgett. I told her she'd moved out. She said she had Curt What's-his-name's number and would call her there."

Turning his back on the presumptuous intruder, Sean stormed into his spartanly furnished bedroom and began stuffing a few things into his backpack. Patti followed him, whining. "What are you doing, sweetie?"

Ignoring the endearment, he finished his task, reached into his pocket, pulled out a key, and tossed it to her. "Stay as long as you like. Lock up when you go and drop the key in the mailbox."

"You're leaving?" she asked incredulously.

"I'll be staying with Bridgett at Curtis Sloan's place while you're here. His number is on the fridge. I'm sure you already have her cell number.

Patti stood in the doorway and watched him go, silently threatening. *This is not the end of it. You have to come home for Page's wedding this weekend, my dear, stubborn Mr. Cody. And then you'll have to deal with me. I'll make it impossible for you to refuse. Struggle as hard as you want, you big, handsome fish, but you won't get away from me. I want you, and I always get what I want. I won't give up until I do.*

Driving the motorcycle at break-neck speed, Sean wheeled through the maddening rush-hour traffic, oblivious to the honking horns and shouted insults following in his wake. Had he been any less skilled at maneuvering the huge bike, he would never have made it safely to his sister's townhouse. He finally realized that he was driving too recklessly when he nearly collided with a small boy on a tricycle.

The little fellow was pedaling slowly across the entrance ramp of the housing complex's parking lot when Sean wheeled the Harley off the road, ignoring the "Slow, Children at Play" sign. He missed the rear wheel of the trike by mere inches, scaring both of them. Skidding to a halt, he called out to the boy, who was wiping at the tears streaming down his grubby face. "Sorry, kid. You had the right of way. I was speeding and not looking where I was going. You okay?"

Offering the big man a grateful smile, the lad sniffed, nodded in the affirmative, and started cranking the pedals of his small three-wheeler, leaving Sean reprimanding himself. *Shit, that was close. See what anger will get you? Now start acting like you've got some damned sense.* Taking a calming breath, he slowly steered the cycle into a parking spot near Curtis Sloan's building.

Still shaken up by the near miss, Sean pulled off his helmet, shouldered his knapsack, and slowly made his way to the condo his sister shared with the attorney. He tapped lightly on the door. Seconds later, the portly lawyer opened it, his friendly face breaking into a welcoming grin. "What a surprise! Come in. Come in." He ushered the pilot inside and offered, "Let me give you a hand with your stuff."

"Thanks." Sean handed him the backpack and helmet.

Curtis hung the bag on a low branch of a brass hall tree, that stood watch in the corner of the entry foyer, and balanced the heavy headgear on the top prong. "Bridgett's in the galley cooking us up some barbecue. I'm sure there'll be plenty, if you want to join us."

"That would be great. I'll give her a hand. There's something I need to discuss with her."

Curtis nodded in understanding. "Right through there." He pointed in the general direction of the kitchen. "I'll be in to set the table in a bit. Help yourself to a beer. There's a cold six-pack in the fridge."

Bridgett greeted him a bit too warmly, which gave Sean the strong impression that she was expecting him. Before he could voice the complaint that was burning his tongue, she ordered, "Wash up, grab a knife, and chop these." She tossed him two large onions.

Patiently biding his time, the big man did as he was told. Just as he was about to ask her why she'd allowed Patti and her brood to invade his home, Bridgett took a well-aimed jab at him. "It didn't take you long to get fed up with your house guests."

Grunting his disgust, Sean grumbled, "By the time I got in, Patti and her brats had completely trashed the place. It'll take me weeks to put things back in order. What in the hell possessed you to let her in?"

Giving him her customary, that's-a-stupid-question look, she defended, "I didn't have much choice. Patti caught me on my way out to the car with my arms loaded. She and her delightful children invited themselves in before I had a chance to protest. What should I have done – run her out?"

"Uhh…yeah!" the angry man snarled.

"Come on, Sean, you know as well as I do that no one forces Patti Martin Sanderson to do anything she doesn't want to do. Once she planted her narrow butt in your apartment, it would have taken a stick of dynamite to get her out." The idea tickled Bridgett's fancy and set her to giggling.

"I'm glad it amuses you to know that I have

nowhere to sleep."

Bridgett laughed again. "Hardly! I'm sure there's a spot reserved, just for you, in your very own bed. You'll have to bunk in with your glamorous visitor, of course, but I know she'll make you feel real welcome."

Sean glared at her. "Screw that."

"Exactly."

"Shut up! This isn't funny. I want no part of that woman, and I'd be grateful if you'd stop pushing us together."

"Hey, I'm pleading 'not-guilty.' Granted, I was responsible for calling her up and inviting her over when we were home. But I had nothing to do with her unexpected visit today, so don't lay the blame for that at my feet."

The onions stung his nose and eyes, making them water. He sniffed. "You were the one responsible for letting her into my place, without my permission, so you and Curtis are stuck with me till they leave."

"No problem. The couch is pretty comfortable." She added the chopped onions to the butter she had simmering in a small skillet.

Sean washed his hands again and helped himself to a bottle of beer. He took a long swig and wiped his lips with the back of his hand. "You know what's weird?"

"Besides coming home to find an endlessly scheming woman, and three helplessly spoiled kids, in your home?"

"Yeah, besides that." He couldn't help grinning at her. "Patti said a woman called for you just before I got home. She told her that you'd moved, and offered her the number, but the caller said she already had it. That's strange, don't you think?"

Bridgett nodded in agreement. "If she knows me and Curt well enough to have his home number, then she should already know that we've moved in together, so why would she call your apartment looking for me?"

"Same question crossed my mind." Sean shrugged his wide shoulders at the mystery. "Have you been home all afternoon? Has anyone called?"

"Yep, I've been here, and nope, the phone hasn't rung."

"Oh well," he said, dismissing the call as inconsequential. "Doesn't matter."

"Hey, I had something unexpected happen today, too," Bridgett announced brightly. "Take a look at that" She pointed at a small package lying on the countertop.

Sean reaching for the clear vinyl case and rolled it over in his hand, immediately recognizing it. "Where did this come from?"

"The airline sent it over this afternoon. Apparently, the guy who picked up my rental car in downtown Roanoke, you know, that day, found it on the seat. He must have assumed it was mine, but in the typical, inefficient baggage-handler style, it took him over four months to get it back to me."

"What're you going to do with it?" the tall man asked his sister, trying to appear nonchalant.

"Me?" She raised one eyebrow at him. "I'm not going to do anything with it, but you are going to return it to its rightful owner."

"Like hell I am," he snarled.

"Stop being such a damned, stubborn fool, and think about it for a minute," Bridgett urged, as she stirred the remaining ingredients into the tangy barbecue sauce she was preparing. "This gives you the perfect excuse to drop in on her."

Sean's full lips were firmly pursed. "I have no desire to 'drop in' on that woman, now or ever, and I wish everyone would stop pushing me at her."

"Everyone?" Bridgett looked puzzled. "Who else has been trying to get you to see Diana?"

Sean groaned. "Vic mentioned it, and so did the illustrious Justin North, heir apparent to the NSE dynasty. He took a short hop with me today and suggested that I visit his aunt.

"Really?" She grinned indulgently.

"Yeah, made me promise to contact her."

"Good for Justin. I've never met this wonder kid but I like him already." Bridgett stirred the bubbling sauce into the shredded pork that she had waiting in a large Dutch oven. Then she covered the pot and left it to simmer. "He's right, Sean. You need to see Diana and clear up all the crap."

"There's nothing to clear up."

"Baloney!" his sister barked. "Diana loves you. I've tried and tried to tell you, but your huge ego and your stupid pride, keep getting in the way. I'm going to give it one more shot and you're going to listen and believe." Bridgett's dark eyes fired angry sparks at him. "Diana made up all that stuff about not being able to trust your motives for proposing to her. I know she did, because I'm the one who forced her to do it."

Sean was still unconvinced but he didn't protest, so she pushed a little more. "I used every dirty trick I could think of to drive a wedge between you. It didn't take me long to find the one that worked – too well."

"Yeah? What was that?" The man tried to remain skeptical, but felt his resolve slipping.

"I played my trump a bit too soon, I guess, but it took the trick. Diana folded her hand as soon as my Cody-heir card was on the table."

"That's a cute metaphor, Bridge, but what the hell does it mean?"

"I played on her guilt, by suggesting that marriage to her would force you into an unfulfilled life of childlessness. I also indicated that the family would hate her for letting the Cody name die out without an heir, and even hinted that it was likely that you'd do the same, eventually. It wasn't in so many words, mind you. I'm much too clever for that; but basically, it's what I made her believe." It was the brother's turn to shoot daggers at his sister. He thought of the things Diana had told him, about her longing for children and her husband's selfish refusal to consider adoption, and he understood why Bridgett's ploy had been so successful. "You sold her a load of bullshit."

"Of course, I did. I can be very convincing." Stepping toward him, she placed a long arm around Sean's broad shoulders. "I'm not proud of my behavior, but at the time I thought I was protecting you. Now I know I was wrong. Diana loves you. "Use that," She pointed to the little bag, "as an excuse to go see her. Give her a chance to apologize. She knows you weren't after her money, but that was the weapon most likely to wound you and drive you away, so she used it."

There was a long pause before Sean spoke, shrugging off her arm. "Worked like a charm."

"Yep. The lady's good," Bridgett agreed. "She's been playing that rich-bitch role for a very long time. She's got it down cold."

"Maybe, but I think she's given up the 'Ice Queen' role for good."

"What do you mean?" Bridgett asked, curiously.

"Justin told me that Diana turned over her interest in NSE to him."

"She gave up her fortune?"

"Seems so." The big man shook his dark head sadly.

"Which proves my point. She was planning to abdicate the North Star crown regardless, so she couldn't have been seriously concerned about any designs you might have on her money. Forcing that ugly scene, making enemies of the Cody clan, and breaking your heart in the process, would have been completely unnecessary. If she'd really believed the stuff she said, she could have just waited for you to dump her when the cash cow dried up. The thing is, she knew you didn't care about the money, so she used your pride, and your ego, against you in a deliberately calculated way."

A hint of a smile graced the pilot's full mouth. He chewed his bottom lip thoughtfully. Sensing that he might be coming around, she urged, "Go on, Sean. It'll be an hour or so before the barbecue is ready; and dinner will keep. Ask Curtis. I'm sure he knows where Diana's living."

"I have the address," he admitted, patting his pocket. "Justin give it to me."

"Then what's stopping you?"

Grabbing the small case, and dropping a quick kiss on his sister's cheek, he lifted his helmet from the rack and bolted to his waiting motorcycle, scolding himself. *Don't think you idiot. Just follow your heart. Bridgett's provided you with the perfect excuse to do exactly what you want to do. So, use it.* And he did.

NINETEEN

Less than half an hour later, Sean pulled the huge bike into the semi-circular drive of a modest sized, flat-roofed brick ranch. The small vinyl case in hand, he steadied himself with a deep breath and headed toward the front door, his knees shaking. Get it together, man, he ordered. His heart pounding with anticipation and anxiety, he reassured himself. *What are you worrying about? You can't make things worse than they already are, and the breakup wasn't your fault. You didn't doubt her.*

He wanted to convince himself that he had no culpability, but his efforts failed miserably. The last words he'd spoken to Diana rang in his head, and his heart twisted again. *How could you say such a horrible thing? What if she refuses to forgive you? She could, you know, and who could blame her?* Steeling himself, he rang the bell.

An unfamiliar female voice called from inside, "Diana, you'll have to get that, I'm up to my elbows in crabmeat."

Taking a step back, he watched the graceful woman approach through one of the vertical, etched-glass windows bracketing the door. She glided toward him slowly, elegantly, her thoughts miles away. Her eyes were downcast, watching her path, so she didn't see him staring at her.

The mere sight of her hit him like an unexpected gut punch. He couldn't take his eyes off her. *She's thinner. And sad. There's something else, too.* Dressed in faded jeans and an old, cotton T-shirt, her feet bare, her pale hair hanging in loose waves around her shoulders, she looked much younger than her forty-plus years.

She opened the door and slowly raised her expressionless face to meet his. Her ice-blue gaze touched on him, making him shiver. When recognition dawned, the corners of her bow-shaped mouth drew into a sincere smile that cut through him like a knife. She seemed so shocked by his unexpected arrival, that she continued to stare at him in disbelief. He desperately wanted to offer her a greeting, but his voice had abandoned him.

"Who is it, Di?" Eleanor's bright head popped into view through the doorway. When she saw the couple silently staring at each other through the open portal, she flipped the dishtowel she was carrying over her shoulder and braced a fist on each hip. "Well, well, you must be Sean." Her eyes scanned the impressive length of him, from top to toe, smacking her lips appreciatively. "Where are your manners? Invite the man in, girl."

Ignoring the violent pounding of her heart, Diana offered graciously, "Oh yes, excuse me. Please, come in. It's great to see you, Sean."

"Is it?" he asked skeptically, stepping across

the threshold and into the tiled foyer.
"Of course it is."

"I wasn't sure I was going to be welcome." His
dark eyes looked intently into her pale ones, making
it almost impossible for Diana to think.

"I'm very happy to see you." *What an
understatement! The truth is I'm hungry for the
sight of you.* Her heart leapt for joy.

"Why don't you take your guest out to the
patio?" Elly suggested. "I'll bring you something to
drink. "What would you like, Sean? Iced tea or
maybe a beer?"

Thinking of the unfinished bottle he'd left in
Bridgett's kitchen, he told her, "A beer would be
great, thanks."

"I'm Eleanor Russell, by the way," she added
with a flirtatious wink. "Figured I'd better introduce
myself, since my friend seems to have totally
misplaced her manners."

"Nice to meet you." Sean stuck out a wide
palm and squeezed the woman's much smaller
hand.

Blushing, Diana apologized, "I'm sorry, Elly. I
don't know where my mind is."

With a broad, mischievous grin, the clever
nurse jabbed her friend with a playful elbow.
"That's okay. It's nice to see you befuddled for a
change, Miss I'm-Always-in-Control. And if you
didn't get a little shook-up in the presence of this
gorgeous hunk o' man, I'd know there was
something very wrong with you."

Watching the scarlet flush move downward

from Diana's high cheekbones until it reached her pale throat, Sean decided that he liked this clever, feisty woman. He chuckled, a pleasant, infectious sound, deep in his chest.

"Off with you, then," Eleanor urged again, waving toward the French doors. "Go enjoy the view. I'll bring the drinks."

Outside, Diana crossed the wide brick patio, and stood her back against the protective railing. Sean could see the lake behind her, sparkling in the evening sun. Hesitantly, she asked him, "What brings you to my door? After the way we left things, I know you didn't drop by to inquire about my well being."

Holding out the small case that he'd tucked under his arm, he told her, "I came to return this."

Disappointment shadowing her expressive face, she replied softly, "I see. Thank you."

Ignoring the hard knot tightening in his belly, he tried to make small talk. "You have a nice place. Great location."

"It was my mother's. She loved it here."

"I saw your nephew today. He told me you'd quit NSE, and gave me your address."

Obviously not wanting to broach that subject, she took the proffered bag from him and asked, "Where'd you find this?" Then she lay the kit aside, dismissing it.

"The American Airlines guy came across it when he picked up Bridgett's rental car, you know, that day. You must've left it on the seat."

Nodding in understanding, Diana told him. "It's kind of you to take the trouble to return it, particularly after the way I treated you."

"It's no trouble," he denied.

That said, they fell into an awkward silence which was broken, yet again, by Elly Russell's excellent timing. "Here we go." She handed a mug of foamy brew to the pilot, and a tall, icy glass to her friend. "No alcohol for you. Not in your condition. Drink your o.j."

Diana shot her a withering glare. "Thanks."

"My pleasure." Tossing her former roommate a challenging, so-sue-me smirk, she disappeared back inside, calling behind her, "Just holler if you need anything else. I'm gonna put the finishing touches on dinner. Sean, I'll expect you to join us."

Once she was out of earshot, Sean asked, "Are you ill, Diana?"

The sound of her name, uttered from his precious lips, echoed in her head. "Heavens no. I'm fine, just a little tired. Eleanor likes to play the good nurse." Lifting the glass in a mock salute, she smiled into his eyes. "Good old Vitamin C, fights off colds, you know."

"So I've been told."

For a long while they sipped their drinks, each taking the measure of the other. Diana seemed to be mustering up the courage to tell him something. Finally, she said, "It's quite a coincidence that you stopped by today, actually."

"Yeah?" He was beginning to feel encouraged by the way the conversation was unfolding. At least she hadn't shown him the door, yet.

"I called your apartment this afternoon to let you know that I still have your leather jacket. I guess it was in the car Bridgett used to drive me to the airport. Curtis must have loaded it onto the NSE jet, thinking it was mine. Anyway, I wanted to return it to you. I shouldn't have kept it for so long, but…"

"You called my place today?" he asked, interrupting.

"Yes, about an hour and a half ago," she acknowledged, checking her watch.

A heavy, twisting dread clutched at his gut and clawed its way upward. "You didn't leave a message."

"I was taken off guard when Patti answered. At first, I thought she was Bridgett." Diana appeared to be fighting back tears, but she pushed on, her voice thready. "Your wife thought I was asking to speak to Bridgett. I thought it best not to correct her misunderstanding. I didn't think leaving a message for you would be a wise move."

"My wife?" The cruel look of victory that he'd seen cross his former girlfriend's face, as she'd hung up the telephone, made sense now.

"Congratulations." Diana seemed to be choking on the words. "I hope you'll be very happy."

Inwardly seething at the determined divorcee's gall, Sean's quick mind searched for the right strategy to use to help him maneuver this unexpected turn of events to his advantage. Then a workable idea hit him.

"Patti and her children seemed to be settled in, based on the background noise. How long have you been married?" Diana probed.

"What would you say if I told you I called

Patti, and proposed to her, the afternoon you left? How would you feel if I said we flew to Las Vegas and were married the very next day?"

The tiny remnants of Diana's shattered heart exploded into brilliant shards of searing pain. It was all she could do to stay on her feet. She leaned against the rail for support. "Why does my reaction matter?"

"You made a production of tossing me aside, of humiliating me in front of my family, so I want to make sure you know that another woman was waiting, eager and anxious, to be my wife." Watching her intently, he added the finishing touch. "My wounded pride wants salving. I need to know if you have any regrets at all." He set his glass down and took two steps toward her, bringing his face close to hers.

You got just what you wanted, my girl, she reminded herself. *So fess up. Be honest with the man. He deserves that much.* Holding her juice in front of her like a shield, she lowered her gaze and stared at her bare feet. Trying to focus on what she needed to tell him, she admitted, "Yes, Sean, I have regrets – a mountain of them. Is that what you want to hear?"

"It's a beginning," he whispered, his full baritone deeply arousing. He took the glass from her and placed it on the rail. "Go on…"

"What do you want me to say? That deliberately forcing you out of my life was the biggest mistake I've ever made? That I'm unbelievably sorry for the cruel things I said? That I didn't mean a word of it? That I did it because I was afraid you'd end up hating me? That it was the hardest, most despicable thing I've ever done? That I love you so much it hurts?" She raised her eyes and let him see the tears streaming down her fair cheeks.

"Diana…I…," he began, but she wasn't finished.

"It doesn't matter what either of us wants, Sean. I can't say any of the things I want to say to you, because you're already committed to Patti, and it's my fault. I can only offer you my deepest and most sincere apology. I don't expect you to understand why I did what I did, so I won't ask you to forgive me, but please know that, at the time, I believed with all my heart that you'd be better off without me."

"And what do you think now?"

"That I was an inconceivable idiot," she admitted, ruefully.

Sean's handsome face broke open in a brilliant, glorious smile.

"Happy now?" she asked, a bit irritated by his apparent delight. He didn't answer her but just stood there staring at her and smiling, Diana thought, like the Cheshire cat. She had to do something to wipe the stupid grin off his face. "If it was an apology you came for, you have it. You have every right to be furious, and I don't blame you for it, but you took a hard shot at me, too. So, do you still wish you hadn't thwarted Stark's plan?"

The smile disappeared immediately, and his maple syrup eyes glistened. "That was my pride talking, not my heart. I wanted to take it back the moment it slipped out. I'm so sorry, Diana. I didn't mean it."

She didn't have the right to ask the question that was on the tip of her tongue, but she couldn't stop herself. "What does your heart say?"

"It loves you." He took another step forward pressing her body backward with his. Her blood thundered in her ears. His rapid, irregular breath tickled the tiny hairs at her temple. The electricity arcing between them was almost palpable.

Laying an uncertain palm on the center of his chest, she pushed gently. "Sean, we can't. Think about your wife."

"Patti! That lying, scheming bitch can go to hell," he growled, ignoring her plea, and kissing her long and hard.

The exchange left her breathless, and vibrating with desire, but still determined to do the right thing. "We can't do this. You're married, now. Remember your vows."

"There's nothing to remember." The broad grin reappeared.

Diana was confused. "But you said that you eloped the day after I left the farm."

"No. I asked you how you'd feel if I told you we'd eloped. I was trying to elicit a response from you, not stating a fact."

"You're not…?"

"Married?"

She nodded.

"No."

"Then why did Patti say that her children were

waiting for 'their father' to get home, meaning you? And why did she call Bridgett her 'sister-in-law'?"

Sean enfolded her into his strong arms, dropped a tender kiss on her hair and explained, "She recognized your voice and lied to warn you off. Worked, too, didn't it?"

Cutting her eyes at him, she returned his smile. "I should be angry with you for manipulating me, but to be honest, I'm too pleased to be mad."

Flashing her a knee-wobbling grin, he elaborated. "When I got in from work today, I found Patti and her spoiled brats squatting in my living room – uninvited and unwanted. I walked out on her and went to stay with Bridge and Curt."

"I would liked to have seen the look on her face," Diana noted, hope soaring.

"It was priceless. I gave my sister what-for, too, because she let that conniving gold-digger into my apartment."

"And what did she say about it?"

"Oh, she defended herself, said Patti didn't give her a choice. Then she showed me your toiletry kit and convinced me to deliver it to you."

"I guess I owe Bridgett a big thank-you for bringing you to my door."

"If you're planning on sending notes, you'd better start making a list, because you'll need to include Vic Baldwin, and your nephew. I had them both on my back today, nagging me to see you. Bridgett just provided me with a good excuse." He pointed at the small vinyl case.

"I've already replaced that, you know," she teased him playfully.

"Even a lame excuse is a good one when it allows you to do something you're dying to do." He waggled his eyebrows at her.

"True," she agreed. "I didn't really want to return your jacket. I wanted to keep it, but I couldn't think of any other reasonable excuse to call you."

"I tell you what," he offered, winking suggestively. "That battered jacket has seen some pretty hard use, so I'll give it to you, as long as you take me along with it."

"Is that a proposal?" Her tone was light, but her heart still thudded.

"Yep. The second one." He held her tightly, laughing. "Before you came along, I never expected to propose to any woman, much less twice – to the same woman! What do you say?"

"I want to say 'yes'," she told him immediately, trying not to think.

"Then do it!"

"There's something else I have to tell you, something that could make you change your mind about wanting me." Staring directly into his warm brown eyes, she tried to convey what was in her heart. "After you hear what I have to say you may want to retract want your proposal. If you do, I'll understand. If you don't, I'll give you my answer,"

"Sounds fair," he agreed, backing up a step and crossing his arms in from of him, clearly worried. "Fire away! What else could possibly come between us?"

"A baby."

"Aw, hell. Not that again," he snorted in frustration. "Bridgett told me that she used the no-kids thing to break us apart, but it's nonsense, Diana. My folks already have a passel of grandchildren, and don't give a damn about producing more. From what I hear, Page is already picking out colors for the nursery, and she and Colin aren't even hitched yet. So, I say let him carry on the Cody name. I'm not sure I want all that responsibility."

"My point exactly," she chimed in.

Confused now, he stuttered, "Wh…what?"

"It's true that I deliberately pushed you away because I didn't believe I would be able to give you a baby, and I convinced myself that you'd be better off with a younger wife. But that's not the problem now. In fact, it's quite the opposite."

"I'm not following you."

Offering him a hesitant smile, she explained, "Well, you need to know that, if you marry me, you'll be getting two for the price of one."

Understanding finally dawned. "You're pregnant?"

"Surprise, surprise."

Swallowing hard, he stammered, "B…but how?"

"The usual way. I can think of four occasions when we made love without the benefit of protection. It could have been any one of them. Take your pick." The memories brought a flush of high color to her cheekbones.

He shot her a don't-be-cute glance. "I know the facts of life, Diana. Shit! I never even thought of using any…anything. I guess I assumed you were taking care of it."

"It didn't occur to me, either, because I thought I was too old for it to matter." She turned away from him and stared out over the lake. "To be totally honest, birth control was the last thing on my mind. I wanted you too much to let anything stop me from making love to you."

"So, we got caught like a couple of horny teenagers," he concluded, swinging her around to face him and squeezing her against the solid, unyielding wall of his chest.

She smiled at his apt analogy.

"You've seen a doctor?"

"This afternoon," she confirmed. "I even have a picture. Do you want to see your son?" Pulling a copy of the sonogram results out of her back pocket, she handed it to him.

"My son?" He couldn't make heads or tails of the printout. "How can you tell it's a boy?"

"Here, let me show you." Pointing to the various body parts of the tiny fetus, she added, "I understand that you usually can't tell the gender of the baby this soon, but it seems that our son is pretty well-endowed. Guess he gets that from his father."

It was Sean's turn to blush. Diana laughed at his rare display of shy self-consciousness. Quickly recovering, he returned the photo to her. Then he guided her toward a wrought iron chair that was placed off to one side of the wide patio. "Sit here." When she did, he knelt before her, taking her hands in his.

Her greedy, tear-filled eyes drank their fill of his cherished face.

"Diana, from the first moment I saw you, I

knew that you were meant to be mine. I will never let you go again. You have no other choice. You have to marry me."

Throwing her arms around his neck, she breathed into his ear, "Yes, yes, yes!" She showered his cheek with feathery kisses, as he lifted her out of her seat and whirled her around and around, until both of them were giddy. When he finally put her down, she had to grab onto him to stop her head from spinning. Then, he set it reeling once more, with a deep, demanding kiss, full of a lifetime of promise.

"You do leave a girl breathless," she breathed. Then her eyes darken and she added, "Sean, I want to be your wife more than I've ever wanted anything, but I have to be sure."

"About what?"

"Are you certain you want this baby? I couldn't stand it if I thought I'd trapped you into accepting a child you had no idea you were creating."

"I want him, Diana." Pausing to consider, he reiterated, "I want him very much. Now shut up and kiss me again."

With a smile as bright as the morning sun, she obeyed him, thoroughly fulfilling his command. This time it was the big man's turn to swoon. "Woman, you are too much. If you keep that up I'm going to drag you inside and have my way with you."

She giggled in response. "What should we do now?"

"I've already told you my idea, but we might embarrass your friend."

"That would be a pretty hard to do," Diana told him. "I'm sure she's been eavesdropping on our entire conversation."

"Then she's gotten herself an earful."

"I'll say."

A thought suddenly struck him and he gave her a playful squeeze. "You know, eloping to Las Vegas doesn't sound like such a bad idea. Let's do it. I can strong-arm Vic into loaning us a company helicopter. My bag's packed and waiting outside on the Harley, and you have your essentials all ready." He pointed to the little case he'd returned to her. "Go throw some underwear and a nightgown in a bag, and we'll take off."

He looked like an anxious kid on Christmas morning. She kissed him again. "On second thought," he purred, his voice warm and suggestive, "forget the underwear and the nightgown. You're not gonna need 'em."

"Neither of you are going anywhere until after dinner," Elly announced from inside, her opportune interruption confirming Diana's suspicions that she'd been listening in. "I've worked my fingers to the bone making crab cakes, and we're going to enjoy them, or else." Though she pretended to be miffed, the pleased smirk that pulled at the corners of her lips told them otherwise.

Taking a big sniff of the tantalizing odor drifting out through the open door, Sean agreed, patting his stomach. "Sounds great and smells wonderful. I'll just give Bridgett a call to tell her I won't be back for dinner."

After offering him another knee-wobbling kiss, Diana left him to phone his sister. Curtis Sloan picked up on the first ring. The portly attorney cheerfully agreed to pass along Sean's regrets to his sister. He was delighted to hear that Sean and Diana had been patched things up. With a "Congratulations and keep us posted," he signed off.

That obligation successfully met, the pilot found the powder room, washed his hands, and joined the women in the cozy kitchen, where the meal was already in progress. Elly took his heaping plate out of the oven and set it on the table next to Diana's. Suddenly ravenous, he dug into the food with relish.

"I do love cooking for a man who really enjoys eating," the nurse admitted, as she watched Sean shovel in yet another huge bite of the succulent crab cake.

Mumbling through the last forkful, he apologized. "Sorry, I'm not using my best Sunday manners. Mom would be ashamed. But this is delicious and I'm starving."

"Being in love does that to a fellow, huh?" she teased him, openly ignoring her friend's vain attempts to stop her from embarrassing the man.

"You could say that," he responded, not at all bothered by her suggestion. Aiming a suggestive wink at Diana, he played right into Eleanor's hand. "Whets my appetite, leaving me hungry for food…and other things."

Cackling with glee, the self-satisfied woman asked. "So, did I hear you correctly? Are you two eloping?"

"Right after supper," he confirmed. "If Diana doesn't back out on me, we're gonna fly to Las Vegas. An old buddy of mine runs a small hotel and casino out there. A little arm-twisting should get us the honeymoon suite. Reaching for his fiancée's hand, he asked, "What do you say, babe?"

A mischievous twinkle in her frosty blue eyes, she answered, "I say it's a wonderful plan, except for the flying part. Helicopters make me nervous."

"We could take the Harley, but you might be a little windblown and saddle sore by the time we reach Nevada, and last-minute commercial airline tickets are too expensive, especially when there's a free option available. I know you're used to the finest things in life, my love, but you'll just have to settle for less, if you're gonna marry me."

"Never," she breathed, squeezing his hand. "You are the best, at any price."

Several toe-curling kisses later, she explained what she had in mind. "I still know how to pull a string here and there. Justin will be happy to loan us the NSE jet for a couple of days. He actually prefers traveling by helicopter. And besides, the trip will be more fun with someone else in the driver's seat."

Liking that idea immensely, he agreed, wagging an eyebrow at her suggestively.

That decided, Diana and Sean pitched in to help Eleanor clean up, only to be repeatedly distracted from the task by a series of longing glances and lingering touches.

"Uh-huh!" Elly forced a cough. "You two need to get out of here pretty damn soon. Watching you is making me hornier than hell." Her fists propped on her hips, she added, "Don't expect me to be here when you get back, either. I'm going home to jump my husband's bones!"

Wiggling out of Sean's demanding embrace, Diana faced her with a laugh, and a thank-you hug. "I don't know what I would have done without you, Elly. You're my rock."

"Rock-head is more like it. Now get out of here!" she ordered. So, they did.

TWENTY

"Come hither, my lady!" Sean called to Diana from the balcony of their penthouse suite.

"Aye, my lord. As you command." Playing along, she joined him. "What is it that vexes thee, good sir?"

Abandoning the playful banter, he told her, "You were too far away." With a deep, throaty sigh, he wrapped one muscular arm around her, as he swept the other in an arc across the panoramic view of the twinkling lights. "That's something, huh?"

"Yeah. Makes me glad I don't have to pay the electric bill."

Her droll observation tickled him, and his hearty laugh rang out.

"What's so funny?" Diana asked him, aiming a friendly punch at his side.

"Just that you would be concerned about that."

"Hey! I might have had more money than I could spend, once, but I've never been a wastrel. You can't hold onto a fortune if you don't pay attention to where it goes and how it's used." Her indignant tone elicited another chuckle from the big man. "Go ahead, make fun. But I have to count pennies, now, right along with the rest of the regular folks."

"I'd say chose-to would be more accurate than have-to," Sean noted. "You chose to give up your interest in NSE, Diana. You weren't forced into it. Justin told me that he begged you to reconsider."

"He even offered to make some of the changes I wanted," she admitted, "but I refused his offer because my heart just isn't in it anymore. And I made the right choice. Justin will be a great CEO." Leveling her gaze, she told him, "NSE was James' dream, not mine. I went along, because my mother needed security. I did too, I guess. But I don't anymore. Now I can stand on my own two feet."

"I hope you'll lean on me, at least a little," he whispered, pulling her close.

"Of course, I will. I already do." She punctuated her declaration with a warm, inviting kiss. For a long time, they stood together, arms around each other's waists, looking out over the colorful skyline. Diana's thoughts drifted back to their whirlwind wedding trip.

As she had predicted, they'd had no problem securing the NSE jet. Justin arranged for the company limo to take them to the airport where the plane waited, fueled and ready. When she'd called him, just before take-off, to thank him for his generosity, he'd told her, "You deserve to be cherished, Diana. Tell Sean he'd better treat you right, or he'll have me to answer to." Thinking of his words now made her smile.

The flight west had been blissful. Only essential staff had manned the plane, which left

Diana and Sean virtually alone in the sumptuous cabin. They'd made extremely good use of the small, well-appointed stateroom occupying the tail section.

A short cab ride had delivered them to the hotel and casino, on the outskirts of the city, where Sean's Corps buddy, Jesse Washburn, managed the front desk. Diana could hardly believe her eyes when she'd first glimpsed the huge ex-Marine, looking very out of place behind the elegant, marble-topped desk. He was even more muscular than Sean, and his dark skin shown like polished ebony against the brilliant white collar of his shirt. As soon as he'd recognized his former Captain, the man had vaulted the high counter effortlessly. After a few seconds of backslapping and affectionate name calling, he'd directed the couple to a suite on the topmost floor.

Jesse had thoughtfully arranged for them to use the hotel's shuttle car. So, they'd stowed their things, and headed out to purchase wedding essentials. At an inviting jewelry shop, owned by a craggy-faced, Native American man, they'd chosen matching silver wedding bands, inlaid with beautifully cut turquoise, and in a tiny, one-of-a-kind boutique, Diana had found the perfect dress.

The gown was very different from anything she'd owned before, but she'd known at first glance that this fairy-like creation was made for her. Its simple, ankle-length slip of rich, purple silk was topped by a sheer overlay in indescribable hues, ranging from orchid to lilac. The dress caressed her curves sensuously. Its scooped neckline showed off

her collarbones and creamy skin, and the flowing
sleeves and fluted hem accentuated her natural
grace.

She'd added a silver necklace and earrings,
inset with amethyst stones, strapped on pewter
sandals, and pinned a small spray of lavender and
baby's in her fair locks. The look of adoration on
Sean's handsome face, as she'd approached him,
was forever etched on her brain.

"You're gorgeous," he'd whispered to her as he
took her hand and tucked it in his. "My fairy
princess."

Though the tears clawing at her throat had
prevented her from telling him so, he'd looked
wonderful too. He'd worn black jeans topped by a
suede vest, crisp white western shirt with silver
buttons and collar tabs, and leather bolo tie.
Snakeskin boots had completed his look, a cross
between dangerous gunslinger, ready for a
showdown, and mischievous boy playing cowboy.
Diana had decided she liked the combination, very
much.

The jaded Elvis-impersonator minister, who'd
seen just about everything come through his
establishment at one time or another, had been
decidedly impressed. He'd led them through their
vows with sincerity and reverence, despite his
unconventional appearance, and had wished them
hearty congratulations, followed by a very
believable rendition of "Love Me Tender."
Afterwards, they had waited patiently while Mrs.
Reverend Elvis took a snapshot, then they'd
returned to their hotel and made love long into the

night.

Thinking back now, Diana found it hard to believe, but each intimate encounter with Sean had been better than the one before. Legalizing their union had only enhanced the desire they felt for one another. As she watched the colored lights flashing against the dark sky, she prayed that would never change.

Instinctively responding to her daydreams, he steered her inside. Grabbing her tightly against him, he showered her face and neck with fiery kisses. "You have on too many clothes," he breathed against her hair, his nimble fingers efficiently removing her panties. Drawing her to the sitting area, he slipped out of his boxers, boldly seating himself on the coffee table, his erection impudently calling to her, and pulled her down on top of him, straddling his lap. Crying out with pleasure, Diana welcomed his delicious intrusion into her body.

Collapsing against the unyielding wall of his chest, she let him determine the rhythm of their lovemaking, raising and lowering herself slowly, driving them both insane with anticipation. He explored her mouth with his, thoroughly and completely. His tongue rained a blazing trail down over the long white column of her throat. Freeing her breasts, he turned his attention to them, caressing each one in turn, teasing her nipples with his hot, demanding tongue.

She dug her fingers into the firm muscles of his shoulders and back, loving the feel of his skin against hers. When they could endure the exquisite torture no longer, he slipped his palms under her smooth, round bottom and encouraged her to climb higher and higher, faster and faster, until she reached the peak of exquisite desire. Sean roared his release, clutching her to him. Diana feared that she would faint from the sheer joy of the moment.

After a long moment, he observed wryly, "I believe we've initiated every piece of furniture in this place."

"I think you're right," she agreed, taking a deep breath, filling her head with his intoxicatingly masculine scent, and added a playful afterthought. "No, wait, I think there's a spot over there behind the dining table, that we haven't tried. Shall we?"

Sean laughed, his smile wide and exceedingly sexy. "Whoa girl. Slow down and give your old man a chance to catch up," he teased. "Aren't you ever satisfied?"

"Actually, I'm very well satisfied, for the moment. I just didn't want to pass up any opportunity," she parried.

"Wanton wench!"

"That I am. And you, good sir, would be well advised to do your best to satisfy my needs." She wiggled her hips against him suggestively.

He groaned, feeling the heat stirring him again. "On second thought, maybe witch is a better word for you. You've put a spell on me. What magic is this?"

"The magic of love," she answered, wrapping her arms tightly around his neck, and caressing his lips with soft, feathery kisses. Feeling his arousal growing again, deep inside her, she observed, "Bewitched or not, you seem to be keeping up with my demands. You may even be a bit overeager."

"Only with you, my lady."

"Oh, so now, I'm your lady?"

"Always."

"Not a wench, or a witch, or even an 'Ice Queen'?"

"Never." To prove his point, he found her lips once more, kissing her deeply.

A long while later, Diana tried to pull her sore, tired body from his embrace. "Just where do you think you're going?" he inquired, his voice still husky with spent passion.

"To take a shower."

"I'll join you," he agreed quickly, rising to follow.

"Oh no. Not this time. We tried that before, and you know where it got us." She put a palm in the middle of his broad chest in a half-hearted attempt to hold him off.

"Of course, I do. Why do you think I'm so anxious to repeat the experience?" His dark eyes flashed eagerly.

"Down boy. I hate to admit it, but you've worn me out. I desperately need reviving. I'll go get a bath while you order us some food. I'm famished." She kissed him softly to ease the blow of her refusal.

"Whatever you say, love," he acquiesced, reaching out an index finger to gently caress the tip of one rosy nipple. "But you'd better be prepared to pay for your supper, and you know what sort of payment I have in mind."

His touch left her skin tingling and her entire

being charged with sexual energy. It seemed impossible for her to get her fill of him, and that thought pleased her immensely. She smiled at him, promising him everything he wanted and more, and forced her feet to move toward the bathroom.

When she emerged a half-hour later, wrapped in the complimentary terry cloth robe, her hair still damp, she found her husband waiting for her patiently, wearing his favorite pair of faded jeans. He rose from the sofa to answer a knock on the door. He admitted the room service waiter and helped him set the food out on the small table, slipping a bill into his hand as he departed. Diana didn't hesitate, but filled her plate, digging into the fluffy omelet and fresh fruit with relish. "Your son wants feeding," she defended, when he laughed at the unladylike way she downed a glass of ice-cold milk. "If I'm going to entertain your amorous attentions and provide you with a healthy, well-grown baby, I've got to keep up my strength."

"By all means, help yourself," he urged her. "We have to make sure you're up to the strenuous activity I have in mind for you later." He attacked his plate with a fervor equal to hers.

"You're not going to scold me about eating too much?"

He flashed her a don't-be-ridiculous look. "Why would I do that?"

"James routinely complained about my appetite. Claimed I was fat and getting fatter. Aren't you afraid I'll get too plump for you, too?"

"When are you going to realize that I'm not like him? In any way?" Sean's maple syrup eyes softened sympathetically, but the edginess in his voice betrayed his anger.

"I'll never mistake you for James, Sean. It's quite impossible, because I love you with all my heart, and to be brutally honest, I never really cared much for James. But his criticism of me still echoes in my head sometimes, so it's difficult for me to believe that a smart, decidedly gorgeous hunk of man, like you, could find me attractive."

"You see what you do to me, Diana. One look and BOOM! I'm all fired up. I touch you and fireworks go off. How can you not know how beautiful you are?" A tear inched down her cheek. He caught it on his fingertip. "I thought I'd made my preference clear long ago. I don't go for skinny chicks. I like my women to have a little meat on their bones." Squeezing her upper arm, he quipped, "You'll do."

She couldn't help laughing. Reassured, she went back to her meal. When she'd finished the last bite, she pushed back her chair and asked him, "Shouldn't we be thinking of getting back? Except for Elly, no one knows where we are, or what we've been doing."

"I sure hope nobody knows what we've been doing. They'd be shocked," he teased. Ignoring his suggestive insinuation, she pressed him, "No one will be looking for me, but what about you? Shouldn't you check in with your family, or with Vic?"

"I told Curtis that I'd be in touch by the end of the week, so he'll head off questions from the sisters, and Vic said I should take a few days off before…" He rubbed his face in distress. "Holy Shit!"

"What is it?"

"Colin's wedding!"

"What?"

"This is Thursday, right?" He jumped up and began pacing nervously.

"Yes, and tomorrow's Friday," she confirmed with a patronizing smile.

"Colin and Page are getting married Saturday night, this Saturday night, and I'm the Best Man. We've got to get home right away. It's a four-hour drive from DC to the farm."

"Calm down," she urged him. "This is not a problem. Go pack your things. I'll call the pilot and let him know we want to leave right away. I'll have him file a flight plan to Roanoke Regional instead of Dulles. You can notify your family, en route, to pick you up at the airport. I'm sure you can catch a ride home, after the wedding, with Bridgett and Curtis."

"Oh no. You're not dumping me with the folks and flying off to safety. If I have to do this, so do you. I'll need the moral support." He could see the look of terror behind her frosty blue eyes, so he improvised. "I hate tuxedos. They scare me."

"Sean, I couldn't," she gasped, his attempt at humor lost on her. "Your family despises me. The last thing you need is to show up at Colin's wedding with me in tow. Go. Do your duty to your nephew, spend a few days with your mom and dad, and I'll drive down to pick you up after everything's over. The timing will be better then."

"Coward," he accused with a growl.

"You bet," she confessed grimly. "If there were any way around it, I'd never face your family. I know I've got to do it, eventually, but let's wait for a better time."

"This is the better time," he insisted. "Everyone will be distracted by the wedding folderol. They won't have time to dwell on us. Relax. It'll be fine." He wrapped a long arm around her and held her close to his heart, stroking her hair. "I won't let them hurt you."

Not being one to run from trouble, Diana sniffed back the tears, straightened her shoulders and said, "Okay. Let's do it."

Morning found them back at the house on Lake Barcroft. Diana changed into a raw silk traveling suit in a becoming shade of pale blue, and added a few things to her suitcase. Thankfully, the waistband of her pants was forgiving enough to accommodate the small baby-bump that had just made an appearance. Then they drove to Sean's apartment in her little Subaru wagon, where he swapped out dirty clothes for clean, and picked up his formalwear. Before noon, they were on their way south.

"We'll have to go straight to the rehearsal," he informed her. "We're cutting it close."

Diana was thankful that she'd taken the time to change out of the rumpled dungarees she'd worn on the plane. In the expensive suit, with her hair twisted up into a sleek chignon, she looked cool and sophisticated. "Just as well. They'll be less likely to lynch me with so many witnesses around. A church is a good place, particularly with a man of the cloth present. Your family won't risk murder in front of their pastor."

Sean was happy to see that her sense of humor had returned. "They might give you a hard time at first, but once they get over it, they're gonna love you as much as I do."

"Maybe." She sounded skeptical. "But what about your 'first wife'? Assuming Patti's going to be there. How're you going to break the news to her – tell her you're guilty of bigamy?"

"Screw her!" he cursed.

"Over my dead body!" she snapped back, adamantly.

They both laughed. The tension between them shattered. "Get some rest, Diana. You're beat. You have to be. How does that old saying go, 'And leave the driving to us'?"

She knew he was right, so she reclined her seat, closed her eyes, and dozed. In what seemed like minutes later, she felt his hand on her shoulder, shaking her gently. "Wake up, love. We're here."

A violent wave of nausea hit her.

"What's wrong?"

"I think I'm going to be sick." Her skin was a pale as parchment.

"Come on. Let's find a restroom."

"No. Just give me a minute." She forced in several cleansing breaths. Grabbing the door handle, she opened it and stepped out. The late afternoon air was unusually cool for late July. A light breeze stirred the trees and felt refreshing against her clammy skin. Sean rounded the car quickly. "Go on inside," she urged him, noting the vehicles already lined up in the gravel parking area. "Everyone's waiting for you. I'll be along as soon as I get my feet under me."

"You sure?" His concern in his dark eyes.

She nodded in the affirmative. "I'll be right behind you."

Watching him stride toward the quaint, white-clapboard church, Diana took several deep breaths, trying to force down the dizzying waves of nausea. She found a clean handkerchief in her pocket, and used it to wipe the beads of sweat off of her upper lip. *Steady girl, it's time. No more procrastinating.* One final gulp of air and she was off, following the man of her dreams into a waking nightmare.

Slipping into the vestibule, unnoticed by the crowd of people who surrounded Sean and eagerly welcomed him, Diana quietly closed the door behind her and waited for someone to acknowledge her arrival. To her dismay, Patti Sanderson's sharp soprano rang out, "What in the hell is she doing here?!" All eyes turned, except those belonging to the shocked minister, who stared at the audacious Matron of Honor in disbelief.

He scolded her, "Please, my dear. This is the house of the Lord. We do not use such language here."

His rebuke fell on deaf ears, as Patti repeated, pointing an accusing finger at the latest arrival, and screeching, "Will someone please tell me what that bitch is doing here?! Who does she think she is?"

Sean dropped the hand he was shaking and

bolted to his wife's side. "Diana's my guest."

"Then you tell her to leave. She's not invited," the enraged woman ordered.

"You should know all about showing up places where you're not invited," Bridgett observed, jabbing Patti in the ribs with a well-aimed elbow. "It's lucky for you that I have better manners and didn't throw you out on your butt."

"I…uh…I never…well…I…" Patti huffed, totally indignant. "That's different!"

"What is she doing here, Sean?" Kathleen asked, haughtily, her head tilted back at an odd angle, so she could literally look down her nose at Diana. "After all those terrible things she said to you?"

Wrapping an encouraging arm around his bride, Sean addressed them. "Since I have your undivided attention and I know you're not going to drop this, let's get it over with." His dark gaze swept the room before he continued. "The scene that many of you witnessed at the house, between Diana and me, was the result of a terrible misunderstanding. We both said things we didn't mean. My pride was wounded. For months, I refused to make the first move, but when I finally did, she apologized and admitted that she still loves me. Then I apologized right back, and asked her to be my wife. This time she accepted."

"No!" Patti screamed in horror. "You can't marry her. You're mine. You've been mine since we were kids, and I won't give you up." Her beautiful face contorted with rage; she sprang at Diana. "What did you do to him, you, you…?" She aimed her long, red-lacquered nails at the defenseless woman's eyes.

Anticipating her attack, Sean grabbed Patti before any damage could be done. She clung to him, pressing her breasts against him. "Please Sean. Tell her it's me you want, not her."

"I'm sorry, Patti. Diana and I are already married." He pushed her away, took his wife's hand in his, and held it up. The matching bands, encircling their ring fingers, winked and sparkled under the lights.

When the stunned murmuring subsided, Sean added, "You and I were over a long time ago, Pats." He saw her cringe at his use of the pet name, so he softened his tone and tried to make her understand, "You dumped me to trade up, or so you thought. It's not my fault that your marriage to the dentist didn't work out. I moved on. Diana is my wife. I love her and I'm gonna do my darnedest to make her happy. You'll just have to accept that."

Wagging a finger in his face now, she spat at him, "I'll never accept it. You're a young, handsome man. She's an old hag. You're infatuated by her money and all the things she can give you, but that won't last. All the money in the world won't be enough to keep you in her bed. You'll get tired of her wrinkles and sagging flesh, and you'll come home, begging me to take you back."

"Don't hold your breath, Pats," he warned her, eyes flashing dangerously.

"Stop using that stupid nickname! I hated it when we were younger, and I hate it still. From now on you can call me 'Mrs. Sanderson'."

"Whatever you say, Mrs. Sanderson." He

bowed mockingly.

Fury undiminished, she whirled in defiance, showing him her back, and flounced away. Page ran to Patti and tried to console her, as she wailed loudly. Patti's mother, a slender, pinch-faced woman, stood in the far corner of the narthex wringing her hands in distress, as she watched her daughter's outrageous temper tantrum.

"Enough!" Sean's deep baritone boomed. "I'm warning you all. If you can't welcome Diana into our family and offer her your best wishes, you'd better hold your tongue. Now, let's get on with the business at hand. We owe it to Page and Colin to put everything else aside and focus on their happiness."

"Here! Here! Well said," Nelson applauded.

J.D. added, "Time's awastin'. Let's get this show on the road so's we can eat."

The relieved minister took his cue from the men, and directed the wedding party inside the sanctuary. Sean tucked Diana into a seat on the back row where she could watch the proceedings in relative safety, before taking his place at the altar. Still edgy and nervous, Diana jumped when she felt a touch on her arm.

She looked up into Mike Cody's dark eyes, so like those of his son. "It's nice to have you in the family, Diana," he told her softly, "You're gonna be good for Sean. I can tell."

"Thank you, Mr. Cody" the surprised woman responded.

"You can call me 'Pop' if you want. I've always wanted someone to call me 'Pop'."

"Thanks, Pop." She smiled at him, tears glistening in her bright blue eyes. With a quick pat on her shoulder, he joined the others at the front.

To Diana's shock, each of Sean's sisters, in turn, followed their father's example, stopping to offer her a kind word or warm welcome. Bridgett led the way, giving her a wink and an encouraging "Chin-up". Sarah Cody brought up the rear.

"I guess I didn't make a mistake about you after all."

"I hope not," the new daughter-in-law volunteered.

Offering her hand, Sarah squeezed Diana's long fingers tightly. "Make my boy happy, will you?"

"I'll do my best."

"Yes, I believe you will."

TWENTY-ONE

The dispute between Bridgett and her mother regarding the location of the rehearsal dinner, had been settled by a compromise. Instead of the church fellowship hall, or a rented space in an expensive hotel, the wedding party retired to the private dining room of a small, family-owned restaurant near Smith Mountain Lake.

An extra place was set for Diana at one of the long tables, next to J.D. Craddock and across from Dwight Young. Though her dinner companions were quite congenial, doing their utmost to make her feel welcome, Diana yearned for Sean's comforting presence. Unfortunately, as Best Man, he'd been placed at the head table, between the bride-to-be and her sister.

The food was plentiful and quite good, but Diana had no appetite. The Matron of Honor's antics soured her stomach. Patti hovered over Sean, bending her head toward him as if the embarrassing scene in the church vestibule had never occurred. She touched him whenever an excuse presented itself, fluttering her long eyelashes and flirting with abandon. Periodically, she'd cast her eye at Diana to make sure she took in every calculated move.

The rehearsal itself had been agonizingly tedious. The endless processional of Sean's sisters, and nieces, and Page's college friends, had seemed to take forever. The minister had been unbelievably thorough, insisting that the bride and groom go over their vows three times. Diana had breathed a thankful sigh when the organist had finally struck up the recessional, only to have her hopeful spirits dashed by the victorious gleam in Patti's eye as she'd marched up the aisle arm-in-arm with Sean. The shameless schemer had even had the unmitigated gall to shoot a challenging smirk at her, as they'd passed by the pew where she waited.

Deciding she'd had enough, Diana excused herself before the desserts and customary toasting was finished and went out to the car to wait for Sean. She lowered the windows and reclined her seat. Then, she closed her eyes and tried to clear her mind of its jumble of vexing images. She was just starting to relax a little, when a tortuously familiar laugh set her teeth on edge.

"What in the hell are you doing in that tin can?" Patti rudely asked, as she stuck her shiny curls through the open window. "Isn't this little car beneath your dignity, Mrs. North?"

"It's Mrs. Cody," the irritated woman reminded her.

"Not for long," the unwanted intruder warned. "Enjoy your time in his bed, because you're not going to be there for long. Like I said before, Sean will get tired of your sagging, flabby body, and when he does, I'll be there waiting."

Fresh out of patience with the determined

woman's dire predictions, Diana took the offensive. "Oh, I do enjoy it – very much, though that's not what I hear about you. Sean tells me you'd be the last woman he'd want warming his sheets. My husband has out-grown you. He prefers a woman who can deliver more than she promises. Of course, knowing how to properly satisfy a man's sexual needs is something that only age and maturity can teach. Given time, even you might get a little better at it."

"Ooh, you…you…you…" Patti huffed.

"You're starting to sound a bit redundant, Mrs. Sanderson. So, if don't mind, I'd like to rest." She feigned a bored yawn. "I need to recharge a bit before tonight."

Patti retreated a step, but held her ground and continued to sputter. Diana watched her, wondering what she might say to get the irritating woman to move on, when Sean approached them, asking, "What's going on here?"

"Nothing much," Diana answered, pleased with her temporary victory. Your ex-girlfriend was curious about the car. She was wondering why we're driving this, instead of something more expensive and luxurious."

"What did you tell her?"

"I hadn't gotten that far, I'm afraid. The conversation got off track." Diana shrugged innocently.

"Oh good. Then you'll allow me to fill in the details?" he offered.

"By all means." He seemed to be enjoying the exchange, so she left him to it.

"Diana relinquished her interest in North Star Enterprises, gave up all of the assets she'd held jointly with her late husband. The Jaguar she used to drive belonged to the company, so that went, right along with the rest of her fortune."

Patti shook her head in disbelief. "You mean she's broke?"

"Not exactly. Diana still has the house her mother left her, and this neat little car." He slapped a broad palm on its top. "It drives like a dream, by the way. And its safety rating is stellar. I much prefer it to your gas-guzzler."

"You want me to believe that you're supporting her now?"

"Believe what you want, but I want you to know that I didn't marry Diana for her money, because she hasn't any."

Meeting his determined gaze with an undefeated glare, Patti hissed at him through clenched teeth. "You think this is over, but it isn't. She thinks she's won, but she hasn't. That fat, old bitch you call a wife has humiliated and embarrassed me for the last time. Beware, my darling Seàn, I'll get what I want. I always do. And she'll pay for what she's done to me. I'm willing to spare your feelings, if I can, but if you get in my way, I'll take you down, too."

"I'm shaking in my boots," he retorted with a sly grin. "I'm fed up with your lies, Pats, and your weak attempts at intimidation." Turning away, he left her standing in the dusty parking lot, shaking in barely suppressed fury.

He slid into the driver's seat, buckled his safety

belt, and fired up the engine. As they pulled out onto the highway, he reassured his wife, "Forget her, Diana. She's just running her mouth. Her threats are empty."

"Don't you worry your handsome head over it. I've already put her out of my mind. Taking anything she says seriously is a complete waste of effort." Diana's words were bold and self-assured, but her energy had been drained by the strain of the confrontation.

"She sure was pissed off. What did you say to her?"

He couldn't see the satisfied smirk that crossed her face. "Nothing much. I just let her know, very subtly of course, that I know something she doesn't' – how to satisfy you in the bedroom."

"You didn't?!" Sean choked out, through waves of laughter.

"I certainly did. I even told her that, with age and experience, she might learn how to please a man too."

"That's priceless. You might have a few years on her, Diana, but I'd bet Patti's been around the block more times than you."

"I wouldn't doubt it for one second. But she doesn't know that, does she?"

"She'll never hear it from me. No matter how many men she's bedded, she'll never be half the lover you are, even with your relative inexperience." He caressed her cheek with the back of his hand.

Sometimes Sean still had difficulty trusting his

good fortune. Glancing at Diana out of the corner of his eye, all soft, and warm, and inviting, he hardly recognized her as the woman he'd watched striding across the tarmac, four months earlier. That woman would never have traded barbs with Patti Martin over the subject of sexual prowess. He decided that he liked this new transformation even better than the first, and that one had been pretty darned good. She'd stirred his blood then too, but not the way she did now. He'd never imagined that it would be possible to reach such a deep level of intimacy, with any woman, that he had with Diana, his bride.

A comfortable silence fell over them as they quickly covered the few miles to the Cody farm. Tires crunching, Sean pulled the car up near the stairway to his garage apartment. "I need to go over some last-minute details with Colin." Even in the weak yellow glow of the dome light, he could see the dark circles under her eyes. "You look beat. Why don't you go on to bed? I'll bring the bags when I come up."

She brushed a kiss across his cheek. "Thanks." Reaching for the infamous toiletry bag, she added, "I'll need this."

Noting that a warm illumination shone out into the thickening darkness from the window above, he noted, "Looks like someone left a light on. You shouldn't have any trouble getting in." He helped her out of the car, kissed her soundly, and headed off with a promise to hurry.

Diana climbed the narrow wooden staircase, opened the door, and stepped inside, surprised to find the room already occupied. "I was praying for an angel, and one walks in. Not that I'm complaining, but what're you doing here, gorgeous?"

"Skip, you silver-tongued devil! I didn't expect you."

"I didn't expect you, either, but that doesn't mean we can't make the best of our good luck. Come over here and sit by me."

The last time she'd been in the spacious apartment, she was much too distressed to pay attention to the décor, so Diana quickly scanned the interior of the comfortable room. It was pleasantly furnished, with a decidedly masculine touch. A queen-sized bed, nightstand, dresser, and chest of drawers occupied the far corner. A sturdy oak desk sat under one of the large windows. An oversized chair, thoughtfully placed beside a floor lamp, was situated next to a well-used but still serviceable couch, where Skip lounged. Along one wall ran a large metal shelving unit, randomly stacked with an odd assortment of books, pictures, football trophies, sports equipment, video games, and one large pair of black combat boots.

Laying her cosmetic case on the corner of the desk, Diana crossed to the sofa and collapsed into the soft cushions with a sight of relief. "Tough day?" the friendly man quipped.

"That's an understatement," she groaned.

Taking her hand, he lifted it to his lips and placed a quick kiss on her knuckles. "Hey, what's this?" Still holding her fingers, he waved her wedding ring in front of her face. "Does that mean what I think it means?"

She nodded and smiled at him.

"Damn! That lucky bastard beat me to the punch." Still pretending to be disappointed, he went on, "Can't say I'm surprised.

"You're not?"

"Nope. After you left here, the guy was a basket case. I've never seen a dude so gone on a chick. I knew he'd track you down and make you his, eventually." He paused to flash her a knowing grin, "Besides, Jesse Washburn called me and told me about your trip to Vegas."

"You marines are nothing but a bunch of nosy old biddies."

His laughter was infectious. The image that formed in her tired brain tickled her funny bone even more. She couldn't stop visualizing the three, very masculine platoon-mates wearing gauzy, floral dresses and bonnets, holding tiny porcelain cups in their big hands, while chatting incessantly. Before long, tears were streaming down her cheeks.

"Hey what's this? You hornin' in on my gal again, Taylor?" Sean grumbled loudly, as he bumped his way through the door, toting their suitcases.

"I was trying my best, but she doesn't seem to be taking my moves very seriously." He glanced at Diana who was still quaking with mirth. "Hurts my feelings, too."

"I'll bet," Sean said wryly.

"Here, let me give you a hand," his buddy offered, jumping up.

"Thanks, man." With the assistance, Sean

found places for the luggage and the hanging bags. "When'd you get in?"

"'Bout an hour ago. You take much flak from the fam?" Skip jerked a thumb toward Diana.

"Not too much. They were pretty great about it actually."

"What about ol' Patster? Bet she freaked."

Chuckling at his friend's colorful vernacular, Sean confirmed, "You'd win that wager."

"That broad's seriously whacked, man. I'd watch my six if I were you. She's the get-even type, and you've already played out that scene once too often." Skip tried to sound casual, but his intent was deadly serious.

"I'm not planning to turn my back on her." Cutting his eyes toward the sofa, Sean was relieved to see that Diana had fallen asleep, her body slumped backward and her head lolling to one side. "Now git lost, you wife-stealing snake. I wanna be alone with my woman."

"Hey, you can't throw me out. In the immortal words of Richard Gere, 'I got nowhere else to go.' His handsome face was contorted to go along with the very bad impression. "Every bed in the big house is already taken," Skip complained. "And I refuse to bunk in the barn, not with a perfectly good sofa right here."

Watching Diana as she slept, Sean relented with a sigh, "Okay, you can have your usual spot. Doesn't look like I'm gonna see any action tonight anyway." He slipped a muscular arm under his wife's knees and another around her shoulders, lifting her with ease. She mumbled something unintelligible. Carrying her limp form to the bed, he whispered, "You know where to find a pillow and a blanket."

Almost ten hours later, Diana rolled over and stretched her tired muscles, trying to get her bearings. The last thing she remembered was sitting on the sofa talking with Skip. She noted that she was still wearing her silk trousers and blouse, and wondered why Sean had carried her to bed without undressing her. A muffled snore erupted from across the room in answer to her unspoken question.

Fuzzy, sun-streaked curls were visible, sticking out from beneath a light comforter. Slipping out of bed very quietly, Diana located her suitcase, removed a few things from it, and tiptoed into the small bathroom. When she emerged a bit later, the sofa was empty. The coverlet was folded neatly on one end.

"Time to face the family," Diana decided, gritting her teeth. She found most of them hovering in the kitchen. The upcoming wedding had disturbed the usual routine of the farm, and despite the lateness of the hour, Sarah and her girls were still cleaning up the remains of breakfast. They stopped what they were doing to welcome her, and to stick a heaping plate under her nose.

"Better eat up," Missy warned her. "We're not cookin' anymore today. The next food you'll get will be at the reception." She waved a dish towel at Skip, who was greedily shoveling heaping forkfuls of hot biscuits and sausage gravy into his mouth. "There's room over there by that scalawag, if you've a mind to sit, but be careful of the flying elbows."

Her stomach heaved and churned, making it impossible to swallow even a few bites of the delicious food. She stopped pushing it around on her plate when the back door swung open, and Sean walked through. His face broke open into wide smile when he saw her. Circling the table, he kissed the top of her head. "Mornin' love. Feeling better?"

"I was, until the cooking smells hit me," she whispered.

Giving her a sympathetic look, he encouraged her, "Try to get down, if you can. It'll make you feel better."

She did and he was right. When the nausea subsided, she willingly joined in the fevered rush of pre-wedding preparations. She spent the afternoon applying makeup to flawless cheeks, and brushing shining hair into elegant, upswept dos. The Cody women were almost ready to leave for the church when Diana realized that she was still wearing faded jeans and a worn T-shirt.

Rushing out to Sean's apartment, she found him struggling with his bowtie. "Let me do that," she offered. With a few deft twists, she tied a perfect knot. Then she stepped back to admire her husband's magnificent form, and let out a long appreciative whistle. "You look good enough to eat!"

"Later," he promised, wrapping her into a big bear hug and slapping her playfully on the rear. "You'd better move that sexy fanny. You're very late."

"I know. Sorry. I won't a minute." Pulling her own wedding dress out of the closet, she laid it on the bed, and searched her suitcase for suitable undergarments. "Do you think this will be all right?" She pointed to the purple and lavender frock. "Maybe I should have brought something more elegant and glamorous."

"The dress is perfect, Diana," he assured her. "You're likely to outshine the bride."

"That's nonsense, but I'm glad you said it." She kissed him soundly.

"Come on, Sean. We've gotta go!" Colin's voice, edged with the tiniest hint of desperation, sounded from below.

Sean hesitated, looking first at her and then the door. Diana could see that his best man responsibilities were weighing heavily. "That boy's beside himself with worry. Page will have his hide if he's late. Would you mind if I went on? You can catch a ride with Skip. He's finishing up the milking for Dad and Nelson."

"Go on. Colin is your first priority today. Don't worry about me. I'll be fine."

Flashing her an appreciative grin, he ran out, coattail flapping. After a lightning-quick shower, she added color to her face, brushed life into her fair locks, and donned the fairy-like creation, Then, Diana went in search of a ride to the white, clapboard church. She found Curtis and Skip waiting for her on the back porch of the farmhouse. Her attorney stared at her open-mouthed, and Sean's friend leered at her suggestively, as she walked across the yard toward them.

"Wow!" Curtis breathed, his face reddening.

Skip whistled appreciatively. "Patti Martin's gonna turn green when she sees you."

"I doubt that very much," she retorted skeptically, her blue eyes twinkling with pleasure. "Thanks for the compliment, anyway."

"Your husband is an-A-number-one, certifiable fool to leave you in my very capable, but very lecherous, hands." Skip stuck out one calloused palm. "If you think you can trust me to keep them to myself, you can accompany me to this shindig." The aging surfer looked dapper in his fashionable, olive-green suit, with his unruly locks combed into a semblance of order.

"I'll take my chances."

"Just so you'll feel safe we'll bring old Curtis along. Right, Curt?"

"Uh yes," the portly man agreed, his eyes still glued to Diana. "Thank you, Mr. Taylor."

"Hey man, it's just 'Skip'. Mr. Taylor's my dad." Skip led them to his stereotypical, classic woody station wagon. Diana slid into the front passenger seat, noting that the back of the car was full of surfing and snowboarding paraphernalia.

Sloan, dressed in his usual corporate gray, took the back seat and told her, "I don't think I've ever seen you looking so lovely, Diana. Are you happy?"

"Yes, Curtis. I am."

He patted her shoulder. "Good. I'm glad. You deserve to be happy."

The short ride with Skip was swift and exciting. He took the winding curves as a challenge to his considerable diving ability, speeding around them with tires squealing. Diana and Curtis were very relieved when he pulled into the church parking lot.

The sanctuary was filling up rapidly. Diana was lucky to find an unobtrusive spot on the back pew still unoccupied. She scooted across the slick mahogany bench behind Curtis. Skip followed, bracketing the other side, leaving her feeling like a thin volume wedged in between two substantial bookends.

Leaning her head toward her husband's friend, she whispered, "Thanks for being there for us when we needed you, Skip. You're a great man to have around in a crisis."

"I'll second that," Curtis put in, absurdly. "If you hadn't made your timely entrance into that board room, I'd be sitting here dead."

They laughed.

"Danger is my middle name," Skip quipped. "Enjoyed every minute of it. I hate it when things get too dull."

"I'll just bet you do," Diana said, smiling warmly.

Then the prelude swelled, Skip flashed her an encouraging grin. "Here we go."

The wedding was beautiful. Page had chosen a becoming ivory gown that suited her peaches and cream coloring perfectly. Colin looked stiff, but handsome, in his dark tuxedo. The bridesmaids wore black, drop-shouldered dresses that flattered the dark-haired Cody girls. Unfortunately, the same couldn't be said for the Matron of Honor. Black was definitely not Patty Sanderson's color. It made her complexion look sallow when compared to the more vibrantly-hued faces of the women who flanked her. Diana was surprised that she'd allowed her sister to make such an uncomplimentary selection.

Just as she had the evening prior, the determined woman made a show of leaning heavily on her escort's arm during the recessional. Despite Sean's efforts to shake her off, she clung to him with a determination bordering on obsession. He tried to join Diana several times, but Patti kept maneuvering him back into the crush of well-wishers."

At one point, he gave Diana a frustrated what-am-I-going-to-do look over the heads of the crowd, shrugging helplessly. Skip noticed his buddy's predicament, and advised, "Sean's never going to extricate himself from that swelling mass of humanity, so you may as well come with me. You too, Curt. Looks like Bridgett's pretty tied up, too."

Knowing he was right, Diana followed him reluctantly, hating the fact that her judicious retreat seemed more like surrender. With more than his usual decorum, the ex-Marine wheeled the vintage woody out onto the highway and headed to the local country club.

The social-climbing Martin family held offices on the Board of Directors of the posh facility, so no expense had been spared. Large round tables, covered with crisp ivory tablecloths, and set with centerpieces of varying shades of blue, were scattered around the perimeter of a huge, parquet dance floor. A fifteen-piece orchestra blasted out a mix of contemporary favorites and hits from the past, with an occasional country-western ballad thrown in. Liquid refreshment was freely poured, and the buffet table was heaped with delicacies.

Skip led the way, reading place cards, until he located their table on the far side of the room. He held Diana's chair for her, offering, "I'll get us something to drink." When he returned, an older couple was joining their little group. He had just started to make introductions when the wedding party entered, accompanied by a trumpet flourish. Page and Colin took a spin around the dance floor, looking deliriously happy, while Patti clung to Sean's sleeve, blowing kisses.

The stately woman who was seated across the table from Diana watched the entourage with obvious delight. Turning to her husband, she announced, "Don't they make the loveliest couple? And isn't it wonderful to see our Patti back with her Sean? I always thought they belonged together."

"It looks like we'll be attending another Martin-Cody wedding soon," the man replied, patting the woman's fingers.

The stricken look that flashed across Diana's fair face needled Skip into immediate action. "Excuse me folks. We haven't been introduced. I'm Skip Taylor, a Marine buddy of Sean's."

"It's nice to meet you. I'm Page's uncle, Norris Martin, and this is my wife, Laverne."
After handshakes were exchanged, Skip continued, "This is Curtis Sloan, Bridgett's good friend."

"Hello, Mr. Sloan." Norris nodded to the quiet attorney.

"And this lovely lady is Diana Cody."

"Cody?" Laverne asked, clearly puzzled. After a second or two, she added, "You certainly don't look like one of the Cody's. You must be an in-law."

"Yes," Diana confessed, grinning at Skip. "I am."

Before she could explain further, the mischievous man jumped in, anxiously delivering the line. "Diana is Sean's wife."

TWENTY-TWO

As soon as he could manage it, Sean extricated himself from his Best-Man responsibilities, and crossed the floor to claim his wife for a dance. Diana immediately accepted his invitation, smiling into his eyes, as he whirled her around and around. The news of their recent marriage had swept the room like wildfire. All heads turned to stare.

Watching the newlyweds, Patti seethed. Sarah Cody's openly-voiced approval of the match fanned the flames of her fury. *This has got to stop!* her brain screamed. Scooting out of her chair with effortless grace, she set her well-rehearsed plan into motion.

"It's time," she whispered as she passed her sister, who turned to her groom and asked him to join her on the dance floor. Halfway through the song, Page prompted Colin. "Let's cut in on Sean. I want to dance with my new uncle-in-law, and you need to get to know Diana."

The groom agreed innocently, guiding his bride deftly toward Sean and Diana. Tapping the big man's shoulder, he asked, "May I?"

"It would be my pleasure," Sean offered

gallantly, handing his wife over to his nephew, and accepting the tiny hand of the petite bride.

Colin's steps were executed flawlessly, but he moved stiffly and with obvious discomfort. The slender groom was inches shorter than the tall woman he led around the dance floor. They both knew they were very mismatched, and decidedly conspicuous. Letting his self-consciousness feed hers, Diana searched the room for her husband.

When she finally located him, holding Colin's bride gingerly, like a delicate porcelain doll, she couldn't stop herself from laughing, shocking her partner. "I'm sorry," she apologized though the fit of giggles. "I can't help it. Look at Page and Sean. Aren't they just too funny? I wonder if we look just as ridiculous."

Getting caught up in her mirth, Colin relaxed. "And, I was just thinking that no one could possibly look more absurd than we do. Guess that disproves my theory."

"Hey, you wanna blow this joint?" Diana quipped, feeling inexplicably light-hearted.

"What-da-ya have in mind, sweetie?" her partner asked playfully,

"I could use some fresh air."

"Lead the way," the groom urged. As they wound their way out of the banquet hall, and through a set of sliding doors, which opened onto a balcony, neither Colin nor Diana noticed that they were being followed.

"What's this? Have you no shame?" Patti's irritating soprano rang out. "Sean wasn't young enough for you, so you have to go after my little sister's husband? It's the man's wedding day, for God's sake. What in the hell is wrong with you?"

Shocked by the vicious, and totally undeserved attack, Colin defended himself and his companion. "Come on, Patti. Don't be silly. We just needed a little air."

"Shut up and get out of here," she ordered him, paying his peacemaking attempt no mind. His jaw working impotently, Colin backed away, leaving Diana to fight this battle without him. When he was out of earshot, the older Martin sister renewed her offensive. "Now you're gonna pay attention to what I have to say for a change, or I'm going back in there and tell everyone that I saw you trying to hit on poor, clueless Colin."

"What do you want, Patti? I do hope it's something new. I'm getting really tired of listening to that old recording you keep playing over and over." Diana faced down her adversary with barely suppressed disgust.

"Oh, it's definitely something you're not expecting. To be perfectly honest, it's something I didn't plan on at all. I was hoping to bring Sean back to his senses without it; but unfortunately, you've made it necessary for me to use all of the weapons I have at my disposal."

"Get on with it," Diana snapped. "You've tried using your youth, beauty, and sex appeal, but to no avail. What else could possibly make Sean leave me for you?"

"A baby," Patti said smugly.

"What?" Diana was taken completely off

guard. A wave of nausea hit her.

"I'm pregnant with your husband's child."

"No!"

"Yes, I am," the scheming woman confirmed. "The last time Sean was here. When you were tagging along, trying to occupy his time, he still found a few minutes to make love to me. Actually, he couldn't keep his hands off me." Patti's eyes shimmered feverishly. "As soon as he saw me he wanted me, and we took up where we'd left off, years earlier."

Shaking uncontrollably, and barely able to keep from retching, Diana responded, "Then the two of you have a lot to talk over." She reached for the handle and slid the door open.

"Wait. Where're you going?" Patti asked, a decidedly suspicious edge to her shrill voice.

"To find Sean, of course."

"No you don't. Not yet. First, I want to know what you're going to do about this."

"Me? I'm not going to do anything about it. It's between you and Sean." Though it took an unbelievable amount of strength to do so, Diana kept her own tone calm and reasonable.

"I figured a woman like you, a woman used to having everything her way, would throw a man out if disappointed her, cheated on her."

"That shows how little you know about me."

"I can't imagine that you still want him, now that you know you're only getting my leftovers." Patti grinned evilly, showing a bright line of tiny sharp teeth. "And that he'll always be tied to me, because of this baby." She rubbed her flat stomach and grinned.

"Yes, well, the truth of your claim is yet to be proven." Diana was determined not to let the woman see how her claims wounded her. "Just answer one question for me. If Sean was as anxious to rekindle that old flame with you, why did he marry me?"

Seeing the stubborn set of Patti's mouth, she knew the woman was not in any mood for logic or reason. "On second thought, forget I asked. It's irrelevant. As I said, the matter is between you and Sean. You're talking to the wrong person."

"Maybe so, but since you've stolen him away from me, you owe me one small concession at least," Patti insisted.

"Heaven's above! What now? You've tried every conceivable trick to catch him, all of which have failed. I'm sure this is just another ridiculous ploy. But since you have a such a selective and convenient memory, let's get this over with once and for all. Please, by all means, tell me what you want." Diana couldn't disguise the desperation that clutched at her throat.

"I want you to give Sean an honest chance to make things work with me. It's the least you can do, considering that he was mine first, and I am the one carrying his baby." Glaring at her intended victim, red-tipped nails splayed out over her hips, Patti pressed her point home. "I can give him the real family he deserves. Our marriage won't be an empty farce.

"I don't know what you've done to him, what kind of spell you've put over him, but I do know that before he left home and went back to D.C., before you brainwashed him, he was mine. If it weren't for you, I'd be planning our wedding, a wedding that would give our child his name."

Turning away, Diana refused her. "You'll get no promises from me. It's up to Sean. Now, please excuse me."

Sean saw her reenter and rushed to intercept her. "I've been looking everywhere for you. What were you doing?"

"Finding out what a busy boy you've been," she snapped cryptically, taking her irritation at Patti out on him.

"What are you talking about?" Sean was clearly confused by her words and her obvious anger. His dark eyes searched her fair face, hungrily, looking for clues.

"Ask your girlfriend," Diana told him, deliberately jerking her arm out of his grasp. "I'm going to find Skip and get him to drive me back to the farm."

"Diana, what's going on? What's wrong?"

Ignoring his pleas, she strode away, showing him her proud, straight back. When she located Skip, lounging against the bar, she asked him to take her to the Cody homeplace.

She'd almost made good her escape when Sean appeared, stopping them as they reached the car. "You're not running out on me. What's the problem?"

"I told you to ask the lovely Mrs. Sanderson," she ordered him.

"I tried," he said, shrugging helplessly, "but she seems to have disappeared."

"Then wait for her to reappear. They say a bad penny always turns up. In the meantime, I'll be at the house, packing. Come on, Skip."

Shooting his pal a sorry-man look, Skip opened the door for her. As he rounded to the driver's seat, he told his friend, "I'll stall her till you can pin down old Pat-ster."

"Thanks, pal," Sean replied, sprinting back toward the clubhouse.

Patti watched the scene in the parking lot from her perch on the darkened balcony, smiling with pleased satisfaction. She waited for a few more minutes before she went back into the crowded ballroom to allow Sean to find her.

When he did, the confrontation was not pretty. "Dammit, Patti. What in the hell did you say to Diana?" he accused, grabbing her arm in a vice-like pinch.

"Ouch! You're hurting me," she whined, pulling away.

"I'm going to strangle you if you don't answer my question."

"Sean, please, everyone is watching."

"Let them watch." His dark eyes burned with such angry fire, that the woman glimpsed, for the first time, the capacity for violent action that he kept so fiercely in check.

It frightened her, but didn't dissuade her from pursuing her chosen course with determination. "I'll tell you, in private."

Taking her elbow, he dragged her out of the ballroom and into a deserted hallway. "We're alone. Now talk."

Swallowing hard, Patti admitted, "I'm pregnant."

"What?" he asked incredulously.

"You heard me. I'm expecting a baby."

"And you led Diana to believe I'm responsible."

Turning doe-eyes on him, the practiced manipulator let huge tears spill out and slide down over her perfect ivory cheeks. "I told her we made love when you were here at the end of March."

"Why, Patti?"

"Because I love you, Sean, and I need you."

"Bullshit," he snarled and demanded, "Who's the father?"

Wringing her hands, Patti sobbed, "It doesn't matter. I can't ask him for help because he's already married."

"So am I! You don't seem to have any qualms about expecting me to dump my wife and raise another man's child."

"You were mine first, before that fat, old bitch stole you from me. And you weren't married when my baby was conceived."

Her fuzzy logic clearly made no sense to Sean. "What in the hell does that have to do with anything? I'm married now."

"Everyone knows that was a stupid mistake. You two don't belong together. You could leave her and no one would think badly of you, especially after they hear the reason."

"As simple as that, huh?" he barked, shaking his head in disbelief. "Why don't you ask the man who's really responsible for your predicament to dump his wife and marry you?"

"Because that would cause a scandal. He and his wife have been married for years, and they're both pillars of the community. My goodness, he's even a deacon in our church."

"Sounds like a real saint. So why did he screw you?"

Feigning embarrassment, Patti scolded him. "I hate it when you talk like that. It's crude." Taking a deep breath, she explained softly. A lone tear squeezed out and rolled down her cheek. "I was crushed when Ron left me, and very vulnerable. He reached out to me, in his role as my deacon and offered me a shoulder to cry on. We just got a little carried away."

"I'd say."

"But you see, Sean, it's really not important who fathered this baby."

"Why's that?" Sean asked her, incredulously.

"Because the only thing that matters is who will love it the most," Patti announced to him triumphantly.

The scheming woman had spent hours strategizing. No matter what Sean said to her, she would never reveal the identity of this baby's father. To do so would risk being labeled the temptress, the evil seductress, who led an honorable man into sin. The narrow-minded, parochial residents of this rural community would despise her for it and she knew it. On the other hand, a marriage of convenience to her high school boyfriend would shock no one, and some would even envy her.

"He loves his wife, and he's already raised his family, so he wouldn't want to start over. Most importantly, I don't love him; I love you. And we're perfectly suited to each other. We were always meant to be together, and it's time we became a family."

"You've wrapped this all up in a tidy little package. I leave my wife, marry you, and raise this kid, along with the rest of your spoiled brood, with no one the wiser."

"Yes!" She flashed him suggestive smile, that was designed to slip her straight into his heart through his libido.

"And you keep your good reputation, instead of letting the whole county see what a slut you really are." Sean's dark eyes snapped furiously. "There's only one little problem."

"What's that?"

"I don't love you. I love Diana."

"You did love me once, and you can love me again. I just know it." She let her voice take on a pleading, desperate tone. "Please, Sean. You have to do this for me. You owe it to me."

Sean held his head in his hands while her grating whine sliced through his eardrums and straight into the inner recesses of his brain "What makes you think I owe you anything?" he demanded. "You dumped me, remember? You threw me over for good old Doc Sanderson, a man who could give you the life you thought you deserved."

"So?" The meek façade melted away as she allowed the real Patti Martin, conceited and spoiled to the core, to come out. "You were the first man to have me, Sean. I gave you the precious gift that a woman can only give once – to the one man she truly loves – forever. You do owe me."

Sean's laughter filled the room.

Patti was incensed. Angry red blotches crept up her neck, marring the peaches and cream perfection of her face. "This isn't funny!" she screamed at him, stamping her foot.

When his mirth subsided, he told her softly, "You were no virgin when we... How should I put it so I don't offend you? When we... did it."

"I was so," she argued adamantly.

Ignoring her denial, he added, "You don't know truth from lies any more, do you? If either of us is owed a reward for sacrificing our virginity, it's me," He paused and stared at her intently, daring her to look away. "I might have been a rookie, but I could tell that you already had a few notches in your belt. You were the seasoned veteran."

"How dare you say such a thing?"

Sean shrugged one shoulder expressively. "I wasn't that naïve. You didn't fool me, Pats. You were no ignorant, nervous first-timer, despite your claims. I'd heard the locker-room talk. You used sex as bait and I wasn't the first fish you'd caught."

Realizing that the approach was getting her nowhere, the devious woman deliberately switched tactics. "So what? It doesn't matter anyway. You're going to divorce the rich bitch and marry me, whether you want to or not."

"It's been a damned long time since anyone forced me to do anything I didn't want to do," he assured her. "So just how to do you plan to make that happen?"

"I've already set everything into motion, and there's nothing you can do about it." Her smile broke out again, smug and self-assured. She studied her long nails arrogantly. "Your bothersome wife is already packing-up to leave you. Once she's out of the way, I'll tell your mom and dad that I'm pregnant with your baby. They'll make sure you do right by me."

"I'll deny it. Do you really think my folks will believe you?"

She shrugged. "They might not, but it won't matter, because everyone else will. Your family has to live in this community, Sean. My parents have tremendous influence. Daddy can exert pressure on the bankers that hold the lien on your precious Cody farm. If they want to keep their land, your folks will have to support me."

"We'll see," he growled, pulling her toward the door.

"Where are we going?"

"To stop this insanity before it goes any further.

As Patti had predicted, Diana was, at that very moment, trying to convince Skip to help her load her bags into the station wagon. And as he'd promised, Skip was stalling her retreat.

"Are you going to just stand there or are you going to give me a hand with this?"

"I'm gonna just stand here, because you're

making a stupid mistake. Running away won't solve anything, Diana. I think a wise man once said that, or something like it."

"I'm not running away. I'm just getting out of the way so Sean time can straighten out the mess he's in," she said, defending her impulsiveness. "Now outta my way!" Hoisting the large suitcase, she tried to elbow him aside.

"Put that down," Skip insisted, jerking the bag out of her hand and setting it down with a thud. "It's too heavy for a woman in your condition."

"What do you know about my condition?" She stubbornly hefted the luggage again.

Once more, he took it from her. "Shit, Diana, it's pretty damned obvious that you're pregnant. About four months along I'd say."

His astute observation took her completely off guard. "Did Sean tell you?"

"No."

"Then how'd you guess?"

"Experience. Before I joined the Corps, I was an OB nurse."

Shaking her head incredulously, she giggled. "You never cease to amaze me. Why in the world did you give up medicine for the Marines?"

"I figured it was the safer choice – screaming women in the throes of childbirth, or men with guns – I picked the latter."

His wry humor released the bands of anger and fear that were squeezing her heart. She laughed until tears rolled.

"There, that's better." He pulled a handkerchief out of his pocket and handed to her. "Now, sit down and tell me what's got you running away again."

Figuring that escape was hopeless, she acquiesced reluctantly. "You win. I'll sit, but don't think I don't know you're stalling me until Sean gets here."

"We're on to each other. I get it. Now tell me what's up."

Before she could begin to explain, heavy footsteps plodded up the narrow wooden staircase outside. Sean threw open the door and stepped inside, towing a screaming mass of cinnamon-gold curls and swirling black taffeta.

"Let me go, this second!" Patti screeched.

Obliging her, Sean dropped the slim wrist he'd had encircled with his long fingers. "As you wish," he sneered, positioning his considerable bulk between her and the exit.

When she bolted for the open door, he blocked her and threatened, "Oh, no you don't. You're not getting out of here until you tell my wife the truth."

"I already have," Patti huffed indignantly, her arms folded across her chest, her bosom heaving.

"No, you told her that you're carrying my baby."

"That's right."

Pulling her closer to Skip and Diana, who hadn't budged from their seats on the overstuffed sofa, he probed, "So when did this alleged impregnation take place?"

"You already know the answer to that," she lied, her tone deliberately petulant.

"Indulge me, please. Tell Diana when, exactly, that this supposed intimacy between us took place."

Huffing again, as if she were totally bored by the exchange, she said, "When you were home, in March."

"Be a little more specific," he insisted, clenching and unclenching his fists. "We couldn't have done it in the house; there were too many people around. And the only time we were alone together was when you insisted that we take a drive. Are you suggesting that we screwed in your tiny sports car? I'm good, Pats, but not that good. I need a little more room than that to maneuver."

Anticipating the question, the wily woman answered without blinking, "No, silly, I'm not suggesting any such thing. We made love later that evening."

"Come on, Patti. Everyone saw you leave. There was no 'later that evening'."

"On the contrary," she corrected. "I came back to the farm after your family had retired for the night."

"You did?"

"You know I did."

"And that's when we…"

"…made love." She finished for him. "That's right."

"Where?"

"What do you mean where?"

"Where in the hell did we find a private place to screw?" Sean was almost yelling.

"I told you earlier that I despise such crudeness. I insist that you stop talking like that around me." She raised her perfect nose to the ceiling and shook her hair haughtily.

"Then answer the question. Where did this alleged 'love-making' take place?" Sean was insistent. "Certainly not in this room, because Skip was in asleep on the couch."

"Sean, you already know all this. Why are you humiliating me this way?" Patti bravely pushed him, refusing to give up.

He glared at her, daring her to defy him. After a long moment of heavy silence, she relented, "Okay, okay." Leveling her eyes at Diana she spoke softly, a sly grin pulling at the corners of her mouth. "Sean and I made love in the barn. In tack room."

"The tack room," Sean confirmed, a delighted gleam shining in his dark eyes.

"Yes. I remembered that, when you're home, you always take on the chore of bedding down the horses, so I circled back, hoping to catch you in the barn. Luck was with me. I found you passing out feed and filling water buckets. You were delighted to see me. Before I knew what was happening, you pulled me into the tack room and we made a baby."

"That's your story?" he asked, grinning widely.

Patti hesitated, studying him. The sudden change in his affect clearly worried her, but she forged on with determination. "Yes, and as they say, I'm sticking to it."

"Good. Then you can go. The family farm is safe," he told her bowing deeply, and sweeping a mocking gesture toward the door.

"I can what?" Patti tried to reengage him, but he'd already dismissed her and turned his attention to Diana, who had found her way into his arms. The insistent woman grabbed his sleeve and forced him to face her. "You are not dismissing me!"

"You've just proven that your story is a complete concoction," he told her softly, his voice coolly controlled. "I feel sorry for you, Pats. You have no power over me and you can't force me to do anything. I'm not only dismissing you; I'm ordering you. Get out." Turning his back on the indignant woman, he folded Diana in his arms and kissed her.

Taking pity on the confused woman, Skip placed a hand in the middle of her back and urged her toward the door. "Let me explain. Interestingly enough, part of your story is true. Sean was in the tack room that night, making love to a beautiful woman. The trouble is – that woman wasn't you."

Finally realizing that her complex scheme hadn't allowed for that one unlikely possibility, and knowing that she'd pay for the miscalculation, her shoulders sagged. "I see."

Not one to accepting defeat easily, she squared them again, ratcheted up her pride and fired one last volley. "I'm very disappointed in you, Sean. Fooling around with a married woman. What will your family say when they find out you're an adulterer?"

"You've got balls, Patti. I'll give you that," Sean told her, grinning at her audacity. "Not much of a threat, though, since it comes from a woman who's carrying a married man's bastard,"

"Yes, well." She let the insult roll off with a flip of a curl. "I can give you a baby, too, Sean. Can she say the same?" Patti pointed an accusing finger at Diana, clearly determined to fight this fight until the end.

Smiling into his wife's adoring eyes, he answered, "She can and she will, in about five months."

Struck speechless by that shocking revelation, Patti slunk away, slamming the door behind her so hard that the windows rattled. Sean grabbed Diana and hugged her in relief. She offered him a welcoming kiss, forgetting for a moment that they weren't alone.

Skip cleared his throat to remind them that he was watching. "Guess I'd better look for someplace else to sleep tonight. Maybe I'll try out the tack room. Seems to be a popular place. Maybe I'll find a good-looking babe to share it with me."

Sean chuckled. "Yeah, man. We got pretty comfortable there." He wiggled an eyebrow at Diana suggestively. Then he asked his buddy, "How'd you know about that, anyway? We thought we were being pretty darned discrete."

"Couldn't sleep. Went for a walk to clear my head. When I heard some mighty interesting noises coming from the vicinity of the barn, I went to investigate. I'm a pretty smart fellow, actually, contrary to appearances. Didn't take me long to figure out what was going on in there. And that goofy, love-struck look you had on your face when you came up to bed, verified my hunch." Grabbing his pillow and blanket and heading for the exit, he winked at Diana and nodded toward Sean. "I have to admit, it's what I would have been doing, if that big lug hadn't beaten me to it."

EPILOGUE

Before they left the Cody farm, the newlyweds announced their happy news. Sarah and Mike Cody were elated, as were Sean's sisters, who hugged Diana and cried. The brothers-in-law slapped the father-to-be on the back and offered him nuggets of sage advice. When it was time to depart, Diana was surprised that she didn't want to leave, because, for the first time in her life, she felt like she was part of a real family.

It only took a couple of weeks for them to get settled into the comfortable house on the beautiful little lake. Sean's Harley Davidson seemed very much at home sharing the garage with Diana's compact wagon. They'd had no trouble moving his belongings from his apartment in the beat-up, four-wheel-drive truck he used for commuting to and from Baldwin Aviation, in bad weather. Diana had teased him about the ancient pick-up, which was so faded and rusted that it was difficult to determine the vehicle's original color, but he'd taken the kidding in stride, proudly declaring that the dilapidated truck "still has a lot of life left in her."

They'd fallen into a routine that seemed to suit

them both, Sean flying hops to New York, Boston, or Atlanta, and Diana preparing for the arrival of their baby. Still, she could hardly believe that her life had changed in such a marvelous and satisfying way, and she thanked God every day for her loving husband, and for the unexpected blessing He'd given her. Never had she dared imagine that such happiness could be possible for her.

And she was truly happy, even though she wished her mother could have lived to see her grandson. Unfortunately, she knew that it was only after her mother's death that she'd had the courage to begin living her life to please herself. In a way, her mother's death had made her grandson's life possible.

The intimate moments they shared continued to be immensely fulfilling, exciting, and full of surprises. One night after making love, they lay entwined, satiated, languid, and warm. In a deeply sensuous voice, that still made chills run up her spine, he asked her, "Tell me about your first time."

The question surprised her. "What? Why?"

"Because I know it wasn't with James. I have this hunch that you didn't wait until you married to him. You were too beautiful and desirable. I want to know about all the guys who tried to get you into the sack and failed – and about the one that succeeded. You made me tell you all about my 'conquests,' don't you think I deserve to know about yours?"

"I don't know all about your experiences," she hedged. "I'm pretty sure Patti was your first. And honestly, I know more about your relationship with Sheila than I'd like to, but that's about it. You mentioned a few others, but you were deliberately vague," she stalled, pushing down the painful memory his request elicited.

"You're right. Patti can lay claim to my virginity. Sad to say." He didn't try to hide the distasteful grimace that slid across his handsome features. "After she dumped me, I had a few short-lived flings. Some were a rebound thing. Most were just recreation. None were serious. Then there was Sheila, my second big mistake." He sighed. "It's embarrassing to admit, but that's all there is to know. So, it's your turn. Who was he, this man who charmed you into bed and took the prize? Should I be jealous of him?"

Laughing softly, she explained, "Hardly. He wasn't man, and there's absolutely no need for you to be jealous of him."

"He was a kid? A teenager? How old were you?" he asked, incredulously. "Don't tell me you fooled around in high school. I know you, Diana. You weren't that sort of girl."

"No, I wasn't, but it happened anyway."

Despite the reluctance in her voice, and in the protective way she withdrew from his embrace, Sean pushed her, "What happened, Diana?"

"It's a long story I've never told anyone, and it's late."

He refused to back down. "I want to hear it, and I think you need to tell it."

"If I do, you'll owe me a secret in exchange. It's only fair," she bartered.

"Deal. A secret for a secret. Tell on."

Swallowing hard, she began, "His name's Rick Longley. He was the star pitcher on my high school's championship baseball team. Everyone looked up to Rick. He was the unchallenged leader of the most popular clique. I'm sure you had one like it in your school, the circle with all the jocks and cheerleaders."

He nodded. "Sure did. I was in it."

"I bet you were," she chuckled nervously. "I hope your crowd was never as mean and despicable as these guys. They were always playing dirty jokes on the students who didn't fit into their little world of athletics and beer drinking. I was the victim of one of their little wagers."

Sean opened his mouth to ask a question, but she laid her fingers on his lips, silencing him. "No, don't say anything or I won't be able to do this." He nodded silently and she continued.

"Like most of the girls, I was crazy about Rick. But I didn't think he even knew my name. I was a measly sophomore, Honor-Society geek, from the wrong side of the tracks. He was a big-shot senior, and the undisputed king of the hallways. I couldn't believe my good fortune when he asked me out.

"I said 'yes' immediately, and for almost three weeks, he made me his pet project. He carried my books, drove me home from school, took me out to dinner and movies, and told me I was beautiful and that he loved me. I was in heaven. When he asked me to the prom, I was elated. Mom spent an entire paycheck, money we needed for rent, to buy me a dress."

Wiping at a tear that leaked out from under her long lashes and dropped onto his chest, he voiced a suspicion. "Let me guess. You never made it to the prom."

"Nope," she confirmed. "He picked me up and drove me to a secluded spot near the railroad siding, telling me that everyone 'does it' on prom night. He insisted that he was so 'worked-up' that we'd both have a terrible time if he didn't 'get some relief.' 'Get it over with before the prom' was what we needed to do, he claimed. 'Take the pressure off' so we could relax and have fun. I can't believe it now, but I actually fell for his line, and felt sorry for him. And despite the fact that I didn't really want to…"

"You let him make love to you," Sean finished for her.

"I wouldn't call it making love. He ripped my panties and shoved himself inside me. It hurt so much that I begged him to stop, but he wouldn't. Luckily, he only pushed a couple of times before it was over."

"Shit, Diana, that's rape!" Sean was seething. "The guy should be hung up by the balls."

"You haven't heard the worst, yet," she told him. "When he was done, he forced me out of the car and left me, taking my torn and blood-stained panties as a trophy. Then he picked up his real date, the captain of the cheerleading squad."

She turned misty eyes on him. "It was all done on a dare, a wager. Rick had been bragging that he could have any girl in the school, so some of the other guys on the baseball team bet him they could find a girl he wouldn't be able to get – me."

"You should have reported the bastard to the cops."

"Probably. But I couldn't. I didn't want anyone to know what a stupid fool I'd been, and I couldn't let my mother find out about it."

After a long pause, Diana continued. "Mom cleaned house for the Longley's, Sean, and for several of their friends. I couldn't report what happened, because she would have lost those jobs. So, I took my time walking home. She had waited up, of course, to ask me how it went. I lied. I told her it was like a fairy tale. And I guess it was – but only the terrible part, without the happily-ever-after ending.

"A day or so later, I told her that Rick and I had broken up. I think she suspected I wasn't telling her the truth, but she never questioned me about it."

Pulling her into a tighter embrace, he kissed the top of her head. "Oh, my dearest love, I'm so sorry. What a horrible, horrible thing. I could find those guys and beat them up for you. I'd particularly like to get my hands on old Rick, the pitcher. I bet I could make him do some big-time begging."

She laughed. "I bet you could. My hero!" She poked a long finger between his ribs, making him squirm. "Where were you when I needed you?"

"Uh…" he teased, scratching his head. "In kindergarten."

She laughed harder, and felt the tension draining out of her muscles. "Well, I appreciate the offer, but there's no need for you to come to my rescue now. It was a long, long time ago. I'm over it, for the most part, and I've had my revenge.

"At the time I was completely humiliated. I couldn't face anyone, not even my closest friends. For the next two years I avoided everyone, spending my time completely alone. I guess that's when the 'Ice Queen' made her first appearance. I put on that protective armor and pretended that nothing anyone said or did could hurt me. At first, she was just an Ice Princess. Living with James perfected her and put the final touches on the frost.

"I have to give the old gal credit. She served me well. That frigid wall definitely kept people at a distance and helped me feel safe. A few people chipped their way through it, though, like Eleanor, but I always kept the persona handy, just in case I had a use for her. Until James, she was very successful in keeping the men away."

"Don't I know," Sean admitted. "She did her best to run me off, too, remember?"

"Thank the good Lord she didn't succeed. I would never have forgiven her for leaving me miserable and alone, longing for you."
That declaration earned her another kiss. After she caught her breath, Diana added. "It took me a long time to get over my fear and distrust of men. I guess that's why James's proposal seemed so perfect. He didn't pretend to love me and he never tried to charm me. He just laid it all out – pro and con – honest. All business. Sex wasn't mentioned, so I figured it wasn't part of the deal. But what did I know? You see how that turned out."

When she fell silent, he asked her, "So what happened to Rick the snake? How'd you get that revenge you mentioned?"

"Now that's a funny story. Not ha-ha funny. Ironic funny."

"Tell me."

"After high school, Rick got a baseball scholarship to a big university. Unfortunately, he was a terrible student and a big party animal. He got thrown off the team and had to come running home to work for dear old dad. Mr. Longley owned the local used-car mart. I say owned, because I bought out Longley Motors. It's Grayson Motors now. Rick works for me."

Sean slapped his thigh appreciatively. "You mean he did work for you, before you gave up your interest in North Star."

"No, he works for me, present tense. This was personal. I didn't want James or his company involved in any way. I bought it with my money and I still own it."

It was Sean's turn to laugh. "And you turn the screws from time to time, just to make sure he knows who's the boss."

"I do. It's about time for me to take a trip home to check up on the old guy. You can come with me and meet him. He's lost most of his gorgeous, wavy hair, but he's grown a huge beer belly to compensate for it."

"Sounds like a real stud." Sean quipped.

"Couldn't prove it by me, but his three ex-wives might be able to give you the scoop." His sensuous lower lip beckoned her, so she savored a kiss. "You see, there's absolutely no need to be jealous of him, or of any other man. You're my one and only love."

"Good. Speaking of jealousy, there's something I've been meaning to ask you."

"Ask away, but you're not going to make me forget that you owe me a secret."

Scrunching up his nose, his eyes twinkling with mischief, he asked, "Why were you ready to bolt when Patti made her little announcement? Were you that uncertain about me, or was it possible that you were just a little jealous?"

"I was totally green," she admitted, punching him. "But I didn't doubt you, not for a second. I never believed Patti, but I wasn't sure what she might be capable of, so I decided that it would be best if I made myself scarce until you worked it out. I wasn't running away from you, I just didn't have the courage to watch the happiness that I'd finally found with you, being torn apart by deceit."

"No one will ever come between us again, Diana, I promise you that. And as long as I have breath, no man will ever hurt you again. Since I first laid eyes on you, I knew there'd never be another woman for me." The sincere truth of his words shot straight into her heart.

"Nor will there ever be another man for me," she said firmly, adding, "Now, it's your turn. Tell me a secret."

Giving her a playful squeeze, he asked, "What do you want to know?"

"You said that when we got to know one another better, you'd explain how you got these scars." She ran a gently finger across the blemishes on his eyebrow and chin. "I think we know each other pretty intimately now, so fess up. Do they have anything to do with your nightmares?"

"Hardly," he admitted, chuckling. "Those dreams take me back to the night when I got separated from my platoon in the jungle. It was pitch black, no moon. The canopy was so thick I couldn't see the stars. I had no idea where I was, but I knew I was surrounded by hostiles. I stumbled around, feeling my way. It was daybreak before I caught up with my men.

"I relived that night for years, surrounded by the jungle, lost and helpless, waking up in a cold sweat, but since I met you the nightmares are almost gone. Making love to you every night wears me out too much to dream." He kissed the tip of her nose.

"That was a great story, Sean," she teased. "But it won't get you out of telling me a secret. How did you get those scars?"

"Another embarrassing high school tale," he admitted, sighing heavily. "I was at football practice. The coach had the team running sprints up and down the bleachers. I was the captain, and the captain always set the pace. I was staring at the cheerleaders, trying to make a good impression. I lost my footing and fell. The rest of the team went down behind me like a row of dominos. Luckily, no one else was hurt, but it took five stitches to close up the eyebrow and nine for the chin. I was a mess. I got a lot of teasing about it, too."

"I can just imagine the nicknames," Diana interjected, giggling.

"Fumble-foot was the nicest."

"Thank-you, love," the happy woman told her husband. "For sharing that with me. It's nice to know that you have normal human frailties. Seems we've both done some things we're not too proud of."

"You can say that again," he agreed.

"You're the only person who knows about Rick. I've never confided in anyone."

"Not even Eleanor?"

"Not even Eleanor."

"I'm glad."

"Why?"

"Because I want to be the one person in your life who knows everything about you," he said, holding her close.

"You are," she assured him, finding his mouth with hers. After a long, deeply stirring kiss, she added, "And there's one other thing I want you to know about me right now."

"What's that?"

"I love you and I need you, right here." Lifting her body above his, she guided him home once more.

As Sean looked up into Diana's adoring eyes, two liquid pools of blue-hot fire, he finally knew, for sure, that the "Ice Queen" was gone forever, melted away by the warmth of his love.

About the Author

Donna Minnix Proctor began writing romantic fiction in the 80's, on a dare. Since then, she's penned historic, contemporary, and sci-fi/fantasy romances. In collaboration with her husband, Cary, she's co-authored dozens of religious plays and skits. In her 30+ year career as a Health Educator, Extension Agent, and Nonprofit Executive, Donna has numerous magazine articles, publications, and a column in "The Roanoke Times" to her credit. In her spare time, Donna enjoys performing in community theater and riding her purple Harley Davidson Sportster. The Proctors are from Vinton, Virginia. They currently reside on Briarwood Farm in Franklin County, where they provide a happy home for two geriatric horses and four rescued pets.

9 781087 871363